STARTING POINT

TURNING POINT SERIES : BOOK THREE

N.R. WALKER

After going past the point of no return and finally reaching breaking point, the only thing Matthew Elliott can do now is start over.

Matthew Elliott is a recovering man. As an ex-cop and ex-fighter, his new job teaching kids at the local community gym about drug awareness and self-defense, is a little bit of both. His new focus on helping street kids is helping him heal, and with Kira by his side, he's making strides.

Brother and sister, Rueben and Claudia, are homeless kids and they're very much alone. As they strike a chord with Matt, he does everything in his power to help them.

But when Ruby and Claude need more help than he bargained for, it stops being about work, and starts being about home.

The day he met Kira, Matt's life changed direction, and it's only now he realizes that everything he's been through was a lead up to this. It was never about endings. His life, his purpose, was just beginning.

COPYRIGHT

Trademarks Acknowledgement

The author acknowledges the trademarked status and trademark owners of the following wordmarks mentioned in this work of fiction:

Ford: Ford Motor Company

Nike: Nike, Inc

iPad: Apple, Inc.

LA Times: Tribune Company

Glock 17: Glock Ges.m.b.H.

Sesame Street: Joan Ganz Cooney and Lloyd Morrisett

Oscar the Grouch (Sesame Street): Joan Ganz Cooney and Lloyd Morrisett

Dr. Phil: Harpo Productions, Inc.

Karate Kid: Columbia Pictures Industries, Inc.

UFC: Zuffa LLC

For my Blanket Fort girls.
This book would not be here without you.

STARTING POINT

N.R. Walker

TAMARA COULTER WAS MY PSYCHIATRIST. She reminded me a bit of Diane Keaton: middle-aged with gray-brown shoulder length hair and a kind face. She was very smart and soft spoken, but her words were carefully chosen and usually fired with perfect aim.

She was the best the LAPD had to offer, and I'd been seeing her twice a week for six months. We'd covered a lot of ground, from the death of my mother to my going under-cover, how I'd lost my hearing in one ear, how I'd almost lost Kira.

We talked about actions and consequences, but most of all, we talked about guilt.

From my first appointment, Tamara had talked about guilt. How it can paralyze or catalyze one into action. How it, more often than not, led to resentment and depression. She'd told me we'd be focusing more on guilt so I'd gone home and researched all I could, that way, at my next meeting, we could discuss it properly.

I have a photographic memory—a mind for details. Years as a detective did that. I'd read all the documents on guilt and other associated emotive behaviors I'd been able to find, which probably annoyed my doctor more than was productive. Too much time and the Internet were not a good combination.

Tamara had been surprised and amused, but in my attempt to be prepared and dedicated to getting help, I'd also shown her what she'd come to suspect—I was a control freak.

Apparently.

So then we talked about that too.

Actually, there wasn't much we didn't talk about.

I had to realize the doctor didn't have the ability to take away my guilt. Only I could do that.

Tamara had said I needed to acknowledge that as part of my therapy, I had to seek absolution from whom I'd hurt. I'd argued that that seemed a little redundant to me. "So I have to make Kira feel guilty, in order to absolve my guilt?"

"How so?"

"If he doesn't forgive me, I can't get better. That's not fair on him. What if he's not ready to forgive me? What if he can't? You're saying that he has to, no exceptions, or I carry this burden forever? What kind of horrible responsibility is that?"

"Do you think he should forgive you?"

"I don't think it's right to ask if he *should* or not. That's not fair. I want him to, yes. But if he *should* forgive me? That's something only he can answer." I'd taken a breath and exhaled loudly.

Tamara had waited, the way she does, knowing I'd keep talking.

"I think he has forgiven me, yes. For the life of me I can't figure out why, or by what grace of whose god, but yes, he has."

"Have you forgiven you?" she'd asked.

"I'm working on it. Every single day. It's not something I'm going to wake up one day and be magically cured of. You know that, Tamara. You know I could spiel off some textbook answer so you can tick all the right boxes, but that's not how this works."

Tamara had smiled. "No, it's not."

"Then why make me say it?"

"Because it's better for you to say it than for me to keep saying it. I know you've studied all you can on this, Matt. I know you're capable of telling people what you want them to hear. You did, after all, exactly that to a team of department psychologists about going undercover."

"I lied to them."

"Yes, convincingly. I read their files on you. You knew exactly what they were going to ask, what they were going to look for, and how to be credible in your responses."

"Do you think I'm lying now?" I'd asked. I'd kept my emotions in check. I'd even given her a small smile.

Tamara had looked at me for a moment. "No. No, I don't. I think you're working very hard at getting better," she'd said.

But I was pretty sure she wondered every now and again if I was telling her what she wanted to hear. Sometimes she'd look at me as though she was looking for some telltale sign of my lying to her. Most of my appointments with her involved debate and banter, and I wondered what today's appointment might entail.

Today was a scheduled appointment, and I'd been looking forward to it. I had something to share. I was smiling. I hadn't stopped smiling yet.

I knocked lightly on the open door. The woman looked up from the file in front of her and smiled. "Matt, come in."

I closed the door behind me and sat in my usual seat.

"You're in a good mood today," she said brightly as I sat down.

My smile got wider. "I am." Then I told her, still getting a thrill to say it out loud, "I asked Kira to marry me."

Her eyes widened, and her grin matched mine. "I take it he said yes."

"He did."

"That's really good news, Matt," she said.

"I can't tell you how happy I am," I said, knowing I sounded like a school kid, and not really caring. "It's not a magical fix, and I still have a long way to go. I know that. I'm not pretending this is going to fix anything overnight, but it's a good thing, yes? We've not set a date or anything. We're just taking it one day at a time."

Tamara was still smiling. "It is a good thing," she said. "And it's good you're both aware that while it's a positive step, it's still good to be cautious." She tilted her head, in the way that she does. "Did you think I wouldn't agree?"

"I didn't know what you'd think," I answered honestly.

"You sounded like you were waiting for my approval or my disapproval."

"I tend to babble a bit when I'm nervous or excited," I told her. "But I didn't want you to tell me we weren't ready for this kind of commitment."

Tamara was still smiling at me. "You didn't plan it? Was it a spur of the moment thing?"

I nodded. "We were at Mitch and Anna's wedding."

"Ah," she said with a nod.

"And after the speeches, and while Mitch and Anna danced, I just looked at Kira. I couldn't take my eyes off him. He signed, asking if I was okay. I signed back saying I was fine. And then I signed the words 'Marry me' across the reception hall," I told her, knowing my grin was ridiculous. "He didn't answer me straight away. We danced first, and we joked about his mom, how it'd keep her happy if she at least had some colors to work with when she planned the wedding. Kira said he thought blue and silver would be nice. Just like that, he picked out the colors to our wedding, well, for the invitations anyway. I asked him if that meant his answer was yes, and he said yes."

Tamara was grinning with me. "Sounds very romantic."

I sighed, trying not to smile, which was futile. "We kept it quiet though. We didn't want to take anything away from Mitch and Anna."

"Did you tell Kira's parents yet?"

"Tonight," I told her. "We'll tell them tonight. They were up at the cabin this last week, so Kira called them and told them to come around for dinner tonight."

"Do you think they'll be happy?" she asked. She always asked questions, like every answer was a test. It used to bother me, but I was used to it now.

"I think so." Then I amended, "Well, I hope so. They've been very good with me in the last six months. I think I've earned back some trust with them."

Kira's parents were often a topic of conversation between Tamara and me. She knew how much I loved them, and how sorry I was that I'd hurt them.

"I'm sure you have," she said. "The fact that Yumi calls you *her Matty*, I'm fairly certain she'll approve."

I nodded and shrugged one shoulder. "I just feel some-times, not all the time, but I wonder how long I have to feel like I failed them."

Tamara looked at me for a long, quiet moment. "That's an interesting choice of words, Matt," she said. "You said you wonder how long you have to *feel* like you failed them.

I'm sure they've forgiven you, but yet you still feel as though you owe them."

"I think I will for a long while," I told her. "And that's not a bad thing. A little remorse every now and then means I'll never take it for granted."

Tamara raised one eyebrow thoughtfully, which told me she didn't really agree with me. "Do you feel like you need to earn their trust again?" she asked. "Have they ever said that?"

"No, but I'd just feel better if there was something I could do that would tip the scales, you know? Make it better."

"Like marrying Kira?"

I shook my head. "No. Please don't reduce my love for him as some ploy to win favors with his parents, because that's not fair."

Tamara almost smiled. "That was a very good answer."

"To a poorly worded question."

Tamara smiled again. "Yes, it was. I apologize."

The corner of my mouth curled into a half-smile. This was the kind of relationship we had. We'd cross boundaries, prodding for reactions. Dr. Coulter knew I had the ability to keep my emotions in check and not react when someone else would. She'd dealt with enough detectives to know that. She was a little surprised I'd managed to fool the psych evaluations to go undercover, so she'd been wary with me from the beginning. But I swore to her, all pretenses were left at the door.

I'd explained to her, I was there to get better. I'd promised Kira I would do this, and I had every intention of keeping my word.

So our relationship was professional but brutally honest. "It's part of the guilt, yes?" I asked. "That I feel bad for what I've done. But there's no time limit, is there? No expiration date, so to speak."

"No, there's not," she answered simply. "You've apologized, and you're working hard at righting your wrongs. That's all you can do, Matt. It will take time."

I sighed. "I swore to them that I'd work on it forever, and I will. I just feel sometimes that they look at me, and they're remembering what I did, what I put them through." Then I admitted, "I just want to move forward."

"Is getting married going to do that?"

"Move forward? Yes. I want to spend my life with him," I told her adamantly. "I want him to know I'm serious, and that there will never be anyone else for me."

"Tell me, how are things going at the club?" she changed subjects like I'd predicted. "Really good. The guys are working so hard. Boss really runs a tight ship."

"How's Arizona?"

"He's doing really well," I said. "He's just moved into a nicer place. His wife's happy, so he's happy. He just wants to do right by her and his little girl."

Tamara smiled again. "He's become a good friend of yours."

"He has."

"Do you see your old police partners much?" she asked. "We haven't talked of them much lately."

"They call into the club every now and then," I replied. "And we try to catch up on weekends when they're not working. Kira sees them at his work at the gym. I talk to Mitch on the phone when I can. They work different hours, and I know what that's like."

"But you all make the effort."

"We do."

Tamara's smile faded a little and she looked at something in the file in front of her. "It's been a while since we talked about the kids at the club? How are they doing?" She titled her head. "Claude, isn't it? The child you mentioned before?"

I nodded. "They're okay. She's okay."

"You worry about her in particular."

"I do. I mean, I've always known kids live on the street. Everyone knows that, and as a cop, I saw it all the time," I explained. "But it's different now."

"Because you're seeing it from a different perspective."

"I am," I agreed. "But... I don't know... I worry about them all, but especially about Claude. She's a young girl on the streets... I know those stories don't always end well."

Tamara sighed. "Then you know what may very well happen to her."

"You can't know that," I said sharply. "You can't just presume she'll end up some drugged out whore or dead in a dumpster."

"Matt," Tamara said cautiously. "My concern is you, and I'm worried that if something were to happen to her, that you'd feel responsible."

I looked out of the window and bit my fucking tongue.

"You can't fix everyone, Matt."

"I don't want to fix *everyone*," I said, looking back to her. "Just her."

"Yes... No. I don't know. She's just a kid."

"You have enough to worry about with your own health, Matt."

I nodded but said nothing. She was right, but fucking hell, so was I. I didn't want to argue with her or deal with unresolved shit today. I was still on a high from Kira saying yes to marrying me. I had even been excited to come here and tell Tamara, but it seemed wasted. I looked at my watch, then back out of the window.

"Matt, you don't agree with me," she said. It wasn't a question.

"Not really."

"Would you like to discuss it?"

"No, not today," I said, finally looking at her. "These last few days have been some of the best I've had in a while, and I'd like to be able to appreciate that without arguing." I shook my head. "I think I'm entitled to a little bit of happiness, yes?"

"Of course you are," she said, in a tone that just pissed me off. All sweet and placating.

I stood up, cutting our appointment in half. "Look, maybe today's not the best day for this."

"Matt, we can talk about whatever you want," she said, her tone still not wavering. Always calm and calculated.

I stopped, knowing walking out wasn't going to help anyone. I bit back a sigh, but instead of sitting back down, I went and stood at the window instead. I didn't speak first, but I also didn't leave.

After a little while, Tamara said, "So, when you break the good news to Kira's parents tonight, are you telling them over dinner in a restaurant or telling them at home?"

I smiled, despite my sudden downturn in mood. She knew exactly what topic would make me stay. "Dinner at home. I was going to cook, but Kira thought it might be safer if he did."

And so we talked then about dinner and cooking and how I still sucked at it, leaving the session on a lighter note. As the meeting was wrapping up, Tamara reminded me of my next appointment. "I'll see you and Kira on Thursday."

"Yep, we'll be here."

"Matt, I'm sorry to put a dampener on your mood earlier," she said. "You were right. You deserve this happiness, and we should have focused on that today. Good luck tonight."

I gave her a genuine smile this time. "Thank you." I got to the door but stopped before I walked out. "We're going to revisit a few things I tripped up on today on Thursday, aren't we?"

She laughed quietly. "Yes, we will. But for now, go and enjoy dinner with your fiancé and soon-to-be in-laws."

I grinned at her words. *My fiancé.* "I will."

***

I WALKED in through the front door and found Kira in the kitchen. He was wearing cargos and a black T-shirt, which matched the color of his hair perfectly. "Hey," I said, putting down the brown paper bag of groceries so I could kiss his cheek.

"Hey," he said, leaning his cheek out for me to kiss. Then he looked up from the chopping board at me for a moment. "You look happy."

"I am happy."

"How was your appointment with Tamara?"

"Good," I answered, then told him how it had taken the shine off my day for a short while, but I was smiling again by the time I left. "She said she'd discuss it in more depth on Thursday when we go in."

Kira nodded and continued chopping the bell peppers. "No worries," he said.

It was great to see him smile again so freely. He had such a beautiful smile, and for a long while, I was the reason he didn't. But in the last six months, since we'd been working through our problems, he'd been smiling more and more often. It still warmed my chest to see it.

"What do you need me to do?" I asked. "Your mom and dad will be here soon."

"Did you get the pie?" he asked, eyeing the paper bag.

"I did. And everything else you asked for."

"Then you can set the table," he said. "I just have to finish this salad and we're done."

When I was almost done setting the dining table, there was a knock at the door. Before Kira could leave the kitchen to let his parents in, I stopped him. "I'll get it." Then as I turned and walked two steps toward the door, the room tilted, my head spun, and the next thing I knew, I was on the floor.

CHAPTER TWO

FUCKING VERTIGO.

The floor was on an angle, and even with my face pressed against it, it still wasn't where it should be.

Then strong hands were on my shoulders, and Kira pulled me onto the sofa. There was another knock on the door, and Yumi's voice followed. "Boys? You there? Why you make us wait? You better be dressed in there. I not want to see that."

I smiled, despite the buzz in my head and the queasy feeling in my stomach. Kira was kneeling in front of me. "One sec, Mom!" he called out. He looked at my face, concerned. "You okay?"

I nodded. "Yeah. I must have turned too quickly or something. Sorry."

He kissed my forehead as he stood up. "Don't apologize."

Kira let his parents in, and when Yumi and Sal saw me sitting on the sofa, they knew straight away what was wrong.

"Oh, Matty," Yumi said, rushing over to sit beside me. "You okay? You look pale. Did you fall?"

"I just turned too quick, that's all," I said quietly. "I'm fine."

This was the part I hated. Fucking vertigo from my middle ear injury which I'd received from fighting in unsanctioned, underground cage fighting. I'd almost lost Kira—I'd treated him so badly—and yet, he was nothing but concerned and attentive. The vertigo was a direct consequence of my actions, a physical reminder of what I had done, as was the deafness in my right ear. And every time I had a dizzy spell or a fall, Kira and his parents doted on me.

But this time, I refused to let the guilt eat at me.

I wouldn't let it fester. I wouldn't let it control me. I wouldn't let it come between me and Kira again.

I hated the fact that it served as a reminder, for me and Kira, that I'd betrayed his trust. And I did feel as though every time he helped me through an episode, it was like a step backward.

But still, I knew it would hurt him more if I allowed the guilt to consume me again.

Yumi put her hand to my face. "You sure you're okay?"

I smiled at her. "I am. It wasn't a full-blown vertigo episode, just a bit dizzy, that's all. I just need to sit for a minute, then I'll be right as rain."

"Okay," she said. "I'll just go see Kira in the kitchen." With a pat on my leg, the tiny woman jumped up and darted through the door.

Sal sat down across from me. He raised his hands and spoke in sign language. "Did you fall?"

I nodded and signed back to him, "Yes. I went to get the door, and the ground wasn't where it should have been."

Sal frowned. "Are you hurt?"

I shook my head slowly. "No. I'm fine, really," I signed. Then something occurred to me, something I should have thought about long before now. *Oh, dear God.*

Sal was adept at reading people, and when my eyes met his, I could tell he knew something was up. "What's wrong?" he signed quickly.

I swallowed hard, and with a quick glance over my shoulder to double check we were still alone, I turned back to him. "I need to ask you something," I signed, then kind of laughed at just how nervous I was.

He narrowed his eyes, curious. "Yes?"

"I should have asked before now, and I'm very sorry I didn't," I signed quickly, probably getting a word or two wrong. "I guess I'm not asking permission, but I'm asking if you'd mind terribly if Kira and I got married?"

He laughed, then signed slowly, "You must be nervous, because that didn't make sense." Sal's reaction was not one I had been expecting.

I barked out a laugh and nodded. I didn't think I'd got the words right. I wiped the palms of my hands on my thighs. I exhaled through puffed cheeks. "I am nervous, yes."

Sal grinned at me, then his smile slowly faded and his eyes widened. I could almost see the pieces coming together in his mind. "Married?" he signed. "You and Kira?"

Before I could answer, Yumi and Kira walked into the room. "Dinner's ready," Kira said, then looked slowly between me and his father.

Yumi picked up on the mood in the room too. "What you two talk about?"

I stood up slowly, making sure my head didn't spin. "I just had to ask Sal something," I told them, knowing Sal would read my lips.

Sal stood up, and as his gaze fell on Kira, he grinned.

Kira glanced at me and raised one eyebrow in question. So I told him, "I was trying to do this properly, but my sign language isn't as good as I thought."

"What you ask him?" Yumi asked, looking up at the three men who towered over her. "Why you not ask me?"

My eyes darted to Kira's, realizing this conversation was about to happen right now. "I wanted it to be a surprise..."

Kira looked genuinely shocked, even a little emotional. "Did you just ask my dad?"

"I tried—"

"Tried what?" Yumi interrupted. "Ugh, you boys!"

Kira stepped in beside me and put his hand on my lower back. "Mom, we were thinking blue and silver as a color scheme."

Yumi stared at us blankly. "For what?" Then she glanced round the living room, trying to find a clue of what we were talking about.

Kira smiled at his mom. "For the wedding invitations." Then he turned to his dad. "Matt asked me to marry him, and I said yes."

I guess in my head, I'd imagined Yumi throwing herself at us or at Kira, at least. But she didn't. She just stood there, as though she'd not heard what Kira had just said. Or that she wasn't too pleased with what she had heard.

"It's okay, Yumi," I started. "I know I haven't been perfect, and I'm really working on being a better person for Kira, but I love him and I know I hurt him *and* you and Sal, but I promise—"

My words stopped cold with the first of her tears. "Oh, please don't cry," I whispered, not really meaning to say it out loud.

Kira left my side and wrapped his arms around his

mom's tiny shoulders, and I was about to panic at her reaction when Kira turned to face me. He was smiling.

I looked at Sal then, who was also smiling. "Speechless?" he signed.

Kira nodded.

Sal chuckled and the big man threw his arms around me. When he let me go, he turned to his wife and put his hand on her shoulder. Yumi pulled away from Kira and smacked his arm. "You make me cry!"

Then she turned to me, and still teary-eyed, she hugged me. "Oh, Matty."

Sal hugged Kira in congratulations, and Kira asked him, "Did Matt really ask you for permission to marry me?"

"Sort of," Sal answered. "He tried, but his hands were shaking. All I got was something *right, terrible,* and *married.*"

Yumi, now tucked into my side, swatted her hand at Sal. "You leave my Matty alone."

"Mom," Kira said. "We thought you might like to organize it."

"The wedding?" she asked quietly.

"Well, yes," Kira said. "When we're ready. We haven't talked about dates or anything. We're not in any great hurry, are we?" he asked, looking at me.

I shook my head. "Well, I'd marry you tomorrow, but I'd also wait years. Just whenever it's right."

Kira smiled warmly at me, as though I'd said exactly the right answer.

Yumi looked up at me, then to Kira. "You really want me to?"

"Yes, Mom," Kira answered.

Then she started to cry again and nodded into my chest.

"We can discuss the rules later," Kira added.

"Rules?" she asked, standing up straight, dabbing her eyes with her sleeve.

"Yes, Mom. Rules," Kira said with a smile. "But we don't have to go through that now. How about dinner first?"

We sat at the table for one of my favorite dishes Kira cooked. It was a meatloaf style dish, with vegetables in it and some kind of sauce that was a Franco family secret, apparently. It was savory, spicy, and sweet somehow.

"This is so good," I said. I scooped up another forkful. "I tried to copy it once."

Kira looked at his parents and shook his head slowly. "It wasn't pretty."

"Or edible, for that matter," I said with my mouth half full.

Yumi gasped. "That's why you want to marry my Kira! For the family recipes!"

I laughed and swallowed my food. "Yes, yes, you got me. That's it, the only reason."

Sal grinned and put down his fork so he could sign. "I don't think the recipe would help Matt's cooking."

Kira laughed really loudly, and Yumi's lips twitched as she obviously tried not to smile. I just shrugged. "True," I signed. "I can make eggs on toast," I said and signed at the same time.

Kira tilted his head thoughtfully. "Well..."

"I said I can make them. I didn't say they tasted any good," I clarified.

Kira laughed and Yumi scolded him. "You leave my Matty alone."

"Thanks, Yumi," I said.

She frowned at Kira. "He can make coffee. And the bed. I see him make the bed one time."

Kira laughed again, and I sighed dramatically. Sal chuckled and signed, "And you want to be part of this?"

I smiled at him and nodded. "I do. But it's okay. If they keep it up, they won't get any of the pie I made."

"The pie you *bought*," Kira corrected me.

"Bought, made, same thing."

The usual banter continued, and when our plates were empty, I offered to make everyone coffee to have with the pie. I placed the coffee pot on the table and bought out a tray with cups, sugar, and cream. I put the pie in the middle of the table. "Pecan and caramel," I said.

"That's my favorite," Yumi said.

"I know. That's why I bought it," I told her. "I wanted everything to be perfect."

Yumi sat back in her chair and sighed with a smile. "Because you wanted to tell us you were getting married."

"Yes," I answered. "And because if you thought maybe it wasn't such a great idea, then at least we'd have pie."

"Why you think we wouldn't think it was a good idea?" she asked. "Matty?"

"Well," I said slowly. "Given what I put you all through..."

Sal shook his head. "We've forgiven you," he signed. "Kira has too. Maybe it's time you did."

I smiled and swallowed hard. "I'm working on it. I really am. I want to be the best man I can be, for Kira," I said, looking at Sal so he could read my lips. Then I signed, "He deserves the best I can be."

Kira startled me, suddenly appearing at my right side. I hadn't heard him move, which was something we were both still adjusting to. He kissed my cheek. "You'll do," he said with a smile. "Now cut the pie."

I served each of us a slice and poured the coffee. When

I handed Yumi hers, she said, "Okay so, boys, tell me these rules you make me do."

"Well," Kira started. "We don't have a date yet, so no pressuring us." He took a spoonful of pie into his mouth and chewed thoughtfully. "Nothing big, fancy, or too expensive. It's not a competition with the ladies at your book club."

"Bridge club," she corrected him.

Kira kept going, "Matt and I are paying for everything, so don't get any ideas about having to spend a cent. But apart from that, I think that's covered everything." He looked at me. "Matt? Anything to add?"

I sipped my coffee then put my cup on the table. "Well, maybe we should pick out our suits," I said, looking to Kira. I turned to Yumi. "The rest is your department."

"The rest?" she asked, her eyes widening.

"The rest?" Sal signed. "Everything?" He looked hard at Kira, then to me. "What are you doing to me? Do you have any idea how much I will suffer?"

"Oh, shush," Yumi said, which was rather funny, considering he never spoke.

I smiled. "Okay, Yumi, another rule. Be kind to Sal. Don't torture him too much with all of this."

Sal leaned back in his chair. He looked genuinely afraid. "I need more pie."

I laughed. "We have a spare room," I signed to him.

"Hey!" Yumi chided me with a pointed finger. "I saw that."

I stood up and walked around to her side of the table, leaned down and hugged her. "But I bought your favorite pie!"

I looked up in time to catch Kira sign to Sal. "Just be grateful he didn't cook it."

"I'm not that bad a cook," I said, pretending to be

offended. "It's just that my areas of talent are not in the kitchen."

Yumi swatted my arm. "I not want details," she said, shaking her head.

Kira gave me a warm smile, and I ran my hand up his arm as I walked past him to the kitchen. I put the pie back into the white cardboard box it had come in, and when I slid it in front of Sal to take with him, he smiled. "Is this bribery?"

"Whatever it takes."

"He not eat all that," Yumi snapped. "Not good for his cholesterol."

Sal signed something quickly, which I didn't quite catch, but it looked like he told her he'd eat what he damn well wanted. Kira laughed anyway, Sal grinned, and Yumi sighed. "Now I have you to take my side, Matty."

"I don't take anyone's side..."

"No," she said sharply, putting her hand to her chest. "You take *my* side."

Sal burst out laughing, and looking at me, signed, "Welcome to the family."

As much as they joked, those words warmed my heart.

When Sal and Yumi were leaving, they hugged us both. Yumi was more excited now, and at least the tears had stopped. She had spent the last half hour talking about research on menus, venues, fabrics, and what websites she could look at, and as Sal ushered her out of the door, he just rolled his eyes and sighed.

Kira closed the door behind them, leaned against it, and looked at me for a long, quiet moment. "I can't believe you asked my dad for permission."

"Not permission," I amended. "But I wanted to try and do it right. I got the words wrong, though," I admitted.

He pushed off the door and walked over to me. He slid his hand along my jaw. "I've never seen my mother speechless."

"I thought for a minute she was going to say no."

Kira smiled. "Never. She adores you." He kissed me softly, but then he pulled away. "What would you have done if she'd said no?"

I thought about that for a long moment. "I'd marry you anyway, but it wouldn't be the same without having your parents' blessing."

"When dad said 'welcome to the family' it kind of stuck with you, didn't it?" Kira asked quietly.

I nodded and leaned my face into his hand. He kissed my forehead, my temple, my cheek. Such gentleness, such love—it still amazed me that this man was still with me.

And I would never take him for granted again.

"I love your parents," I whispered. "And I love you." I looked into his eyes and said, "I don't think you realize just how much you're giving me."

He smiled. "My parents?"

I nodded and closed my eyes. "A family."

"Oh, Matt," Kira murmured and slipped his arms around me.

I sighed against him and simply enjoyed his embrace, his strength, his warmth. "Not just any parents. *Your* parents. *Your* family. They're amazing."

He kissed the side of my head. "To bed?"

I nodded against him. "Though you'll need to be gentle with me."

"Are you still feeling dizzy?" he asked, concerned.

"No. I ate too much pie."

Kira laughed, took my hand and flipped the lights off as he led me to bed.

"HEY, ARIZONA," I said, smiling at the huge man. He was wiping down the gym equipment before we opened, like we did every morning. I hadn't seen him since Friday. "I missed you yesterday. Everything okay?"

The tall man stood up to full height and smiled. His teeth looked so white against his dark skin. "Lashona had a doctor's appointment."

"Is she okay?" I asked.

"Oh, man, she's so good." His grin got wider. "She's gonna have a baby!"

I'm sure my smile matched his, and I gave him a hug. "Oh, Arizona, that's excellent news!"

He laughed. "It's still only early days. Twelve weeks, to be exact. We were fairly sure before, but the docs say not to tell anyone till that first trimester is done, and anyway, he confirmed it yesterday."

"I'm really happy for you, man," I said again. "I have some good news too."

Arizona's eyes lit up. "Whassup?"

"I asked Kira to marry me."

He grinned again. "Really? Yeah? Did he say yes?"

I nodded and laughed. "He said yes."

He looked down at my left hand. "Where's the ring, man?"

I looked at my ring-less finger, then back to Arizona. "Do guys wear engagement rings? Because I haven't got a clue."

"Well, I didn't when me and Lashona got engaged, but we didn't have no money for shit like that," he replied. "But I dunno. I wear a wedding ring now. When I'm not workin', that is."

"I didn't even think of rings," I admitted. "To be honest, I'm not sure Kira's the ring-wearing type."

Just then, Boss, the short, gruff man in charge of the center, walked over. He looked at the both of us like we'd sprouted second heads. "Quit ya smilin'," he barked at us. "You'll scare the shit outta the customers lookin' like that."

I laughed at him. "Good morning, Boss. *How was your weekend, boys?* Fine, thanks for asking. How was yours?"

"Don't get smart, Elliott," he said flatly. "I got something I want you to have a look at. You got ten minutes?"

I looked at my watch. "Sure. I have to open up soon, or those kids will be knocking my door down," I said.

"They can wait," he said seriously. "This is more important."

CHAPTER THREE

I LOOKED through the papers he'd handed me. They were spreadsheets. Financials on the first six months trade of the Harbor Fight Club.

"Got them last night," Boss said. "The admin lady gave 'em to me. Do they say what I think they say?"

I nodded and looked from the paper in my hand to him. "Yeah. We're not trading real well."

"What do we do?" he asked. "I'm a trainer, not an accountant. What the hell do I know about running a business—"

I put my hand up to stop him mid-rant. "Boss, no need to panic. We knew this would be tight, and we knew we'd have to do some self-funding. They're not about to shut the doors on us or anything. We just need to create more income."

He ran his stubby fingers through his gray hair. "How do we do that? People that come here ain't got no more to give. And I can't lay any of those boys off. It'd kill 'em to lose this."

I clapped my hand on his shoulder. Despite his rough

exterior, despite the way he barked at everyone, Boss was a genuinely goodhearted man, who really loved the FC. "We'll fix this. We need to call a meeting, brainstorm a bit, put all our ugly mugs together, and come up with some ideas. It'll be okay, Boss. We're not losing anything."

He exhaled loudly, and after a pause he nodded. "Figured you'd think more rational than me."

I smiled at him. That was as good as a compliment coming from him. "I'll round up these boys and see about calling a little meeting, huh?"

"What should we tell 'em?"

"Everything." My answer obviously surprised him. "Boss, no secrets. We're a team, yeah?"

He rolled his eyes. "Is that what bein' a cop taught ya? Team work and bonding and shit?"

"Yep. But don't worry. I won't make us hold hands when we sing 'Kumbaya.'"

He glared at me and snatched the spreadsheets out of my hand. "Get the fuck out of my office, Elliott."

I laughed as I walked back out across the gym floor to my 'office', or so I called it. It used to be an old kitchen and storeroom when it was privately run by Leon Tressler—the man I went undercover to take down. But we'd cleared it out, cleaned it up, and it was now like a community meeting room for the local kids.

The room itself was pretty big—fifteen by twenty feet of open space with a sink and kitchenette cupboards along one wall. We had some mismatched chairs, a table, and I had some plastic pamphlet holders on the wall near the window for all the brochures on subjects that affected these kids. I wasn't sure if they ever took any—from the stock levels I could safely say not many were missing—but if anyone ever needed information on drug use, STIs, teen pregnancy, or depression then they knew where they could get it.

Like every morning, I tidied up and restocked the kitchenette supplies. It was just cheap powdered chocolate, instant coffee, and powdered milk. I paid for it out of my pocket every week, which didn't cost a lot, but the kids that came in loved it. I'd bought a pile of old coffee mugs from the thrift shop and had a rule: you use it, you clean it.

And for a bunch of kids who didn't respect much, they respected that.

The ages of the kids that came in ranged from six or seven up to eighteen and even adults. Weekends were busiest, but after-school hours were busy too. I could also determine from the hours some kids came in, school was not on their to-do list.

All in all, I had about twenty familiar faces that I saw most days, another twenty on top of that maybe once a week or less. I ran self-defense classes a couple times a week, for kids who were interested, and had community nurses come and do talks on sex and drugs.

I helped them on the gym floor and helped Boss out ordering stuff and organizing the day-to-day stuff. I was still on 'light-duties' because of my vertigo. Even though the episodes were getting fewer, learning to live with hearing in one ear was something I was still getting used to.

I found myself turning my head to the side when talking to people, so I could hear better. Large open spaces with a lot of people, particularly in the gym, were harder than in smaller rooms, simply because noises seemed to get lost. Sometimes, like the other night with Kira, I'd find myself being startled by someone suddenly appearing on my right side, though most people at the club knew and were pretty good about it.

The kids had all thought me being deaf in one ear was lame until they'd found out how it had happened. I hadn't told them—maybe Cody or Jamaal had. It didn't really matter. A group of them had asked me directly, with a lack of tact only kids have. "Is it true?" one of the older kids had asked. "Was it from getting your head smashed in a cage fight?"

"Yes, it was."

"Did you save Arizona's life?"

"Well, I guess I did," I had answered. "But it was my fault he was in there with me."

"Does it hurt?"

"Nope. I get dizzy sometimes, but that's all."

"From being deaf?"

"No. Damage to the inner ear causes balance issues," I'd told them. "When I got hit, it messed up the inside of my ear."

Claude—the young girl I'd told my shrink about—had looked at me with her head tilted. "Is you okay?" she'd asked, all concerned.

I'd smiled at her and told her I was fine.

Claude, whose real name was Claudia, was also the one I was worried about. I mean, I worried about them all, including her brother Ruby, but her in particular.

The fact she—a small child on her own, or sometimes with her brother, who was only a few years older than her—walked off the streets of LA into a fight club at seven-thirty in the morning looking for something warm to drink was what concerned me. Like today, she walked into my office like she owned it, wearing the only clothes I'd ever seen her in.

"Hey, Claude," I said with a smile.

"Hey, Matt," she replied.

"No school today?"

She gave me a non-committal shrug for an answer as she made herself a hot chocolate. I'd asked about their family once before and she'd shut down on me, so I knew not to push that subject. I wanted her and her brother to feel comfortable here, to have a place they felt welcome.

Instead of asking questions she didn't want to answer, I picked up one end of the table and said, "Here, help me with this."

She put down the mug she'd claimed as hers and picked up the other end of the table. It wasn't heavy by any means, and even though she was tiny, I treated her like I would any of the kids.

"Whatcha got on today?" she asked, walking back to collect her hot cocoa.

"A bit of a meeting with the other guys when they get here," I said. Looking at my watch and seeing it was almost nine, I amended, "In about five or ten minutes, then I'm meeting with a lady from Hillvue Community College, and then this afternoon I have some sessions with you and the others."

Claude nodded. "Busy."

"I try to be," I told her. "I try and meet with another community venues at least once a week. I take this place very seriously, and I want them to take it seriously as well."

"That's pretty cool," she said, before sipping her drink.

"You like having somewhere to hang out?"

"Yeah," she said casually. "It's cool here. I like it."

"What exactly do you like about it?" I asked. "I mean, some feedback would be good. We're gonna have a meeting shortly about what we can do to improve this place, so any suggestions would be great."

"From me?"

"Sure. You come here. You do some training. You and Ruby use the facilities. Why not you?"

Claude's face lit up. "Seriously?" She took another drink and thought for a long second. "Well, shit. I can't think of anything."

I considered chipping her about her language but thought better of it. "Well, have a think and let me know later. I gotta grab these boys before they start lessons." I walked to the door, leaving the young girl alone in my office. Before I walked out, I turned back to her. "Hey, Claude?"

"Yeah?"

"If you're gonna stick around, can you finish sorting out those pamphlets and brochures for me?"

"Yeah, yeah." She tried to act like it was no big deal, but there was a smile in her eyes that told me otherwise.

I grabbed Arizona, telling him about the meeting, and Cody and Jamaal as they walked in too. "Hey, guys. We need a minute," I said, nodding toward the office.

"Sure, Matt," Cody said. "Wassup?"

"Boss wants to see us."

Jamaal groaned. "Well, this can't be good."

"Come on, it's not that bad." I led the way to Boss's office. He was at his desk, looking at the same spreadsheets. Chewing on his lip and with furrowed eyebrows, he looked worried and nervous.

"Boys," he said. "Come on in."

The four of us filed in to what used to be Tressler's office, which now belonged to Boss. "We got the financial reports for the first six months, and it doesn't look good. We need some money."

He had the tact of a wrecking ball.

Arizona, Cody, and Jamaal all paled, and it was a very

concerned-looking Arizona who spoke first. "What? Are we gonna lose our jobs?"

I stepped forward and put my hand up. "Whoa, stop. Jesus, Boss, you can't say it like that."

"It's the truth, ain't it?" the old guy said gruffly.

"Look, guys," I said, facing my three workmates. "What Boss is saying is *kind* of true, but exaggerated. It's not that bad. We're doing okay, but we just need to tighten up where we can." I looked at Arizona. "No one is losing their jobs, okay? We just need to think of some ways to increase the income for the club, that's all."

Then I clarified, for the benefit of everyone in the room, "When Boss asked me to take a look at the figures, it was my idea to bring you guys in on this. You're a part of this business, so your input is important. Some ideas on how we can get some money or increase our turnover and cash flow would be great."

"What the hell do we know about runnin' a business?" Cody asked.

"You're on the floor with our clients every day, man," I said. "Ask them what they like. What we're doing right, what we're doing wrong, what they want to see more of."

"Well"—Cody scratched his head—"Tressler made money from hosting fights..."

Arizona looked around Jamaal and glared at Cody. "You lost your freakin' mind, boy?"

Cody's eyes widened and darted to mine. "No, no, I didn't mean underground fights, man. That's not what I meant."

I gave him a smile. I knew he didn't mean anything by it. "Legal income. It can't be illegal in any way or the City will shut us down. And preferably an idea of something where no one nearly dies."

"I meant real fights, like a tournament or something, That's all I meant," Cody said.

I nodded. "That could work. We'll need more of a plan than just that, though. Is that something you could work on, Cody? Get some ideas together?"

The young man nodded. "Suppose. Just ideas though. Nothing too special."

"Maybe we could set up a legit tournament or something," Jamaal said. "Like a charity day or family day. I know that sounds kinda lame, but when I was a kid, I spent the holidays with my cousins, and in their town they used to have these family days where they closed off the street and had these stalls and shit. It was so cool, for a kid, ya know? No one does that shit anymore."

"I like the sound of it," I said, smiling at his enthusiasm.

"What kind of insurances you think we got?" Boss cried. "We need to make money, not spend it."

I looked to Boss. "We'll look into it," I told him. "I'll make some phone calls and see what has to happen. But it could be real good for us, the club, and the kids, ya know?" I looked back at Jamaal. "That could really work."

Arizona shook his head and smirked at me. "I'm gonna start callin' you Mike fuckin' Brady."

I laughed. "Just as long as we don't sing those songs we used to at camp, right? Like 'Kumbaya.'"

The three men stared at me blankly, and I realized none of them would have ever gone to camp. "Never mind."

Boss laughed behind me and clapped his hand on my back. "Different world here, Elliott. You don't wanna hear this lot sing anyway. Probably a good thing you're half deaf."

I chuckled at him. "Yeah, small blessings, huh?" Then I turned to the other three. "Okay, so the plan is this—I'll do some homework on having a community street day in conjunction with a tournament and see just what's involved. You guys talk to the customers, see what they'd like to have improved, and have a think yourselves about where you want this place to go."

Cody and Jamaal practically bounced with excitement as they walked out, and Arizona stayed back for a second. He was smiling. "You do realize you just rounded us up and gave out orders like you're still a cop, right?"

Boss snorted, and I laughed. "Yeah, but the strategic planning and morale talks worked, yes?"

He held out his fist, which I bumped with mine. "Sure did." Then he sighed. "Don't know what I'll do if this place shuts down."

"That's why we can't let it get to that," I said. "That's why we're acting now, so it doesn't happen. Okay?"

The big man nodded. "Just lemme know what you want me to do."

"I will."

He got to the door then stopped. "You know, if you want me to work later every day and run classes in the evenings as well as weekends, any extra shifts, I'll do it."

I gave a nod. "We'll see." Then I looked at Boss. "That goes for me too. If we need someone to do extra shifts..."

"You're supposed to be on light duties," he said. "And you're not even on our payroll."

"All the more reason to use me," I said. "And I'll see my doctor about my limitations and see what I can do. I won't push myself, but if I get the all clear..."

Boss sighed and gave a nod as he sat back down at his desk. "All right." Arizona left, and when I got to the door, Boss called out, "Elliott?"

"Yes, Boss?"

"What you did back there, with the boys, was good.

Arizona's right. You're good at organizing the team stuff and makin' 'em feel good about the place... They look up to you. They were unsure to begin with, when they found out you was still a cop, but you've earned their respect by doin' what you're doin'."

"Thanks."

"Don't get a fat head or anything, you hear?" he said, back to his gruff self. "And don't go tellin' them I said somethin' nice or they'll all go expectin' it."

I bit the inside of my lip to stop from smiling. "Wouldn't dream of it."

He grunted at me, which was my dismissal, so I went back out to my office and found Claude was still there. "Hey, my little assistant is still hard at work."

She grinned and stood back from the wall of brochures. "I rearranged them for ya. I put the girl stuff on this side and the boy stuff on this side and put 'em to match by color. I figure if they look different and we change 'em up once in a while, then people might take a second look, yeah? Might even pick one up."

I held out my fist to her. She looked at it for a while before she bumped her fist to mine. "You are one very smart kid."

She seemed proud of her work or pleased with my compliment. I wasn't sure which.

"Well," I told her. "I'm gonna run through some defense programs for you kids. Wanna help?"

Claude nodded eagerly. "Sure."

I went over to my desk in the corner. "Pull up a chair." I took out my folders and waited for my little assistant to get comfortable. "Right," I said, pointing to the charts and database tables in my folder. "These show what week we're up to and which program we're on. Right now, we're up to week seven, and see here?" I asked, pointing to the week seven column. "These are the moves I'll be teaching this week."

She glanced at the paper for a second then looked at me. "I didn't think you put that much thought in it. I just thought some kids turned up and you got 'em to do stuff."

I laughed. I loved the tact of kids. Brutal honesty. "There is a method to what I'm doing," I said. "Each week we learn new things, and in a certain order. You know, like in *Karate Kid*—wax on, wax off."

She stared at me blankly. "Huh?"

I chuckled. She'd obviously never seen that movie, the new or old version. "Well, it's kinda like painting. If you wanted to paint a tree, it'd make sense to try and draw it first, yeah? To make sure it all looks right before you add the paint."

"I guess."

"Well, that's what I'm doing. I'm teaching you how to draw before I'll let you paint."

She shook her head. "You know, all you had to say was self-defense requires skills with different stages."

I snorted. "Sorry. Forgot who I was talking to."

Claude rolled her eyes. "I'm nine, you know. I ain't five."

"I'll keep that in mind."

She sighed. "What else do you have to do?"

"Well, I need to finish this." I tapped the papers in front of me. "Then I was going to use the gym for an hour or so, have some lunch before my meeting with the community college, then run a session or two for any kids that turn up. That's my plan for the day."

"Hmm," she hummed. "Sounds pretty boring."

I laughed. "Well, if you're not busy for the day, young lady, how about you just try keeping up?"

The little girl smiled. "Deal."

And so I had got myself a shadow for the day. She helped me do some filing and tidying first off, then we did some restocking. I showed her where the supply closet was, where we stored all the cleaning products, paper towels, and toilet paper. "We need to make sure everything is stocked at the beginning of every day, in both bathrooms," I told her as I loaded up rolls of toilet paper in my arms.

She scrunched up her nose. "That's kinda gross."

I chuckled at her and handed her two rolls. "You can take those into the women's bathroom," I said and loaded on two more rolls.

I stood outside the entrance door and waited.

"Just sit 'em on top?" she called out.

On top of what, I didn't know. "Yep," I answered anyway.

She came out empty handed, so I presumed all had gone okay. I walked to the door of the men's bathroom. "I won't be a second." I walked inside, put the toilet paper in the cubical stalls, and was checking the paper hand towels when Claude walked in.

She leaned against the door, looked around the large room, and folded her arms. "What the hell, man?"

"What the hell, man, what?"

"Why's this one three times the size of the women's room?"

I laughed and clicked the hand towel dispenser back into place. "Well, it was originally a fight club, and there weren't any women fighters back then."

Claude put one hand on her hip and raised an eyebrow.

"You know," she said, pursing her lips. "We have equal rights now. It's the twenty-first century."

I grinned at her. "I heard that rumor, you know, about it being the twenty-first century and equal rights and all that." I put my hand on her shoulder and turned her around. "Come on, you shouldn't be in here. Out with you."

We walked out and back across the gym floor, and Arizona smiled at us. "You got yourself a helper?"

"Yep. She's just been lecturing me on equal rights."

Arizona stifled a laugh. "Keep up the good work, Claude."

I rolled my eyes at him and kept ushering the little girl toward my office. "Come on, squirt. Lunch time."

When we walked back into my office, Claude went straight over to the small kitchenette. "I'll just have another hot chocolate," she said.

Of course she didn't have any lunch with her. She came in here empty handed. It was hard seeing kids come in here, knowing they didn't have a nice home or proper food. I took out my lunch container from the small fridge and put it in the middle of the table. "You should eat something," I said simply.

"This hot chocolate is real good," she said.

"So are the salads Kira makes," I replied. "Fresh greens, peppers, cucumber, carrot. But you're right. Hot chocolate probably is better."

She eyed the container on the table, and I knew she wanted it. I wondered just how long it had been since she'd actually eaten anything fresh if a vegetable salad looked appetizing to a nine-year-old kid. "You're welcome to it."

She came over to the table like she couldn't have cared less and peered into the plastic container. She took it immediately, snatching the fork, and speared some greens and peppers. I watched as she ate it, like she hadn't eaten in days. If I was hungry before, I'd just lost my appetite.

I actually felt a little nauseated.

"Is there rice in this?" she asked with her mouth half full.

"Brown rice," I corrected her. "Kira is a bit of health freak. Each meal should have the right portions of nutrients, vitamins, protein, and fiber," I said with a smile, almost as a joke. "He only eats healthy stuff."

"It's good," she said while she chewed. She looked at the almost empty container and swallowed her mouthful. Reluctantly, she handed it back to me.

"It's yours," I told her. "Eat up. We're in the gym next. You need your energy."

"Is Kira your boyfriend?" she asked with her usual level of tact.

"Well, actually, he's my fiancé now, but yes, my boyfriend too."

She nodded and kept eating. She obviously knew, like most of the kids did, that my partner was a man.

"Does that bother you?"

She shrugged and speared the last of the salad with the fork. "Nuh." And she kept on eating like I'd asked her if she was bothered by the color of my shirt. "It's the twenty-first century, remember?"

I laughed at that. I held out my fist, which she bumped with hers, still holding the fork. "I like you, kid."

She slid the empty container back onto the table. "Tell Kira I said thanks. It was real good."

"Come on, time to hit the gym. You can go slow at first. We'll be going for an hour, so pace yourself."

"Why do you exercise so much?"

I quickly rinsed out the lunch container and wiped it

down. "It's good for your body. You have to look after your body. It's the only one you've got."

And that's pretty much how the day went. I did an hour or so on the bike and treadmill, then practiced jabs with Arizona, then Claude did too.

She had fun. Asked a hundred questions and seemed to absorb everything she learned. She sat quietly through my meeting with the community college while I tried to garner as much information on free courses and things the local kids could get in to. I explained our goals to help the kids learn and better themselves, and I think I made a good contact.

Janelle, a middle-aged lady with purple hair, was impressed with my Narcotics Division background and my new direction of teaching kids about drugs and trying to better their lives. I asked, if I could get a group of kids together, maybe we could visit the college and take a look around. Janelle thought that sounded great, and she left with promises that she'd be in touch.

"That went well," Claude said with an approving nod. "You really gonna take some kids up there?"

"Sure," I said, putting away my folders and locking the cabinet. "Maybe Rueben would be interested?"

"Maybe." She shrugged again.

I wondered where her older brother was. They were never too far apart. I'd asked once already today and she'd chosen not to answer, so I left it alone. But about half way through the defense class I ran for the kids in the afternoon, Rueben came in.

Without disrupting the class, I gave him a pointed nod toward the other kids, silently asking if he wanted to join in. He quickly got into formation with the others, picking a spot next to his sister, and finished the class with her.

When the class wrapped up, Rueben gave his sister a bit of a hug. "Thought I might find you here," he said to her.

"You took all day, Ruby," she chided him. "I was here all day."

Rueben scanned the room until he saw me. "She wasn't too much trouble?"

"Not at all," I said, walking over to them. "She was my little helper."

The older boy, all of twelve or thirteen, looked at his little sister and smiled. "As long as you don't get in his way."

She rolled her eyes. "Matt said I was *helpful*, Ruby, not in his way."

"Come on," he said to her, putting his arm on her shoulder to lead her out through the doors. But then he stopped and turned back to me. "Thanks, Matt. I appreciate it."

I checked my watch. "Kira will be here soon to pick me up," I told them. "Do you guys need a lift home?"

"Nah, it's cool," Rueben said. "Thanks anyway."

Then Claude frowned. "How come you don't drive?"

"I do," I answered. "Sometimes. If Kira's working late, I'll drive myself, but if he's finishing work around the same time, he'll swing past and pick me up. I'm not supposed to drive too much," I admitted. "Doctor's orders."

"Because of your ear, right?" Claude asked.

"Because of the vertigo, yes."

"That must suck."

I smiled. "It does. But it could have been worse."

"If you say so."

I chuckled at her snarkiness. "Well, Claude, you did good for your first day on the job. Wasn't too boring for ya?"

She shook her head. "Nah, it was fun."

"Will I see you tomorrow, or are you going to school?"

She raised an eyebrow at me, like I had no right to ask.

I added, "You know, just so I know if Kira has to make two lunches instead of one."

She tried not to smile. "Maybe." And with that, she waved her hand, said, "See ya," and she and her brother walked out the door.

I followed them out about ten seconds later, but when I looked up both sides of the street, they had already gone. I climbed into the waiting car and said hello to Kira.

"Good day?" he asked, probably curious about my smile as he pulled out into traffic.

"It was," I said "Productive and kinda fun. I had a helper today."

"A helper?"

"Claude. She was just hanging around, so I told her she was my assistant for the day." Then I added, "She loved your salad, by the way."

"She ate your lunch?"

"Well, she didn't have any," I said. "Actually, by the way she scarfed down a vegetable salad, I don't want to think about the last time she ate."

"Matt..."

"What?" I asked. "She's just a kid. I wasn't just gonna eat in front of her."

"I know, but you can't start feeding the kids. If you do it for one, you should do it for all of them, and Matt, that's—"

"I know," I said, cutting him off. "It's not my responsibility. But it kind of is, Kira. Claude comes in and fills up on hot chocolate like it's the only thing she'll have all day, and that's hard to watch, ya know?"

Kira slid his hand over the console and took mine, giving my fingers a squeeze. "I know."

"Anyway, I told her I'll bring another salad for her

lunch tomorrow if she turns up for work." I could feel Kira's eyes on me as he drove, and although I deliberately didn't look at him, I squeezed his hand. "I know what you're going to say, babe, and I get it, I do. But she's just a kid."

"They're all just kids."

I nodded. "I know. It's harder than what I thought it would be," I told him honestly. "For years when we encountered kids on the street, they were just nameless faces. Each of them was different, and sure, they each had a story to tell, and I guess we were kind of jaded as cops…"

"But they're not nameless anymore?"

I looked at him then, and when his eyes left the traffic and found mine, I nodded. My voice was quiet. "No, they're not."

"Matt, you're doing a good job," he said reassuringly. "You knew there'd be issues you'd have to deal with."

I exhaled loudly. "I know, I know." I tried to shake it off. "How was your day? Tell anyone you're a spoken-for man?"

"I've been a spoken-for man for a year and a half, thank you very much," he said with a smirk. "Did I tell anyone we got engaged? Yes."

I smiled automatically. "Who?"

"Chris," he said. "Being my boss, I figured I should tell him first. Then Abby and Jeff, the other trainers that were on today."

"Any clients?" I asked, wondering if any of my old workmates knew.

"Thought I'd leave those honors to you. Mitch isn't back yet."

"No, he has another week on his honeymoon."

"And Anna will kill you if you call him," Kira said with a half-grin. "For anything."

I laughed. "She might have told me that."

"She *did* tell me that."

I snorted out a laugh. "I have to tell him first, out of all the guys. Oh, but I told Arizona, but he one-bettered me."

Kira looked at me and smiled. "What'd he do?"

"He and Lashona are having another baby." I shook my head. "You should have seen him. He was still grinning when I left."

We pulled up at the house, grabbed our gym bags from the back seat, and went inside. "What did you want to do for dinner?"

"You haven't eaten all day, have you?"

"Not since breakfast."

"Oh, Matt."

I pulled a pint of yogurt out of the fridge, grabbed a spoon, and ate it straight from the carton. "Oh," I said, "I almost forgot. Boss got some half-yearly financials through and kinda panicked about the money side of the business, so I suggested a think-tank of sorts with the boys. Anyway, we're thinking of holding a sort of fundraising, family day." I shoved another spoonful of yogurt in my mouth and swallowed. "I gotta do some homework, see what we can find out, but it was a pretty good idea."

Kira smiled warmly at me, but he didn't say anything.

"What?"

"Just you."

"What about me?" I asked, wondering where he was going with this.

"You used to say you loved being a cop, but you never smiled then the way you do now when you talk about your day."

I put the lid on the yogurt and opened the fridge to put it back. I leaned over to him and kissed him softly. "That's because I'm happier doing this than I was being a cop." I turned back to the fridge and pulled out the raw chicken. "How about I cook dinner?"

Kira took the dish of chicken out of my hand, and when I looked at him, he shook his head. "How about *I* cook dinner?"

I pouted. "I'm not *that* bad a cook."

With his free hand, he took my chin between his thumb and forefinger and pulled me in for a quick, hard kiss. "But, baby, you're not that *good* a cook either."

CHAPTER FOUR

"COME IN, GENTLEMEN. TAKE A SEAT." Tamara smiled, closed the file in front of her, and gave us her full attention.

We walked into the psychiatrist's office and took our usual seats—with Kira on my left so I could hear him—and Tamara wasted no time. "You're both looking well. Kira, I believe congratulations are in order," she said. "Tell me, when Matt was here earlier this week, you were going to tell your parents that you were engaged. How did that go?"

"Very good," Kira answered. "We rendered my mom speechless. And then she cried, but they were happy tears."

"They were," I said, looking at Kira. Then looking at Tamara, I told her, "I had an episode of vertigo when I was going to the door to let them in, and that kind of ruined the moment a little, but it was all fine."

"What happened?"

"I was setting the table, turned to go to the door, the room spun, and I hit the floor," I said. "Kira picked me up and put me on the sofa."

"Did that upset you?" she asked.

"No," I answered immediately. Honestly. "Like I said before, vertigo is something I'm learning to live with. Is it frustrating? Yes. Is it embarrassing? Yes, it can be. Do I blame anyone for it? No. Do I resent myself for needing Kira's help? No." I sighed. There was no malice in my tone. I was simply stating a fact. "It just is what it is. Like being deaf in one ear. It's a... condition I have, something I have to live with. That's all."

I reached over and took Kira's hand, and he squeezed my fingers. "It's true, Tamara," Kira said. "Matt's really very good about it. Takes it in his stride, doesn't get angry or shut down on me. Same with the hearing loss. It's just something we deal with."

"True," I agreed. "And like I've told Kira before, I doubt I'd have dealt with losing the hearing in one ear so well, if it weren't for his family. Sal's completely deaf, so concessions for that and sign language are just part of the daily norm."

"I agree," Tamara said. "I'd imagine it's helped a great deal." She looked between us and smiled. "You two have come a long way."

"It's because I tell him everything now," I said. "Probably too much. I talk about what's going on at the club all the time." I looked at Kira. "Does it drive you crazy?"

Kira chuckled and shook his head. "Not at all. I love hearing about it." He looked at Tamara. "It's a nice change from police work where he couldn't really talk about the day to day stuff. And it kind of helps when I visit that I know what's been going on."

"You visit the club often?" she asked.

"About twice a week," he answered. "If I'm working an afternoon shift, I'll call in for an hour or so. Sometimes just for a chat with the other guys if Matt's busy."

"And you're finding the change of pace suits you, Matt?" she asked.

"It's really good," I answered. "To be honest, it's welcome. I mean, I'm busy most of the day and there's always something to do, but it's not as demanding as being a cop, that's for sure." Then I added, "One of the kids, Claude, the one I told you about before, she said what I did sounded boring."

"How's she doing?" Tamara asked, her head tilted to the side.

"I haven't seen her in two days. She spent the whole day with me on Tuesday, but I haven't seen her since."

"Do you worry?" Tamara asked.

"Of course," I said with a shrug. "But kids come and go. Some of the other kids said they've seen her and Rueben, Claude's brother, so they're around. Maybe they're busy at home. I don't know. They'll come in when they can."

Tamara gave me a small smile, and I knew we'd be talking about this again in my next session. Then she looked at Kira and started talking through some trust exercises we would quite often do. In the beginning, after I'd got out of hospital, some of these sessions had been tense—particularly on my behalf. I had been worried I'd say the wrong thing or upset Kira even further. But six months on and these sessions were sometimes fun. We'd laugh a bit and get the giggles between us, and even Tamara would find herself smiling at us.

Today was one of those days. For the rest of the hour, we had questionnaires that Tamara had written just for us that we had to complete on each other. Some of the questions were serious, like the ones about what we wanted for each other by getting married, and what our expectations were, and we had to answer what we thought each other would want and expect.

But some questions were funny, and the fact we got nearly all them correct and we could laugh about the ones we got wrong, really just showed how well we knew each other. How far we'd come.

We left the session in a good mood, and when we got to the car, I stopped Kira from getting in. "Can I ask you something?"

Kira was still smiling, but his eyes were cautious. "Sure."

"Did you want to get rings?" I asked. "You know, engagement rings? I mean, I don't even know if guys wear them. I guess there's no reason why we can't. It's just that I asked you to marry me and forgot about the rings."

Kira's smile widened to a grin. Then he scratched his head. "Um, I don't know... it's not like I can wear one at work. Not without damaging the ring or my finger."

I'd reasoned that very thing, but it still stung that he didn't want to. "Oh."

"Do you want to?"

"Well, no, it's okay..." I started to say no, but stopped. No more lies. "Yes. I do. I want to wear something that says I'm with you."

"Like a shirt?"

I pushed his shoulder. "Shut up. You know what I mean."

He laughed and got in the driver's side. I opened the passenger door and, with a sigh, got into the car. But when he'd pulled into traffic, instead of turning left to go home, he went straight ahead.

"Where are we going?"

"To look for something that says you're with me."

I grinned at him. "Really?"

"If you want it, then yes."

"I do," I said. "I just don't know what."

"What do you mean?"

"Well, I've been thinking about it. I thought about maybe getting a tattoo," I said.

Kira jerked his head around to see me instead of the road.

"Watch the traffic, babe. And I'm not discounting that idea, but you know what? As silly as it sounds, I think I'd really like to get a ring."

Kira smiled but seemed surprised. He pulled the car into a spot and pointed up the sidewalk. "There's a jewelers just up there."

We got out of the car and headed in the direction he'd suggested. I was so excited, but as we got to the door of the jewelers, Kira stopped and pulled me aside. "A tattoo? You thought of getting permanently inked?"

I nodded. "Yep, permanent and meaningful."

He seemed a little lost for words. Eventually, he said, "What would you get?"

"Well, it would need to be something symbolic, and I was thinking—you'll probably think this is stupid—but I was thinking of getting a warrior." Then I elaborated, "A Samurai warrior, but he would hold a Spanish shield." I shrugged and looked up the sidewalk. "You know, to represent you: Japanese and Spanish and a fighter. Like I said, it's probably silly..."

Kira lifted my jaw so I looked at him. And there in the broad light of day, in full public view, he kissed me.

"That's not silly," he said quietly. "Matt, that's... I really do love you."

I smiled. "I love you, too. So maybe I should get both?" I

asked with a laugh. "The tattoo *and* a ring?"

Kira laughed and opened the door to the jeweler's. He walked in and stood aside, holding the door open for me. I walked inside, still smiling, and the lady behind the counter greeted me. "Gentlemen, what can I help you with today?"

"Rings please," I answered.

She showed us a few trays of silver and gold bands, and I picked one that was a beveled edge, polished tungsten something-or-other as the woman told me, but I didn't care. I just liked it. I tried it on and they had the right size, so I told her I'd take it.

"We'll have two," Kira said.

I looked up at him. "Really?"

Kira looked at the saleslady. "I'll need a necklace or something to go with it, please."

He chose a black leather strand that, when worn with the ring secured on it, sat just above his sternum. It looked fucking hot.

And something was very clear.

"I'll have a leather necklace too," I said. My voice was quiet but sure.

"Matt?"

"I want to wear it. I really do," I told him. "But not until we're married. I want to wear it for real."

Kira's lips twitched, as though he was trying not to smile, but his eyes gave him away. "You're unbelievable. It was your idea to do this!"

"We don't have to get them now," I said quickly. "We can put them on lay-away or come back later..."

Kira put his hand to the ring that was still hanging around his neck. He looked from me to the saleswoman. "We'll take them now."

I grinned like an idiot, and the poor lady behind the

counter couldn't help but chuckle at me. "Did you want to wear the necklaces now? Or shall I box it all up for you?"

"Box them up, please," I said.

"You sure?" Kira asked. He looked as though he found my enthusiasm amusing.

I turned and faced him, so the saleswoman couldn't see my face. I bit my lip. "I think we should try them on at home."

He understood what I meant.

"We'll take them to go," he said.

I paid, and five minutes later we were on our way home. I was still smiling and Kira kept glancing at me as he drove. "We only have two hours before I have to go to work, you know."

"Plenty of time," I said. When we got home and walked inside, I pulled the small black boxes from the paper bag. "You really need to wear this." I pulled out the leather strand and then his ring, and threaded it through. He was standing close to me and I could almost feel his eyes on me. "Take your shirt off," I said, my voice gruff.

I looked up at him as he pulled his shirt over his head. He had a smug smirk, but his eyes were dark. "You really liked it on me," he said. "I could tell in the store."

I couldn't deny it. "I did." Then I whispered, "Turn around."

I held either end of the leather necklace, lifted it over his head, and tied the two ends together. I traced my fingers along his shoulder, and he turned back around slowly to face me.

The ring sat on his chest—dark silver on black leather. But it was more than that. It was the ring he'd wear when we were married. I touched it lightly, feeling the cool of the metal under the rise and fall of his chest. "It's beautiful."

Kira surprised me by taking my face in his hands and kissing me deeply, thoroughly. His hands, his lips, his tongue—there was an urgency, a passion in his touch, his kiss. He fisted my shirt, only pulling his mouth from mine to rip the shirt over my head before quickly kissing me again.

With a soft groan, he slowed the kiss and pulled my bottom lip between his. His eyes were still closed, his full lips were wet and red. "Matt..."

"Mmm," I hummed. "You can kiss me like that any time."

He chuckled and opened his eyes. "Your turn," he said, and licking his lips, he took the box. "Turn around for me."

I did as he asked and his adept fingers ran across my skin. I felt an overwhelming sense of love and peace as the cool metal ring was placed above my heart.

I automatically touched the ring, and Kira turned me by the shoulders so I faced him.

"Kira," I said, suddenly overcome by emotions. My eyes sprung with tears. I wasn't embarrassed—in fact, I raised my chin proudly. "I'm so happy right now."

Kira traced his fingers along my jaw with the touch of a feather. "Then why the tears?"

"Happy tears," I said. "Overwhelmed... I'm so grateful for you. I can't explain what it means that you want to marry me."

"Matt," he murmured.

Even after these last six months of me battling demons, guilt, and insecurities, he never faltered. He was my absolute rock. "Kira, please take me to bed."

He took my face in his hands, gently this time, and kissed me softly. Then he took my hand and led me to our room.

Sex between us was different now. Since *then*, when I'd

been undercover and would basically beg him to hurt me. *We* were different now. We were more open with each other, communicated better, and there was a closeness now that wasn't there before.

And how this overflowed into the bedroom was no different.

Gone was the rough sex, *the fucking*, and in its place was eye contact and hand-holding, soft kisses and whispers of love. We still had passion, and there was still urgency and need, but different emotions fueled us.

I bottomed mostly—it was just what felt natural between us, and to be honest, I preferred it. Kira did too. He was a natural top, and without fail, he took care of my pleasure before his own.

Kira undressed me, he kissed every inch of skin he could reach, he prepped me, and he filled me. My legs fell open for him and his hips rolled into mine. He was buried deep inside me. He held one of my hands and his other hand wrapped tight around my cock. His open mouth pressed to mine, his tongue teasing, tasting. He knew which buttons to press, what turned me on, what made me come.

With long, deep thrusts inside me, with low moans and his tongue in my mouth and his hand squeezing, pulling and twisting, my orgasm spilled between us.

Kira leaned back, flexing his hips into me, beckoning every ounce of pleasure from me he could. And only when I was boneless and blissed out, did he realize his own pleasure.

He held my hips and thrust into me. When he was buried to the hilt inside me, he leaned over me once more and rolled his hips, again and again. The ring on the necklace swung between us in time with his thrusts.

"God, Kira," I groaned.

"You feel so good." He grunted. "I don't want this to end."

I took his face in my hands. "It never has to. You can have me forever."

And with a final thrust, his body flexed and stilled as he filled the condom inside me. He collapsed on top of me with a groan and a chuckle, and after a moment, he pulled out of me. Rolling off me, he quickly wrapped his arms around me.

"You look so good with that leather band around your neck," he said with a kiss to my temple.

I chuckled. "Do you have a leather kink I don't know about?"

He laughed. "No, but I so have a 'he belongs to me' kink."

I burst out laughing and leaned up on my arm so I could see his face. "Well, it's just as well that I do belong to you."

Kira smiled and touched the ring on the necklace around my neck. "I'm really glad you suggested this."

"What? The rings or the sex?"

He grinned. "Both."

I looked down at the smeared, drying messes on our stomachs and the condom on his now softened cock. "We really need to get cleaned up," I said, but as I tried to roll off the bed, Kira stopped me.

He looked me in the eye seriously. "Matt, I love you and you mean the world to me."

He quite often told me this, like it was his job to remind me. "I know," I told him. I leaned in and kissed him. "And I won't ever doubt it again."

"Go start the shower," he said with a smile. "I'll join you in a sec."

I hadn't even got under the water and he was behind me. I soaped up and he rubbed me down, skimming his hands over my body as the water washed me clean. He kissed over my right shoulder and up my neck to my ear. It was weird—it still made me shiver, it still gave me goosebumps when he gently bit down on the lobe, but I heard nothing.

There was no whispers, no soft moans. Not in my right ear anyway.

But then his lips found my left ear and he whispered, "You're done. My turn."

He was even sexy bossing me around in the shower. I returned the favor, soaping him up and washing him down, planting soft kisses across his shoulder blades, and when he turned around, the sight of the ring resting on his chest took my breath away.

He must have seen the look in my eyes, because he said, "If we don't leave soon, we'll be late."

I smiled as I kissed his collarbone, and the water washed over both us. "You might get into trouble for being late to work, but I won't."

Kira growled and bit my shoulder. "Not fair." He shut the water off, stepped out of the shower, picked up a towel, then threw it at me. "Anyway, those kids wouldn't let you forget it, and neither would Boss."

"True."

He kissed me lightly before he walked out of the bathroom. "Five minutes, babe."

Exactly five minutes later, we were in the car and headed to the Club. Kira pulled up where there was a spot, not too far from the doors to the fight club.

"Who are those two?"

"They're the two guys I've told you about."

"The two guys who've been hanging around outside?"

"Yep. That's them."

"Is that Rueben?"

I looked out of the windshield to where the small African-American boy was talking to the two men on the corner of the block. "Yep."

"Does he know those guys?"

"Don't know. I've seen them hanging around a bit. They don't come into the club, so I don't really see much of what goes on outside of it," I said.

"They look like trouble," he said quietly. "I mean, what kind of adults hang around kids like that?"

"The ones with not-so-nice objectives. The type that shouldn't be on the streets."

Kira was quiet for a long second, his brow creased, and he looked at his hands. "Matt... you're not a cop anymore..."

"That's why I'm not involved in any way," I told him. It probably should have bothered me that he thought I was involved, but it didn't. He had every right to ask. "And I *won't* be involved in any way. If I think they're a threat to anyone, I will put a call in to the department. I promise you, Kira, I won't put myself or anyone I love in jeopardy again."

He looked at me and smiled. "I believe you."

I looked back out to where Rueben was. He seemed happy enough—he was smiling anyway. "But right now, those two guys are just innocent men on the street. Maybe they live close by. I really don't know."

Kira nodded. "It's okay, Matt. You don't have to justify anything."

"I know," I told him. "And you don't have to justify asking. I will tell you anything. No more secrets, remember?"

Kira smiled again. "Like the tattoo you wanted? Were you going to tell me about that?"

"No," I said with a snort. "It was a secret."

This time, Kira laughed. "Maybe we should talk about that some more."

"You keep bringing it up," I said with a grin. "I'm starting to think you're rather taken with the idea?"

"I wasn't," he said, looking a little embarrassed. "Until you mentioned getting one that reminded you of me."

"Well, I do rather like the idea of having you permanently etched into my skin."

Kira's head fell back and he groaned. "Get out or I'll be late. I'll see you at about a quarter-past nine."

I snorted. "You know what else we mentioned once the other night but haven't since?"

Kira looked at me, somewhat nervously. "No, what?"

"A dog. At the wedding, I mentioned kids—which was just an errant comment, by the way—and you said we should probably start with a dog."

"Oh, God," he mumbled. "We're going to be looking at dogs, aren't we?"

I grinned hugely and nodded. "Dogs and tattoos."

Kira laughed out a sigh. "Go on, get out of the car. Before you bring up any other life-changing suggestions."

I gave him a grin for good measure then got out of the car. As I walked up to the front doors of the fight club, Rueben walked over too. "Man, you are in trouble!" he said.

I smiled at the kid. "What for this time?"

"Claude's been here all day, waitin' for you to show up."

"I told her I was doing a late shift and I'd be here in the afternoon!"

The little guy shook his head pitifully. "Well, she's reorganized everybody, and you're in trouble."

I laughed and put my hand on the boy's shoulder, leading him to the door. "Well then, come on. I better get this over with."

CHAPTER FIVE

CLAUDE WAS FEISTY. All four and a half feet tall and full of sass. She greeted me with her hand on her hip and a raised eyebrow. "Where th' hell you been?"

Boss, who was standing behind her, grinned. He didn't have to say anything when a pint-sized spitfire could say it for him.

I looked at my watch. "I'm on time! I said three o'clock!"

Claude rolled her eyes. "Lots to do today, Matt."

"She's been waitin' all day for you, man," Arizona said, walking up to me. The big man smiled. "Keepin' all of us organized too."

I smiled at the little girl. "Good to see someone's in charge, Claude."

She beamed. "What are we doing first, Matt?"

"Well, I'll just put my bag in my locker, then you and me are going to go to church," I said. "We have an hour before our first class."

Ruby, who had been quiet up until this point, laughed. "Church? What the hell for?"

"Yeah, Matt?" Claude chimed in. "What are you takin'

me there for? Do you need to talk to God?"

Arizona bit back a chuckle, and I smiled at Claude. "Not to God. Well, not this time anyway, kiddo," I answered. "I need to talk to the priest."

"The what?"

"The man that works there," I said, simplifying my answer.

"Right then," she replied, standing there expectantly. "Well, come on. We're running out of time."

I went over and threw my bag into my locker. "All right, squirt. Keep your hat on." I shut my locker door. "You're worse than my old boss, and he was like a military drill sergeant."

Rueben laughed, and Claude eyed her big brother. "You comin' Ruby?"

"Nah," he said dismissively.

"You'll be here when we get back, right?" she asked.

"Sure," he said.

She nodded, happy with that, and I walked to the door and held it open for her. "Come on. God forbid if I'm running late."

"You probably shouldn't say God if we're going into a church," she lectured me as she walked out, making the guys in the club laugh.

I shook my head at the little girl but stepped in stride beside her, and we headed toward the old church on the corner of the next block. She wore the same simple clothes —a pair of shorts and a shirt that looked dirty, and her shoes were old and looked a bit too small. There definitely were no brand names and were most likely second hand when she'd got them new. Her black curly hair was wiry and wayward, but it added to her charm.

"What are you going to see this man for?" she asked, as

we made our way up the sidewalk.

"Well, you know how we're trying to organize some fundraising?" I asked.

Claude nodded, so I said, "Well, we're going to see if he wants to help out."

Claude looked up at me, and her big brown eyes narrowed. "I didn't think churches had money."

"I'm not going to ask him for money," I said, stopping at the steps to the church. I pointed toward the door. "I'm going to ask him if he wants to get on board with us."

I opened the heavy wooden door and waited for Claude to walk in under my arm, then I followed her. It was a large rectangular-shaped room, with stained glass windows and wooden pews in rows. It was empty and even a little cold. Claude seemed hesitant so I headed up the aisle first, and the small girl followed close behind me.

We were met by a curious, middle-aged man. He was well-dressed for this part of town, wearing gray slacks and a white business shirt, and his thick, short brown hair was kind of slicked down. He smiled warmly, and wrinkles creased at the corners of his eyes. "Can I help you?"

"I'm looking for Father Michael?" I asked. Boss had given me a name, or the name he thought belonged to the man who'd been the priest here for the last ten or so years. Boss wasn't a religious man, or so he'd explained, but he thought that was the name someone had given him.

The man in front of me smiled again, but it was cautious this time as he eyed me then Claude, who was still close behind me. I recognized the look. From my years as a cop, I could tell this man was street-wary. I concluded he was the man we were here to see before he confirmed it. "I'm Father Michael," he said.

I extended my hand and smiled. "I'm Matthew Elliot,

and this here is Claudia."

He shook my hand and smiled more genuinely this time. "And what brings you to Saint Andrews?"

"Well, as you probably know, the fight club on the next block has been taken over by the City of Los Angeles."

"Yes," he said. "And are you in favor of this recent development?" he asked, obviously not sure of my purpose.

"Very. I'm proud to say I had a hand in closing the drug-ring down," I told him. "Leon Tressler was a grub and is well-placed behind bars."

Father Michael's eyes widened. "You're *that* Matthew Elliot?"

"I am," I told him. "And we now run drug and self-awareness classes and fitness courses for the local kids. I'm trying to get schemes set up for kids, to give them a chance when no one else would."

"It's very admirable," he said.

"It's very costly."

He smiled knowingly. "Whoever is generous to the poor lends to the Lord, and He will repay him for his deed," he said, rattling off some biblical quote. Then he added, "But if you've come looking for funds... the church simply has none to give."

"No, not money. Advice," I told him quickly. "We have some government funding, but it's not enough to keep our doors open. We're looking into additional sponsorship, but we're trying to get a community fundraising day together."

"And you want *advice?*"

I nodded. "Yes, and your support."

Father Michael looked at Claude. "Do you like the new club?"

She nodded. "It's pretty cool," she said. "Matt here treats me pretty good."

"Claude here is my second-lieutenant," I said with a smile. "She keeps the place running smooth—don't ya, squirt?"

She rolled her eyes, and the priest tried not to smile. "I can see you're trying to do good with these kids," he said to me. "I think we can work together on this. I'm open to suggestions. We're not busy here like we used to be," he went on to say. "Times are tough."

"They are," I agreed.

Then Claude said, "If you want people to come in, Mr. Michael, maybe you should make it look like fun." The little girl looked around, then up at both of us. "It looks scary."

I smiled at Michael, and he nodded, most seriously. "I will take that into consideration."

Claude nodded, like her work here was done. "It couldn't hurt."

The priest looked at me. "Second-lieutenant, yes?"

I nodded. "Yep."

We talked for a little while longer, about ideas and legal requirements, with Michael promising to come into the club one day and see for himself. And when we headed out of the front of the church to leave, the two skinhead-looking men were on the sidewalk again. They were only walking past, but I could tell from the look that crossed Michael's face, he didn't like them.

"Do you know much about them?" I asked.

"Tyler James and Darius McInnes."

The names meant nothing to me. I'd not heard of them before. "I've only seen them around. But they seem to hang around the kids a bit."

"Tell the kids around here to steer clear of them," he said softly, but his warning was clear.

I nodded. "I will," I promised. "Come on, Claude. Work

to do, remember?"

She ran over to me and with promises to be in touch, we went back to the FC.

Like every other afternoon, I ran some health and fitness classes for the kids that turned up, showing them some exercises and a few new self-defense moves. I also tried not to think about how most of them left, without parents or siblings, onto the darkened LA streets.

Just before closing time, when all the kids were gone and Arizona was with his last client, I picked up the phone. I didn't use the phone much anymore. If I was at home, it was fine, or if the club was quiet and it would be a quick call, it was okay, but putting a phone to my only functioning ear limited all auditory sensors to the phone call and nothing outside of it.

"Kurt Warner," he answered his phone abruptly.

"Hey, Kurt, it's me, Matt."

"Elliot!" he replied, his tone now cheerful. "Let me guess. You miss us, and given Mitch is still on his honeymoon, I'm your next best option."

I snorted into the phone. "You should be a detective."

He burst out laughing. "What's up?" he asked, getting to the point of my call. "How's things? You and Frankie looked tight at the wedding, so I'm presuming all things are good on that front?"

"All things are great on that front," I said, smiling as he called Kira 'Frankie'. It was the name all our police friends still used for him. I considered not saying any more until I'd spoken to Mitch, but my no-secrets policy extended to everyone. "I um... I asked him to marry me," I said, my smile widening. Without making a conscious decision to do so, my hand went to my new necklace, feeling the metal band that hung from my neck.

"Oh, man, that's so good," he responded genuinely. "I'm so happy for you! Though all these freakin' weddings are gonna send me broke."

I laughed. "You've got plenty of time to worry about that."

"No immediate plans, huh?" he asked. "Oh man, Mitch doesn't know, does he?"

"No. Kira said Anna will kill me if I call him while he's on his honeymoon."

Kurt laughed. "We got told the same."

"Good to know she treats us all equally," I said with a laugh.

"Rach'd do the same."

"How is Rach?"

"Good, man," he said. "She's real good."

"No plans on asking her to be your bride?"

"Well, no." Then he added, "We're more of a live-in-sin kind of couple."

I smiled but thought I may as well get to the purpose of my call. "Anyway, I was hoping you could do me a bit of a favor," I started. "Normally I would ask Mitch, and he'd either do what I asked or flip me off."

"Okay."

"I have the names of two guys that I'd like you to do a background check on, if that's okay?"

"I'm listening," he said cautiously.

"Darius McInnes and Tyler James. They're two guys that have started hanging around outside. They don't come in, but they seem to target the local kids." I sighed. "Maybe it's nothing, and I didn't really give them much thought, but I was talking to the church priest today and his reaction to them was fair warning."

"Hmm," was Kurt's response.

"Hmm, what?"

"Well, a few things," he mused. "If they're not drug-related, I don't know how much I can find out. But you know this, so I'm presuming you've cause enough to be concerned. Which brings me to my next concern—if *you're* questioning it, then chances are they're up to no good."

I smiled at that. "Well, like I said, it wasn't my intuition about the two guys. It was the priest's reaction to seeing them. He seems to be a pretty switched-on kind of guy."

"And the names?"

I repeated them, "Tyler James and Darius McInnes."

"Needles and haystacks, man."

"I know."

"I'll see what I can find out for you."

"Thanks," I said. "I know it's a long shot and they're small-fry, but I'm grateful. Maybe it'll turn up nothing. *Hopefully* it'll turn up nothing."

Now it was Kurt's turn to snort into the phone. "When have *you* ever raised an investigation that turned into nothing?"

I barked out a laugh. "Say hi to the guys for me."

"Even Berkman?"

"Especially Berkman."

There was only laughter then a dial tone in my ear. I hung up the phone, and it was then I heard another familiar laugh in the gym. Smiling, I walked out of my office to the main floor area and found Kira and Arizona talking, laughing.

"Hey," I said in greeting.

"Hey," Kira replied. "Arizona was just telling me about your little sidekick, Claude. She was giving you a hard time today?"

"She gives me a hard time every day."

"You finished for the night?" Arizona asked me.

"Yep. I just got off the phone to Kurt."

"Everything okay?" Kira asked.

"Yeah, it's all fine," I reassured him. "Just wanted to ask him a few things." I gave Kira a smile but knew he'd ask me about it when we were alone. I looked at Arizona. "You done here? I'll help you lock up. Need a lift home?"

"Nah, man, I drove," he said. "I'll just check the bathrooms," he said, walking to the amenities door.

"I got the windows," I called out. It was procedure to check and double check all doors and windows before we left each night. When the place was secure and the alarm was coded, we said goodbye to Arizona and headed home.

"What did Kurt have to say?" he asked. We'd not even gone one block.

"I asked him to do a background check on two guys that have been hanging around."

Kira smiled, but then he glanced from the road to me, and realizing I was serious, his smile died. "Matt."

"I told you before. I'm not involved. I just asked the question, and they're going to look into it, not me," I said. He didn't look too convinced, so I said, "Kira, baby, that's why I called Kurt. I don't *want* to be involved. Truly, I don't. It was just that the priest at the church warned me to keep the kids away from them, so I thought I'd just ask the boys to check on it. What they find, or what they don't, is outta my hands. I promise you, Kira, I'm not involved. But I can't have some losers at the club scouting kids to run drugs—"

He reached out and grabbed my hand. "Matt, it's okay. I believe you. I do."

I gave him a quick smile and sighed. "I don't blame you

for asking the questions, babe. You've earned the right, and I have nothing to hide. I'm not involved."

"You care, Matt. It's what makes you, you." Then after a few moments silence, he said, "I haven't earned the right."

I snorted. "Yes you have."

"How long are you going to think you owe me?"

Well, that was simple. "Every day of forever."

Kira smiled, looking from the road ahead to me. The seriousness was now gone. "And just what does that entail?"

"Back rubs, massages, breakfast in bed, awesome blow jobs."

Now he laughed. "I can live with that."

THE NEXT WEEK was much the same. I kept busy at work, kept my appointments with Tamara, and spent my nights wrapped around Kira. Some nights we opted for no TV and simply talked—about his work and mine, his family, my therapy sessions, about the news, about the back garden. It didn't matter what we talked about, the fact was... we talked.

They were my favorite nights. We'd cook dinner. Well, he'd cook and I'd clean up, and we'd just talk.

It wasn't exciting, it wasn't overly romantic. It was probably mundane and probably boring to some, but to me it was perfect.

We needed to get back to basics. We needed to learn how to trust and how to be a couple again, and communication was paramount in that.

It gave us an intimacy I'd never thought possible.

It was like falling in love all over again.

It was Tuesday night, we'd eaten dinner and had moved to the sofa. Kira took the mail off the coffee table and laid back with a sigh, exhausted from his long day at work. I climbed over him, settling myself in between his legs with my back to his front, my head on his chest. I shuffled in till I was comfortable, making him laugh and groan. "You all right there?"

"I am now."

He wrapped his arms around me and the pile of unread mail sat square on my chest. I opened the first few bills, nothing unexpected, but the last envelope was plain white, and when I opened the letter, we both saw the familiar logo on the top right corner. It was the pathology results from my last lot of bloods taken after my stay in hospital. Cage fighting was a high-contact blood sport and there was a risk of contamination. I'd had extensive testing when I'd been admitted to hospital, then three months after, and again at six months.

The first and second results had come back fine, but it was still daunting to open the letter for a third time. Kira slid his hands over mine and we read it together, him squeezing my hand as we read the results. All was clear—I had a perfect bill of health.

I exhaled in relief and taking his hand, brought it to my chest. "I still can't believe I came away from those fights unscathed."

Kira leaned forward and kissed the side of my head, above my useless ear. "Not completely."

"I have my health, and I have you," I replied.

As we lay there in silence, Kira ran his fingers through my hair. I tossed the mail onto the coffee table. "Kira," I said softly, but seriously. "I want to tell you something."

He tensed underneath me, the briefest of reactions, but

it was enough to remind me that I'd caused him reason to be wary of my confessions.

Unprotected sex was something we'd talked about before, but given the bloody nature of MMA fighting, with the cuts, the blood, the contact—even my job as a cop came with risks of contact—so unprotected sex hadn't been an option for us.

But now it was. I wanted to give him everything. I wanted him to know it was just for him. Neither of us had ever experienced it before, and I wanted to prove to him I trusted him with my health, with my body, with my life.

I took his hands and wrapped his arms around me. "Well, it's not really telling. It's more asking, but I just want to put something out in the open, and you don't have to answer me or decide anything. I just want you to think about it, and you can let me know when you're ready."

"Okay," he said, still hesitant, but more curious now.

"When you're ready," I said, "or only if you want to, now that we have these latest blood results, I was thinking, or wondering, if you've thought about... you know... not using condoms."

I always rambled when I was nervous.

He was silent, so I shuffled and rolled over to face him, so I could look into his eyes and ramble some more, telling him not to worry, but a slow smile spread across his face.

"You're cute when you're nervous," he said.

I huffed out a sigh of relief, and put my cheek to his chest. "It's not something you need to decide right now," I said softly. "No pressure."

"But you want it?" he asked.

I looked up at him and nodded. "One day. To have you, and only you, inside me. No barrier between us." He still didn't answer, so I told him, "It's okay if you don't, babe. It's something we both have to agree on and make an informed decision about."

Kira traced his fingers down the side of my face, and his eyes looked intently into mine. "Can I have time to think about it?"

"Of course. As much time as you need."

"I want to," he added. "I really do, but I'd like some time to think about it. And I want you to know any hesitation on my part is not a lack of trust." He held my face a little firmer and stared at me, almost daring me to claim otherwise. "You know that, right?"

I smiled. "I do. I know it's a heavy topic to just dump on you, but just with getting the letter and results... I just want you to know that it's something I'd consider if you wanted."

He leaned forward again and pecked his lips to mine, and I lay my head back down on his chest and sighed contentedly.

Then Kira's hands started to skim my sides, across my shoulders, my lower back, over my ass. His touch became firmer, and his cock stirred against my stomach.

"You really shouldn't have told me to think about it," he said and lifted his hips for effect.

I laughed into his shirt, and he rolled me over so we were both on our sides. We were crammed onto the sofa, which was funny enough, but then he tickled me, making me laugh and squirm.

Tickling fingers became fumbling hands and sure mouths and searching tongues. Kira took me to bed and fucked me. He used a condom, of course, but as he lay over me, he grunted into the back of my neck that one day he wouldn't have to. That he'd slip inside me, just him, and he'd bury his seed deep within me.

His words alone brought me undone.

CHAPTER SIX

I HIT send on the text and put my phone on the diner table and looked at the two faces looking back at me. "So what will it be?"

"Nothin' for me," came Ruby's reply. He slid the unopened menu back across to me. "You don't need to be buyin' us anything."

Claude tried to hide the disappointment, but in silence agreed with her brother. I had no clue how long it'd been since these two ate anything.

"Well, how about I just order you both something, and if you decide you want to eat it, you can," I said, and without waiting for a reply, I ordered two burgers and fries and two lemonade sodas.

"Aren't you eating, Matt?" Claude asked. "You didn't order anything. Or is the food here really bad and you won't eat it?"

I laughed at her tact, or lack thereof. "The food here is just fine. Kira and I have plans for tonight, that's all."

"If you're goin' out, why you wastin' time here with us?" Ruby asked.

"I'm not wasting time," I told them. "I'm buying you guys dinner. I had to wait for Kira to pick me up anyway, so I texted him to tell him I'd be here instead of the club. No big deal."

Claude smiled across the table at me. Her wiry, tight curly hair was like a dark halo around her angelic face. "Where you going?" she asked. "With your man."

I smiled again at her. I usually found myself smiling at the things that came out of her mouth. "Date night. We're going to the movies. Kira's turn to pick what we watch, so it will probably be crap." Then I added, "Don't tell him I said that."

Claude laughed and even Ruby smiled at that. He was so protective of his sister, always serious, so it was good to see him smile. I'd learned early on not to push the questions they didn't want to answer, so while I really wanted to know where their mother was, or where they lived, or why they were never home—if they even had a home—or when and if they ate, I didn't ask.

One wrong question and these kids shut down and backed off, and I couldn't risk that.

I really liked them. I wanted them to have a proper chance. A better chance than what life had given them. It was something I think my shrink was stuck on, like there was some hidden guilt trigger and this was me trying to right the wrongs I'd done.

I could see why her psychological brain made that leap, but for me it wasn't like that at all. I just didn't want kids like Ruby and Claude to think everything in the world was against them. If I could give them a few happy moments in a world that was kind of dreary, then I would do that.

We talked about the fight club, of course, and the upcoming fundraising day and tournament. Claude was excited about it, whereas Ruby only seemed agreeable because his sister was all huge smiles and animated hands. The waitress served the two lemonades just as Kira walked through the door.

He spotted us straight away, and I could tell from the look in his eyes that he was curious to my being here. Then he saw who I was sitting with, and he gave me a "what are you up to now" look before he sat down next to me. "Hey, guys," he said. He patted my leg under the table.

"Hey," I replied with a smile.

"Hello, Kira," Claude said cheerfully. "What movie are you going to see?"

Kira's eyes shot to mine. "I'm not sure yet," he said cautiously.

"I told them we were going to see something," I explained.

"Actually," Claude said, all bright eyes and huge smile. "Matt said you're having a date night and your taste in movies is crap."

My mouth fell open. "Hey! Where's the camaraderie?" I asked Claude. "I thought my second lieutenant was supposed to have my back?"

Kira laughed. "Is that what he said?"

Just then, the waitress returned with two plates of burgers and fries. She slid them onto the table in front of the two kids, and their eyes went wide. Without another word, they both started to eat.

When they were about half way done, I said, "Well, we better get going if we plan to catch a movie."

Ruby put down his half-eaten burger and swallowed what was in his mouth. "Thank you," he said. It was a quiet, humbled, genuine thanks.

Then Claude chimed in, "Yeah, thanks, Matt. Will I see you at work tomorrow?"

"You sure will," I told her. "And don't be late."

Claude rolled her eyes at me, then I turned to Kira and said, "You ready?"

The look in his eyes was brief, but I saw it. It was a very quick "should we leave them here alone" kind of look. "Yeah," he said hesitantly.

"Okay then," I said, standing up. "You two take care. Enjoy your dinner. We're off to see some crap movie."

Claude laughed again. Ruby gave me half a smile and a nod as Kira and I were leaving. He drove and was quiet for a few blocks. "Are they okay?" he asked. "I mean, should we just have left them there? It's almost eight at night. And you bought them dinner?"

I smiled and put my hand on his thigh. "They'll be okay."

"How do you know?"

"I don't," I amended. "I just hope they will."

Kira was quiet again after that, as though my answer didn't sit well with him. We went into his favorite sushi bar for take-out rolls and still made the nine o'clock movie. He still hadn't said much since we'd left the diner, but as we were waiting in line for tickets, he frowned and his brow creased. "Rueben didn't seem too happy to be there," Kira said. "Tonight, in the diner. And you didn't answer me before. Did you buy them dinner?"

"Of course I did," I told him. "And no, Ruby probably wasn't too keen to be there. He looks after her, and he's a proud kid, so it probably stung to have someone provide something, ya know? But Claude was all excited for it. They were both still at the club when I finished, and I knew Claude hadn't eaten, so I suggested a burger. Ruby wouldn't have come if it weren't for the fact that Claude was getting something to eat."

Kira frowned. "Watching them eat... It was...sad. They scarfed half the meal and left the rest," Kira noted, as though that confused him.

"Well, Claude was with me all day. She came in just before nine, made herself a hot chocolate for breakfast, I gave her my salad for lunch, and that was dinner. They're probably keeping half their burgers to have tomorrow. They would have waited until we left, wrapped what was left in a napkin, and shoved it in their jackets."

Kira's frown deepened, and he looked over at the ticket counter. The idea of those kids stashing food wasn't very pleasant. With a gentle pat on his arm, I walked over to the cashier and ordered two tickets. When I got back to Kira, I gave him a smile. "How do you compartmentalize that?" he asked. "How are we supposed to just walk away from them, knowing they have no food, no anything?"

I put my hand on his arm again and smiled sadly. "Years of being a cop, I guess. It's a fact of life. It's not easy, and I'm not dismissing it, because it does matter—*they do matter*—but like you've said before, we can't fix all of them."

"Just two."

"I'm not trying to fix them. Just showing some kindness. That's all." Then I asked, "Is that wrong?"

Kira shook his head and looked around the cinema foyer. "No, not at all. I guess it just hits home when you watch them eat like it's the first thing they've had in a week."

"That's why I bought them dinner."

"You're a good man."

I snorted out a laugh. "Well, I don't know about that, but I'm trying."

Kira finally smiled. "You're doing just fine."

"Come on, let's get this movie over and done with."

I WAS HOLDING the punching pads for Arizona, while he was giving three-punch-jab combinations. He was strong, he hit hard and it was a good workout. As we'd got more into the coaching side of this fight club, our own training and practice sessions were restricted by time, so when we did step into the ring and spar, it felt great.

Arizona didn't fight competitions anymore, just like he didn't fight underground for money. He didn't have to. He had a paying job, with benefits. Now boxing was for fitness and for fun.

I'd been egging him on to stop hitting like a girl and have a real go, so when he surprised me with a kick to my thigh, I dropped the punching pad, and he laughed.

I liked that we joked around when we could. I picked up the padded mat and pulled out my mouth guard. "You kick pretty hard," I taunted him. "For a girl."

Arizona laughed this time, but I put my mouth guard back in and goaded him to try again. "Is he giving you a hard time?" I didn't notice the two guys walk over to the ring until one of them had spoken.

I looked over then, to find Mitch and Ricky standing at the edge of the boxing ring, watching us. "Hey!" I said. Then I pulled out my mouth guard and tried again. "Hey! Here's the newlywed man himself!"

Mitch grinned at me, and as I ducked through the ropes of the ring and jumped to the ground, I put my arms out wide.

"If you think I'm hugging you when you're all sweaty, think again," my old partner said, still grinning.

I ignored his jibe and hugged him anyway. "Good to see you, man. You look great. Married life agrees with you." He did look good—relaxed, suntanned. "How is your beautiful bride?"

"She's great," Mitch said, smiling wider at the mention of Anna. Mitch reached out and touched the ring on my necklace. "And I hear of big news with you, too?"

Now my grin matched his, and I clapped my hand on his shoulder. I looked at Ricky. "Berkman keep you busy without Mitch around?"

The younger cop groaned. "You know him well."

I laughed and looked back at Mitch. "What brings you here? Did you miss me that much?"

"Have you got a sec?" he asked. "Somewhere we can talk?"

"Sure," I said, nodding to my office. I called out to Arizona, "We done, man?"

"Yeah, you hit like a girl anyway," he called back with a grin.

I snorted out a laugh and led Mitch and Ricky to my office, where Claude was sitting at my desk, organizing and reorganizing whatever she wanted, apparently.

"Hey, squirt," I said to her. "Can you give us ten?"

The little girl got up from the chair, and after eyeing the two men with me, she raised an eyebrow at me. "Are you in trouble, Matt? Did they come here to arrest you?"

"No, ma'am," I said. "This is my old partner Mitch, and his new partner Ricky. They're just here to talk."

Claude nodded suspiciously. "Mm hm. 'Course they are."

We watched her leave, and once she'd gone, Mitch said, "Is she in charge?"

"Yep."

He laughed and parked his ass on the table near the window. "You asked Kurt to find out some intel on two guys that have been hanging around," he said. It wasn't a question.

"Yeah. They seem a little suss," I told him. "To be honest, it wasn't my initial reaction to them. We have a lot of people that hang around, some live local, some don't, but if they don't come in here, I don't pay 'em much attention. I got talking to the priest from the church down the road, and he made mention that they were bad company."

Mitch nodded. "Your priest is right. Darius McInnes has done time for drug trafficking and some pretty serious assault charges." Then Mitch sighed. "He's also been flagged as an associate of Nazi Lowriders, Matt."

"What the hell do white extremists want with a thirteen-year-old black kid?" I whispered.

Mitch's eyes fell to the floor. "They pick up street kids, Matt. Get them hooked, give them a hit if they mule and carry. These kids are disposable, Matt. They don't give a fuck." He shrugged. "No one cares. No one misses a homeless kid."

"I do." I ran my hand over my face and waited for him to continue.

"We're gonna look around, see how deep it goes," he said. "But yeah, their names have come up in certain circles."

"Narcotics and gangs?" I asked. "Jesus Christ."

"They seem pretty diverse."

Mitch was being evasive in his answers, which told me two things—one, he wanted me to know these guys were bad news, but two, couldn't say outright what it was because it was now an open case. And I was no longer a cop.

"Thanks, Mitch," I said. "I appreciate the heads up."

"No worries. Just wanted you to know."

"Nothing like having a honeymoon and then jumping straight back into work," I said with a laugh.

Mitch rolled his eyes. "Always more bad guys, Matt." Then he said, "Who was the kid?" He gave a pointed nod to where Claude had disappeared to.

"That's Claude. Claudia," I added. "She's my second lieutenant."

"Is she here often?" he asked.

"More often than not." Then I said, "Her and her brother have it kind of tough, so I don't mind if she hangs out here."

"And she's here with you?"

I nodded. "Yep. Keeps me and the boys in line. She's a little firecracker."

Mitch's look of disbelief gave way to a smirk and a shake of his head. "Jeez."

"What?"

"Things are really different for you now, aren't they?" he said. "Not you. You're still the same, but you're running a different ship."

"I am."

"You happy?"

"I am," I repeated.

"That's good," he said with a genuine smile.

"Are you?" I asked him, unable to stop smiling back at him.

"I am," he said with a laugh and held out his hand for me to shake in the way sportsmen often did—the way brothers did—which I gladly took.

"You just don't want to admit how much you miss me," I joked with a pat on his shoulder.

He pulled back and tapped my face. "Don't make me regret coming to see you." Then, as though he thought better of tapping the side of my face, he clapped my shoulder instead. "Hey, how's the ear?"

"Ear's okay," I told him. "Still the same."

"Still dizzy?"

"Sometimes. Not too often. Usually if I turn suddenly or stand up too quick. Or sometimes for no reason whatsoever."

Mitch's brow furrowed a bit, then he sighed. Before he could say anything about my deafness, there was a knock on the open door. It was Ruby. He eyed Mitch and Ricky cautiously but finally looked at me. "Hey, Matt, is Claude here?"

"Yep. She was in here five minutes ago, so if she's not with Arizona, check with Boss."

The kid gave a nod. "Thanks." He turned to walk away but stopped. "And thanks again for dinner," he said quietly. "You really made Claude's night."

"Really?" I asked. "Because she's been giving me a hard time all day."

Rueben laughed. "Sounds about right."

He walked off in search of his sister, and when I turned back to Mitch, he was wearing that stupid, shit-eating grin. "Man," he said, shaking his head. "You buying kids dinner now?"

"Just them, just once," I said. "I don't think they eat real often," I added.

The smile soon slid from his face.

I nudged him with my shoulder. "It's a different world here, man."

"I can see that," Mitch replied.

"They don't go to school?" Ricky asked.

I shook my head. "Not many do around here. I've made a contact at the local community college, which is great for the older kids, but not much help for Ruby. He's twelve or thirteen and doesn't go to school."

"Don't authorities make kids go to school?" Ricky asked.

I smiled. "These kids can smell authority," I told them. "And they disappear. I don't want them to go to ground. At least here, they're safe. We let 'em hang out, hope they see some good for a change." I shrugged. "You'd think there has to be something a kid can do to stay out of trouble."

Mitch smiled. "You'll figure it out. You always do."

"Hope so. Ruby's the one that I've seen those two thugs talking to. I try to keep him busy, off the streets, but I can only do so much," I admitted.

"Matt," Mitch said with a sigh. "You're doing a lot. Probably more than what we do as cops."

I snorted. "I seriously doubt that."

"Maybe not in the big picture," he agreed. "But in the lives of these people, you are."

I smiled at his compliment. "I'm trying."

"Very fucking trying," he joked. Then his smile faded. "But you're right, Matt. You should try and keep kids away from McInnes and James."

"Received and understood," I said with a nod.

Mitch's eyes darted over my shoulder then quickly back to me. "I think someone is waiting."

Not hearing anyone approach, I turned to find Claude in the doorway with a none too pleased look on her face. "Haven't got all day, Matt," she said with that sassy pout.

Mitch laughed, and even Ricky failed at biting back his smile.

"Righto, squirt," I said.

My old partner snorted. "Jeez, no wonder you don't miss Berkman. You have a mini-Berkman right here."

Claude raised her eyebrow at him then walked out the door while giving him the stink eye, and Mitch grinned. He clapped my shoulder. "On that note, we'd better get back to it or the real Berkman will have our asses in a sling."

As they walked toward the door, I said, "Oh, don't forget! Last weekend of next month is the day we want to have our community fundraising day. I'll let you know if it's gonna happen, and you all need to be here." Then I added, "Tell Berkman I said I want to see his sorry face here too."

We said our goodbyes, and I followed them out to where Claude was not-so patiently waiting. "I thought Ruby was here?" I asked, looking around and not seeing him anywhere.

"Just came in to tell me he'd be back later," Claude said. "I can stay here with you, yeah?"

"You sure can."

"What are we doing first?" she asked.

"Well, I need to make some phone calls. Boring stuff like insurances and public liability for our fundraising day. Then we can head out and see some of the local businesses and folks around the neighborhood."

"Sounds like a plan," the little girl said.

I followed Claude back into my office and sat down at my desk. I pulled out my notepad of contacts and numbers while she sat patiently and smiled when I looked at her. First, I spoke to the contacts the department heads had given me about insurance and public liability. I'd spoken to them before a few times, and it seemed we were actually going to do this.

Finally given the green light, I hung up the phone and

my smile must have given me away. Claude's eyes lit up. "Can we do it?"

"We sure can," I replied, holding up my hand for her to high-five, which she did with a laugh.

"I'm gonna go tell Boss," she said, then darted off the chair and out of the door.

I made a few more calls, confirming details and securing the fundraising day as a legitimate event. All T's were crossed, all I's were dotted, now the real work could begin.

When I hung up the phone, Claude, Boss, and Arizona were standing in the doorway. With the phone to my only functioning ear, I hadn't heard them come in. I gave them a smile. "It's all a go," I told them. "Paperwork will probably tie me down for a week, but we have the green light to go ahead."

Boss shook his head. "Don't know whose ass you kissed in that police department, but someone in there must like you."

I laughed. If Claude wasn't there, I'd have made some smartass comment about me and ass, but I thought better of it. "Well, regardless of *how* it's happening, it *is* happening. We'll need to pull all the guys in for another meeting tomorrow." I looked at Arizona. "Can you organize that?" Then I looked at Boss. "Can you set some time aside tomorrow, and we'll go through all the financials, budgets, and allowances? We're gonna have to spend some money to make money, but between us, I'm sure we can streamline it."

Both men nodded. "Yeah," they agreed in unison, then went back to what they'd been doing before Claude had interrupted them.

Claude put one hand on her hip. "What about me?"

"You," I told her, "are coming with me. We need to go talk to the other local businesses."

"But you already asked 'em," Claude reminded me.

"I know. But now we can tell them it's a definite date and we're moving forward. Most of the groundwork has been done, but now we just need to step it up. And then we need to go speak to other local fight clubs about setting up some tournaments." We walked toward the front door and I held it open for her. "We've only got six weeks, squirt. We need to get organized."

So that's what Claude and I did. We called in to see the other local businesses who had shown interest, and we paid Father Michael a visit again. Ruby came back into the club around eight and collected Claude, and Kira picked me up at nine.

I was excited to tell him that we'd finally been granted permission to close the street off for the fundraising day. There were other businesses that were keen to get on board with stalls, and the FC was going to put on public displays of the kids doing their thing and even an exhibition tournament. "I want people to see that these kids are doing something, that they're learning something here. And I don't know," I said with a shrug, "that we have a purpose."

Kira's eyes darted from the road to me. His smile became a grin, but he didn't speak.

"What?"

"You just love it, don't you?"

I didn't even have to answer. My returning smile said it all. We talked all the way home, through a late night supper, then as we got into bed. Mostly we talked about my work, about his work, and the people we worked with. I mentioned how Claude had again spent the day with me, and a flicker of something unsaid flashed across his features.

"What?" I asked. We were lying in bed, facing each other, so I reached out and took his hand. "Lately when I mention Claude or Ruby, it's like you want to say something but don't."

Kira sighed. "I know you like them and you spend a lot of time with them, in particular Claude. And yeah, they're good kids, but I do worry that if something happens to them, or if they move on, or just stop coming in, you'll get hurt."

I lifted his hand to my lips and kissed his palm. "I probably would be hurt," I admitted. "But you know what? That's okay. I shouldn't stop being nice to them just to protect myself from a what-if scenario."

"No, you shouldn't," he said softly. "Because you've got a kind heart, Matt, you wouldn't do that."

"So what are you saying?"

Kira squeezed my hand. "I don't know," he hedged. "It's one thing to show kindness on a professional level, but sometimes I worry it's getting personal for you, and I don't want you to get hurt." He squeezed my hand again. "Maybe just put in a little distance."

Personal.

Distance.

As much as his words stung, Kira was right. I took his suggestion on board, because it was valid—it was likely that any of the kids I dealt with would stop coming in at some point, and I would feel their absence greatly.

But three days later, the one to close the distance with Claude and make it personal, wasn't me at all.

It was Kira.

CHAPTER SEVEN

JUST LIKE ALWAYS, when I worked till nine, Kira would be waiting in the car out the front of the FC. Only this time he was across the road, which wasn't too unusual if he had to get fuel or if he picked up something for dinner. I ran across the darkened street, but when I got in to the passenger side Kira didn't start the car.

"What's wrong?"

Kira nodded toward the side alley where the dumpster bin was, and it was then that I saw what he was watching. Movement in the darkness. And when the person moved into the streetlight to the front of the bin, I saw who it was.

Claude.

"Jesus," I mumbled, grabbing the door handle to get out.

Kira's hand on my arm stopped me. "Just wait. If you run over there now, you'll frighten her. Let's just see what she does."

I looked at Kira, and he was staring out of the window. He never took his eyes off her. "I've been watching her for three minutes," he whispered. "She doesn't know we're here. I think she was waiting for the lights to go out in the club."

"What for?"

"I think she's gonna sleep in that dumpster."

My heart squeezed. "Oh, God."

"Is she homeless?"

"I don't know," I answered quietly. "If she does have a home, she's not looked after properly, that's for sure. She wears the same clothes all the time, and she doesn't eat much..." My words died off. "Oh, Jesus..."

Then Claude moved from the shadows, and we watched in silence as the small girl edged around to the front of the dumpster in the darkened night and lifted the lid. My heart broke into tiny pieces when she climbed inside and pulled the lid back down.

I pushed my door open, but Kira was already out of the car and half way across the street. He was a few steps ahead of me by the time we reached the dumpster, but he didn't hesitate. He flung the bin lid back, eliciting a scream from the small girl inside it.

"Hey, Claude," I said, hoping she'd recognize my voice, as scared as she was. "It's me, Matt."

The bin was half full of garbage bags and flattened cardboard. She was sitting on top of the rubbish, trying to push herself into the back of the dumpster, away from the threat. Away from us.

"It's me, squirt," I said again.

"And Kira," Kira added.

Claude pulled a bag of garbage closer, as though it would somehow protect her. "What do you want?" she squeaked.

"I just want to talk," I said, using a placating tone. I really wanted to get her out of the dumpster but needed her to know we meant no harm. "I just want to know you're okay."

Even in the darkness, I could see her eyes dart between me and Kira. "I'm okay." She spoke so quietly, I barely heard her.

"Where's Ruby?" I asked.

The little girl looked at me for a long moment. "I don't know."

I sighed and took a deep breath while my heart rate slowed down. "Okay, Claude. You're okay."

"He's normally back by now," she said, her voice sounding so removed from the forthright little girl I knew.

But then Kira spoke, "Claude, you need to get out of this bin, okay? You trust Matt, don't you?"

The little girl looked at Kira, then to me and back to Kira. She nodded but was still wielding the bag of garbage like a shield.

"Then you can come home with us," Kira said, surprising me more than Claude. "We have a spare bed. You can sleep in it. Or on the couch. Whatever. You'll have a hot shower, some food, and Matt will bring you back here first thing so Ruby doesn't miss you when he gets back."

Kira's tone was a little sharper than I was used to hearing from him. His jaw was clenched, and whether he was mad at Claude or at the situation, I really wasn't sure.

"Kira," I warned.

"She's not sleeping in a fucking dumpster!" he bit back at me, as though Claude wasn't a few feet in front of him. He exhaled loudly, obviously regretting the outburst. "Please, Claude," he added, much softer this time.

I held out my hand. "Come on, Claude."

"You won't take me to the police or to a shelter?" she asked. "You promise?"

"I promise," I answered.

She hesitated for the longest moment but cast the garbage bag aside and grabbed my offered hand. I pulled her out while Kira kept the lid open, and I held on to her. I didn't want to risk putting her on the ground, only to have her run away. She was so slight, she barely weighed a thing, and she clung to me as though grateful for the human contact.

It broke my fucking heart.

I put Claude in the back seat and climbed into the front as Kira slid in behind the wheel. It was deathly quiet for a few blocks. No one spoke, but I kept turning around and giving the little kid a reassuring smile. Kira stared out of the windshield never taking his eyes off the road. His reaction was baffling to me.

Normally so open and warm, he was pissed off and cold. I didn't understand it.

Claudia was first to break the silence. "Have you got ice cream?"

"No," Kira answered flatly. "It's not good for you."

I stared at Kira and blinked at his words. "No, but we can get some," I amended. "Did you want some?"

"Nah, it's okay," she replied nonchalantly.

"How about we grab some drive-through," I suggested, thinking it would be quicker, easier, and I presumed all kids liked takeout. I doubted Claude would care either way.

"I'll cook something," Kira said, his tone still harsh. But then he looked at me, as though he realized how abrupt he'd sounded, and gave me a tight smile. "It's okay. Won't take me long. I don't mind."

I gave Claude a smile, then turned back around in my seat for the rest of the drive home, trying to let the events of the night make sense in my head. A few minutes later, without another word spoken between us, we pulled into our drive.

Kira mumbled something about starting dinner, then got out of the car and walked up the steps. He stopped at the front door, as though we were an afterthought. I held Claude's door open and waited for the little girl to climb out. She just kind of stood there, awkwardly, uncertain, and for a moment I thought she was about to turn and run.

"Come on," I said, trying to reassure her with a smile. "You can have a hot shower and then watch some TV while we cook dinner, okay?"

By the time Claude and I had walked inside, Kira was already in the kitchen. I grabbed a T-shirt and a towel then showed Claude the bathroom. "We can wash and dry your clothes so they're ready in the morning," I told her. "One of my shirts is the best I can do for PJs. Is that okay?"

She nodded and shrugged. "I guess."

I rummaged through the cabinet drawer and found a new toothbrush. I held it out to her. "For you."

She took the toothbrush, and as I turned to leave her alone, she stopped me. "Matt, is Kira mad?"

"No," I answered reflexively. "'Course not." I waved my hand toward the shower. "Feel free to use the shampoo and conditioner. It's only boy stuff, so it might not smell real pretty, but it'll have to do."

She kind of smiled, so I pulled the door and headed toward the kitchen.

Kira had sliced up some left over beef and scraped the slivers of meat into a saucepan on the stove. From the bottles on the counter, I gathered he'd thrown in some soy and mirin into some kind of broth.

"What are you making?"

"Nikujaga."

"Huh?"

"Niku—" he started to say again but stopped. "It's a type of stew. It's Japanese. We don't have any saki, so it won't be right," he said. He peeled a potato with firm, rigid strokes and sliced it with just as much anger.

"Kira," I said softly. "Can we talk about this?"

He continued chopping, and I gathered his silence was in order to get the words right in his head. But his words never came. He sliced carrots, peas, and shallots, then added them to the small pot. He never said a word.

"Kira."

"Later, Matt," he said sharply. Then he sighed. "Later," he said again, softer this time.

"Are you mad at me?" I asked.

"No."

"Are you mad at Claude?"

"What? No," he said, shaking his head. "God, no." He turned back to the saucepan, put a small plate inside the pot —which was weird—and put the lid on. I wanted to ask what the hell he was cooking but didn't think it was the right time. His shoulders were tight, and he ran his hand through his hair, then turned around to face me. Just when I thought he was going to tell me what he was so clearly strug- gling to say, someone else spoke.

"Matt?" Claude's voice called out from the hall.

I hadn't heard the water turn off. "One sec," I yelled back to her, then spoke quietly to Kira. "You okay?"

He nodded. "You better see what she wants."

"Okay."

She was standing in the hall holding her dirty clothes, wearing my shirt that came to her knees, with a towel wrapped around her hair. She looked tiny.

And scared.

"Feel better?" I asked brightly, my outward confidence belying the internal insecurity I felt. I had no clue what I was doing. What the hell were we thinking? Bringing a small kid back to our house? I mean, fuck! The ramifications could be catastrophic.

Maybe this was what Kira was livid about. Maybe he saw what I didn't. Maybe he was right. Fuck.

"Um, what do you want me to do with these?" she asked, holding out her dirty clothes.

"Um, how about I do you a swap?" I asked. Walking to the linen closet, I pulled out a blanket. "Here, wrap this around you to keep yourself nice and warm, and I'll put your clothes in the wash."

I flicked out the blanket and draped it around her little shoulders. It was hardly cold, but I figured it would make her feel safe. She was, after all, now in a strange house with two strange men.

Oh, fuck. What have I done?

"How about we see what's on the TV" I said, leading her toward the sofa. "Park yourself up there and you can flip through the channels. I'll just go put these in the wash."

I left her to it, then I threw her clothes in the washing machine, adding extra soap, hoping it would get rid of the ingrained dirt and smell. When I walked back out to the living room, Kira was handing Claude a drink. She peeled her hands out of the blanket. "Thank you," she said softly.

As he walked back into the kitchen, he said, "Dinner won't be long," to either me or Claude. I wasn't sure.

His reaction was baffling, and I knew we would talk it through, maybe when Claude was asleep. Right now, we had to focus on the little girl, who, if we'd not intervened, would have spent the night alone in a dumpster.

"Whatcha watching?" I asked, nodding toward the flat screen.

Claude shrugged. "Not sure." She picked up the remote and kept scrolling through the cable channels. I don't think she had any idea what she was watching. She obviously wasn't too familiar with any shows on TV.

We stared at the screen for a while, until Kira walked in carrying a tray with two bowls. He put the tray on Claude's lap. "It's hot, so be careful," he said. His tone still had an edge but had softened somewhat. Kira took one bowl off the tray and handed it to me. It was a mix of shredded meat, potato, noodles, and vegetables in a broth.

Claude looked into the bowl. "What is it?"

"It's nikujaga," Kira told her. He sat down on the opposite sofa. "It's something my mom would make for me."

She lifted the spoon to her lips and sipped the broth. She hummed. "It's real good."

"It's Japanese," Kira said. "It's what my mother would call a—" He glanced at me, and his voice softened. "—a comfort food."

I smiled at him. He'd been indifferent to Claude being here but made a point of making a meal his mom probably made for him when he wasn't feeling well. It was confusing, if anything, but I didn't question his gesture.

I stirred my dinner, although I was barely hungry, and sipped the broth. It was tangy and sweet and somehow soothing.

"Are you not having any?" I asked Kira.

He shook his head. "I had a late lunch." I doubted that was exactly true. I guessed, like me, he'd lost his appetite as well.

Claude, on the other hand, devoured hers. We watched as the little girl, with her tiny arms poking out of her blanket cocoon, took mouthful after mouthful of meat, vegetables, and noodles until she couldn't eat any more.

I took her plate on the tray and slid it onto the coffee table. "Feel better?" I asked her.

She nodded. "It was really good, thank you," she said, looking at Kira. "Matt always says you're a good cook."

Kira kind of smiled at that, and I figured now was the best time to bring this up. "Claude, where was Ruby tonight?"

She shrugged. "I don't know. He said he'd be back, but he's not normally that late."

"Have you spent other nights alone?" I asked.

Claude shrugged again, like it was no big deal. "Sometimes."

"Where do you stay?" Kira asked. "If Ruby's not there."

Claude didn't answer for a while. A dozen emotions flickered across her face—among them sadness, anger, defiance. I wondered if she'd been told not to say anything on the subject.

"Claude," I said softly, "where do you go, even if Ruby's with you? Where do you sleep? Have you guys got a home? Or a mom or dad?"

The little girl's gaze went to her lap and she tucked her arms back into her blanket, as though the question made her cold. Again, she didn't answer for a long moment, and I guessed she didn't want to.

"It's okay," Kira said quietly. "You don't have to say anything."

She stared mindlessly at the television for another long moment, and just when I thought she'd shut down completely, that we'd pushed too far, her tiny voice cut through the room.

"No one wanted us."

No one wanted us. I allowed those words to turn over in my head, not quite believing what I'd heard.

"Me and Ruby," she continued. "It's just us."

"Oh, Claude," I said, my voice barely a whisper. "That's not true."

She looked at me, then, and smiled bravely. "Yeah. It is. It's just been me and Ruby for a while, and that's okay. We do okay."

"I'm sure you do," I replied, trying to smile.

"Ruby says we shouldn't go to the shelters because they'll put us into homes and separate us," she said, as though it was something all nine-year-old kids should know.

"He's pretty smart, your brother," I said, trying to cheer her up a little.

"He is," she agreed brightly. "He finds us somewhere warm and dry and so no one finds us. One time he found whole packets of cookies that someone didn't want. They were chocolate, and I ate so many I got sick."

Kira stood up from the sofa, snatched the tray off the coffee table, and walked into the kitchen. Claude didn't see it, but I did—the way Kira's lip trembled and how he set his jaw, how his nostrils flared, how his eyes were wild and glassy.

"You must be tired, huh?" I asked Claude. "We have a spare room. You can sleep in there."

She shook her head. "Here's okay." Then she simply lay down on the sofa, pulling a cushion under her head. Not that I wanted her to sleep on the couch, but if that was what she wanted...

"How about I get you a pillow and another blanket? We've got a busy day tomorrow, you and me," I said.

I grabbed a pillow and a blanket throw from the spare

room and made her a makeshift bed on the sofa. "You all right, squirt?" I asked.

She nodded, and before I could walk into the kitchen, she asked, "Do you think Ruby's okay?"

I gave her my most convincing smile. "I'm sure he is. We'll find him first thing in the morning, okay?"

Claude nodded again and closed her eyes, so I walked into the kitchen to find Kira with his hands on the counter top and his head bowed.

I rubbed his shoulder. "Babe, are you okay?"

He turned to face me and ran his fingers through his hair. He shook his head and exhaled loudly. "No one wanted her, Matt. That's what she said. That no one wanted her. It's not right that a kid even knows what that means." His eyes welled with tears. "It's not right, Matt."

"I know."

"She's eaten food from a trash can," he whispered. "She ate food that someone else threw away." His tears threatened to spill. "Matt, that's just," he groaned. "It's so wrong."

I took his face in my hands and pressed my lips to his forehead. "Kira, babe." I wiped a stray tear. "I thought you were mad."

"I was," he said, exhaling loudly. "I mean, I am. I'm so mad at this whole mess. It's not fair, Matt. She's just a kid." His eyes glistened with fresh tears. "She was going to sleep in that dumpster."

I ran the pads of my thumbs over his face and kissed his temple, his cheek. "I know."

"Do you think her brother's okay?"

"I don't know. I hope so."

"We have to do something."

"I know."

"What *can* we do, though?" he asked. "She said herself they won't go into a home in case they get split up."

"Claude's safe tonight," I offered.

"Is that enough?"

"It's a start."

"Matt—"

"Sshhh," I said, kissing him quiet. "It's the best we can do today, and it's a start."

Kira sighed and leaned his forehead on mine. His eyes were closed, his eyelashes were wet. "When did you get so smart?"

"It's all I can do," I said softly. "The enormity of homeless kids, Kira, it's too much. If you let yourself be overwhelmed by it all, it'll break your heart. But one or two kids, one day at a time..."

He gave me a watery smile and sighed. "I can't believe I cooked her nikujaga for dinner."

"It wouldn't have been my first choice for a kid, but she loved it."

Kira smiled, though it was still traced with sadness. "It was something my mom used to cook," he said again. "It was something she'd cook if I'd come home wet and cold or if I'd had a bad day... I wanted Claude to... It was the first thing I thought of to give her. I thought if I were her, what would I want to eat?"

I kissed his cheek, then his lips. It was the most lost for words, the most torn I'd seen him in a long while. "Then it was perfect."

Kira pulled me against him, slid his arms around my back, and sighed again. "Where's her parents?" he asked.

"I don't know," I admitted, pulling back so I could see his face. "Every time I've asked, she's gone quiet on me. What she said tonight is the most she's ever told me about that part of her life, so I really don't know. But I think tomorrow I should try and find out."

THE NEXT MORNING when I woke up, Kira was already out of bed. There was the sound of conversation coming from the kitchen. And a smell that had me out of bed in a heartbeat.

Bacon.

I walked into the kitchen, still half asleep. Kira was standing at the stove, while Claude sat at the table. She wore her now-clean clothes from yesterday, her unruly hair was exactly that, and her smile was bright.

After she'd fallen asleep on the sofa, Kira and I had double-checked the windows and doors were locked, and we must have checked on her a dozen times—just to see if she was okay. She had slept soundly. We, unfortunately, had not.

We'd eventually got into bed and talked a bit more about Claude and Ruby, what their lives must be like, and when Kira did eventually fall asleep, it was fitful at best. I spent most of the night as the big spoon to a very restless little spoon.

He was up before me, standing all sleep-rumpled at the stove, turning strips of bacon in a pan. I smiled back at Claude, and standing behind Kira, I kissed his shoulder. "Bacon?" I asked. "How come I never get bacon?"

"You don't eat breakfast," he replied.

"I eat bacon."

Kira chuckled, though he still didn't turn around. "Claude, can you set the table, please?" he asked. "Plates are in that cupboard," he said, pointing the tongs to that particular cupboard door. "Knives and forks are in the top drawer."

Kira was undoubtedly moved last night by the weight of this little girl's troubles, but here he was giving her orders. Claude happily hopped down off the chair and did as she'd been asked. I retrieved the juice and milk from the fridge, grabbed some glasses, and we sat back down at the table, facing each other.

"Sleep well, squirt?"

"Sure did. Did you?" she asked. "'Cause you look tired."

"I'm okay," I told her. "I always look like this before I have coffee."

Kira pulled a tray out of the oven and set it in the middle of the table. "These have been keeping warm," he said. There were poached eggs and slices of toast, and he put the plate of bacon on the table alongside the tray, and sat down.

I couldn't believe it. "Wow."

"Don't get used to it," Kira said. "Claude was hungry. I thought she might appreciate a cooked breakfast rather than yogurt and fruit."

Underneath the table, I ran my foot along his, as silent thanks. I transferred some bacon, eggs, and toast to my plate, as did Claude, and I watched as she took her first mouthful.

"Oh my God," she said, still with food in her mouth. "Kira, your dinner was good, but breakfast is *real* good."

Kira smiled, but it was short lived. He did little more than push some bacon around his plate with a fork. "Claude, can I ask you something?" he said.

She looked at him, then at me and continued to chew her food.

Kira took her silence as a yes. "I get why you don't want

to go to a shelter or to a home. I get that. I really do. You don't want some authorities splitting you and Ruby up, and that's fair enough. But, Claude, sleeping in a dumpster is never a good thing..."

Claude put down her fork and swallowed her breakfast. "Not everyone's got a home, ya know. Sorry it bothers you, but me and Ruby are doin' the best we can." She pushed her plate away. "Anyways, Ruby says it's best to stay hidden. Where no people can see me or take me. And the bins are warm and dry. You might not like it, but it don't matter none what you think."

Kira frowned. "I'm not judging you, Claude," he said patiently. "I am worried for you, that's all. Next time Ruby's not there, or if you're alone or scared, or if it's raining, you can go to the FC and ask for Matt, okay? They're open till late, and if he's not there, they can call him. Okay?"

Claude blinked a few times and frowned. "I'd like to go find Ruby now. If that's okay." Her voice was quiet.

Even though it was too early for the club to open, fifteen minutes later, showered and dressed for the day, we were on our way to the FC. With a few hours before Kira had to work, he insisted on coming with us. Claude had one of my old backpacks filled with my shirt she'd slept in, a bottle of water, some food Kira had given her, plus the wrapped leftover bacon and toast for her brother. If we could even find him.

I didn't dare say anything to Claude about the likelihood of Ruby not being found. It scared me to think of what would happen to her if he went missing.

But my concerns were unfounded.

We'd no sooner got out of the car and were opening the doors to the club when Ruby came running across the street.

He was obviously worried and relieved to see his little sister. He threw his arms around her. "My God, Claude, I was so worried. Where the hell were you?"

I looked over at the direction he'd come from and saw the two people Ruby had been with, Darius and Tyler. The two men Mitch had warned me about it.

And they were heading straight toward us.

CHAPTER EIGHT

"COME ON, GUYS," I said quickly. "Inside." I unlocked the door and held it open for them, but before I could follow them, the two men were behind me. I turned to face them, and they stopped about four feet from me. Both men smiled, more menacing than pleasant.

"Sorry, we're not open for business yet. You'll need to come back in an hour or so," I said. I stood with my head slightly turned, facing my good ear toward them.

"We're friends with Rueben," one of them said.

"We're not open," I repeated.

Kira now stood beside me, and the two men in front of us saw they were evenly matched in number, and with another sneer, they turned and left.

"You okay?" Kira asked quietly.

"Yeah, I'm fine." Turning to look at him, I asked, "Are you?"

Kira nodded, though he looked rather disappointed. I pulled the front door shut and locked it. "They've gone," I said softly.

I thought he was upset with me, but he clapped his

hand on my shoulder and turned around to where Claude and Ruby had disappeared into my office. "Let's go see what Rueben has to say for himself."

"What the hell do you mean you slept at Matt's place?" Ruby cried, just as we walked in. He glanced up at us. "What the hell, man? What did you do to her?"

I was shocked at his outburst. "Hey," I said, resisting the urge to point my finger at him. "The only thing we *did to her* was give her dinner, a hot shower, and a place to sleep. What *we* did was pulled her out of the damn dumpster last night because she was scared and alone."

The boy sighed, his frustration and relief evident in his slumped shoulders. "I was coming back," he said weakly.

I sighed as well and leaned my ass against the table. "It's all right, Ruby. Claude had fun, I think. She watched some TV, helped set the table. Isn't that right, Claude?"

The little girl nodded and smiled brightly. "Yeah, and look, Rube," she said excitedly, rifling through her new backpack. She pulled out some foil-wrapped bacon. "I saved you some of this. Kira cooks real good."

Ruby took the parcel of food and opened the foil to look inside. "Kira cooked you this?"

Claude nodded. "Yep. And dinner last night. I mean, it was a stew type thing, and it looked like something died in it, but it tasted so good."

I laughed at Kira's expression. "Like something died in it?" he repeated.

"Well, kinda," Claude said, not even sorry. "But it was the best thing I ever tasted. Almost better than this bacon."

Ruby smiled, finally, and bit into a piece of bacon. He spoke with his mouth full. "I'm sorry about before. I didn't mean anything, I mean, it wasn't personal. I just couldn't find her, and I was so scared that something bad had happened, and well, it's just that when she said she'd spent the night at your place..." He shook his head.

"Claude," I said. "How about you and Kira go stock up the bathroom supplies for me. Can you show him where I keep it all, please? I just want to have a little chat with Ruby."

Kira gave me a nod, knowing it was an excuse for me to speak to Ruby alone. Once they'd gone from the room, and even though Ruby wouldn't look at me, I said, "Ruby, I won't lie to you, she was scared as hell last night. I was scared for her, and for you," I added. He looked at me, then. I continued, "I'm glad you're okay. I really am. And it really was no problem having Claude stay over. Kira's already told her that if, for whatever reason, you can't be there, she can stay with us. Just for the night."

Ruby bit off some more bacon. "I can look after her."

"I know you can. And, Ruby, you're doing a great job. You really are. She adores you. But you gotta promise me you'll stay away from those two guys. I don't care what they're promising you, what they're telling you they can do for you. Those guys are bad news, Ruby. No good will come from it, I promise you. You know what I'm saying?"

He nodded, but I could tell he wasn't interested.

"You know I spent years in Narcotics in the police, and I can't tell you the things I've seen..." I exhaled loudly. "Ruby, I want better than that for you."

The small kid didn't look at me, but at least he nodded.

"Ruby, you can have a better life than that," I told him. "If you want, I can try and get you a traineeship or a scholarship or whatever it is I can get for you. You'll have to work hard, but you can do it. You can have a better life," I said again. "It'll be hard work, Ruby, *real hard*, but you'll go to school and so can Claude. We'll find you some place to live, where you can stay together and go to school. Does that sound good?"

He shrugged and nodded again, still not convinced.

"Do you want to give Claude a better life?"

He looked at me again. His shoulders sagged and his hands, still holding the wrapped food, fell to his side. The fight in him was gone. I'd hit a nerve—maybe it was a low blow, but I had to do everything I could to get him to see which was the better path to choose.

"Of course I do," he said softly. "Of course I want her to be safe and to have a home." He looked at me, and there was a haunted look in his eyes, much older than his thirteen years. "I'm doing the best I can."

I clapped my hand on his shoulder. "You're doing great, Ruby. But let me help you."

He didn't answer me, but he didn't say no either.

I took it as an opportunity to push a little harder. I needed him to know it was something I understood. "Ruby, can I tell you something?"

He gave a nod. "Sure."

"My mom died when I was seventeen," I told him quietly. "I didn't have anyone else. Just me. I was completely alone, but I was lucky in one regard. I had some policemen come by and check on me, and they offered to help." I exhaled loudly. "I could have ended up in a home or a ward of the state."

"But you didn't?" he asked.

I shook my head. "No. I was almost eighteen anyway, and they kept tabs on me. I was lucky. I had a home, and that's more than most people. I was real lucky; I know that."

"They helped you how?"

"They didn't just help me, they saved me," I told him.

"As soon as I could, I joined the police and got myself a new family."

Ruby's eyebrows knitted, and he frowned. "You want me to be a cop?"

I smiled at him. "If you want to be, you can. But I was thinking a little closer to this family," I said, looking around the gym.

Ruby looked at me, not sure what of what I meant.

"Let me see what I can do about scholarships and MMA. I've seen what you can do these last few months. You have talent, kid, and I reckon you'd have a shot at a place in the program. But it'll take real hard work and a lot of dedication."

Ruby bit the inside of his lip. "You reckon I could do it?"

I smiled. "Hell yes, I do."

"Will you coach me?"

"I can teach you stuff like nutrition and how your body will adapt and all that boring science stuff, but I think Arizona would be a better boxing coach. Or even Boss. But how 'bout we check with the big fella and see if he wants a new student? How about that?"

I thought pairing him with Arizona would be a good idea. Arizona was a good man, and I wanted Ruby to see that an African-American guy, who came from nothing, could make a life for himself. Arizona would make a great mentor for Ruby.

"I can't," he said softly after a long silence.

"Why not?"

Ruby shrugged and looked to the floor when he spoke, "I appreciate you tryin' and everything, Matt, I really do."

"Rueben, why won't you at least try?"

"It's not that simple."

"No, it won't be," I agreed. "It will be hard, but good things don't come easy, Rube."

"No," he said, looking up at me this time. "It's just that I'm not real good at the school stuff. I haven't really done much of it, ya know, and if I have to take tests and stuff, then I may as well just not waste anyone's time."

"Let's just get one thing straight," I said seriously. "You're not a waste of anyone's time, Ruby. Not now; not ever. So if you can't read and write very well, then you can sit your ass in here and learn. When you're not out there with Arizona, you'll be in here with me. If we have to get books and stuff from the local library, then that's exactly what we'll do. Not just you, but any kid that wants to join in. You wanna know something, Ruby? Life sucks. It's unfair and cruel, but every now and then something good comes along, and you fucking grab it with both hands. You know what I'm saying?"

He looked at me, and there was a sadness in his eyes. Not just a sadness, but there was an old soul in those eyes, a kid that had seen too much, learned and lived through things no kid should ever have to. It was a hollow darkness. But inside all that, there was a flicker of hope. There was a need for acceptance and a want to not be forgotten. This kid, all of thirteen years old, needed something to hold on to.

"Will you do it?" I asked quietly. "Will you at least try?"

Ruby seemed to think it over seriously, and in the end he nodded. "Okay," he said.

I grinned and held out my fist, which he bumped with his and rolled his eyes. "But just so you know," he added, "I'm doin' this for Claude. Not for you, not for anyone else."

I nodded, though I was still smiling. "Of course."

"Then we better go see what Claude has Kira doing and

wait for Arizona to get here," I said. Looking at my watch, I continued, "He'll be here in about ten or so minutes. And I'll need to get some paperwork started and make some phone calls, huh?"

Ruby nodded again, but he looked happier.

We walked out into the main floor area of the gym in search for Kira and Claude. We heard Claude's voice from the women's bathroom, giving orders to Kira. I smiled at Ruby and leaned against the wall. "You two done in there?"

The little girl walked out first, her self-importance evident in the way she raised her chin. "Just showing Kira how it's done. He gives me chores at his house; I give him chores here."

Kira, who was now behind her, rolled his eyes, but there was a smirk threatening to give him away. "I have to go to my real job now," he said to Claude. He gave a nod to Ruby. "See you guys later."

"I'll walk you out," I said, and as we got to the front door, we could hear Claude telling Ruby how she had to set the table and fold her blanket in the morning.

Before I unlocked the door so Kira could leave, I gave him a smile. "Thank you for being so understanding," I said quietly. "I thought at first, the way you kept giving Claude orders, that you were mad, but you weren't."

Kira shook his head. "Not at all." Then he shrugged. "I don't want her to think it's a free ride, ya know? I don't want her to think she can just turn up at our place and be waited on, hand and foot. I want her to respect what she's doing, even if it's just setting a table. If she's going to stay at our place, even if it's just one night, then she can contribute and pull her weight." He looked over to where Claude and Ruby were still talking. "I wanted her to feel important."

I bit the inside of my lip to stop my spreading smile.

"What?"

"You'd make such a great dad."

Kira's mouth fell open and his eyes widened. He snorted. "Oh, um..."

I smiled at his comical reaction. "Not right now," I added. "But someday."

Kira exhaled through puffed cheeks. "I thought we were gonna start with a dog?"

"We will," I agreed. "Maybe we could check out some shelters this weekend or the next?"

He shook his head at me, and a slow smile graced his beautiful lips. "I'll see you this afternoon after five."

"Does that mean we have all afternoon to ourselves?" I asked. "Just us? No work, no doctor's appointments, no cooking..." I said, waggling my eyebrows at him. Then I whispered, "Hours in bed, takeout for dinner, more hours in bed..."

Kira smiled just as Arizona walked up to the front doors, arriving for work. I unlocked the doors for him. "Hey, man," I said holding my fist out for him to bump with his.

Arizona nodded to Kira, then looked at me. "You're in a good mood this early," he replied. "Whassup?"

"I need to talk to you about taking on a new student," I told him. "I might have talked Ruby into going full time, as a bit of a scholarship thing. I haven't worked out any details, but if he goes back to school, we can teach him MMA, and then by the time he's old enough for college, he'll be good enough for a full scholarship."

Arizona smiled and shook his head. "You got it all worked out, haven't ya?"

I shrugged. "The kid needs a break."

Kira grinned at me. "Is that what you talked to Ruby about this morning?"

"Yep."

"And *you* think *I'd* make a great dad," he said with a grin. He tapped his open hand on my waist. "I'll see you this afternoon," he said and walked out.

"Did I miss something?" Arizona asked, his eyes wide. "Did he just say something about being a dad?"

I laughed. "Yep. We're gonna get a dog."

Arizona rolled his eyes. "Oh, man. I thought you were being serious," he said as we walked over toward Claude and Ruby.

"We are!" I told him. "We're gonna check out the rescue centers."

"I meant about the baby," he said.

I laughed at him. "I think we'd be better off with the four-legged variety."

"Whatcha doin?" Claude asked.

"Just never you mind," I told her with a smile. "The question is, what are you guys doing?"

"I hear you might want to start some serious training?" Arizona interjected, looking at Ruby.

"Will you, Ruby?" Claude asked with wide, hopeful eyes. "Will you do it?"

Ruby's eyes met mine briefly, then he gave a nod to the big man next to me. "Yeah. Matt seems to think I could handle it."

"There's some schoolwork that needs doing, too," Arizona said. "That's part of the deal, you know that, right?"

Ruby nodded again. "Yeah. So Matt said."

"You ready to start on some basics today?" Arizona asked.

The boy shrugged. "I guess."

"Good." Arizona smiled proudly. "You're now my first appointment for the day, but I gotta get some things set up for the day first. Gimme twenty minutes." Then he looked at Claude. "You come with me, squirt. We got work to do."

"I already put the toilet paper in the girl's bathrooms," Claude told him as they walked off. "I made Kira put it in the boy's."

I pointed to my office, signaling to Ruby he was coming with me. I was trying not to smile as I sat down at my desk, but I was so excited that Ruby was gonna give this a shot. "I've got some forms that we need to fill out," I said, rifling through my files.

I slid the single piece of paper onto my desk, and Ruby sat back in his seat, as though trying to put some physical distance between himself and the form.

"I'll fill it out for you," I told him. "We can only give 'em what we know, okay?" I said, trying to put him at ease, as though it was no big deal.

I picked up a pen. "Full name."

Ruby blinked a few times and looked at the offending piece of paper. Anyone else might have thought the kid didn't know his own name, but I knew better. He didn't want a paper trail where some authority might be able to track him and his sister down and take them away. But as if he'd waged a war inside his head, whatever side opted for the truth had won. "Rueben Vaughn."

I wrote his name in the boxes then read the next question.

"Date of birth?"

"September sixteen," he answered.

"Do you know what year?"

His face pinched. "I'm thirteen..."

Knowing math wasn't on his to-do list, I quickly wrote the year of his birth on the form and moved to the next question.

"Address…" I said out loud, then wished I hadn't. I didn't give him time to answer. "How about we put the club down as your address. That way if anything comes for you in the mail, it'll come here and we'll keep it for you?"

Ruby nodded. "'Kay."

"Phone numbers. I'll just put the club down again and my cell number as well," I added, writing as I went.

"Parent or guardian," I said.

Ruby looked out into the gym room instead of answering.

"It's okay, Rube," I said again. "Claude told me it was just you and her. And that's okay," I added. "These programs are designed for kids just like you. Some have folks, some don't. I can just leave it blank."

"Don't I need some permission or something?" he asked, still looking away from me.

"There are special circumstances allowed for in programs like this," I said. "It'll be fine. I can have a chat with Janelle. She's the lady at the school that organizes all this, and we'll get it sorted out."

He nodded, so I asked the next question. "Last school attended?"

Ruby answered quietly, "Marvin Elementary."

I wrote it down like it was just another piece of information, but it was difficult to hear. This poor kid really had had a hard life.

I read out the last question, "Any known medical problems, medications, that kind of thing?"

"Nuh."

"Cool," I said, giving him a smile. "Paperwork is done. Now go find Arizona and see what he wants to do with you. Tell your sister, if she doesn't want to watch, she can help me in here."

Ruby looked to the table and nodded. "Thanks again," he said quietly. "For this." He motioned toward the piece of paper on the table. "And thanks for looking after Claude last night. I was coming back…"

I pressed him for some kind of answer. "Did you want to talk about where you were last night?"

He shook his head. "No," he whispered. "I'm okay."

"All right," I said, not wanting to ruin anything we'd accomplished this morning. "That's fine. What I said before still stands—if you or Claude need somewhere to crash for a night, somewhere safe, you just let me know."

He nodded again and disappeared through the door. I looked back down at the form I'd just filled out for him, and it saddened me. There were so many blank lines, empty spaces, where a world of information should have been. Proof that he'd lived a life all thirteen year olds should, proof that someone loved him, cared for him, gave him the best they could. But for Ruby, it was all but blank.

It was so unfair.

Claude's words from last night sounded in my head. *'No one wanted us.'*

I picked up my phone, scrolled through my contacts until I found Janelle, then pressed dial. She answered on about the fifth ring, and after I'd reminded her of who I was and where I was calling from, I told her about a new prospective student. I explained he was younger than the other kids I'd applied for, but this kid was an exception to the rule.

"Why's that?" she asked.

"Well, he's thirteen," I admitted. "And last night I pulled his nine-year-old sister out of a dumpster where she had intended on sleeping the night. Ruby won't tell me where he was or why he left his sister alone, but I've offered him this as a chance to change his and his sister's lives, and he's interested."

Janelle hummed into the phone. "He's too young to sit for his high school diploma."

"I know. But he can barely read or write, so I was hoping you might have a school program he could do to help get him on par."

"We're not a government school with a full curriculum. We run intermediate courses to help older people get their diplomas—"

"Yes, but you have the means and the tools, and I've told him he can sit in here with me while he learns. Please, Janelle, this kid has had adult after adult let him down and abandon him. I won't do that to him. I won't tell him he's not worth it. If he's made to go to a normal high school, he wouldn't last a day. But if I can get him this, he stands a chance. If I can get him an education, then he can secure funding for his fighting gear, and when he gets his high school diploma, I can try and get him an MMA scholarship at college. It's a few years away yet, but it needs to start now. Someone needs to show him that someone cares—"

Janelle's laughter cut my rant short. "You're nothing if not determined, are you, Mr. Elliott?"

I took a deep breath. "I can't let him down."

I heard her groan, but then she spoke as though she was smiling, "Let me see what I can do. If you say he can't read or write very well, then maybe I could push for an introductory course to English first to see how he goes, then we'll know what we're dealing with and where to place him in relation to high school standards."

I grinned into the phone. "You're fantastic," I told her. "Thank you, thank you."

I promised to hand deliver the application myself later

that day and even bring Ruby with me so she could meet him. Janelle said if we left it till tomorrow, she'd have some kind of prelim schoolwork organized for us to take with us so Ruby could make a start. I promised we'd be there.

I disconnected the call, and I sighed. But the smile on my face waned the longer I stared at Ruby's almost-blank enrollment form.

I took my phone and, this time, dialed a familiar number. I probably shouldn't have done it—it probably breached his trust—but I wanted to help in every way I could. And for me to help both Ruby and Claude, then I needed to know exactly what I was dealing with.

"Matt? Is that you?"

I smiled at the sound of his voice. "Yeah, Mitch, it's me."

"What's up?"

"I met your two drug runners this morning."

"Matt." His tone was pure caution. "I told you to stay away from them."

"I did," I told him. "They came here. They were following one of the kids who was coming in, and I stopped them at the door."

"Same kid as before?"

"Yep. Ruby."

"Hmm," he hummed.

I knew that sound. It meant something didn't quite add up, but his mind was connecting the dots anyway. I knew how Mitch's mind worked. I'm sure he wanted to ask me a ton of questions, but as a civilian, protocol didn't allow it. Not without making it official, anyway. Instead, he asked, "Is the kid okay?"

"Yeah."

"Did they threaten you?"

"No."

"Good," he said with what sounded like a sigh of relief. "So what can I do for you?"

"I need some information."

"What kind of information?" came his tentative reply.

"I want a full history and background check."

There was a second of silence. "On who?"

"I want to know everything you can tell me about a Rueben and Claudia Vaughn."

CHAPTER NINE

THE MOONLIGHT CAST a silver glow across the room, across the bed, and across Kira.

We lay on our sides facing each other. The leather strand that held his engagement ring, which hung around his neck, weighed down toward his armpit. Reaching out, I took the ring, feeling the cool weight of it in my hand. I marveled at the beauty of the ring, and what it signified.

"I love you, Matt," Kira said. He would quite often tell me, out of the blue, but seriously. He'd always look me in the eye and tell me he loved me, like it was something I was likely to forget. As if I could, ever.

"I love you, too," I replied.

"You feel okay?"

"Yeah, I'm okay."

Kira had picked me up from work, we'd had dinner and I'd told him all about getting Ruby signed up for the scholarship program. Kira had offered to drive me and Ruby up to the college in the morning to get his paperwork finalized. I'd kissed him lightly on the lips and whispered in his ear how much I'd like to thank him.

We'd been fooling around on the sofa and my head had started to spin. Not in a good way, but in a vertigo kind of way. It had been getting late anyway, so Kira had taken my hand and slowly led me to bed. He'd undressed me down to my briefs while I'd sat on the edge of the bed with my eyes closed. He'd pulled back the covers, then while he'd stripped down, I'd slowly lain down before he'd joined me.

He traced his fingers along the scar above my eyebrow, I still held his engagement ring, and we simply reveled in the silence. Sometimes the quiet moments between us were the most intimate.

"You really like it, don't you?" he asked.

I turned the ring in my hand, making it catch in the silver moonlight, then looked to his eyes. "I can't wait until you wear it."

Kira smiled and touched the ring that hung around my neck. "Did you want to pick a date?"

"For what?"

"The wedding," he said with a chuckle. "I'm sure Mom wouldn't mind."

Despite the lopsided tumbling in my head, I smiled. "I'd marry you right now, but I think we'll know when the time is right."

Kira's eyes widened. "Are you saying no?"

I threw back the sheet and sat up, though my head spun and pulled me sideways. Kira caught me and laid me back down on the bed. "Whoa, where are you going?"

"Taking you to find a priest or a minister or someone who'll marry us."

"Now?"

"Right now," I said, still trying to get up.

Kira laughed and kept his hands on me, holding me down on the bed. "No you're not. You can't even sit up."

I pulled his hands off me, but he rolled on top of me and pinned me with his weight. He was still smiling. "You're not going anywhere."

I loved feeling his full weight on me, but my head was still spinning in the opposite direction to the room. I closed my eyes to ease the revolving in my head.

Kira moved to get off me, but I hitched my thigh and hooked my leg around his to keep him exactly where he was. His hands were on my face, and he kissed my closed eyelids. His hardening dick pressed against my thigh, and my hips responded by flexing into his.

"Matt," he whispered with another kiss to my lips. "You're not okay."

"I am now."

Kira shifted his weight, and his erection now pressed against mine, making me moan. He laughed softly and kissed me again. "I'm sorry. My body reacts to you."

Without opening my eyes, I ran my hands over his chest and up his neck to cup his face. I pulled him in for a proper kiss.

He hummed into my mouth as my tongue met his, and we got lost in the kiss, but when he groaned, then pulled away, I finally opened my eyes.

Kira rested his weight on his elbows, one hand on my head, his fingers in my hair, his other hand framing my face. His eyes were dark, full of want and desire. He licked his lips and groaned low in his throat.

"What's wrong?" I asked him.

"You're not well," he said. His voice was husky. "We shouldn't be doing this."

I rolled my hips into his, feeling how turned on he was. I ran my hand over his ass, pulling him harder against me.

"Matt," he started to protest again.

I pushed him off me a little, so Kira leaned up just enough for me to move, but instead of sliding out, I rolled over underneath him and settled back on the bed face down. "If you want me, then have me."

Kira groaned again, and needing just one more reason to give in, I lifted my hips and pulled my briefs down, exposing my ass cheeks.

Kira laughed as he leaned over me, trailing his lips up my shoulder to the back of my neck. He held his body weight off me, his knees on either side of my hips. "Matt," he said, before kissing my shoulder again, "if your head starts to spin..."

"You always make my head spin."

His smiling lips pressed against my neck, then he murmured in my left ear, "I promise I'll be slow."

I shivered at his words, at the gravel in his voice. The bed dipped as he fumbled with his briefs, and I groaned when he trailed his cock along the crack of my ass. I thought this might be it; I thought he might take me bare—without a barrier between us—just him.

I moaned without shame, lifting my ass, urging him to do it. He slid his cock down to my hole, kissing my shoulder, my neck, behind my ear. My head was still hazy, with vertigo, with sensation. When I rocked my hips back, Kira grunted, but then he was gone. He knelt back, pulled my briefs down my thighs and off my legs. I half expected him to crawl back up my body and finish what he'd started, but then he was off the bed, taking off his own underwear. I heard the bedside drawer open followed by the familiar rustle of foil.

I didn't even care that he wasn't about to bareback me, I just wanted him inside me. If he wasn't ready, if he wasn't ever ready to do it, I wouldn't mind. I just needed to feel him where I wanted him the most.

I pressed my useless right ear into the pillow and watched in the moonlight as he rolled a condom down his rigid cock. He slicked himself with lube, and I closed my eyes in anticipation.

I smiled when he ran his hands over my ass. I moaned when I felt the cool liquid drip down my ass crack, and my blood warmed when his fingers slipped into me.

Then his warm breath was in my ear. "Do you feel okay?"

"God, yes," I answered. My head was still fuzzy from vertigo, still spinning. The room was lopsided, and even lying down, I felt like I was falling. But fuck, what he was doing to me felt so damn good.

I thrust my hips, pushing onto his fingers, fucking, wanting.

Then his hand was gone and was soon replaced with the thick, hot, blunt head of his cock in the crevice of my ass. Kira's hands were on the bed beside my head, his full weight pushed me into the mattress, and his cock pressed my hole, pushing, breaching, and oh-so-slowly, slipping inside me.

Kira's mouth skimmed the back of my neck, his breath stuttering in my ear. "Oh, my God, Matt." His voice cracked, and he moaned long and low as he pushed deeper into me.

I reached up under the pillows to grip the top of the mattress, and Kira ran his hands up my arms to hold my fists as he rocked into me. Slowly. Deeply.

I lifted my ass for him, giving him more of me, all of me. He gave me every inch of himself, so his balls sat heavy against my ass.

Rolling his hips, he rocked into me, and with each thrust, he nipped my shoulder, then followed with sweet, soft kisses.

I raised my ass in time with him, and his thrusts got quicker, harder. His hands squeezed mine as we gripped the top of the mattress, and his moans became grunts.

Kira got harder, his cock swelling in my ass, and with a final thrust, he cried out, moaning, convulsing, as he came. "Fuck," he groaned in my ear, collapsing on top of me, skimming his lips, his nose, his forehead over my shoulder and the side of my head.

I would have stayed like that forever, but eventually Kira rolled us over, sliding out of me at the same time. He held me tight, still planting kisses on whatever skin he could reach. "Your turn."

"Uh-uh," I hummed. "No need. That was just for you."

"Matt," he said, sounding surprised, worried. "Are you sure?"

"Very."

"Do you feel okay? Is your head spinning too much? Do you feel nauseated. Shit, Matt, you should have told me to stop."

I chuckled and snuggled into his chest, pulling his arm around me so he could hold me. "I feel great. Head's still fuzzy a bit, but I feel great. I love it when you do that."

Kira raked his hand over my back, up to my hair. "But I didn't make you come."

"I didn't have to," I mumbled into his chest. "I just love it when you fuck me."

Kira barked out a quiet laugh. "You're such a bottom."

I pulled back from his embrace and my eyes took a moment to focus. "I am," I said, feeling myself blush. "For you."

Even in the moonlit room, Kira saw it. He kissed my heated cheek. "I haven't seen you blush like that in a while."

I ducked my head back to his chest. Kira gave me a squeeze and sighed contentedly against the side of my head. "Shower?"

"No, I'll just stay right here."

"Are you too dizzy to get up?" he asked me seriously.

"A little dizzy. A lot comfortable."

"I'll bring back a washcloth for you," he said, then with a kiss to my forehead, he was gone.

I heard the shower start but must have dozed off. I woke up to a warm, wet cloth and gentle hands. When he was done, he climbed in beside me, and his shower-warm, soap-scented body wrapped around mine, lulling me back to sleep.

I'm not sure how much later it was, but my restless pillow woke me up. I pulled him in tight, but he sighed. "Matt? Matt?" he said, gently tapping my arm.

"Mm?"

"Matt? Are you awake?"

"Yeah, what's wrong?"

"Do you think they're okay?"

"Who?"

"Claude and Ruby."

"Um..." I was too sleepy to catch up. "Um, what?"

Kira leaned up on one elbow. "I can't sleep. I mean, we're in here, safe, warm, protected, and they're out there somewhere. God only knows where."

I sat up slowly, mindful of the vertigo. "Kira, babe, what are you saying?"

"Well, aren't we responsible somehow? I mean, we know they're sleeping on the streets, or in a dumpster, for all we know, and we're not doing anything about it. We're here, and those kids are out there alone somewhere."

"What did you want to do?"

"I don't know," he said, clearly frustrated.

"Did you want to go for a drive?" I asked. "We could drive the streets around the club, but there's no way of knowing where they are." I looked at the alarm clock on the bedside table. "Kira, babe, it's past midnight. They'll be holed up somewhere, sound asleep. If we go looking now, it might draw attention to them."

With a loud sigh, he lay back down. I did the same but put my head on his chest.

"It just bothers me, that's all," he said finally.

"That's because you're one of the good guys," I said. "You're thoughtful, kind, forgiving..."

"Forgiving?"

"Very," I answered. I lifted my head off him and, lying back on the bed, pulled him against me instead. I dragged the sheet and blanket up over us, tucking it in around him, and gave him a squeeze.

"Matt," he said softly.

"Shush." I kissed the top of his head and tightened my arms around him.

"Matt."

"Go to sleep, babe."

After a long moment, he said, "Uh, Matt?"

"Yeah," I mumbled, almost asleep.

"You're squashing my arm."

"Oh," I said, shuffling and wriggling until his arm was free. "Better?"

"Yeah." Then when I was almost asleep again, he said, "Matt?"

"Mmm?"

"Will you tell Claude and Ruby they can stay here if they need to?"

I smiled and kissed the top of his head again. "I already have."

He was quiet for a while, but he exhaled deeply and his breathing steadied. Then he spoke again, his voice croaking with sleep, "Matt?"

"Yeah?"

"You're one of the good guys too."

KIRA CAME to work with me and helped while I got a few things set up before the other guys got there. There was something relaxing about being there before it opened—it was quiet, it smelled familiar. It wouldn't be long and there'd be a hive of activity, talking and noise, but early in the morning, it was peaceful.

Boss arrived first, and as he walked in, he looked at Kira. Without stopping, he said, "Hope you're volunteering your time because we can't afford you," and kept walking to his office.

Kira laughed, but kept wiping down the weight benches.

Arizona was next to arrive, bumped fists with me, then with Kira. "Hey, man," he said to Kira. "Good to see you here."

"Yeah, Matt's a slave-driver," he said with a smile. He wouldn't admit to wanting to be here to see if Claude and Ruby turned up unharmed.

Or in fact, turned up at all.

"How did it go with Ruby yesterday?" I asked him.

"It went okay," Arizona replied. "We mostly did prep stuff, introductory stuff, and talked about schedules and shit like that. I mean, he's been coming here for a few months, he knows the basics. He's only young, but jeez, he's got a natural talent."

I smiled, relieved that it'd been a productive first session. "I think so too. Inside the ring'll be easy for him. Outside it, not so much."

Arizona nodded. "Yep. I just hope he can stick to the program."

"Me too."

Arizona went on to say, "He said he had to be back first thing. You got some paperwork thing with him."

"Yeah, I wanted him to meet with Janelle, the lady at Hillvue Community College who's organizing his school program," I told him. "I just thought if he saw there's a group of us who want him to do this, he might be more inclined to stick to it."

"You really pushin' for him?" Arizona asked, but it wasn't really a question.

"I am," I agreed. "I mean, I want all the kids in this program to do well, but I want Rueben to see he has choices, ya know?"

Arizona gave me a huge grin. "I know exactly, man. Exactly. And I'm guessin' that's the reason you put him with me."

I smiled and clapped my hand on his shoulder. "Not just a pretty face."

"Hey," a smiling Kira said, butting in at my compliment to Arizona.

"I didn't mean it like that," I quickly corrected. "It means he's got brains, not that he had a pretty face."

"Hey!" Arizona chimed in.

I threw my hands up. "I won't win this," I said, then turned to walk into my office.

Kira and Arizona both burst out laughing.

I left them to it, to make a start on some paperwork in my office, though every time I heard animated chatting or laughing between Kira and Arizona, it made me smile.

I heard Jamaal's voice, and realized it was time for the club to open. The next voice I heard was a very excited Claude. "Kira!" she cried. "You're here!"

"I am," he replied.

"Where's Matt? I want him to see. Look at what I got!" she shrieked.

Immediately intrigued, I got up from my desk and walked out into the gym room. Claude was beaming and proudly showing off a new pair of running shoes.

Probably a size or two too big, bright white and purple and sparkly. They weren't any expensive brand name. They weren't anything special when it came to sneakers. But they were new.

It was hard not to be excited for her. She was just about to burst. But there was a nagging thought in my head.

How on earth did she get them?

"Ruby got them for me," she said, as if reading my thoughts. "We went into a shop and everything! They is a bit big, but Ruby said I'm only gonna grow."

By the look on his face and his silence, it was pretty obvious Kira was having similar thoughts to mine. "Oh, man!" he cried, excited, reacting perfectly. "They are the prettiest shoes I have ever seen!"

"I know, right?" she said. "Matt, whaddya think?"

"I think they're pretty special," I said, giving her a smile. Regardless of just how she'd gotten them, I didn't need to ruin her moment. "There's a treadmill over there you could try 'em out on."

She stared at me like I'd lost my mind. "I want them to stay new! I ain't gonna run in 'em."

Ruby walked cautiously over to where the four of us were. He handed Claude the backpack I'd given her.

"I was showing 'em my shoes, Ruby," Claude said. She hadn't stopped smiling yet.

Rueben looked at his sister with what I could only describe as a saddened pride. Like he was protecting her innocence, whether futile or not, the best he could. "They're somethin' special, Claude."

I noticed he didn't have new shoes. He still wore the too-small, threadbare runners he always wore. Regardless of where or how he'd got the money, it was hard to be judgmental and negative when he'd spent every cent he could on his sister.

"You ready for a big day, Ruby?" I asked, changing the subject. I checked my watch. "We've got thirty minutes to be up at the community college."

"Yeah, I'm ready," he said, though he hardly sounded convinced.

"Good," I said. But then I turned to Claude. "Hey, squirt, how 'bout you go make yourself a hot chocolate. I've got something I want to talk to Ruby about, is that okay?"

Claude shrugged and, still smiling, skipped her new shoes into my office.

I tapped my hand on Ruby's shoulder. "I've got something I want to show you. Come with me." I motioned for Kira and Arizona to come with me and led the kid into the locker room.

"Take a seat," I told him, pointing to the long bench that ran down the center of the room.

"I didn't steal them shoes," he said quickly, defensively. "If that's what you's are here to ask me. I didn't steal the money either."

"Hey," I said, putting up my hands. "That's not what this about. We've got something for you, which we give all new committed fighters that join this club."

Ruby looked between me, Arizona, and Kira. He took a steadying breath. "Okay."

"You get your own locker," I told him.

His eyes widened in disbelief and he smiled. "For real?"

"For real," I agreed. "If you agree that you're committed to this course and to doing some schoolwork as part of the deal, then it's all yours. You can keep your stuff in it."

His smile faltered. "I ain't got no stuff."

"You sure about that?" I asked, smiling at him. "Number forty-two. Open it."

Ruby stood up and hesitantly stood in front of the locker, as though whatever was inside it was both exciting and forbidden. He opened the metal locker door and smiled at what he saw. His eyes went to mine.

"Not just me. Arizona as well."

"Oh, man," the kid said. He pulled out what was inside. "Are you for real? Are these mine?"

I looked at the black fingerless MMA gloves he was holding. "All yours. The towel was a gym towel, but it's now got your name on it too." It really wasn't much to give him, but for a kid who literally had nothing, it was special. "And if you stick it out for the first few weeks, we'll get you some proper shorts."

Ruby was grinning now, which was not something I saw him do often. "I'll stick it out, just you watch."

"The first sign of you slacking off or not turning up or not doing your schoolwork," Arizona said, "then you lose the locker, all right? It's a privilege you earn to keep, ya hear?"

Ruby nodded. "Yeah, man, I hear."

"Good," I told him. "Now you get washed up. We'll be in my office waiting for you so we can go meet your new teacher. Then this afternoon you can try out those new gloves, okay?"

He smiled at us. It was a humbled, grateful look, and it was easy to forget the kid was just thirteen.

Before we walked back into my office to where Claude was, Kira stopped me. He whispered, "If he didn't steal that money, then where did he get it from. Fuck, Matt, I hardly slept a wink last night because I worried about them, and now it turns out he's stealing stuff? I mean, I know it's tough and he has to do whatever he can to survive, but that's not right. God, what if he snatched some lady's handbag? He must have got about fifty bucks—"

"He didn't steal the money."

"You don't believe that, do you?" Kira asked. "Oh please, Matt—"

I cut him off, "He didn't steal the money from a little old lady, Kira." Sometimes I really hated knowing what I knew. Years in the Narcotics Division of the LAPD shed light on a very hard, cold reality.

I looked at Kira and sighed. "Kira, babe, Ruby's a drug mule. He runs drugs for cash."

CHAPTER TEN

KIRA PALED. "HE'S WHAT?"

"A drug mule," I repeated quietly.

"How do you know?"

"The pieces fit," I explained. "Those two skin-head guys that hang around, how he disappears some nights, the cash. It makes sense."

Kira opened his mouth, then closed it. Twice. He shook his head. "Fifty bucks is hardly income for that kind of thing." Then his eyes widened. "Is it? Is it really? He's risking his life for fifty bucks?"

"Babe, fifty bucks to kids like Ruby may as well be a million dollars. And you know what he did with it?" I asked, still trying to keep my voice down. "He bought his kid sister a pair of shoes and some food."

Kira turned his head sharply to the wall and took a deep breath. "We have to do something."

"I am!" I said. "I'm trying to give him a fresh start. An education, a career. It's all I can do."

"Hey," Ruby said, interrupting, and probably

wondering if we were arguing or why we were having a whispered conversation. "I'm ready."

I gave him a smile. "Cool. Let's do this. I'll just grab your paperwork and we'll go." I quickly grabbed his application and called out to Claude. "Come on, squirt. You can come too."

She jumped up, quickly washed her hot chocolate cup out, then dried it while I waited at the door for her. I liked how she still did her jobs, even in a hurry to leave. She put the mug in the cupboard then raced over. She threw the backpack over her shoulder and skipped over to where Kira was waiting with Ruby. "Is you driving us?" she asked, looking up at Kira.

He grinned at her. "I am."

"You not workin' today?" she asked.

"Afternoon shift."

She seemed happy with that explanation and went off with him to the front door. Looking at Ruby, I gave him a pointed nod after Kira and Claude. We followed them out, and walking around the corner to where the car was parked, I wondered if McInnes and James saw us, if they saw us with Ruby, and if there would be any ramifications if they did. I scanned the streets, as inconspicuously as I could, but there was no sign of them.

The car trip took all of ten minutes, but there wasn't a word spoken the whole time. Kira was obviously troubled by my suspicion of how Ruby had come into some cash—the whole situation with these kids bothered him a great deal. With our joint therapy session with Tamara coming up, I knew it'd be something we'd discuss at length.

We arrived at the college, and after checking at the administration office, we found Janelle. Kira and Claude waited outside while Ruby and I went into her office. She looked busy but was happy to see us.

"I really want to thank you for taking the time to meet with us," I told her.

"No problem," she replied quickly. Then she looked at Ruby and directed all questions to him. She basically asked him if he understood what the program meant and, if he stuck it out, what it could offer him. "We know it's not easy," she went on to say. "There will be times when you will want to quit, when it's too hard, but, Ruby, not many kids get this opportunity."

"I know," he answered quietly.

"Matt here has pushed pretty hard to get this for you," she said.

Ruby shot me a quick look, but then his gaze fell to his hands. "Yeah."

"Now all the academic stuff will be going through me, but all the physical stuff, the training, and the MMA sched-ules will be done through the Fight Club," she said. "You're not the only one from Matt's club that's doing this, but you are the youngest. Younger than what we'd normally allow, but Matt was persistent."

Ruby looked at me again, and this time I gave him a smile but spoke aloud for Janelle's benefit, "He's now got himself a locker and a few basics, and we're gonna work on getting him some more gear. It's more of a work-hard-get-rewards system."

Janelle seemed impressed. "Sounds good. Ruby, I have put together a starter pack of work for you to go through. You'll have a week to get it done, come back next week, hand it in, and take the next week's work with you."

Ruby nodded but looked a little overwhelmed. "'Kay."

"I think you'll handle it just fine," she said. "If it's too hard, we'll knock it back a gear, or if you find it too easy, we can adjust. You've got Matt and the other guys who are learning as well to help you. If you're really struggling, you need to let us know and not just quit, okay?"

"I'm no quitter," he said, quietly but defiantly.

I looked at Janelle. "No, he's not."

She smiled, more genuinely this time. "So, we'll see you next week."

Still looking at his hands, Ruby gave a nod.

"You will," I spoke on his behalf.

Janelle handed Ruby his schoolwork in a simple plastic sleeve, and as we walked out of the office, Claude was full of questions. "Whatcha got, Rube? Is that homework? Have you got homework, Ruby? Can I help you with it? Can you show me? Maybe I can help you some."

We started to walk back to our car, and I patted her head. "No you won't, squirt. Rueben has to do his own work."

"Are you really gonna make him do schoolwork, Matt?" she asked brightly.

It was hard not to smile at Claude. She was always full of energy. "I sure am. And if you're not careful, I'll find you some to do too."

"Good luck with that," she said.

I laughed, and even Kira smirked at that. As Claude and Ruby got into the car, I asked Kira quickly, "You okay?"

He nodded, but his smile didn't quite look right. Again, it was a relatively quiet trip back to the club, aside from Claude looking through Ruby's papers.

Kira was quiet until we got back to the gym. He held the front doors open and waited for the two kids to go inside. I saw him scout the street, presumably looking for the two men who had paid Ruby, but they weren't there. I'd already looked.

"You gonna stay here a while?" Claude asked Kira, looking up to him as she walked beside him.

"Yeah," he answered. "A little while."

We walked into my office, and I clapped Ruby on the shoulder. "You can keep your folder in your locker," I told him. "And you can sit in here anytime, day or night, and get some work done, okay?"

Rueben nodded. "Thanks, Matt. For this"—he held up the folder—"and for the gloves."

"You wanna go try 'em on? The gloves?" I asked. "I can run through some sets with you if Arizona's busy right now."

Ruby nodded and brightened. "Cool."

"Wait," Kira said, before Ruby got out of the door. "Rueben, wait." Kira seemed a little stuck for words. "Tonight... I'm not sure what your plans are for tonight, but I'll be picking Matt up just after nine... If you and Claudia want somewhere to stay... just for tonight, you can stay with us."

Well, this was news to me. I withheld my surprise, so when Ruby's gaze shot to mine, he'd think it was completely okay. But I'm not sure it was. I wanted these kids to be safe, and I wanted them to have a real chance at life. I just wasn't sure that was at our house.

Ruby said nothing, but Claude asked, "Is that okay, Matt?"

"Sure it is, squirt," I told her. "Just for tonight."

"Will Kira cook again?" Claude asked, with a bright-eyed innocence. "Because he cooks real good."

"Claude," Ruby whispered, gently shushing her.

"Anyway," I said, trying to act like it was no big deal,

"you've got all day to think about it. I'll be leaving for an hour or two after lunch, but I'll be back for afternoon classes. If you're here when we finish up, then I'll spring for a burger and a bed. Your choice."

Ruby pulled Claude by the arm, said another quiet thanks, and walked out into the gym room. Kira, who was leaning against one of the tables, ran his hand through his hair and sighed. "I'm sorry," he said. "I should have asked you first."

"You don't need to ask me," I told him. I stood in front of him and put my hand on his arm.

"We'll need to find them something more permanent, Matt," he said. "I know they can't stay with us long-term, but even just a night or two is better than nothing. Until we find them somewhere they can stay."

"Last time I mentioned some government-funded housing, they took off and I didn't see them for two days."

"I know," he said with a resigned sigh. "We just have to do something."

I leaned in and gave him a quick kiss. "You're a good man."

"I better get to work, or I'll be a fired man," he said, pushing off the table to stand close enough to me that I could feel the warmth of his body. "You're doing a good job here, Matt," he said softly. "You got a session with Tamara at one?"

"Yep."

Kira nodded. "We can talk later tonight, okay? About today, about your session."

I smiled at him, at his want to keep the communication between us on track. "Of course."

He looked so... helpless.

"Kira, babe, we'll sort something out. It might take a day

or two. I'll ask around, and see what I can suss out. There'll be something that suits."

He finally nodded and gave me a sad smile. "Okay."

I spent the morning organizing some advertising and marketing of our community fundraising day. We had permission to close off the street, we had local businesses on board, we had some food stalls, kids' games and activities, we even had some carnival rides lined up. And there were three other clubs willing to join us for an exhibition tournament. The weeks were closing in on us, but it was slowly coming together.

It took me about an hour going over details with Boss, trying to keep his stress levels down, reassuring him this could work. We'd have kids doing classes out on the street, showing techniques and skills, showing that we had purpose. I had talked to one of the merchandise reps, our biggest supplier of fighting gear, to sponsor some gear for the day. We scored some shirts for our kids to wear, so we looked like a team, and some to sell.

Our biggest ploy was for the community to see us as valuable. We needed to break down that drug-ring stigma that had plagued this place from when Tressler had run it. I wanted people, parents, teachers, local professionals to see us as an important step for these kids' futures.

Well, that was my dream anyway.

I then spent a good hour on the treadmill and even managed a sparring session with Arizona. It was good for Ruby to see. He sat with Cody, and Cody vocalized our moves, telling him why we did what we did.

After we'd showered, Arizona sat in my office with me and we ate a late lunch. It was good to catch up with him outside of the ring. He told me all about Lashona's pregnancy progress, just beaming from the inside as he described the latest scans.

I'd told him about Claude staying on our sofa the other night, and I told him of Kira's offer earlier that day. He nodded thoughtfully. "It's a tough one. It's hard not to become attached..."

"But?" I prompted, knowing he was censoring his comments.

"Just be careful, that's all. It's never easy when there's kids involved."

I nodded. "Yeah. I know. On one hand, they're resilient as hell, and on the other hand, they're as fragile as glass."

Arizona gave me a slow-spreading smile. "Sound like a dad already."

I scoffed at that. "Not likely."

"Got yourself a dog yet?"

"Nah, maybe this weekend or the next."

Arizona chuckled. "You watch. Dog'll be first, then a kid. Just you watch."

I shook my head. "Man, I don't think I'm geared for kids."

"Bullshit," he replied. "I've seen you here with the kids that come in."

"Yeah, so why would I want more when I've got about twenty to look after here?"

Arizona laughed this time, shaking his head like I was missing the obvious. Then Cody called out from the door, "Hey, Matt!"

"Yeah."

"Cab's out front."

"Thanks," I told him. I held my fist out to Arizona which he bumped with his own. "I'll be back after two."

"Have fun."

I scoffed. I had a feeling this shrink appointment wouldn't be fun at all.

———

"WHAT'S BOTHERING YOU, MATT?" Tamara asked.

I sighed, and I let my head fall back. "Kids."

"The kids at the club?" she clarified. "Claude?"

"And her brother, Rueben." Then I added, "And how Kira struggles with it."

"Struggles with what?" she asked.

"With how they live. I think Ruby has gotten himself in with the wrong crowd, and there's a pretty good chance he's doing drug drops for cash," I said. "I'm really pushing for him to do this scholarship-type course, so he can get his high school diploma, and then maybe an MMA scholarship at college, but he's so young..."

"How does that make you feel?"

Always with the feelings. Instead of rolling my eyes, I answered her question, "Frustrated. Sorry. Angry that kids that young have to deal with stuff most adults couldn't cope with. That they weren't given a proper chance."

Tamara was quiet for too long. Her usual way of prompting to fill the silence.

And stupidly, I did. "Kira asked them if they wanted to stay at our place tonight."

She raised one eyebrow. "Really?"

"Yes."

"And you're okay with that?"

"Of course I am," I told her. "I don't know, Tamara. I get the feeling you're stuck on these kids. Every time I mention them, you get all passive–aggressive ..."

"Passive–aggressive?"

I sighed. "It's like you're judging me or something."

Tamara was quiet again, though it seemed more thoughtful this time. "I'm not judging you, Matt. I'm trying to get you to question things you wouldn't normally question. It's my job to help you question decisions—past and future—analyze those decisions and set about the best course of action—"

I put my hand up, palm forward, to stop her. "I read the manual."

Tamara smiled and exhaled slowly. I wondered just how much self-control it must have taken for her not to sigh. Or throw something at me.

"I'm sorry," I told her.

"You're under stress," she rationalized. "You're allowed to express your concerns, Matt. It's the very reason you come here."

I took a calming breath and ignored her objective rationale the best I could. "Can I ask you something?"

"Of course."

"My six-month review must have been up by now," I said. It was a statement, not a question. "So can I ask what your recommendation was?"

Tamara smiled. "Matt, you knew this was a long-term endeavor. And you've become impatient that things aren't moving quick enough? Is that the problem?" she asked, her tone still neutral. "If the problem is with me, I can find you another therapist if you'd prefer?"

"I don't want another therapist," I snapped back at her. "I don't want to have to start again. I want to get better, and I'm prepared for it to take a long time—after all, I was pretty fucked up, and that's gonna take some fixing. I just think there's an issue here with the kids I'm trying to help, like you're waiting for everything to fail."

"Like *I'm* waiting for it to fail?" she asked. "Or is it *you* that's waiting for it all to fail?"

I opened my mouth, to rebuke her stupid fucking question, but couldn't. I snapped my mouth shut, stared out of the window, and said nothing.

"Time's up, Matt," she said.

I almost thanked God out loud.

"Your meeting on Thursday is a couple's session with Kira. Will you want to discuss what we've talked about today with him?"

"Sure," I said, still staring out of the window. "I tell him everything that you and I talk about anyway," I added.

"Okay. Good." This time she sighed. "Matt, I want you to know, I don't have any problems with anything you've done or are trying to do—especially with those children. I think you've come incredibly far in a short time, and you should be proud. So today wasn't a great day. And that's fine—it's perfectly normal. But, Matt, if you're looking for me to tell you that you don't need to have these appointments, I can't do that. I'm not here to tell you what you want to hear, Matt. I'm here to do my job, and that's to help you get better. I want you to move forward, to have a happy and fulfilling life with Kira—and with kids, if that's what you want. And I have no doubt you'll have exactly that. Matt, don't sell yourself short. Give yourself the time it takes to heal."

I stopped short of saying "what-the-fuck-ever" and said nothing instead.

I caught a cab back to work, and instead of going into my office, I got changed into my gym gear and hit the tread-mill. Normally the steady beat of my feet on a treadmill would clear my head and relax me, but not today. The other guys gave me space—maybe it was the angry determination on my face, or maybe it was because of how fast I was running.

I guess they knew if I was pissed off, the best thing to do was to leave me alone.

It wasn't long before I could feel the sweat running down my back and a familiar burn in my chest and legs. When I finally hit stop on the machine and jumped off, Arizona came over.

"Man, you okay?"

I wiped my face and took a mouthful of water. "Not really."

He eyed me cautiously. "Wanna talk about it?"

"Not really," I said tightly. Then I sighed, frustrated with myself for being so bent out of shape over something so stupid. "My fucking therapist," I started. "God, she makes me so fucking mad."

Arizona smiled, as though relieved. "Man, I got half an hour to spare. Want me to spot for you while you kick the shit out of the pads?"

I grinned at him. "You'd do that? Really?"

"Well, it's either that or I could call Kira and tell him to come haul your ass outta here."

I set down my towel and water bottle in the corner near the pads and scoffed at his joke. "Yeah, right."

Arizona picked up a rectangle thigh pad. "I ain't jokin', Matt. I wouldn't hesitate. I've seen you pissed off and I seen where it got ya. There's no way I'd let you throw it all away again."

His words threw me for a second. Not just because they were true but because he was keeping an eye on me, and if I even looked like having a setback, he'd be the first in line to help me.

"Come on," he said, getting my attention. He patted

the kicking pad before he lifted it against his body, bracing for impact. "Take it out on this instead. Kick the living shit outta this instead of beating yourself up. I can take it."

I kicked the padded mat Arizona held, not too hard, and he shook his head. "Come on! You can hit damn harder than that!" He squatted down a little, anchoring his center of gravity, bracing himself. "Don't hold back."

I kicked again, harder this time—two short taps with my right leg, my shin hitting square on the pad.

"Better," he said. "Now kick like you mean it! You come in here wanting to beat the shit out of yourself because your doctor pissed you off, so fucking kick like you mean it."

I grinned at him and he braced himself, grimacing a little as though my grin was familiar. And frightening.

And I let him have it.

I kicked high, low, hard, and harder. Arizona lifted the padded mat in time with me, calling shots, correcting me, urging me to let it go. When I'd kicked enough, he called, "Hands," and with bare knuckles, I punched, jabbed, deflected.

"Keep on your toes," Arizona grunted at me, like I was one of his students, and for the next thirty minutes, I had a full cardio workout and one-on-one stress and anger management.

Arizona threw the mat into the corner and wiped his face down with his towel. He'd had as good a workout as me. "Fuckin' hell, man," he said, taking a deep breath. "What the hell did she say to you to get you so pissed?"

I snorted out a laugh. "She just presses my buttons," I said. Then, figuring I owed him more than a blasé brush-off, I explained, "Every time I talk about what I'm doing here, I get attitude from her."

Arizona frowned. "What for? Leaving the police and now doing this?" He glanced around the gym.

"Nah, more to do with the kids."

He stared at me. "What the hell?"

"I know!" I said, running my towel over my face and through my hair. I took a sip of my water. "I'm trying to do something right here, ya know? And it's like she's judging everything I do." I shook my head and sighed. "I don't know. Maybe I'm imagining it."

"Well, how angry you were wasn't imagining it. I've seen that look on your face before."

I laughed, a little embarrassed. "Thanks," I said. "You really helped me out. I owe you one."

This time Arizona laughed. "Man, you don't owe me nothin'," he said.

A few kids came in, waiting for their afternoon session with me.

Arizona nodded toward them. "You feelin' up to runnin' class for these guys? 'Cause I can put 'em through their paces."

I gave him a smile and held my fist out to his. "Nah, man. I'm good. But thanks."

He bumped my fist with his. "Okay, see ya tomorrow," he said, then went off to talk to Amil.

I herded the kids into our usual corner and ran through my class with the sixteen kids that had turned up. It was a good, full session with a lot of familiar faces, though Claude and Ruby didn't show.

Afterwards, I grabbed a shower and caught up on emails while I waited for Kira to finish work. When it got late and Amil and I were closing up, Kira came in, and I saw him quickly scan the club, presumably looking for Claude and Ruby. "Hey," he said with a smile. "Kids not here?"

I shook my head. "Haven't seen them since lunch time."

Amil walked over to us and gave me a hesitant, apologetic smile but spoke to Kira, "Arizona wanted me to tell you, in case Matt didn't, that Matt here was really pissed off this afternoon, and that he hadn't worked out like that since... since... well, before, when things weren't so great."

Kira turned to face me, but I was staring at Amil. "Man, really? What the hell?"

Amil put both his hands up, palms forward. "Hey, don't shoot the messenger. I'm just doin' what the big fella told me to do." Then Amil shrugged. "He was worried, man."

So now, of course, Kira was worried too. "Matt, what happened?"

"It was nothing, really," I told him. "My session with Tamara wasn't exactly progressive. Or even amicable, really."

Kira still looked alarmed. "Are you okay?"

His initial response wasn't about the appointment, but if I was okay. "Yeah, I'm fine," I reassured him. "I came here, hit the treadmill to run it off, and Arizona put me on the punching pads. He held them while I punched and kicked the crap out them until I felt better."

"Did it work?"

I nodded. "Sure did."

Kira smiled, relieved. "We can talk about Tamara later, if you want?"

"Sure," I said, returning his smile. I didn't want him to worry unnecessarily.

He looked around the empty gym, then to Amil and then to me. "You guys done?"

"Yep. Just let me switch off the lights in my office," I said. We double checked the windows, locked the doors, and left the gym with Amil.

When we were almost to the car, Kira turned around. I spun on my heel, looking for whatever he'd heard. I hadn't heard anything besides traffic and the sounds of a usual LA night, but Kira obviously had. He was staring toward the alley at the end of the block.

"Matt!" a little voice called out, which I heard just fine this time. Then two small figures ran out of the darkness—Claude first, wearing my old backpack and a huge smile. Ruby followed his sister but looked a little less enthused. "Thought we'd missed you," Claude said. "We were late, and I told Ruby you'd be gone if we didn't run."

"Hey," I said, trying to sound like I wasn't a mix of relieved they were here and worried about where they'd been. "I was gonna buy you guys dinner. Thought you stood me up!"

Kira glanced at his watch, and I was sure he had a hundred questions he *wanted* to ask, but instead he settled for, "You two crashing at our place?"

Claude looked up at him. "Is you gonna cook that nikujaga?"

Kira's eyes widened. "You remembered what it was called?"

"'Course," she replied simply.

Kira opened the door to the back seat of the car. "Come on. Get in," he said. "It's late and the air is getting cool."

After the two kids had climbed in, Kira walked around to the driver's door. He looked over the top of the car at me with an expression that clearly asked "what the freakin' hell are we doing?"

I shrugged and got into the car. As soon as Kira climbed in behind the steering wheel, Claude said, "Still no ice cream, right?"

"Right," Kira replied, pulling the car out into traffic.

Claude spoke cheerfully, mostly bringing up the last time she stayed with us, obviously for Ruby's benefit. He would give little more than a slight nod and a tight smile, clearly here with us at his sister's insistence. He was a tough kid, but if Claude wanted something and it was in his power to give it to her, he wouldn't hesitate.

Even at home, I tried to prompt conversation with Ruby, but all I got in return was closed, clipped answers. He sat with Claude on the sofa while she chatted brightly, and Ruby looked like a caged rabbit.

"Claude?" Kira called out from the kitchen. "Can you come here, please?"

She looked up at Ruby. "He probably wants me to set the table," she said, almost beaming with self-importance.

After she'd walked into the next room, I sighed to get Ruby's attention. "You're liking your training sessions with Arizona?"

He nodded once. "Yeah."

"Had a chance to look at the schoolwork yet?"

"Nope," he said quietly.

"We might do that tomorrow, hey?" I said. "In the morning, we can go through all those papers, and I can help you with where to start."

Ruby nodded. "'Kay."

Claude walked back into the room, carefully carrying two coffee mugs. She was grinning as she put them on the dining table. "Rube, we got hot chocolate. Kira said it's the good stuff, not that awful stuff at the gym." Then she quickly looked at me. "He told me not to say that."

I laughed, and when Kira came out carrying two plates, he was smiling too. "Thanks, Claude."

"That's okay." She grinned cheerfully as she sat at the table.

Kira put the two plates down. "Grilled ham, cheese, and tomato sandwiches," he told them. "Not quite the nikujaga I cooked the other night, but it'll have to do."

"It'll do just fine," Ruby said. He stood up and walked over to the table, then sat down. "Thank you very much," he said humbly.

He was so uncomfortable, it was radiating out of him. Kira gently clapped his hand on Ruby's shoulder. "No need to thank me. Just be thankful Matt didn't cook it."

I sat down at the table and sighed. "I'm not that bad a cook," I said. "I mean, I'm not great..." Then I had an idea. "Squirt, tomorrow morning, you and me are on breakfast duty. We'll show 'em I can cook just fine."

Her eyes lit up, and she spoke with her mouth full. "What are we making?"

"Ruby? Any suggestions?" I asked.

The grilled sandwich stopped halfway to his mouth. "Me? Um... It's not up to me."

Not wanting to push him too much, I looked at Claude. "Okay, squirt. Your choice."

"Pancakes!"

"Pancakes?" Kira repeated.

Claude nodded then bit into her sandwich and chewed quickly. "With syrup and everything."

Kira's nose scrunched up. "Pancakes aren't very nutritious."

"Hey," I said to Kira with a smile. I motioned between me and Claude. "*We're* cooking breakfast. So pancakes it is."

Kira rolled his eyes, ignoring me and Claude completely and spoke to Ruby instead. "Is the sandwich good?" he asked, earning a nod from Ruby. "I'll make you both another, then you guys can have a shower and get cleaned up, watch some TV before bed. How's that sound?"

Ruby swallowed the last of his sandwich, took a sip of the hot chocolate and nodded. "That sounds good," he said softly. "Thank you."

Kira made more sandwiches, while Claude and I discussed breakfast. Ruby was quiet again, just sitting there in silence, a stark contrast to his loud and chatty sister.

And when they'd eaten enough and showered, they moved to the sofa and, as Kira had suggested, watched some TV. It wasn't long until Claude was curled into her brother, sound asleep, but Ruby bit back yawns and blinked back the tiredness he obviously felt. It was as though he was too scared to close his eyes. It was sad that a thirteen-year-old kid was so wary, so downtrodden by life, that he'd fight sleep all night so his kid sister could rest peacefully.

Looking at the young boy fighting to stay awake, Kira said, "I'll just grab you some blankets and a pillow."

Claude was happier to sleep on the couch, and Kira and I had decided after that first night if or when Claude and Ruby stayed, they'd crash on the sofa. Yes, we had a spare room, but we didn't want to give these kids any sense of permanence—safety, yes. Permanence, no.

It was, quite simply, a line we didn't want to cross.

But I knew Ruby wouldn't sleep a wink where he was.

"How about you two take the spare room," I said, more of a statement than a question. I could feel Kira's eyes on me, but I didn't look at him. I spoke to Ruby, "You can take Claude and shut the door, give yourself some privacy."

Ruby eyed me cautiously for a second and finally gave me a nod. "Thanks."

"You'll have to share a bed," I told him. Figuring they'd slept on cardboard boxes and in dumpsters, I didn't think he'd mind. I smiled at him. "Hope Claude doesn't snore too much."

Ruby almost smiled.

"I'll go pull back the covers," I said, still not looking at Kira. "You right to carry Claude?" I asked him.

"Yeah, I got her," Ruby replied.

I went into the spare room, flipped on the lights, and pulled back the duvet and blankets. I switched on the bedside lamp and stood aside in the doorway while Ruby carried his still-sleeping sister into the room.

I waited until he'd laid Claude in the bed—she stirred a little, but Ruby whispered something and she settled—and I flipped off the light. Ruby's eyes shot to mine, but then he realized the room was still lit by the much softer bedside lamp. I gave the poor kid a smile. "I'll shut the door. Try and get some sleep. If you need anything, just yell," I said.

He nodded, so I slowly closed the door.

Kira was at the end of the hallway, leaning against the door. His arms were folded and one eyebrow was raised in question. "Matt... I thought we agreed—"

I walked up to him, put my hand on his arm, and spoke quietly so Ruby wouldn't hear. "Did you see how scared he was? Kira, babe, he would have sat up, wide awake, all night while Claude slept, just to make sure she was safe."

"I saw," he admitted.

"At least in the spare room with the door shut, he'll feel safer, and who knows? He might actually get a decent night's sleep." I ran my hand up his arm and pressed my palm against his chest. "I know we agreed about them sleeping on the sofa, and I'm sorry. I should have asked your opinion before I offered it to Ruby. I'll make some phone calls tomorrow to some housing for at-risk kids and even go around and visit some if I can. I'll try and find them somewhere they'll feel safe, and somewhere that promises not to split them up."

"Matt, it's okay," he said, a soft smile playing at his lips.

"Are you sure?"

He leaned in and kissed me sweetly. "Yeah."

I slid my arms around his back. I sighed contentedly, almost melting into him. "I'm so lucky to have you," I mumbled into his chest. "You're really rather incredible, you know that?"

Kira chuckled. "Yeah, I think someone told me that once."

I pulled back to look at him. "You're the best thing to ever happen to me."

He pressed his lips to mine, kissing me again, and cradled my face in his hands. "You're the best thing to ever happen to me too," he said, staring into my eyes. "I love you, Matt."

I smiled at him. "Love you too." I ran my hands up his back. "Maybe I should just show you how much I adore you."

Kira smiled, but then he glanced at the spare bedroom door and shook his head. "Not with two kids in the next room."

I turned to look at the offending door, then looked back at Kira. "Oh, man. Really?"

"Yes, really," he said. "What if they... *hear us*? It's not like you're very quiet."

I scoffed and pulled his chin between my thumb and finger, kissing him quickly. "Because you make me loud."

"Me?"

I nodded. "The noises I make are your fault."

Kira grinned beautifully and chuckled. "They are some very good noises. Normally, I'd say the louder the better."

I pulled our hips together. "Maybe you should put something in my mouth, down my throat, so I'm not loud."

He shook his head. "Yes, well, still not doing anything when there are kids in the next room. That thought kinda creeps me out."

I kissed him with smiling lips. "What about on the sofa?" I asked. "That way, they're not in the next room."

"No, but they could walk out while we're... That's worse!"

I laughed at him. "I'm definitely looking into alternative accommodations for them tomorrow."

Kira chuckled, trying not to laugh out loud. He took my hand and led me to our room. We got ready for bed, and much to my dismay, Kira got into bed with pajama bottoms on. He told me I should do the same, and I was still pouting when my cell phone rang.

I reached over and grabbed my phone from my bedside table, then read the caller ID. It was Mitch.

It was a quarter-past eleven at night, so my initial thought was that something was wrong. "Hey," I answered the call. "Everything okay?"

"Yeah, man, fine here. How are you?" my old partner asked.

I slid my thumb across the speaker button and put my phone between us on the bed. It was easier for me to hear that way without holding the phone to my only functioning ear. "You're on speaker," I told Mitch. "Kira's here with me."

"Didn't interrupt anything, did I?"

"Uh, no," I said. "Sadly, you're not interrupting anything."

Kira smacked my arm. "Hi, Mitch," he said, leaning into the phone.

"Hey, Frankie," Mitch replied. "Keeping him in line?"

"Trying."

"Berkman got you working late?" I asked.

"No, someone wanted me to find out some background information on two kids, remember?"

"Oh, give us a sec," I said, keeping my voice down. I got off the bed, and walking to the door, I motioned for Kira to come with me. When we were in the kitchen, away from hearing-ears, I put the phone on the table between us. "Sorry about that. Did you have any luck?"

Kira was looking at me, clearly wondering what was going on. So I quickly explained, "I asked him to find out what he could on Claude and Ruby." Then, I spoke back into the phone, "Sorry, Mitch. What did you find?"

"Well, it's not a very happy story," he started. "It took a few phone calls. Child services, department of education, housing and welfare."

I looked at Kira, and seeing concern on his face, I reached out and took his hand. I gave him a nod, letting him know I'd expected this much. I looked back to the phone. "And?"

Mitch exhaled into the phone. "Rueben and Claudia Vaughn. Father, Lamar Vaughn. Mother, Candice Vaughn. Lived in Mid-City—not overly wealthy, but they were doing okay. Father was a construction site supervisor, mom worked part-time in retail, both kids were enrolled at Marvin Elementary, good attendance record."

"What happened?" I asked.

"The GFC," Mitch answered. "Lamar Vaughn was retrenched in mass cuts across the construction industry late in 2009. Candice Vaughn lost her job not long after. Lamar held a few different jobs over the next two years but never for long. Bank foreclosed on them two years ago. The school reported no fixed address after that, unofficially listed as living in their car.

"We kind of lost track of them for a little while," he went on to say. "Kids stopped going to school and no one had no way of contacting them, but then Candice applied for welfare, citing some bogus address. Apparently Lamar couldn't handle it and skipped out on them. Left the three of them to fend for themselves. They spent some time in a women's shelter, but after a spate of attacks from other residents, they left. Matt, from what we can tell, Candice ended up hooking. Probably for money to feed her kids."

He stopped talking, letting us absorb this information. I pressed my fingers into my eyes. "What ever happened to her?"

"She was found dead a year and a half ago. It was a drug overdose, accidental or not, no one knows."

"And Lamar?"

"Totally off grid. Disappeared. No social security registrations for employment, no bank accounts touched. Just gone." Which meant, in cop terms, it was highly likely he was dead. Given the circumstances, one could presume suicide.

Kira sighed, and I squeezed his hand. "Any other relatives?"

"Nope. Not that I could find, anyway," Mitch said. "Rueben and Claudia were registered at a Saint Augustine shelter for a few weeks, but then they tried to organize foster care and maybe having to split them up, and they weren't seen again."

This time I sighed, and my head fell back. "Fucking hell."

"Matt, are these the two kids at your club I met the other day?"

"Yeah, it's them. Ruby and Claude."

"Are they okay?"

"Mitch," I said, "those two kids are asleep in our spare room right now."

There was only silence for a while. "Shit, Matt," he replied eventually. "The eldest, Rueben, he's the one those skinheads were talking to? The one you were concerned about?"

I nodded, though he couldn't see. "Yeah."

"Jesus, Matt. Be careful."

"I'm not involved in this in any way," I told him. "That Darius McInnes and Tyler James are not known to me. They don't come into the gym, and I certainly don't go seeking them out."

"Matt, you have one of their runners in your house!"

He'd just confirmed what I'd assumed all along. "I have two kids from the gym, Mitch, *two homeless kids* asleep in my house. What are we supposed to do? Let 'em sleep in a dumpster?"

"Ugh," Mitch almost growled into the phone. It was his frustration growl. I knew it well. "You're gonna draw unnecessary attention to yourself, Matt."

"Maybe if those two drug guys see people looking out for these kids, they'll leave 'em alone. They won't be such easy targets," Kira said. "If they know someone's looking out for them."

"They don't care, Frankie," Mitch said quietly. "Those kids are disposable to them, nothing else."

"I'm not drawing any attention, to them or to us," I said.

"Look," he said, "we're working on them, Matt. But you know there's a right and a wrong time. We can't rush this without the right evidence, Matt, or they'll walk. You know that."

I sighed. "Of course I know that."

"I'll try pushing Berkman," he said. "Not that *that* will get me anywhere. It used to work for you, of course…"

I laughed. "Because he liked me." Then I was serious. "Mitch, I'm not asking you to do anything that will jeopardize your case. I would never do that," I told him. "I'll just keep these kids off the street the best I can."

"Until when?"

"Until you catch all the bad guys."

Mitch snorted into the phone. "There's always more bad guys."

"That's what makes us good guys so special."

Mitch was quiet for a long moment. "Just be careful, Matt."

"I will," I told him. "And thanks."

"No problem," he answered.

"Give your gorgeous wife a kiss from me," I added.

"I will."

"Oh," Kira said. "Tell Anna I'll call her about lunch on Friday."

"No worries. See you guys later."

Mitch disconnected the call. Kira and I sat at our kitchen table, and for the longest time, we never spoke. The jokes about finding Claude and Ruby accommodations because we wanted to have sex, were long forgotten. He threaded his fingers with mine. "Do you think they know?" he asked.

"Know what?"

"That their mom is dead."

I rubbed my thumb over his hand. "I don't know."

"I mean, Claude just said no one wanted them, like she thinks her parents just walked away from them."

"Babe," I said. "I don't know. Maybe Ruby knows more

than Claude, but he's about ready to bolt as it is. I don't want to push by asking questions."

"True," Kira said sadly. "It's just horrible, isn't it?"

"What is?"

"The whole thing."

Keeping hold of his hand, I stood up. "Bed time," I said, leading us back to our room.

"I'm not showered—"

"I don't care," I interrupted. "I just want to get into bed with you."

Wearing just his pajama bottoms, Kira climbed into bed. I stripped down to my underwear and joined him.

I slid over to him, wrapped my arms around him, and Kira held me back just as tight.

"Matt," he murmured above my left ear. "I can't even imagine what those kids have been through, being so alone like that."

I could. All too well.

And it was that thought that kept me awake most of the night.

CHAPTER ELEVEN

"KEEP STIRRING IT, SQUIRT," I told Claude. She had the whisk in the pancake batter. "We need all those lumps out. No one likes clumps of flour in their pancakes."

"My arm's tired," she complained.

"Here." I handed her the spatula. "Be careful not to touch the pan with your hand. It's hot."

"Well, derr," she said. "That's because it's on a cooktop."

"Don't 'well derr' me," I said, whisking the batter quickly. "I was just sayin'."

"Why don't you have a pancake waffle maker machine?"

I looked down at the little girl, who was wielding the spatula at the frypan. "Because we don't eat pancakes. This is a special occasion."

"Is it special because me and Ruby's here?"

I nudged her with my hip. "Well, derr."

Claude put her free hand on her hip and looked up at me. "Don't 'well derr' me," she repeated my words back to me, then looked over to Kira and Ruby, who were sitting at the table watching us, and rolled her eyes.

Kira had cut up fruit to have with our pancakes, Ruby had set the table—after being instructed to by his sister— and it had been a relatively pleasant morning. We'd been up early, Kira had gone for a run, but I'd stayed at home so Ruby and Claude didn't think we'd left them. I'd tidied up and done some laundry while I waited for the two sleepy-heads to get up.

It was obviously the first time in a long time they'd slept in a bed, because even in a strange house, they'd slept like logs.

So it was a late breakfast for us, but we didn't mind. Kira didn't have to be at work until early afternoon, I had no urgent appointments, and Ruby was scheduled with Arizona after lunch, so we were in no rush.

We ate the pancakes topped with cut berries and maple syrup, and Claude declared that, in defense of my honor, I could cook just fine.

It was kind of nice, and even Ruby seemed to relax. He laughed as Claude told Kira. "Those grilled sandwiches last night were real good, but Matt's and mine pancakes are the best."

"But look at the mess!" Kira replied.

"The mess don't matter none," Claude told him. "'Cause we cooked, you two clean. Ain't that right, Matt?"

I bumped fists with her, and our laughter was cut short by a knock at the door.

Ruby's eyes went wide and his body tensed. I could see him gauging the distance between himself, his sister, and the back door, calculating his risks on getting him and his sister out. Always had an escape plan. It was instinct.

"Boys!" a familiar voice called out. "You in there?"

I exhaled in relief, and Kira smiled at Ruby. "It's just my mom."

Kira stood up, still smiling—though now somewhat forced—and in sign language, said, "It's my mom. Shit, it's my mom!" as he stood up. "Coming, Mom!" he called out.

Well, this was about to get interesting.

As Kira opened the door, I could hear Yumi mumbling something about not wanting to catch the two of us in bed, then her voice got louder as she walked toward the kitchen. "What you boys cooking? Something smells good..."

Yumi's words trailed off when she walked into the kitchen, with Kira and Sal behind her. She saw Claude first, then Ruby, and finally her widened gaze fell on me. Claude leaned in closer to me, almost hiding behind me, while Ruby looked as though he was getting ready to run.

"Mom," Kira said. "This is Claudia and Rueben. They stayed here last night." Kira sat down at the table, in the seat next to Ruby, and seeing how nervous the kid was, Kira patted him on the back. "These are my parents."

"Hello," Yumi said cautiously, and Sal, who was just as wary as Yumi, gave a wave behind her.

"Hi," Claude said. Her voice sounded so tiny against the awkward silence.

Yumi's attention went from Claude to Kira, and she signed, "What's going on?"

Kira replied in sign language. "Mom, not now."

"Hey, guys," I said to Ruby and Claude, collecting the dirty plates and standing up. "How about we go out to the backyard? You guys can help me with something." I put the plates in the sink and held the back door open for them to walk out first. I signed to Kira, "Is this okay?"

He nodded. "Thanks."

Kira would need ten minutes to explain the situation to

his parents and another ten minutes to explain to Yumi why we had never told her before now.

I knew she'd be okay with it but probably more upset that we'd not told her we'd had kids stay at our house before. I just hoped he would tell them not to bring up the subject of school, home, or their mom and dad.

"Why were they talkin' with their hands?" Claude asked, looking up at me and squinting in the morning sun.

"Kira's dad, Mr. Franco, is deaf."

"Like you?"

"Kind of. He's completely deaf, whereas I can hear in one ear."

"How come you don't talk with your hands?" she asked, moving her hands in karate-like chops.

I laughed. "Well, I do sometimes. When I'm talking to Kira's dad, I do. But I can still hear a bit."

Claude stopped in the middle of the yard. "You know, if you wanted some time to tell 'em about us, you just had to say," she said. "You don't need to be makin' stuff up to get us to go outside."

I smiled at her. "Well, I actually do need your help. We're thinking of getting a dog, so I need you guys to help me check out the fences and fix any holes where a dog could fit through."

Her eyes lit up. "A dog? For real?" she asked loudly. "What kind? What will you call her?"

"I don't know if it will be a girl or a boy," I explained. "We haven't even looked yet."

Her excitement never waned. "Where will you get it from?"

"There's a few animal shelters we could look at."

"Today?"

I laughed. "Probably not today."

"Tomorrow?"

I laughed again, and Ruby chided his sister. "Claude," he murmured.

When she looked at him, he shook his head as though telling her to drop it.

"Not sure when," I told her. "But we need to make sure he or she can't escape." We scouted the fence line, looking for possible holes. I was pretty sure the fences were fine, but it would at least give Kira enough time to talk to his parents.

"You might need to put something under this," Ruby said, pointing to the side gate. "Depends on the size of the dog, I guess, but a small one could get out under that."

I walked over to where he was and saw he was right. "I think we have some old bricks or pavers in the garden shed," I said.

"Let's get 'em," he said and walked toward the small shed in the corner of the yard. After following him, I opened the shed and found the old bricks that were stacked there. I handed two to Ruby and two to Claude.

"You right to carry them?" I asked her.

She raised one eyebrow at me as her answer and skipped excitedly behind her brother.

Ruby fit the bricks along where the bottom of the gate didn't quite meet the ground. It was probably a tripping hazard, and I would no doubt do something more perma-nent later, but seeing Ruby doing something constructive, something that made him feel important, was pretty sweet.

I held up my hand for a high five. Ruby rolled his eyes like it was uncool, but he high-fived me and I could tell he was trying not to smile.

The back door closed loudly, which sounded like Sal. Over the time I'd known him, I guessed he obviously couldn't hear it slam, so I just got used to it. Maybe it was his way of letting us know he was there.

We came around the corner of the house to find it was Sal. He signed, "Hi."

I signed back, "How's it going in there?" Then I said out loud, "Is Kira surviving?"

Yumi called out from inside. "He's the deaf one, Matty, not me."

I grinned at Sal and formally introduced him. "Claude, Ruby, this is Kira's dad, Mr. Franco." I looked at both kids. "He can read your lips when you talk."

Claude was first to look up to Sal. He was a tall man and she looked tiny compared to him, but she smiled brightly. "Hello."

Ruby gave a more subdued, "Hey."

When Sal looked at me, I asked him in sign language, "Did Kira explain?"

Sal nodded, then signed back, "Everything." It was fairly obvious the big man found hearing about these kids' life as hard to hear as we did. He clapped his hand on my shoulder, the way a father would a son.

I looked from him to the two kids. I gave them a smile. "We better get going soon, hey?" I asked. "Arizona and Boss'll be wondering where we are. How about you go in and grab your bag?"

Claude and Ruby went inside, and Sal signed, "They've had it tough."

I signed back, "They have." I exhaled loudly, and signed, "I don't know if I'm doing the right thing."

"One thing, Matt," he signed. "You are all heart." He tapped his chest. "That's never wrong."

"Thank you," I said out loud.

We walked into the kitchen, just as Claude and Ruby

were coming in from the living room. Claude held my old backpack to her chest.

"I'll take these guys back," I said. "I've got some work to do before classes this afternoon," I told Kira.

"Are you right to drive?" he asked.

"Yeah, I'm fine. If I start to feel dizzy, I'll pull over and call you."

He nodded and gave me a warm smile. "Okay." Then he looked around the kitchen. "I'll clean this up."

"Uh, Ruby?" Claude said. "You were supposed to help clean this up."

"It's okay," I said with a smile.

"But Kira said," she countered. "Those were the rules."

"There were rules?" Yumi asked.

Kira stood up from the table. "It's okay, Claude. I got it this time."

"I'll just grab my bag," I said.

When I came back out, Claude was talking about dinner.

Yumi spun around to look up at Kira. "You cooked nikujaga?"

Kira ran his hand through his hair. "It was cold and late, and I don't know why I cooked that."

"I used to make that for you," Yumi said quietly.

"Oh, God, Mom," Kira said, putting his hands on her shoulders. "Please don't read too much into that. I just wanted to cook something to warm her up, that's all."

Yumi sniffled and her eyes brimmed with tears. She looked at Claude and Ruby. "My *sobo* would cook that for me."

Kira looked over at the rest of us. "Sobo is her grandmother." Then he shook his head, a mix of amusement and embarrassment. "You okay, Mom?"

Yumi nodded. "You such a good boy," she said.

"Okay, we'll go," I said, trying not to smile. Then I signed to both Kira and Yumi, "Sorry to leave in a hurry. I think it's too much for Ruby."

"It's okay," Kira signed back.

I walked over and kissed him, a quick peck on the lips. "I love you," I said, not caring who heard me say it. I even gave Yumi a kiss on the cheek.

I smiled at Sal, and as we walked out of the door, I told Kira, "I'll call you later."

After we'd been in the car for a few blocks, Claude, who was in the back seat, said, "You kissed Kira in front of his parents! That's kinda gross."

I laughed and looked at her in the rearview mirror. "They don't mind."

"They seem nice," Ruby said, looking out of the window. I almost didn't hear him.

"They're the best people I know," I told him. "I'm not sure where I'd be if it weren't for them."

Ruby looked at me then, as though he was going to say something but decided against it.

Figuring the subject of parents wasn't a good one, considering what we'd learned last night, I chose the topic of conversation. "So, we gonna have a look at those papers Janelle gave you today?"

"I guess," Ruby replied.

"Come on," I said, trying to gain some enthusiasm from him. "It'll be fun!"

Ruby gave me a raised, 'have you lost your freakin' mind' eyebrow, and it was only when Claude said, "School sucks," that he smiled.

I pulled the car up near the gym. "Well, you gotta get used to it. It's part of the deal."

"Yeah, yeah," Ruby grumbled.

We got out of the car, and as we made the short walk to the gym's front doors, Claude looked up at me and asked, "You feel okay, Matt? You not dizzy or nothin'?"

I opened the front door and held it open for the two kids. I grinned at Claude. "I feel good, squirt."

Claude and Ruby walked inside, and when I scanned the street, I saw two familiar faces watching me.

Darius and Tyler.

They made no attempt to hide watching me. I considered waving, but remembered Mitch's warning not to draw unnecessary attention from these two. So I went inside and closed the door behind me.

We said a quick hello to the guys, and I told Claude to help Boss and Arizona while Ruby made a start on his schoolwork. He grabbed his paperwork from his locker, and when he came back into my office, I had one of the tables pulled aside with a chair, and handed him a pen.

Knowing Ruby as well as I did—even as little as I did know—I figured he was the type to want to go through at his own pace, without feeling like I was watching over his shoulder.

"I've got stuff to do here too," I told him, sitting down at my desk. "Give me a yell if you need. Any question, big or small, okay?"

He mumbled, "Yeah." He sat down and started on the first page, reading. I saw him write something on the paper and smiled to myself, proud that this kid was trying.

I pulled out my checklist for the fast-approaching fundraiser and ran through all the last minute details. I made a list of people I wanted to call, to double check and confirm we were all still on track. I ran through the radio advertising proof and emailed the confirmation from my phone. I'd never done this kind of work before, and while it was a steep learning curve for me, I enjoyed it.

I looked up at Ruby, to find him staring out of the window. "You okay, Rube?"

My voice must have surprised him. He startled, but quickly straightened out his papers. "I don't think this is gonna work," he said. "Thanks for all your help and for tryin' and all." He wouldn't look at me, but he stood up. "But this ain't for me."

I was quick to walk to his table and stopped him. "Hey, what's up?"

"Nothin'," he said. "I just can't do this kinda shit."

I looked down at the papers and saw the problem. There was some writing, though it was big, messy, and very childlike. Words were spelled wrong and some had angry lines through them. "Rube, this is okay," I told him. "We knew it wasn't going to be easy, but I'm here to help."

He shook his head. "I shoulda known it was a bad idea."

"It's not a bad idea. It's just gonna take some work. Here," I said, pulling up a seat next to his table. "Sit back down and we'll go through these. Look at this one." I pointed to the first question. "You got it right! And the second one!"

"I'm no good at it," he said, defeated. "My writing's shit."

"Ruby, you haven't been to school in a while, so it's gonna take a while to get back into it. It's kinda like skipping rope," I told him, something he could relate to. "It's fine if you're doing it all the time, but as soon as you stop doing it every day, you're gonna find it real hard when you start again, yes?"

"I guess.".

"Well, reading and writing's no different," I told him.

"It's just a different muscle group you're workin', that's all."

Ruby nodded, like he understood that analogy, but when he looked back at the papers, he frowned. "Some words I can't read," he mumbled.

"Then I'll help you," I told him. "You just need to ask me, Rube. It's okay to ask for help sometimes, okay?"

He didn't answer.

"So let's take a look at question number five," I said, not giving him a chance to back out.

He needed a gentle push, but he needed reassurance too. And the truth was, as we went through the questions, Ruby could verbalize the answers. It was just the writing he struggled with. He was smart, and given that his last schooling was the fifth grade, he was doing very well.

I made a mental note to buy some math and word posters to put up for the different age groups. I should have thought about that before. "You know what we should do?" I asked him when we were done.

"What's that?"

"Maybe two nights a week, after the classes I run for the kids in the afternoons, maybe we should have school class time in here."

"For me?"

"Not just you," I told him. "But yes, if you're interested." He didn't object outright, so I continued, "A few of the other guys doing the classes like you might find it helpful too. And who knows? You might find it easier to all work together."

He frowned and shrugged. "Maybe."

"They don't find it easy either," I told him. "You gotta understand, Rube, it's a struggle for everyone. So don't think you're the only one who finds it tough, okay? I mean, it's hard enough for kids who have homes with beds, and moms or dads, who go to real high schools... It's not easy for them either, but you guys... well, I can tell you this much—the kids that come in here and are willing to put themselves through this for a chance at a better life, these kids, kids like you, are the real fighters. I don't think you realize just how strong you are for even wanting to do this. You should give yourself some credit. Because it's not gonna be easy, Rube. But you're not alone, and I promise you, with some hard work and dedication, you will win. Okay?"

He looked at me, then back to the table, and he bit the inside of his lip. "Can't read too good," he said softly.

"I will help you."

"Learn to read?"

"Sure," I said. "Why not? It's no different from me teaching you footwork or fitness. It's just another skill. I'm teaching, you're learning."

He still didn't look convinced.

"Look, Ruby, I know it's scary, and it'd be a helluva lot easier to just walk away and do nothing. But, man, you can do this. I've seen you in the ring. I've seen you train with Arizona. I don't think there's anything you can't do."

He nodded this time. "You don't give pep-talks too often, do you?"

"Was it too much?"

He snorted. "Um, yeah."

I clapped my hand on his shoulder and smiled at him. "Well, too bad. I meant every word."

Ruby looked a bit happier.

"You cool with it? You're gonna stick it out?"

He hesitated, but he nodded once. "I guess."

"Good," I said, standing up. "Arizona will be looking for you. You better get out there and show him you mean business."

Ruby smiled and went out into the gym area in search of his coach. I stood in the doorway and watched as he said something to Arizona before he went into the dressing room to get changed. Arizona shot me a look and smiled before he went back to the guys he was training. Whatever Ruby had said made Arizona happy.

Figuring I could do with a good workout before lunch, I got changed and hit the treadmills while Arizona ran Ruby through his warm-up routine. He ran him through some techniques, then put him in the ring with Zach.

Zach was another kid I'd organized to get his high school diploma through the local community college. He was sixteen, lived in a hostel house, and hadn't been to school in years. I think he'd been hooking for a few years, though he would never admit it.

Unfortunately, stories like that were all too common with these local kids.

As Zach and Ruby sparred in the ring, Arizona corrected their stances, their posture and their sequences. I spent some time on the punching bag, going through my own punch-jab routines.

I was in my own world and had my right side to the door, which is probably why I didn't hear anyone come in. I noticed that Ruby and Zach had stopped sparring first, and I followed their line of sight to see Arizona, who was now talking to two guys.

Darius McInnes and James Tyler.

It didn't look like a pleasant conversation.

I left the punching bag swinging in midair and walked straight over to stand beside Arizona. Arizona must have asked what they were doing here, because the smaller guy, James, said, "We's just seein' what goes on in here."

Darius smiled at me. He was obviously the leader of the

two, and a particularly unattractive guy—maybe mid-twenties, shaved head boasting scars, tattoos up his neck, he was missing teeth, and his eyes were hard and cold. He had gang tattoos over his knuckles and wore a T-shirt that showed prison tattoos up his arms, and the most disturbing—a swastika on display for the world to see.

"Just curious to see what a white fella like you is doin' in here with folks like these," Darius said.

I remembered what Mitch had said about them being neo-Nazi fascists. Without taking my eyes off Darius, I said, loud enough for the boys to hear, "Ruby, Zach, hit the showers." There was no movement behind me, and Darius's eyes flickered to where Ruby was standing in the ring behind me, and he smiled. "Ruby," I said, louder this time, "take Claude with you."

Darius smiled at me, as though pleased that I was even mildly threatened by him. Ruby and Zach jumped out of the ring and walked toward the dressing rooms. I looked over then and saw Ruby grab his sister by the shoulder and lead her through the doors.

I turned back to Darius and smiled. "Anything we can help you with?"

He sneered at me. "This is a community club, yeah?"

"Sort of."

"So we can be in here if we want," he replied smugly.

"Sure. Subject to police records and random drug tests."

Darius grinned at me, then, showing his gapped smile. He knew I was lying about the testing, but he also understood I was having a shot at him about using drugs.

"Well then where do we sign up?" he asked with a shit-eating grin.

The whole gym was quiet now and watching the four of

us. I could almost feel the wrath buzzing out of Arizona. He leaned forward. "We're too busy."

Darius ignored him and sneered at me instead. "You need a leash for your nigg—"

I stepped in front of him, with my face barely an inch from his. I spoke through clenched teeth, "Finish that sentence and you'll be eating meals through a fucking straw."

Cody and Jamaal were suddenly beside me. Any one of us would defend Arizona. Like my cop partners, these boys were my team.

Darius kept the stupid smile on his face, but he looked as though he was weighing up his options as he darted a glance at each of us.

I lifted my chin and stared him down. "Any one of these boys could kill you, right here, four different ways without using their hands," I said, almost in a whisper.

"I ain't scared of no nigger-lovers," he spat out.

Then Boss was somehow between us, pointing his stubby fingers at the two unwelcome men. They were taller than him and two of them to his one, but Boss didn't seem to care. "Get the fuck outta my club," he snapped at them.

Darius and James sneered at us, but they turned around and walked out, mumbling obscenities as they went.

Boss called out to them as they got to the door, "And if I see ya's hangin' around, I'll call the cops on ya for bein' a pain in my ass." Then he turned around to the four of us. "What the fuck was that, Elliott?"

"They were looking for trouble," I told him simply.

"And you were gonna knock 'em into next week for that?"

"No," I corrected him. "But I was gonna teach them some manners for disrespecting Arizona."

Boss sighed loudly but then eyeballed Arizona, Cody, and Jamaal. "Back to work," he said gruffly. "And you," he said, looking at me, "you go back to hitting the shit outta that punching bag. You take your anger management issues out on that and not some dumbass off the street."

I gave a nod to Cody and Jamaal, and asked Arizona, "You all right?"

"Yeah, man," he said. "You?"

"Yeah, I'm cool," I told him.

"Thought you were gonna snap," Arizona said. "Haven't seen you go off at someone in a while."

"If he had of kept going, I probably would have," I answered honestly.

"Man, it ain't nothin' I haven't heard before," he said with a smile.

"That doesn't make it right," I said.

"Probably not," he said, trying to play it cool, trying to placate me. "Thanks for having my back, anyway."

"Always," I replied. "Partners, right?"

He grinned, a big, white, toothy grin. "Right."

I went to walk back to the punching bag but stopped. "Oh, and Arizona?"

"Yeah?"

"If you want to snitch on me to Kira for losing my shit and save you looking up his number, I'll be calling him later..."

Arizona laughed. "Nah, it's okay. I've got him on speed dial."

I snorted. "Hey, have you got my back or his?"

"Both, my friend. Both."

Boss, who was looking up between us like a tennis match, said, "You two done?"

"Yeah," I answered. "But, Boss, before you go, a word?"

The older man stopped and waited. "What now?"

"Those two guys," I said, nodding toward the front door where Darius and James went. "We need to keep the kids away from them." Then I admitted, "I have it on good authority that they might be under surveillance by the LAPD."

Boss's jaw clenched, and he spoke slowly. "What have you done?"

"I haven't done anything," I told him. "When Mitch and Ricky called in one day, I mentioned those two thugs and how they're hanging around the kids, and Mitch looked into them. He said they're now persons of interest. I'm not involved, I swear to you."

Boss growled. "Dammit, Elliott. We don't need that kind of shit here."

"No, we don't," I agreed. "And when Mitch cleans them up off the streets, we won't have that kind of shit here." I put my hand to my chest. "*I'm* not involved. The *FC* is not involved. But the kids that come here are. They're targeted and they're singled out."

"Who?" Boss asked. "Which kids? 'Cause if I find out any one of 'em are running drugs, they're out of the program."

And right at that moment, Ruby and Claude walked out of the change rooms. Boss followed my line of sight, then turned back to me. I didn't have to answer. The look on his face told me he knew.

"I'll talk to him," I whispered. "Please don't kick him out, it'll be a death sentence to both of them."

I could almost feel Boss's eyes burning holes in the side of my head. But I didn't look at him. "Hey, guys," I said brightly to Ruby and Claude. "Both of you, my office."

A rather pale-looking Ruby shot glances between me and Boss. "Everything okay?"

"Everything's fine," I said with a smile. "Just gimme two minutes here, okay?"

I watched as the two kids disappeared into my office, then turned to Boss. He shook his head at me. "Jesus Christ, Elliott."

"I just got him signed up to finish school, and I'm working on finding them somewhere to live."

Boss sighed heavily. "It's a slippery slope you're walkin', Elliott."

"Someone has to, right?"

He growled again and shook his head. "Fucking do-gooders. Always gotta make things right."

I smiled at him. "You should meet my therapist. You and her would get on like a house on fire."

"I pity that woman," he said gruffly and turned on his heel. "Sort the kid out, Elliott," he said as he walked away.

When I went into my office, Claude and Ruby were sitting on the table in the corner. He looked at me with a mix of uncertainty and fear in his eyes. "Was Darius in here 'cause of me?"

I sat down on the table next to them and sighed. "Probably." I considered asking Claude for some time with her brother but figured she could probably do with hearing this. "Rube, those guys are no good. I've told you that. They might promise you a lot of stuff, but they're just using you."

He swallowed loudly. "I don't want no trouble."

"I know you don't," I said, giving him a reassuring smile. "Let me try and line up somewhere for you guys to stay. You guys'll have the final say, but how about I find you a few places and you pick the one you like the most."

Claude looked up to Ruby, waiting for him to answer.

His mouth twitched in thought, and he looked at his sister for the longest moment. "Okay," he said with nod. He would agree to anything if it was for her. He turned back to me. "Okay."

I couldn't help but smile. "Good. Well, it's too late today to do anything, but we can look tomorrow. You two can stay at my place again tonight, and we can spend tomorrow morning looking at places. How does that sound?"

Claude smiled brightly, but when she looked up to Ruby, her smile faded. He was frowning.

"Ruby, you okay?" I asked.

"Why are you doing this?"

"Why am I doing what?"

"Bein' so nice to us? Helpin' us out so much?" Then he whispered, "Did you want something from us?"

I blinked in shock at his question, or more so the implication behind it. Did he think I wanted *something* from him? He had no money, no possessions, the only thing he could offer was his body. Something no kid should have to give. "No, Rueben. I don't want..." I couldn't even say it. *Jesus Christ.* "All I want is for you to try."

When he looked at me, then, I saw for the first time just how truly haunted his eyes were. He was too damn young to have lived through what he had.

"Opportunities for anyone are rare, but for a street kid?" I said. "They're almost non-existent. You need to take this, Rube, with both hands. Know what I'm saying? Yes, school is hard, fighting is hard, but it'll be worth it."

He nodded and spoke to the floor, "Was it worth it for you?" he asked. "When you were fighting? You got banged up pretty bad. Was that worth it?"

"I was fighting for the wrong reasons. You're fighting for the right reason."

Ruby looked at his sister, then back to the floor. He nodded. "I know."

"Go in and have a shower," I told him. "I have classes this afternoon, but I'll be going home around seven. You two be here by then, okay?"

Except they weren't.

I finished my classes, and by seven thirty, they still hadn't showed. Disappointed, I grabbed my bag and headed out to my car.

"Matt!" a far-off voice called out.

I turned to find Ruby and Claude coming from the far street corner. I smiled as they got closer. "Thought you guys stood me up."

Claude gave me her usual smile, her mop of curls bouncing unruly from her head. Ruby, on the other hand, didn't smile. He wasn't just quiet. He was distracted.

You guys ready?" I asked, wary of Ruby's reaction.

"Claude is," he said. "I'm not."

"What?" she said, turning to her brother.

Ruby looked at me, deliberately not looking at her. "You and Kira are real good people. She'll be safe with you."

"What?" Claude repeated, this time stepping in front of Ruby. "Ruby? What are you doing? You said *we* was staying, not just me."

"I'll see you back here at the FC in the morning," he said, giving her a quick but tight hug and kissing the side of her head. "You'll be fine, Claude. They'll take real good care of you."

"Ruby, don't," I said, alarmed and genuinely worried for this kid.

He let go of Claude and took a step back. "I'll be here first thing in the morning," he said to me. Then he looked at Claude and tried to smile. "Save me some breakfast."

He turned on his heel and ran back in the direction he'd come. Claude started after him. "Claude, wait," I said, wanting to grab her arm, but scared to touch her. I put my hand on the backpack she wore instead, and stopped her from running after him. "Claude, stop."

She turned to look at me, her big brown eyes were wide and filled with tears. It was heartbreaking to see. Ruby had disappeared around the corner, and Claude was left all alone.

"Come on," I said. "You and me, squirt. We'll make dinner together. Your choice." I opened the car door and waited for her to get in. Still on the verge of tears, she slowly got into the back seat. I climbed in behind the wheel, and after we'd driven a few blocks, I could see in the rearview mirror that Claude had tear streaks down her cheek.

"You know what we need?" I asked.

She didn't reply.

"Ice cream," I told her.

She was quiet for a long moment, and when I thought she wasn't going to answer at all, she said, "Kira said I couldn't." She'd spoken so softly, I'd barely heard her.

"Well, he's not here," I said.

She didn't say anything to that, but at least the tears were gone.

"What flavor do you want?" I asked. "Chocolate, strawberry?"

Again, silence. We'd gone several blocks when she finally replied, "Vanilla."

I smiled. "Vanilla, it is."

"With chocolate topping."

"Okay."

"And waffles."

I laughed. "Deal."

CHAPTER TWELVE

WHEN I HEARD Kira unlock the front door, I called out to him, "We're in here," so he'd know I wasn't alone.

He walked to the door, saw that Claude and I were cooking, and leaned against the frame. "Well, this looks like trouble."

I smiled at him, put down the stirring spoon, and signed, "Don't ask about Ruby."

"Everything okay?" he signed back.

"Talk later," I signed.

Kira acknowledged what I said with a small nod, then he smiled at Claude. "What are you two making?"

"Dinner," she replied. "Matt said I got to choose."

He glanced around the kitchen. "And you chose mess?"

"I chose spaghetti and meat sauce. Matt made the mess."

"You just keep stirring the sauce," I chided her gently. Then I walked over to Kira and kissed him softly on the lips, not caring that Claude was there. I figured if she was going to stay at our house, then we shouldn't have to hide anything. "You have a good day?" I asked him.

His gaze flickered to Claude, then back to me, but he seemed amused. "I did. And I have to admit, this dinner of yours smells pretty good."

Smiling, I went back to the boiling pasta and gave it a stir. Claude turned to Kira. "Can you set the table, please?" she asked.

My shoulders shook as I tried not to laugh at Claude giving the orders. Kira did as asked, and when we were eventually seated at the table, Kira looked at the plate in front of him. "Spaghetti Bolognese? Really?"

"Claude wanted it," I told him. "I said she could choose anything she wanted. Well, anything that wasn't takeout."

"You could choose anything?" Kira asked. "And you picked this?"

The little girl shrugged and stuffed her first forkful of messy pasta in her mouth. "My mom used to cook this," she said with her mouth full.

"Oh," Kira said softly.

"I don't remember much," she said, shoving in another forkful of food. "But Ruby tells me this was his favorite," she said, looking to the plate in front of her.

"Then we better save him some for tomorrow," I said, giving her a smile.

Claude nodded and kept eating. Kira chewed slowly and swallowed. "Is he okay?" he asked tentatively. "He's not here..."

"He took off and left me with Matt," Claude said. "Must have been something important," she added, seemingly happy to convince herself of this.

"Must have been," I said. I looked at Kira, and he didn't have to ask if it was likely that Ruby was doing something he shouldn't be. We all knew he was.

"Oh," Claude said brightly. "We got ice cream!"

"Did you?" Kira asked, now looking at me and smiling.

"Gee, thanks, Claude," I said sarcastically. "We got you a berry gelato. Ninty-nine percent fat free," I told Kira.

"What did you get?" he asked.

"French vanilla," I told him.

Claude brightened. "With waffles," she said, then threw me right under the bus, "and chocolate sauce."

Kira rolled his eyes, but he smiled as he ate. "Well, this isn't too bad," he said, lifting a forkful of spaghetti. "It's pretty good, actually."

Claude looked at me, and with her mouth full of food, she said, "He sounds surprised."

I couldn't help but chuckle at her, and when we'd finished our dinner, I suggested they go to the living room and watch some television while I cleaned up. I couldn't hear what they were talking about, just a hum of voices and the occasional burst of laughter.

When I had the kitchen back to normal, I took Kira's gelato out to him first. He was lounging casually on the long sofa, and when I handed him the bowl, he sat up straight, looked up at me, and smiled. "Thank you."

"You're very welcome," I said, leaning in and kissing him.

"Ew," Claude said from the single recliner. We both looked at her, and she screwed up her face. "Boy germs."

Kira barked out a laugh. "Boy germs don't bother us, you know, because we're boys."

"Hmm," she mused thoughtfully, then shrugged. "Guess it wouldn't."

"And this is our house, Claude," I told her. "I'll kiss him if I want." Then I asked, "Do you want one waffle or two?"

"Two!" she answered quickly.

"Coming right up," I said with a smile. I knew she

meant nothing bad about seeing us kiss—two men—but I wanted to reinforce our boundaries. This was our house, our rules. We shouldn't have to hide who we are, and as a reoccurring guest, she should respect that.

When I handed her the bowl of toasted waffles and ice cream, her eyes grew huge. "Oh, Matt. Thank you," she said brightly. Then she looked over at Kira. "Should I sit at the table?"

He looked at the plate in his hand and swallowed his mouthful of gelato. "Nah, not tonight."

When I had mine all plated up, Kira was putting his empty plate on the coffee table. So I parked myself on the sofa, leaning my back on his chest, and put my legs up on the sofa.

"You all right there?" he asked.

"Yep," I said then shoved my first spoonful of dessert in my mouth. I think I groaned. "This is so good," I mumbled.

Claude was quiet as she ate, only stopping to lick her lips as she devoured everything on her plate.

After my fourth or fifth spoonful, just as I was about put it between my lips, Kira grabbed my hand and lifted the spoon to his mouth.

"Oh, my God," he murmured. "I forgot how good that is."

Claude laughed. "Ice cream's not good for you," she repeated his words.

"Oh, shush, you," he said and grabbed my hand again, lifting another spoonful of my ice cream above my head, then quickly shoving it in his mouth. His chest vibrated as he laughed.

I finished the last of my ice cream, then leaning over, sat the bowl alongside Kira's on the coffee table, before settling back against him. Kira pressed his lips to the side of my head as his arm fell over my shoulder and across my chest. We sat like that and watched some movie more appropriate for Claude to watch than our regular viewing.

After a little while, she yawned. "You tired, Claude?" I asked.

"I guess," she said.

"You wanna crash?"

"I'll do my bit first," she said. Then she hopped up off the sofa, taking the plates from the coffee table, and went into the kitchen. I heard the clang of plates in the sink followed by running water.

"You don't have to wash up," I said. I lifted Kira's arm off me and got up, before following her into the kitchen. "Hey, Claude, you can leave it."

"You say at the FC, if we use it, we clean it," she replied. "Where did you put the soap stuff?"

"Under the sink. But that's different. This is home, not work."

"I can do this," she said. "It's just some bowls. No big deal." Her eyebrows knitted as though it annoyed her that I didn't trust her or think her capable.

"Okay," I said. "Just be careful with the hot water. It gets hot quick."

She raised one eyebrow at me. "I ain't five."

Smiling, I went back to Kira and sat next to him this time.

He signed, "Is she okay?"

I signed back, "Not sure. She's upset about her brother."

"Is he okay?" he asked, continuing in sign language so Claude wouldn't hear us.

"I don't think so. I'm worried for him. And Boss isn't too happy."

Kira looked confused. "What do you mean?"

My sign language wasn't as good as his, so I worded it the best I could. "Those two guys came into the club today. Confronted Arizona. I stepped in. Nothing happened," I quickly signed, trying to reassure him. "They left."

"Matt," he signed.

"They had a problem with his skin color," I told him, still using sign language. "So I had a problem with them." Then I spoke, knowing I'd never get the words right. "I wasn't about to let them have a shot at Arizona, Kira. He's like a new partner to me now. He's one of my best friends..."

"I know," he answered quietly. "It's fine, Matt. You shouldn't tolerate that. You wouldn't be you if you did."

I smiled at him and slid my hand over his. "They left anyway. Nothing happened."

Kira took his hand back so he could sign. "What did they come in for?"

I looked into the kitchen to see Claude was still busy. "They came in to see Ruby," I signed back. "To let him know they knew where he was, or just that they were watching him. Maybe that's why he left Claude. Maybe that was them telling him they wanted him to come see them."

Claude cleared her throat from the kitchen doorway. "Um, I'm done," she said.

"Cool," I said, "thanks for doing that, squirt. Did you want to sleep in the spare bed?"

She bit her lip. "Um, can I sleep out here?" she asked. "I can just use the sofa, if that's okay."

It was obvious she was tired and probably worried about her brother. "Sure," Kira said. "That's fine. I'll grab a blanket."

When Kira had walked out of the room, Claude asked, "Why do you talk with your hands?"

"Sign language?" I clarified. "Well, Kira's family uses it a lot, and I've picked it up from being around them. And now with my ear, it's something I use a lot more."

She nodded slowly. "I thought maybe you didn't want me to know something and so you was speaking so I couldn't hear."

"Claude," I said gently. "We talk in sign language often."

"Was you talking about Ruby?" she asked, ignoring what I'd just said. "Do you think he's okay?"

"Claude," I started again, and in that split second, I considered lying and telling her he'd be fine, then I considered telling her the honest truth, but she was getting ready for bed and I didn't want to upset her. It was obvious she missed her brother. So, in the end I settled for somewhere in the middle.

I patted the seat beside me, indicating for her to sit. She seemed unsure, but I smiled and waited. When she did sit down, I said, "Claude, those two guys that came into the club, Darius and Tyler, they're no good. They're trouble, and it worries me that Ruby talks to them."

"He does stuff for them," she said simply. "Delivers messages and stuff."

I nodded. She'd just confirmed what Mitch told us. "I know, squirt. And that worries me."

"Why?" she asked innocently.

"Because sometimes they ask people to do stuff they shouldn't do, and sometimes they get into trouble."

"Is Ruby in trouble?"

I shook my head. "Nope. But I want to make sure it stays that way."

She exhaled loudly, relieved at my answer. "I don't want Ruby in no trouble."

"I know you don't, Claude. Neither do I."

"He's smart. That's why he'll stay out of trouble," she said, nodding to herself.

I gave her a smile. "He is smart."

Kira walked in then, no doubt hearing the whole conversation.

"Ready for shower and bed, squirt?" I asked.

She nodded. "Yep. I'll just grab my bag. I still got your shirt from last time," she said. After picking her bag up from in the foyer, she headed to the bathroom. The door clicked closed, and not long after that, the water started.

Kira sat down beside me, put his hand around my neck, and pulled me in for a kiss. His passion surprised me, but I welcomed it, opening my mouth for him. Kira held my face while he tasted my mouth with his tongue in a deep, consuming kiss.

When our mouths finally broke apart, I sucked back a breath, and instead of telling him we should take it down a notch because Claude was in the bathroom, I slid my hand along his jaw and kissed him.

I could get so lost in him. His touch, his taste, his everything.

And this time when he slowed the kiss to a stop, keeping his forehead against mine, he licked his lips. "The shower turned off," he said. "Claude will be out here soon."

"Hmm," I swept my tongue across my bottom lip, tasting him "That was some kiss."

He smiled, and with his forehead still pressed to mine, his eyes closed slowly. "I had to kiss you," he whispered. "I love you, Matt. What you said to her, how you treat her, look after her... You're a good man."

I scoffed at his compliment. "Right."

He pulled back and looked at me seriously. "Can't you see what you're doing? And how good it is?"

"I'm just helping out some kids, that's all."

"Matt, you should give yourself credit," he said with a quick peck to my lips. "You're the first to run yourself down, but the last to acknowledge something positive."

"I thought humility was a good personality trait," I said with a smile.

Kira shook his head at me, then turned to the hallway Claude would soon be coming out from. He whispered, "Now I know we talked before about no fooling around when there was kids here, but maybe tonight we could..."

"Make an exception?" I added.

"Bend the rule a little," he clarified. "Because the way you kissed me just now..."

"The way I kissed you? I think it was the way you kissed me."

Claude walked out to the living room, wearing my old T-shirt, which came to her knees, and a towel around her hair.

"Oh, hey, squirt," I said, standing up. "We'll get you settled in, and we're going to bed too, okay?"

She nodded. "Okay." Her voice was quiet.

She sat on the sofa, and as I flicked the blanket out to cover her, she laid her head on the pillow. I picked up the remote control, but she asked, "Can you leave the TV on?" She was staring at the screen and her voice was tiny. I don't think she liked the idea of sleeping without knowing where Ruby was. Having him disappear into the night was becoming more frequent, and poor Claude was left alone, again. If the TV was a comfort, then who was I to deny her that?

"'Course I can," I said. I flicked through some channels

until I found some cartoons, turned the volume down a bit. "If you need anything, you just give a yell, okay? Or you can knock on our door, okay?"

She nodded and continued to stare at the screen. Her blinks were getting longer and her eyelids were getting heavier.

"Night, Claude," Kira said. "See you bright and early." Kira looked at me then and signed, "I'll go shower."

I nodded. "Okay," I signed back. "I'll just wait until she closes her eyes." I went into the kitchen and pretended to be busy, and four minutes later her little eyelids were closed. I left the TV on and went into the bathroom.

Kira was almost finished in the shower, but I stepped in behind him. "My turn," I said, turning us around so I was under the water. I ran the soap over my body, and Kira followed the streaming water with kisses to my heated skin along my shoulder and neck.

"In here?" I asked gruffly. "Or the bedroom?"

"Bedroom," was all he said.

I shut the water off, and Kira handed me a towel, which I quickly dried myself with and wrapped around my waist. After we walked out of the bathroom, Kira headed left to our bedroom, but I went right, and with a last, quick check on Claude, I quickly tiptoed back to our room. "Just checked on her. She's sound asleep."

Kira, who was in bed naked, said, "And if she wasn't? You're dripping wet, wearing nothing but a towel."

I looked down at myself. "Oh, I didn't really think of that," I admitted with a laugh. I closed the door gently, hearing the quiet click of the latch and threw my towel on the floor. "Now, what did you say about bending rules?"

"That depends," he said. I could tell he was smiling

when he spoke, even in the dark. "How quiet do you think you can be?"

I knelt on the bed and crawled up over his body, kissing up his legs as I went. "Maybe you should put something in my mouth to shut me up."

KIRA SERVED CLAUDE CEREAL, fruit, and yogurt for breakfast, much to her protest over pancakes, but she still ate everything he put in front of her.

So with clean clothes, a full tummy, and a backpack full of crackers and fruit, we took Claude back to the FC. As we drove, I had a sickening feeling in my gut that Ruby wouldn't be there, that he'd never be seen or heard from again, just another street-kid statistic.

But as we walked into the FC, he was there waiting for her. Arizona had opened up and was already in a session with one of his clients, so I didn't interrupt to say hello as we walked into my office.

Ruby gave Claude a hug, then looked up at me and Kira. "Thanks so much, man. I really owe you."

"Did you do whatever it was you had to do?" I asked.

He gave a single nod as his answer, and after Claude had told him all about dinner and dessert, I asked for a minute alone with Ruby.

"She was worried about you," I told him. "It scares her to be without you."

"She's safe with you," he said. "I'm with her almost every night. It's just some nights I can't be, and then she's better off not being alone on the streets, ya know?"

"I do," I told him. But it was time for the hard truths. "Rueben, listen to me. Those two guys will see you nothing but dead, you hear? I don't care what they offer you, what they say they can do for you or give you. I'm telling you, it's a one-way street."

He nodded as though he understood, but I don't think he understood at all. "You've got a session with Arizona today," I reminded him. "And you need to finish your schoolwork with me. Boss said one fuck up and you're out," I told him, not caring about the language. It seemed this kid needed to hear it straight. "You know what I mean, Rube? Don't waste this chance."

He nodded again, but at least this time he seemed to listen to what I was saying. "Yeah."

"I gotta go right now," I told him. "But I'll be back after lunch, and I'll have about an hour or so spare to help you. But you need to be here, and you need to want this, okay?"

Ruby nodded again. "I do want this."

"Good," I said, giving him a clap on the shoulder. "But if I were you, I'd get the session with Arizona out of the way first. He's not one to piss off."

Ruby gave me a half smile.

"We packed some food in Claude's bag. Have something to eat. Then go get dressed and see what Arizona has planned for you today," I told him. "I'll see you after lunch."

I left him to it and had a quick word to Arizona on our way out. "You right here?" I asked.

"Sure. Boss is out back and Cody'll be here in five. Where are you two off to?"

"Going to check out some housing options."

Arizona's eyes widened. "Who for?"

"Ruby and Claude."

The big man smiled and shook his head. "You guys up for citizens of the year awards or somethin'?"

I laughed. "We should be. At least it might get Claude off our sofa."

Arizona's smile strained and he shook his head. "Oh, man."

I gave him a smile. "I'll be back after lunch."

And with that, Kira and I left the FC and went in search of some place warm and safe for two homeless kids to hopefully call home.

"YOU BOTH LOOK A LITTLE TENSE," Tamara said.

We'd just sat down across from her.

"Anything you'd like to discuss today?"

I couldn't help but sigh. "There's no tension between us," I said. "It's just that we went looking for alternative accommodation for some kids this morning, and the places we found weren't exactly charming."

"They were awful," Kira said quietly.

I put my hand on his knee. "Yeah, they weren't great."

Kira shrugged. "But I guess it's a better alternative than sleeping in a dumpster."

"Are there not department authorities that could find placements?" Tamara asked.

"These two kids in particular don't exactly trust government agencies," I explained.

"Is this for Ruby and Claude?" she asked. "The two children you've mentioned?"

"Yes."

"I'm sure we'll find something," Kira said, giving my hand a squeeze.

"They've been sleeping at our place," I admitted. "Not every night, but some. I worry for them..."

"I know you do," Tamara said.

"We stopped at the sporting goods store before we came here. I was a bit hard on Ruby this morning, so I wanted to get something to make him feel good about what he's trying to do. I just bought some gym shorts. They're the MMA brand name, so he'll think they're pretty special."

"Why were you hard on him?"

"He bailed last night and left Claude with me. He said she'd be safer with us, which is true, but then he took off. I know he's up to no good, and I've told him before that I'm pushing his case harder because I want him to get a scholarship, ya know? I want to give this kid a chance, and..." I sighed. "I don't know... It's disappointing, I guess."

"You feel let down," Tamara preempted.

"He's just doing what he knows. He's doing what he thinks it takes to stay alive on the streets. What I'm trying to do is the long, hard way, and I guess to a thirteen-year-old street kid, who's trying to look after his kid sister, it's not soon enough."

"You can't make him," Kira said. "As much as I wish we could." Then he looked at Tamara. "They're good kids, but there's only so much we can do."

Tamara looked at me. "Matt, as a police officer, what would you do if you encountered kids living on the street?"

I frowned at her. She knew damn well what I'd do. She just wanted me to say it out loud. "I'm not a police officer anymore."

She stayed silent, waiting for me to answer her question.

"I'd notify welfare and social services," I said quietly.

She nodded. "Why haven't you done that for these kids? Would the department of social services or child welfare not be better equipped to deal with them?"

I shrugged. "Probably. But you know what? One sniff of

a child protection worker and these kids would disappear. They'd be nothing more than shadows in alleyways. At least this way they're being a part of the community. At least this way they don't think the world's given up on them, forgotten about them."

She was quiet for a long while, which usually meant she was getting the words right in her head before she dropped a bombshell. "Does the abandonment of these kids remind you of how you felt when your mother died?"

I blinked slowly, not really believing what I'd just heard. "What?"

"Do you feel there is a link between wanting to help these kids and you being a kid that was left alone when your mother died?"

"What? No," I answered, probably a little louder than I should have. "Is that what you've been edging around these last few weeks?"

She tilted her head. "What do you mean?"

"Every time I mention these kids at the club, you look at me like you're judging me. You want to know how I *feel*? I *feel* like I have to justify my reasons to you."

"That was never my intention, Matt."

"So we should just forget about the unfortunate street kids because we all have our own troubles, or we're all too busy?" I shook my head. "That's not good enough."

Tamara smiled. "You're a good man, Matt. That's what made you a great policeman. You care about the people."

"If I don't care about these kids, then who will?"

"You're not responsible for them. You can help them, but they're not your direct responsibility." Tamara's voice was calm, as always.

"Is it not irresponsible of me not wanting to help at-risk kids?"

"Not at all. It's a human condition to want to protect a child—"

"It's not a condition!" I cried, unable to hold it in any longer. I got out of my chair and started to pace. "It's not some over-psychoanalyzed predisposition! There's no underlying reason, Tamara. I'm not doing this because my mother died or to atone for any guilt, as much as you'd like to wrap it all up with a pretty psychiatrist bow, that's not what this is. There's no hidden agenda here. I don't know what you call it in a textbook, but I'll tell you what I call it in the real world. It's called doing what's right, damn it! It's called being a human fucking being."

"Matt," Kira said softly but with fair warning. He stood up and walked over to where I was at the window. "Why don't you go for a walk..."

"I don't need to go for a walk," I snapped at him. "I need—"

"You need to calm down," he said quietly.

I ran my hands through my hair and took a deep breath. "I am calm. But I'm also frustrated and angry. I don't think I should have to justify reasons for wanting to help another person. A kid, for that matter. I don't need to go for a walk to calm down—"

"Matt," Kira said, cutting me off mid-rant. "I'd like a moment with Tamara, please."

That stopped me. I blinked in surprise. "Okay," I said, almost in a whisper. I put my hand on his arm. "I'll give you all the time you need." I walked out, using every ounce of self-control I had not to pull the door off its fucking hinges.

How was a doctor so fucking cold? How could she not want to help another person? It was her fucking job!

How could someone just sit there and look for an ulterior motive when a child's life hung in the balance?

I walked down the stairs, out into the fresh air, and took some deep breaths. I walked along the path, down to the parking lot, then leaned against our car for as long as my temper would let me. After a few minutes, I shook my head as if to clear it and went back inside.

I took the stairs two at a time, and as I walked down the hall, I realized the door was slightly open, and I stopped. I could hear them talking. I almost pulled the door shut to give them their privacy, but heard Kira say my name.

"Matt's very passionate about his work and about changing the lives of these kids. It's not just about drug awareness but about education and respect. And in a lot of ways, I think it's more effective on a personal level for him than his work as a cop."

"Do you think he misses being a policeman?" Tamara asked.

"To be honest, I think there are some days he might miss it, but generally speaking, no. I don't." Kira sighed. "Maybe if you came down one day and met these kids, you'd see what he's trying to do," Kira said. "He's a good man. He has the kindest heart. I guess you just see a file full of every wrong he ever did, but he's done an awful lot of right too."

There was silence for a moment. "Ross Berkman is a friend of mine," she said. "When he called me and asked if I'd take on a new client, he said it was a special case. He said this kid was one of the best people he knew, not just one of the best cops, but best people. He said he was almost like a son to him."

My heart rate spiked.

"Kira, did Matt ever tell you about the day his mother died?"

"Just that he was seventeen, almost eighteen. He had no other family. That he probably would have been taken in as a ward of the state, but the cops who came to check on him..." Kira's words trailed away. "Was it Berkman?"

"Yes. Ross was one of the officers who told him his mother died."

"Oh. I didn't know."

"He checked on him every day until he turned eighteen."

"Matt joined the police the day he turned eighteen."

"He did."

"Is that why you think Matt wants to help these kids so much?" Kira asked. "Why he'd prefer to help them rather than turn them over to authorities? Like what Ross did for him?"

"What do you think?"

Kira was quiet, and my heart was hammering. My stomach was in knots. I was just about to open the door so he wouldn't have to answer, but then he spoke, "I don't think it matters *why* he wants to help them. Just that he does want to help them. You might think it's to do with his own mother's death, and I don't know about that. What I *do know* is that Matt's always going to be helping someone, whether it's being a cop or not, it's his nature to serve and protect."

Tamara laughed quietly. "Yes, it is his nature. That's a very apt description."

Then Kira said, "It's people like Matt that change the world. Like they're born to help others. That's Matt. That's what makes him who he is. I can't change that. I *wouldn't* change that. For him, it was never about the fame or prestige of being a cop—it was about doing good and helping others."

There was a long moment of silence. "I better go find him," Kira said quietly.

"Kira," Tamara said. "Matt has come a long way. I know he doesn't think he has, and I know he leaves here some days frustrated, and that can't be easy on you."

"Matt and I talk more now than we ever have."

"And that's great."

"But?"

"But there's still a long way to go. He's doing really well, and even after days like today, when, like he says, I make him angry and frustrated, but it's all progress. He's moving forward. He really is."

"I know."

"You love him very much," she said simply.

"I do," Kira replied. Then he said, "Even after everything we've been through, if I could do my time over, I'd still choose him."

My hand pushed open the door, without me even realizing it. Kira was standing behind our chairs, and when he turned to see me, he didn't need to ask if I'd heard what he said. The tears in my eyes told him.

I didn't trust my voice to speak, so using sign language, I said, "I love you."

Kira glanced to Tamara then smiled as he looked back to me. He closed the distance between us, slid his arm around me, and kissed my forehead. "I know you do," he said.

"Matt," Tamara said. She was smiling at us. "Here, please take this," she said, thumbing through some business cards. She found the one she was after and held out one. "It's the name and number of a woman who runs a house for at-risk kids on your side of town. I can't guarantee she has vacancies, but she's... *sympathetic*... to kids who have had a hard time with authorities like social services. I don't normally recommend her for that very reason, but she might be better suited for your kids."

I stepped away from Kira and took the offered card. "Thanks."

"Tell her I sent you. She'll probably fall over from shock, but she'll know it's a special case."

"Thank you," I said again. "I'm sorry about getting angry before. Maybe you should come down to the family fundraising day so you can see what we do."

"Maybe I will," she said with a smile.

AFTER LEAVING TAMARA'S OFFICE, we had gone a few blocks in silence when I slid my hand over the console to rest on his thigh. "I'm sorry about losing my temper," I told him. "And I'm sorry for eavesdropping. I didn't mean to, but the door was open a bit and I heard my name."

Kira smiled at me. "It's okay. I wouldn't say anything to Tamara that I wouldn't say to you."

"It was Ross Berkman who came to check on me," I blurted out. "He's the one who told me my mom died..."

Kira squeezed my hand.

"I don't know why I never told you that."

"You always said he was like a dad to you," he countered. He looked at me instead of watching the road. "Do you miss him? Berkman, that is."

I shrugged. "I guess. I always moved up with him, through the ranks—he was always my superior."

"Did he arrange it like that?"

I snorted. "I'd never thought of it like that. But probably."

Kira smiled. "Did you want to call him? Or go in and see him?" He checked his watch. "We have some time."

I grinned. "I have an even better idea. We need to find a local liquor store."

Twenty minutes later, I climbed the side fence at Berkman's house and put the carton of Corona beers at his back door. I wrote on the carton itself, "Because I miss your sorry face."

"Do you think you should just leave it at the back door like that?" Kira asked.

"Yep, because when he opens the door, he'll trip over it," I said with a laugh.

Kira rolled his eyes and walked back to the car. I followed him, pulled out my phone and sent Berkman a text.

You need to mow your lawn.

As Kira pulled the car out onto the street, he smiled at me. "Feel better?"

I was still grinning. "I do."

My phone buzzed in my hand. I saw the name and laughed as I took the call.

"What the hell did you do?"

I snorted into the phone. "And you should really put up a higher fence. I mean, seriously, Ross, what kind of security is that?"

He growled into the phone, "Elliott, do I need to—"

"You can thank me," I cut him off. "Because you miss my sorry face."

"You don't even work for me anymore," he said gruffly. "Tell me, how are you still a pain in my ass?"

"Didn't want you to miss me too much."

The call clicked off, and I threw the phone into the console and laughed. "Yeah, he loves me."

After pulling up at the FC, I grabbed the sporting goods bag, and we went inside. Kira had the day off, so he intended to help me with my class, then we'd grab dinner and have a quiet night at home. But first, I had to find Ruby.

He was sitting at a table in my office, laughing with Claude. I handed him the bag, and it was a buzz watching his face as he pulled the shorts out. He tried to play it cool, but his smile got the best of him. "Oh, man," he said, now grinning. "Whatcha get me these for?"

"You need to look the part," I told him. "Especially as we move into the competing phase. You can't step into the cage looking like you don't belong."

Ruby chewed the inside of his lip, probably to try and stop smiling so hard, while Claude bounced on her toes trying to look at what he was holding. He handed her the shorts and she held up the black fighter's shorts with a bright green UFC logo. "These are so cool, Rube," she said. "They kinda match your new shoes! They got green on 'em too."

"New shoes?" I asked, faking an excitement I didn't feel, knowing what that meant.

"Yeah," he answered sheepishly. "I did my session with Arizona, then Claude and me went and got me some new shoes. Mine were too small..." he finished quietly.

I guess in my excitement to give him the shorts and the fact he was sitting down, I missed that he was wearing new high tops. I'm not sure how I could have missed them because they were bright green.

"Jeez," I said, looking from his feet to his face. "I'm pretty sure the airport flight control could use those to land the planes."

Claude's eyes were wide with excitement. "Pretty cool, huh?"

I grinned at her. "Pretty cool."

I considered grilling him on just how he had the cash to pay for the new shoes but decided against it. He had come back to the FC to go through his schoolwork, just like I'd asked, and I didn't want to start by making him feel bad.

"Well, we may as well get this hell started," Ruby said.

Kira, who was still standing beside me, snorted. "Man, I hated school, too."

I could have kicked him in the shins. As it was, I gave him a pointed what-the-hell glare.

Kira smiled and shrugged. "It's true! I hated it."

"But you still went, yeah?" Ruby said.

"Had to," Kira said. "I hated English the most, and even though I was okay at math, I didn't like it much better."

"Oh, man, I hate math," Ruby said as though the thought itself smelt bad. "I got math to do in my paperwork."

Kira nodded sympathetically. "Did you want me to have a look at it with you? Maybe between the two of us, we can knock it over."

Ruby shrugged one shoulder. "If you want." He looked at the table in the corner where his schoolwork folder was. "I guess."

I couldn't stop my smile. So that was Kira's ploy, and it worked. As he and Ruby sat at the table and started going through papers, I looked at Claude and nodded toward the door. "We're just going to see Father Michael. Be back soon," I said, leading Claude out.

"What is we seeing Michael again for?" Claude asked as we walked out onto the sidewalk.

"Well, I just want to finalize a few details about our fundraising day, that's all."

"Isn't it all done yet?"

"Not quite."

Claude looked up at me as we walked down the block. "Did you just want Kira to help Ruby without us bein' there?"

I laughed at her. "You're too smart, Claude."

She grinned and her black curls bounced as she walked. "He does want to try, Matt," she said. "Ruby told me he wants to be part of it, but he said it was hard. The school stuff."

"You know what I think?" I asked. "I think Ruby is smarter than he gives himself credit for. Yep, it's hard, but he's doing great." I stopped at the gate to the church. "He's pretty hard on himself."

Claude seemed happy with this, and smiled as she turned into the church yard. We went inside but were told by a small, elderly lady that Father Michael wasn't in. She introduced herself as a long-time parishioner and sometimes office administrator. "I'll pass a message along, if you'd like," she said. "Father Michael will be back tomorrow."

I told her where we were from and that we'd come back another day. I reassured her it wasn't urgent, and Claude and I went back out into the LA sunshine, heading back to the FC.

"How old do you think she was?" Claude whispered as we walked.

"I'd say..." I pretended to have to think about it. "Oooh, about two hundred years old."

Claude burst out laughing, and it was then I noticed a car on the street. It was a non-descript Ford, kinda banged up, and it blended into the neighborhood. There was one guy in the car. Behind the steering wheel, he was talking on his phone. Well, it looked like he was pretending to talk on his phone, and it all seemed harmless. But something tripped my intuition. Something made the hairs on the back of my neck stand up.

Then I looked up the street and across the road. At the end of the block was a van. And across from the FC, on the other side of the busy street, was a homeless man. He was sitting on the pavement, leaning up against the building, with newspapers and cardboard his only belongings. He was unshaven, wearing ratted clothes, and had a dirty cap pulled down, hiding half his face.

But he did something out of character.

He glanced at me from under the brim of his cap, and in that half a second, I saw his eyes were clear and sharp.

Fuck.

The homeless guy, the car, the van.

I knew what that meant. Something, someone on this street was under surveillance.

To anyone else, everything looked normal. There were dozens of cars lining both sides of the street, the van and the car were not out of place at all. The non-descript homeless man would have been invisible to anyone else. And maybe if I hadn't have caught his eye, I wouldn't have noticed either.

Hell, I didn't notice them on the way to the church. I certainly did on the way back.

I swapped sides with Claude as we walked, putting her closest to the building—the safest place. We walked quickly back to the FC, and I held the door open for her, acting completely normal.

Not so much for Claude's sake but also for the policemen out there. If whoever they were watching—Darius and Tyler came to mind—were watching me, suspicious behavior on my behalf could alert them to the surveillance.

I smiled at something Claude said as we walked inside, and as much as I wanted to turn around and scope the street, I didn't.

I told Claude we'd leave Ruby and Kira alone and go and annoy Boss instead. As we walked into Boss' office, I pulled my cell phone out of my pocket and sent a text to Mitch.

Some warning would have been good.

He responded almost immediately.

Go to church often?

I almost snorted.

I've got about fifteen kids coming here in about twenty minutes. Do we have a problem?

No. You're all good.

Be careful, I told him.

Always.

I pocketed my phone and smiled at Boss. He looked to the pocket I'd just put my phone in then to my face. "Everything all right?" he asked.

"Everything's just fine," I told him. "Squirt and I just thought we'd come help you since had twenty minutes spare."

Boss looked to Claude. "Is that right?"

"Well," Claude said, "Matt said we'd come annoy you, not help you."

Boss sighed then grumbled, "Figures."

"Hey, Claude," I said. "Can you check the supply cupboard for me? See what we're running low on."

She looked between me and Boss. "If you want to speak to Boss by yourself, just say so," she said as she walked out.

I waited until the door closed and we were alone. "The street is under surveillance."

His eyes bulged. "What? What for now?"

"I didn't ask specifics, but it's a narcotics detail. I noticed a few familiar sets on the street, sent my old partner a text, and he confirmed it. Not the club, though. We're okay."

Boss groaned. "Sometimes I think I prefer not knowin'."

I chuckled at him. "Yeah, well, I told you no secrets, right?"

He groaned in answer and ignored me.

So I fished my phone out of my pocket and said, "I need to make a call without Claude."

Boss eyed me curiously as I pulled the business card from my wallet and dialed the number. The phone picked up after the fifth ring, and after brief introductions, I told them, "I'm looking for accommodation for two kids, aged thirteen and nine."

"Hmm," the gruff female voice huffed down the line. "Where did you say you was calling from?"

"I'm calling from the Harbor FC. I run some classes for kids and have two in particular that need somewhere to stay."

"I don't usually take cold calls. Haven't got much in the way of availability..." she started to brush me off.

"I was given your name and number by someone who said you could help."

"Who?"

"Doctor Tamara Coulter."

There was a long beat of silence. "Well, shit."

I grinned into the phone. "She has that effect on me too."

She barked a laugh into the phone, then gave me an address. "Can you swing past tomorrow? Around nine in the morning?"

"Absolutely."

When I clicked off the call, I smiled at Boss and slid my phone back into my pocket. "Just lining up somewhere for Ruby and Claude to stay."

Boss glared hard at me. "I told you to talk to the kid, not find him a house."

"Well, if we want him off the streets, in school, and not running drugs, then he needs to *not* be on the streets." I gave him a satisfied smile. "Anyway, I like helping these kids. It's what I'm here for."

Boss shook his head and threw his pen on the table. "I think I liked you better when you wanted to punch and kick the shit outta people."

I laughed incredulously. "What?"

"At least when you were scowlin', angry, and wantin' to kill people, I knew what to expect. But the way you've been smilin' lately scares me. I dunno if you're really smilin' or if you're about to snap."

I tried not to smile at him and failed. "Boss, I'm in a good headspace. I really am. I'm working on my shit, and being here doing something positive isn't just about working off debts to you and the boys. I actually love doing this."

His eyes hardened under his thick, gray eyebrows, and I could tell he was considering the sincerity of my words. "You ain't got no debts here," he said.

I'd probably used the wrong word. "Not a debt, so much," I corrected. "Even though it kind of is. I almost took a lot away from you guys."

"But you've given a lot back," he said. "And those boys out there think of you as one of 'em now."

My smile became a grin. "I know."

There was a knock at the door, and when it opened, Cody stuck his head in. "Hey, Matt, get your ass out here.

You've got a bunch of bored kids about to riot if you don't show up."

I laughed and stood up. "On my way."

Boss rolled his eyes, but before I left he said, "Hey, we on track for this fundraising day?"

"Yep. I can go through the details with you tomorrow," I told him. "We'll sit down and go through it all."

Boss picked up his pen and went back to the papers in front of him. It looked like the spreadsheets he'd shown me the other week, which he'd probably gone over five dozen times every day.

"You'll wear the words off that page," I said as I walked out.

He grumbled something I didn't hear, but I laughed anyway. When I walked out to the main floor of the gym, Kira and Ruby were just coming out of my office. Kira gave me a quick smile, so I assumed his little tutor session with Ruby had gone okay.

Kira and I went through my class together. It wasn't too unusual if he was at the FC for him to help me. The kids knew him and he knew most of them by name, and I think they enjoyed having a different instructor every now and again.

By the time we were done and ready to go home, Ruby and Claude were gone. Kira told me, "Ruby said they'd be fine tonight. Said he and Claude would be back tomorrow."

"Oh. Okay then."

"Did you want to go look for them?"

I thought about doing just that, and the concern on Kira's face probably should have made up my mind. But I wanted something else more.

"Would it be selfish of me to say I just want to be at home? With you. Just us."

Kira smiled in the way that made my stomach flip. "Yes, probably. But then I think that sounds pretty perfect to me too." Then he added, "I mean, it's not like we're kicking them out or anything. They're not even here."

I grinned at him. "That's right. If they were here, they could stay with us, but they're not... so it's not like we're saying no."

"Exactly!" he agreed with a nod. "And considering I didn't go to work today, I could really use a work out at home..." He cleared his throat. "And it's been a while since you've practiced your grappling moves, and given we'll be home alone, we could bring the punching bag out to the floor..."

"I'll just grab my things," I said quickly.

Twenty seconds later, we were in the car and headed home.

"I THOUGHT we were going to get the punching bag," I said.

Kira walked me backwards down the hall toward our bedroom, his arms wrapped tight around me, quickly covering my mouth with his. He pushed me through the doorway and onto the bed, his tongue never leaving my mouth, his hands roaming all over my body.

"No," he murmured against my lips. "Need you now."

Kira pushed me against the bed, and putting a hand on my chest, he pushed me onto the mattress. He pulled my pants down my thighs in one movement, then he crawled up over my body.

He kissed up my body, nuzzling his nose into my briefs before freeing my hard-on. He licked the length of my cock and continued up my stomach, over my chest to my neck, and finally his mouth found mine.

I pulled his shorts over his ass and slid my hand between us, taking his engorged dick in my hand. Kira groaned into my mouth, his tongue stuttering at my touch.

When our cocks rubbed against each other, I took us both in my hand and let him fuck my fist. He held my face in his hands and thrust harder, rocking his hips, seeking relief from my hand. Kira's tongue invaded my mouth, kissing me deeply, and I could feel his cock harden further against mine.

"Fuck, Matt," he ground out. "Won't last."

"I want to feel you come," I whispered against his mouth. "Your cock against mine."

Kira thrust one final time into my fist, and his whole body stiffened as his cock pulsed in my hand. Hot cum smeared between us as his head fell back with a groan.

He was so fucking beautiful.

His body arched as the aftershocks of pleasure rolled through him, and I came. I bucked my hips, fisting my cock, and when I pulsed hot and thick between us, Kira chuckled into my neck.

"Fuck, we didn't make it far," he said.

"We're still dressed," I added.

Kira laughed and rolled off me onto the bed beside me. "Come on, shower."

"My head's spinning."

Kira leaned up on his elbow. "Is it vertigo? Shit, Matt, I didn't know..."

My burst of laughter cut him off. "Uh, no. It's an orgasm head spin." I writhed as the last of my pleasure twinged at my muscles. "The very best kind of head spin."

Kira laughed, and when he got off the bed, he took my

hand. Slowly pulling me upright, he kissed my swollen lips. "You look like you've been thoroughly fucked. You have that blissed-out smirk and sleepy eyes look."

I chuckled. "Well, the thorough fucking will happen later. Shower and dinner first."

Kira grinned at me, and still holding my hand, with our pants barely around our thighs, he led me toward the shower.

AS WE FINISHED UP DINNER, we talked about our appointment with Tamara. I told him again that I heard what he'd said to her about me and asked him if he had any questions.

"Actually, I do," Kira said. "But it's not about what Tamara said."

"Okay. You can ask me anything."

"Why don't you like her?" Kira asked. "It's not a clash of personalities," he declared, "because I think professionally, as a cop, you would have gotten on like a house on fire. And it's not like you to be so abrupt with someone. So what is it about her that gets under your skin?"

I put my plate in the sink and leaned against the counter. "You know, I've thought about that. A lot. And I don't *not* like her…"

"Then what is it?"

I let out a nervous breath. "She, um, she scares me."

"She what?"

I barked out a laugh. "Yeah, weird, I know. But I think that's what it is. I'm not sure, to be honest."

Kira stood in front of me and put his hands on my arms. "What do you mean? Explain it to me."

I looked into his dark eyes and saw only concern there. I smiled for him, took a deep breath, and said, "I keep waiting for her to tell me I that I'm going to fail. With these kids. I know she keeps stressing caution about these kids or whatever, and I know I'm not in the best place mentally to be thinking about kids and long-term. I should be taking one day at a time and concentrating on us, on you, and on me, not thinking about being a father. Or, in my case, being told I can't ever be one—"

Kira blinked, and my nervous rant died off.

"Wait," he said with wide eyes. "You want to have kids? Like for real?"

"I mean, yeah, I've mentioned kids before, but I'd never even thought about it! Not seriously. Never in my life did I think that was a possibility for me. I never *wanted* it."

"And now you do?"

"Now I... Well, yeah!" I admitted. "I can help dozens of kids at the club and that's okay, but I don't want to be told I'm not good enough to have kids of my own. I mean, I want to help these kids get a better life. I want to help find some of them better places to live, to feel safe, and to get them an education and a future. But kids of my own? Well, shit. Why not? I mean, we could be dads, right?"

Kira's mouth fell open, but then he smiled slowly. "Um, sure...?" he trailed off like it was a question.

"Don't you want kids?" I asked. Then I realized maybe I shouldn't have assumed. "It's okay if you don't. We certainly don't have to—"

This time he stopped me mid-rant with a soft kiss to my lips. "I think it's something we should talk about," he said, still smiling. "Honestly, I think it's wonderful, but I don't think it's something we should worry about right now. Like you said, we should be concentrating on us right now."

"I know we should," I agreed. "I just don't want Tamara to make some diagnosis that I'd never be fit for being a dad."

Kira kissed me again with smiling lips. "Matt, you'll make an excellent dad."

"You think so?"

"I know so," he said. "But maybe we should start with a dog."

I laughed, relieved. We'd been honest with each other, and I felt better that I'd told him how I felt. "So, a big dog or a little dog? A boy dog or a girl dog? Long hair, short hair?"

Kira chuckled. "You can't control everything, Matt. Anyway, I hear the right pet picks you, so I think we'll know when we see it."

***

KIRA and I went for a run in the morning, came home, showered, made out in the shower, made love in bed, and made breakfast together in the kitchen. Right on time, we stopped by the FC to pick up Claude and Ruby and headed to the address the lady had given me for the halfway house for troubled kids.

It was an old terrace-style building, just a few blocks from the FC. There were some kids out front, who eyed the four of us cautiously as we walked up the front path. I knocked on the door and was met by a woman who almost snarled at me until I told her who I was.

"My name's Matthew Elliott. I called yesterday about finding a place for two kids." I stood aside then, so she could see Ruby and Claude standing behind me.

She smiled then. She was about five-foot-four and built like a football player. She had short, gray hair and a hardened face. She reminded me oddly of Boss, but all jokes aside, it was obvious her life, the life she'd dedicated to homeless kids, hadn't been an easy one.

"Come on in," she said. She shook my hand, then Kira's. Her hands were calloused and her grip was strong. Gina Sharp introduced herself to Ruby and Claude and showed us around the house.

"Communal living room and kitchen. We eat in the dining room through there. There's a cooking roster and a cleaning roster. You do your own laundry. I'm here to help, but I ain't no maid," she said as she headed up the stairs. With a quiet look between the four of us, we followed her as she talked. "Bedrooms on the first floor. If you decide you want to stay, it'll be four to a room and a shared bathroom. No doors on bedrooms," she said. "Except for my room. Strictly out of bounds, no excuses."

The house itself was old and there were scuff marks on the walls and floors, but it was tidy. And above all, it was better than sleeping in a dumpster.

Gina went through the rules but said, while she encouraged kids to go to school, she couldn't make them. "My deal breaker is drugs. You take 'em, you run 'em, you sell 'em, you're out. No exceptions, no excuses."

I found myself smiling at her. I liked her. "Sounds good," I said. I looked at Ruby and Claude. "Whaddya think?"

Claude looked to her brother. With a final look around the living room, Ruby shrugged one shoulder and nodded. "I guess."

I grinned and clapped my hand on Ruby's shoulder. "Good man," I said.

"When did you want to start?" Gina asked.

"Tonight," I answered on their behalf.

Gina smiled warmly at the two kids. "You have anything you want to bring over?"

Claude shook her head. "No. I got my backpack with me."

Gina smiled at her. "Well then, you're all set."

I explained that Ruby had classes, both school and MMA, and how he was my scholarship prototype, and that Claude would spend most days with me. I would eventually work on getting her into school, but for now I was happy just to get a roof over her head.

"We can bring them back this afternoon," I said to Gina. "Ruby has a session with Arizona today, and we need Claude's help with something special this morning."

"Like what?" Claude asked. Her wide eyes narrowed. "You aint takin' me to school, are ya?"

I laughed. "Nope. Not today. I have to work this afternoon, so we only have a few hours."

Kira looked at me questioningly but didn't say anything until we'd left Gina's with promises to return this afternoon. We drove back to the FC first, and it was clear that I was more excited about finding these guys somewhere to sleep than they were. It was understandable they were apprehensive, but it was a huge relief for me; at least that they'd be off the streets at night.

When we pulled up at the front of the FC, I told Ruby we wouldn't go in. We had somewhere else to be. We waited for him to walk inside, and I could feel Kira's stare on the side of my head.

"Do I even want to know where we're going?" he asked.

I looked at him, then Claude in the back seat, and grinned. "We're going to get a dog!"

CHAPTER THIRTEEN

"FOR REAL?" Claude said. "A real dog?"

"Yep," I said.

Kira sighed, almost sagging into the driver's seat. "We're getting a dog."

I laughed. "Come on, it'll be fun!"

"And where exactly are we getting a dog from?"

"The animal rescue shelter," I told him. "On Bridge Street." I turned in my seat so I could talk to Claude. "I thought you might like to come with us. It'll be fun. We'll have a look anyway. There might not be the right one."

Kira ran his hand through his hair. He looked kind of worried. "Uh, Matt. Promise me, it's just one. We're getting *one* dog."

"Yes, one," I said. "I said *a* dog."

"It's just I know what you're like," he said. "You'll walk into the shelter and want to take them all."

I looked back at Claude and rolled my eyes, making her giggle.

"And we'll have to get a collar and a leash. And a vet,"

Kira said. "Jesus, Matt. Maybe this is something we should have discussed."

"We did discuss it," I reminded him. "It was your idea!"

Kira shook his head at me. "I think you misunderstood."

"I'm pretty sure I didn't," I said, settling in my seat, rather happy with myself. "And you have this afternoon off work, so it will be a good time for the dog to get used to a new house."

Kira rolled his eyes this time, but he smiled as he drove us to the rescue center. We pulled up in the parking lot, then as we walked toward the front door, Kira said, "One, Matt. One dog."

Grinning, I opened the door and waited for him and Claude to walk in first. There was a lady behind the counter who smiled at us as we walked in. "Can I help you?"

"Yes," I answered. "We want to get a dog."

"Just one," Kira added. "Please don't let us leave here with more than one."

The woman laughed. "Sure. Come this way."

We walked through a doorway, down a short hallway that opened up to a longer corridor lined with caged partitions. It was loud, even for me, and it smelled like wet concrete, wet dog, and dog pee. Each cage had a few dogs in it, of a range of shapes, sizes, and colors, and they all bounced and barked at the mesh.

Claude put her hands to her ears, but she was giggling as we slowly walked down the corridor. The lady explained a few of the breeds as we went along, giving a brief history on a few of the dogs. Some were new, some were at their end of their stay.

"Where do they go when they leave?" Claude asked.

The woman shot me a quick look, then smiled at

Claude, but before she could answer, Kira said, "They go to a new shelter somewhere else, to see if anyone there wants them."

Claude nodded, quickly distracted by the barking dogs on either side of us. The lady smiled again and kept walking. She might have thought we were sparing a child the harsh fact that the animals were put to sleep if no one wanted them, but it was more than that. How could I explain to an abandoned, homeless child that an animal was put down because it, too, was abandoned?

I put my hand on Kira's arm, silently saying thanks for saving Claude from that realization.

As we got to the last cages, we turned back to look at the way we'd come. There were happy little short dogs and proud big dogs, any of which would have made an excellent choice.

But there was one dog in the very last cage. He was in a cage all by himself, lying down, just watching us. He looked like a German shepherd cross, maybe about two years old. He looked... sad. He looked at us for a while and put his head back down on his paws.

I pointed to him. "What's the story with that one? Why's he by himself?"

The lady sighed. "Well, he came in two weeks ago. He's actually in this yard because he's scheduled to be..." She looked at Claude and corrected herself, "he's at the end of his stay."

"Why?" I asked quietly.

"No one wants him."

I crouched down near the wire and called the dog over. "Come here, boy," I called. He put his head up but didn't come over to me. "What's his name?" I asked the lady.

"He doesn't have one," she said with a shrug. "Doesn't matter anyway."

I looked up at her from where I was still crouching down. How could it not matter? "What do you mean it doesn't matter? Because he's being... sent away?"

"It doesn't matter what you call him, he can't hear you. He's stone deaf."

I stared at her for a long moment, then I looked at Kira. He raised an eyebrow at me and smiled. I looked back to the lady. "We'll take him."

She blinked. "You want *him?*"

Ignoring her, I looked at Kira and signed, "We want him, yes?"

Kira smiled and signed back, "Would you take any other dog?"

I shook my head and signed a very determined, "No."

Kira turned to the stunned lady. "Yes, we want him."

"Um," she said, looking from us to the dog. "Normally people have a few sessions with a prospective pet, just to make sure they're making the right decision..." She unclipped a set of keys from her waistband, then took the lock on the gate in her hand. "Having a deaf dog comes with certain responsibilities."

"I'm sure it does," I told her. "But being disregarded because he's deaf isn't fair either." Then I turned to Kira and signed, "We can't let him be put to sleep just because he's deaf."

The lady watched our signed conversation, and without another word, she opened the door. The dog sat up, excited now that the door was being opened. "Spend some time with him. I'll be back in five to check on you."

I crouched down at the door and, patting my leg, called the dog to come over. He stepped toward me, unsure but excited all the same. I gently rubbed his forehead and gave him a good pat, getting a body-wiggle, a wagging tail, and a lick to the face as thanks.

Claude laughed, and Kira shook his head, but he was smiling. I stood up and told Claude to pet him. Kira, who was still smiling, slid his arm around my waist. "You're gonna need to wash your face before I'll even think about kissing you."

I laughed. "Dog slobber never hurt anyone."

By this time, Claude had her arms around the dog's neck, giving him a hug. "Just be careful, Claude," I warned. "We don't know if he's inclined to bite or if he's been wormed or anything."

"He won't bite me," she said. "He's a nice dog."

"He needs a proper name," Kira said. Then he sighed. "And a visit to a vet and a collar and a leash and a bed and a bowl. *Two* bowls, actually, one for water—"

I laughed. "Don't worry about all that. I can get all that stuff."

"Aren't I allowed?" he asked. "I mean, if he's ours, then *we* should." Then Kira knelt on the other side of the dog. "He *does* have a happy face."

"He needs a name," I said. "What do you reckon, Claude?"

"Me?" she asked. "I've never named anything before."

"Well, now's your chance," I told her.

She blinked a few times and stared at the dog. He was still wiggling excitedly, and if dogs could smile, this one was grinning.

The lady that worked there came up behind me and said, "I see things are going well." She startled me. With all the noise of the other dogs, I hadn't heard her come back.

I spun to face her, and luckily for her, I took a step back rather than getting on the defense and putting my fists up. It was moments like this that reminded me of what my instincts were. Kira stood up quickly, but it was fine. As soon as I realized who it was, I gave her a smile. "I think we've found our dog."

She ran through some paperwork, explained some training tips for deaf dogs, some general dos and don'ts, and after we'd paid for him and spent a small fortune on a car harness, collar and leash, and special dog wash and a brush, we were on our way.

In the car, I kept turning around and looking at Claude and the dog, both sitting up and smiling. "Thought of a name yet, squirt?"

"O. He looks like an O."

"An O?" I asked. "What is that?"

"Any name starting with a O," she said, like I'd missed the obvious.

"Oh."

"Exactly," she said.

Kira laughed. "An O name. Right. Any suggestions?"

"Oscar, Otis, Oliver," I started.

"That's not an ex-boyfriend list, is it?" Kira asked quietly.

It made me laugh. "Uh, no. *That* list starts and ends with K."

Kira smiled as he drove, and I turned back to Claude. She was looking at the dog. "I think he's an Oscar," she said, not taking her eyes off him.

"Oscar?" I asked.

"You know, *Sesame Street*. Oscar the Grouch. I used to watch it when I was a kid," she said.

When she was a kid. I almost corrected her, but then

realized even though she was only nine years old, she probably hadn't been a kid for a long time.

"He doesn't look like Oscar the Grouch, though," I said.

"Yeah, he does," Claude said. She waved her hand in front of her face. "He has the same eyebrows."

Kira laughed but covered it with a cough. He took his eyes off the road for a second. "He kind of does."

I found myself laughing as well. "Oscar it is."

When we got home, we hooked the leash onto Oscar's collar and walked him into the yard. It was all so new to him, and he kept running back over to us, all excited, like he somehow knew he had been given a second chance with us. We let him sniff around the gardens, then we took him inside. He was a little apprehensive in the strange house so I took some cut ham from the fridge and snuck him some slices.

"Matt," Kira chided.

"Just so he knows this is a happy place," I said. "That he's safe here, and we won't hurt him."

Oscar all but inhaled the meat and licked his lips expectantly. "You'll create a monster by spoiling him."

I looked at Claude and rolled my eyes. She giggled and took some ham to give to Oscar. "How will you talk to him?" she asked.

"Um..." I hesitated and looked to Kira.

He shrugged. "We'll work out some signals for him. He'll catch on, I'm sure."

"Can you teach me some of your sign language?" Claude asked. "Maybe then I could teach him. If that's okay?"

"I think that's a great idea," I agreed. "Come on, we'll take him out to the backyard and work on some basics."

For the next hour, that's what we did. I think the poor

dog was more confused than educated, but Claude picked up a few words. She was a quick learner. Kira called his mom and told her about the new addition to our house, and it wasn't long until they arrived.

Yumi and Sal brought lunch with them and set a few bags of deli food on the dining table. "Where is this dog?" Yumi asked. "Why you get a dog?"

"We saved him," I told them. "His name is Oscar. Claude named him."

"What you save him from?" Yumi asked.

"He was out of time at the rescue center," Kira said.

"Oh." Yumi petted the dog. Then she spoke to the dog, "You are cute, yes?"

"Um, he's deaf," I said.

Yumi stood up straight and sighed. "Of course he is," she deadpanned.

Sal laughed, and Kira explained that as soon as the lady at the center had told us the dog was deaf, I wouldn't consider another dog. "We need to get him a few things—a bed, some bowls. But he's ours. He'll be our new running buddy every morning and can suffer through Matt's cooking with me at dinnertime."

"Hey!" I said. I leaned over and ruffled Oscar's forehead. "You'll love my cooking. It's really not that bad."

"We're teaching him sign language," Claude announced. "Well, we tried. I don't think he gets it."

Yumi smiled at the little girl. "Might take some practice," she said.

After we'd eaten lunch, Claude took Oscar to the backyard again and tried running through the basics of training. Words like sit, stay, lie down, followed by the actions and some treats as rewards. I didn't know if he learned anything, but he seemed happy to spend time with her.

Sal signed to Kira, "She's here again?"

Kira nodded and signed back, "Just for the day. We picked her up this morning."

"We found her a place," I signed. "For her and her brother."

"We hope it will work," Kira added, signing fluidly.

"I'll take her back this afternoon. I just thought she might like to come along and look at dogs."

Yumi looked out into the yard at Claude, who was still trying to get Oscar to sit on cue.

"She's a good kid, yes?" she asked quietly.

"She is," I answered. "Her brother is a worry, but we're working on him."

"You two are good boys," Yumi said. "Kira, you not work this afternoon?"

"No," he said out loud. "I have all of today off. I'll go and get a few things for Oscar and make sure he's okay, then I'll head down to the FC to pick up Matt. Dinner later. That's my entire day. Why?"

"Oh, no reason. I just ask to be polite."

Sal laughed. "She has folders of wedding stuff she wants to show you," he signed.

"Oh, I'm not going through that by myself," Kira said quickly. He looked a little scared. "Matt has to be there."

Sal laughed again, and Yumi scowled. "It not bite you."

"We did say we were in no hurry, Mom."

"You just need to look," she replied, shaking her head. "I get drink. Who want one?"

I shook my head. "No thanks. I'm fine. Yumi, you can bring all the wedding stuff over here," I said. "I'll look through it with you."

She walked over to me and gently tapped my face. "One of my boys loves me."

I laughed, Kira sighed, and Sal shook his head.

"Look," Claude called out. "He sat down!"

We all looked out into the yard, and sure enough, Oscar was now sitting down in front of Claude. Sal snorted, then signed, "Poor dog probably just got sick of standing up."

BEFORE DINNER, I took Claude back to the FC. We collected Ruby, and I took them to what would now be their new place with Gina. I only stayed for a few minutes, not wanting to overstep any boundaries, but wanting to know they'd be okay. It wasn't easy to just leave them there, but it was better than leaving them on the streets.

Having Kira and Oscar at home was a good distraction. It gave me less time to think about the two kids who were spending their first night in a new place.

"Matt," Kira said, kissing the side of my head. "I'm sure they're okay."

There was no point in trying to act like I didn't know what he was talking about. "I know," I sighed, resigned.

I was leaning against him as we sat on the sofa, and Oscar was dozing on the rug. Considering everything we'd been through—everything I put us through—somehow life had turned out okay.

I had Kira. He was my absolute rock, and I would be grateful for him every day for the rest of my life.

"Talk to me," he urged, tightening his arms around me.

"After everything I've done, all the pain I caused, I still have you," I said. "I have you and my job and a house and some money saved. I mean, it's not perfect, but life's pretty damn good, yeah?"

"Yeah. It is."

"What did they do?" I asked. "What did Claude and Ruby do to deserve the life they've got?"

"Matt, they didn't *do* anything—"

"That's my point," I said, leaning up and looking at him. "It's not fair. They're just kids. They had no say in what happened to them. They didn't choose their lives to be like that. They're just trying to survive."

Kira rubbed my arm and waited for me to continue.

"I don't know," I said, running my hand through my hair. "I fucked everything up and hurt a lot of people, and I still have everything I could want. Those kids never did anything wrong, *anything*, and they have nothing."

"Matt, you can't blame yourself for that."

"I don't blame myself," I assured him. "But there's no..." I searched for the right word. "Karma. There's no karma."

Kira laughed quietly and pulled me back against him. "Oh, Matt," he sighed. "You're their karma." He pressed his lips to my temple. "To each of those kids, you're a whole lot of light in a pretty dark world."

I wasn't too sure about how much credence I gave to *that*, but Kira gave me a squeeze. A comfortable silence fell over us while we watched the TV, then a foul stench assaulted my nose. I almost gagged. "Jesus. Was that you?"

Kira sat up, pushing me off him. "It was you! Fucking hell, Matt. What did you eat today?"

Then Oscar yawned and stretched out on the rug on the floor, looking rather pleased with himself.

"Ugh, take him outside," I whined. I ran to the bathroom and grabbed the air freshener, spraying it continuously as I walked back to the living room. Looking through the kitchen to the back door, I could see Kira. He was waiting for Oscar to do his business and laughing at me while I fumigated the living room.

"He's *your* dog when he farts like that," I grumbled at him. "Not mine."

Kira snorted out a laugh. "I think you can stop spraying that now."

"I can still smell it."

"Yeah, but now the house smells like some flowery shit *and* dog fart."

I stopped spraying and read the label on the spray can. "It's ocean breeze."

"Okay, so it's ocean breeze and dog fart."

"Man, that stunk," I said. "Whatever he ate, he's never eating again."

Kira bought Oscar back inside. The dog padded over to me, tail wagging, and bright, happy eyes. I crouched down and gave him a pat. "Oscar, we have a rule in this house," I said seriously. "Under no circumstances, ever, should an ass smell like that."

I WAS at the gym early the next day. We'd taken Oscar with us on our early morning jog. We'd taken him for a walk last night too, to give the house time to desmell, so he was getting familiar with the leash. This morning, we jogged slowly with him, making sure he didn't freak out.

Surprisingly, he'd taken it all really well.

Kira had bought him a bed and bowls and food. And a list of things we'd more than likely never use, but he was proud of his purchases. He'd set Oscar's bed up in the corner of the living room, and we'd had to leave a light on for him. "Just in case he gets scared," Kira had said. "And we should probably leave our door open, just in case."

"What if sees us... doing stuff?"

Kira had grinned and spoken against my lips. "Then we better make it doggy tonight."

I'd considered rolling my eyes, but thought his suggestion sounded pretty damn good. And the one benefit of having a deaf dog was that he couldn't hear the noises that came from our bedroom.

"Hey, man, what's got you smilin'?" Arizona asked, snapping me from my memories. I hadn't realized I was smiling.

"Nothing much," I told him. "Life's just good right now, that's all."

Arizona grinned a wide, toothy grin. "It sure is," he said.

"We got ourselves a dog yesterday. He's a beauty."

Arizona's eyes lit up. "That's cool."

"How's your growing family?"

"Oh, man. It's so good. My girls are so beautiful."

It was so good to see him so happy. He'd had such a hard life—he used to earn cash in underground cage fights—and here he was with a full-time job, full benefits, a wife and daughter he adored, and another baby on the way. And I was proud to think I had a helping hand in that—not the wife or baby, obviously. The job, the new life.

"What the fuck are you two smilin' at?" Boss barked at us. "We got a world of shit to do and you two are standin' there like circus clowns."

I burst out laughing, which just seemed to irritate Boss even more. "Oh, come on, Boss," I said. "You love us."

Boss pointed his pen at me then shoved it in his mouth like it was a cigar. When he realized it wasn't, he ripped it out of his mouth and pointed it at me again. "I will beat your sorry ass."

I looked at Arizona and, with a straight face said, "I think he's coming on to me."

Arizona busted up laughing and Boss's face was hysterical. It went a high blood pressure kind of purple and a vein pulsed down his forehead. He took two quick steps toward me, and a still-laughing Arizona pushed me toward my office.

Boss was still cursing at me as he stalked off to his office, and I was *still* laughing when Claude and Ruby came in.

"Here they are!" I said as they walked over to me. "How was your first night at Gina's?"

"How's Oscar?" Claude asked excitedly. "I told Ruby all about him. Why didn't you bring him? Did you leave him at home all by hisself? What if he gets scared or lonely?"

I put my hand up, like I was directing traffic. "Stop. Oscar is just fine. Kira bought him a whole store full of chew toys and food and everything you can imagine. We took him for a run this morning, and when we left for work, he was yawning on his bed."

"Oh," Claude said, deflated. "I was hopin' you'd bring him."

"I can't bring him here." Then I repeated my question. "So tell me, how was your first night at the house?"

"S'okay," Ruby said. "Didn't sleep much. We shared with other kids, so I put Claude in my bed so she could sleep."

I gave Ruby a knowing smile. I felt sorry for this kid. He was trying so hard to look after his kid sister, but I was sure he was taking the steps to ensure a better life for the both of them.

"The other kids don't like us much," Claude said.

"I'm sure they're just getting used to you. Give 'em a day or two and they'll be fine. Did you have breakfast?" I asked. All I could hope for was a warm, dry bed and at least one or two meals a day for these kids.

"Yeah, toast. It was okay," Claude said. "Gina said she gets free bread from some shop. It's two days old, but she says when it's toast you can't tell."

I would guess a local house that looks after kids with little to no funding would take whatever freebies they could get. "Go make yourself a hot chocolate, squirt. I'll be in in a sec."

When she'd gone through my office door, I clapped Ruby on the shoulder. "You okay? You look tired."

"I'm okay," he said. "Claude was all excited about your dog."

"She named him," I said.

Ruby smiled. "She said that."

"How about we see Arizona and tell him nothing too extensive today, hey? Maybe just some technical stuff and then some schoolwork?"

Ruby shrugged. "I'm all right."

"I don't want you burning out. It's okay to have a low-key day every now and then. Not every day has to be full on, and you're exhausted, Rube. I don't want you thinking it's all too hard. It's not too hard, okay? We'll just do something less physical today, that's all."

Ruby nodded. I was pretty sure he would have agreed if I'd just told him I wanted him to hit the cross-trainer for four hours straight. This kid was tough and he held his cards close to his chest. I just didn't want him to think what we were doing here, with his training and schoolwork, was too hard, and a life running drugs was easier.

I spent a few hours at work then headed for my appointment with Tamara. I told her about Oscar, and when I mentioned that he was deaf, I expected a barrage of questions and psychobabble about me needing to rescue and fix everything, but she never did. She just smiled. I told her we'd found some accommodation for Claude and Ruby, and how I hoped it would be a permanent thing.

It was a fairly pleasant session with Tamara, which was a nice change. I didn't feel like I was being crucified for every little decision, and it was actually productive. I wanted to tell her I thought maybe I was ready to cut back on our sessions to once a week, but it was something I wanted to talk to Kira about first.

I wanted his opinion and what he felt in his heart. *I* felt like I was ready, but maybe those around me thought differently. I didn't want to go making decisions that affected us without his input. That was a mistake I'd never make again.

I cabbed it back to the FC in time for my afternoon sessions with the kids. It was a good turnout—twelve kids in all Kira got there when we were about half way through, and he quickly stepped in to help me teach the kids. We were almost done when a familiar but unexpected face came in.

Father Michael.

He scanned the open-floor area of the gym, and when he spotted me and the kids in the far corner, he smiled. He stood against the wall near my office door and watched us go through movements and exercises with the kids. When we wrapped the lesson up, he came straight over and shook my hand. "Sorry I didn't get back to you sooner. I only arrived back today and got your message."

"Everything okay?" I asked.

"Oh sure," he said. "I often head over to Saint Xavier's and help out. We all do our part."

"We do," I agreed.

"You're running a good little class here," he said. "The kids seem to love it."

"They do," I said. "I'm proud of these kids. It's not easy for some, but they still keep turning up."

Kira put some floor mats up against the wall. "Kira, I'd like you to meet Father Michael. He's the priest I told you about at the church down the road."

Kira smiled and shook his hand. "Nice to meet you."

"Father Michael, this is Kira. He's my boyf—" I stopped short and corrected myself. "He's my fiancé."

The priest was surprised, but then he smiled. "Nice to meet you too."

Kira shot me a quick glance, probably for admitting we were gay to a priest. "Matt's told me that you offered to help with advice."

Father Michael smiled. "Yes, but looking at the good work he does here, I doubt there's much he could learn from me."

"Well, I dunno about that," I said. "I'm just giving these kids something to look forward to and hopefully teaching them a few things as well."

Father Michael rocked back and forth on his toes and looked around the gym. He seemed uncomfortable.

"Look," I said. "I hope I've not offended you, but I won't lie. And I won't deny who I am or what Kira means to me, so—"

Father Michael smiled and put his hand on my arm. "I'm certainly not offended. God's house has many rooms, my friend. We're all welcome."

His response surprised me. I'd expected to be on the defensive. "Oh."

He laughed. "No, I was just looking around. This really

is a great facility you have here. And all these kids," he said, nodding to the remaining few, "you teach them?"

"Yep. Fitness and health. I run through some self-defense, a bit of boxing, but it's mostly for fitness. I also teach about drug awareness. I've had clinic nurses and health professionals come in and talk to them and show them pictures of what drugs do to their bodies. I've got my first lot of kids lined up with the local community college and have four of them getting their high school diplomas. We've combined school and MMA classes, so the next step will be, when they're old enough, scholarships for college."

Just then, Ruby and Claude came over. "Here's my star. Rueben here is gonna blitz them in the classroom and in the cage. You'll be on the UFC list soon, won't ya, Ruby."

The kid gave me a half smile, and Claude looked up to her big brother with pure admiration. "We're headin' off," Ruby said. "Gina's got a curfew, apparently." He rolled his eyes.

"Need a lift?" Kira asked.

"Nah. We're good. See ya's tomorrow."

Claude turned her big brown eyes to me. "Can you bring Oscar? Please. I can walk him and look after him and nothing will happen to him, I promise."

I grinned at her. "I'll see."

So she turned to Kira. "Please, can he bring him?"

Kira laughed and put up his hands, palms forward. "Don't bring me into this."

Ruby pulled his sister out of the door, and giving us a nod, they disappeared into the LA sunshine.

When I looked back at Father Michael, he was smiling. "Wow," he said. "When you said you were running classes for kids, I didn't realize it was so extensive. You should be proud of what you're doing here."

"Yes, he should be," Kira added. "Though Matt's not the type to take compliments very well."

"Matt," Father Michael said. He looked around the gym one more time and he sighed. "I'm going to make some phone calls. I have some contacts around town that might be interested in what you're doing here."

"Contacts?" I said. I couldn't hide my surprise. "Sounds a bit like *The Godfather*. I mean, don't get me wrong..." Kira gawped at me. I don't know whether he was horrified or shocked. Possibly both.

Father Michael seemed amused. "Close. But I don't threaten to have people's brains on the dotted line."

"No, of course not," I said quickly. "I didn't mean it like that."

Michael laughed. "I find the suggestion of eternity in purgatory much more effective."

Kira burst out laughing. "Nice."

Father Michael smiled, but then he said, "In all seriousness, I do have some people in certain corporate circles who can help you. They quite often look for a good cause to help out financially. Especially around tax time," he said with a smirk. "Leave it with me, and I'll see what I can do." With that, he said goodbye and went on his way.

I was a little stunned. "Can you believe that?" I asked Kira.

He smiled warmly and nodded toward the front doors. "Come on, we need to go. We need to see if our house has been trashed by a dog."

"Oh."

"And," he added, "you're on poo and piss patrol. If he's crapped in the house, you're cleaning it up."

"How is that fair?" I asked as we walked out.

"I never said it was fair," he stated. "I just said it was what was gonna happen."

I pushed his shoulder, making him laugh. "He was your idea!"

"He better not have chewed up the new sofa."

"He wouldn't do that," I said. "He's a good dog. Anyway, you bought him every chew toy known to man."

"Yes, but the new sofa might be the biggest leather chew toy he's ever seen!"

I laughed and opened the passenger door of the car. "Just get in and drive."

Kira kept looking at me as he drove, and a few blocks from home, it got the better of me. "What?"

"It's just good to see you... happy."

"I am happy."

"It's different though. Something else," he said. He shook his head and seemed to think for a moment. "Content. I think that's a better word."

I reached over the console and put my hand on his thigh. "That's because I am. Content, that is."

"These last few days," he said. "It's the happiest I've seen you in a long while."

"I was only saying to Arizona that life at the moment is pretty damn good," I admitted.

Kira pulled into the drive. "I'm really glad to hear you say that, babe," he said. He smiled warmly and tilted his head, and just when I thought he was about to say something sweet, he said, "Because you're on poo and piss patrol, remember?" He laughed and got out of the car.

When we walked inside, we found Oscar sprawled out on his bed, pretty much right where we'd left him. "Did he move at all today?" Kira asked.

I snorted out a laugh, and whether or not he could sense us or smell us, he started awake. "Hey, boy," I said soothingly, although it was of little use. He couldn't hear, but I spoke to him anyway while I petted him. "Did you have a good day?"

"Why are you talking to him like he's a baby?"

I looked from Oscar to Kira. "A baby?"

"Yeah, you spoke in a baby voice," he said, grinning beautifully.

I looked back to Oscar and touched my nose to his while giving him a good pat. "Don't you listen to him. He's the bad dadda, I'm the good dadda."

Kira laughed. "Well, the *good dadda* better go check the smell coming from the laundry."

I did check the laundry and cleaned up the mess on the newspaper I'd put down. It wasn't too bad. The fact he was even a little housetrained told us he'd once had an owner.

How he'd ended up unlicensed and unwanted in a rescue center was anybody's guess. How he'd ended up with us was our gain.

After I was done cleaning up, I found Kira watching over him in the backyard. "He's peed the Mississippi," Kira said. "Poor guy must have been holding it in all day."

"Not all day," I said. "I had poo and pee to clean up."

"We'll have to install a doggie-door," he said. "We can get one this weekend."

Oscar was sniffing around the yard, looking rather pleased with himself. "How about we leave him out here while we get dinner ready. Then we can take him for a run, come back, eat, and have a quiet night in."

"Sounds good," he said. "Any elaboration on quiet?" he asked suggestively.

"Actually, I want to snuggle up to you in front of the TV and watch some crap movie until you take me to bed."

Kira smiled warmly. "Sounds perfect."

"That's because I suggested it."

He laughed, and it was a sound I would never tire of hearing. He kissed the side of my head and walked inside. I followed him in, and we spent the night just as I'd suggested.

After we went for a run, had showers, and dinner, Kira sprawled on the sofa. I made myself the little spoon, wiggling into his side until we both fit lying on our sides facing the TV.

It wasn't long before Oscar wandered over and stuck his nose in my face. "I think he likes me the best," I said.

Kira dug his free hand in my ribs, then reached over and petted Oscar on the forehead. "He's a good dog."

"Of course he is. He's ours."

Kira kissed the back of my head, and Oscar sat in front of us, and rested his head on my arm so he could get pats from both of us. When it got late, Kira took Oscar outside for one last pee before he put him to bed. Then he took me to our bed.

It was the perfect night.

Except for the TV show Kira had made me watch. It was crap.

***

THE NEXT MORNING, Arizona and I were having an early warm-up session skipping rope, when Claude and Ruby came in. Claude was clearly upset. I threw my rope to the wall and met them at my office door. "Claude, I can't bring Oscar here," I said, thinking that was the reason she was sad.

"S'okay," she said softly.

Ruby gave half a shrug and walked off toward Arizona, presumably to start his day of training.

"You okay, Claude?" I asked.

"Some kids took my bag," she said. Her bottom lip started to tremble. It was her one worldly possession. "It was the bag you gave me. With my shirt in it too. The shirt you gave me, Matt, and the bag. You gave 'em to me, and I'm sorry. I didn't mean it."

"Hey, hey. It's okay," I said. "Don't be sad. We can get you another one."

"I don't want another one. I want that one. You gave it to me. It was special."

"Oh, squirt," I said. I gave her a hug, which only seemed to make the tears come harder. "We'll get you another one. You can pick it. And I need to get a present for Arizona's new baby too. You wanna help me?"

She wiped her tears but thankfully was distracted enough to nod.

"Then we can go pick up Oscar. Okay?"

I got a watery smile and a sniffle. "I'm not going back to Gina's. I know it was real nice of you an' all, but they took my bag and I don't wanna go back."

"Claude..."

She shook her head defiantly. "It's not safe there, Matt. I don't feel safe there."

"But you do when you sleep in an alleyway or in an undercover parking lot?" I asked. "Claude, they're not safe."

"But at least we don't get our stuff stolen. Those bigger kids picked on me and they took it. I didn't tell Ruby because he'd fight 'em, and he'd get into trouble and I don't want him in no trouble."

"They picked on you?"

She nodded. "They stood all around me and took my bag."

"I can go see Gina and get it back."

She shook her head and her eyes welled with fresh tears. "Please don't make me go back."

I pulled her against my side again and patted down her unruly curls. "It's okay, squirt." I wondered when the last time this kid was hugged or when she had some human contact that was not her brother. The one thing I'd learned from depression and isolation was that human contact, human touch, could heal a wounded soul. "Do you need a hug?"

Her eyes widened, and she blinked a few times, but then her lip trembled again. I leaned down so I was closer to her height and pulled her in for a big hug. I think I shocked her at first, but she soon relaxed.

"I'm sorry I lost your bag."

I pulled back and kept my hands on her shoulders. "Don't you apologize. It's not your fault, okay?"

She nodded eventually but was still sad.

"Come on, we have a lot to do today," I said, trying to brighten her mood.

Claude was still quiet as we got into the car, and after we'd driven a few blocks of silence, she said, "How come you're driving?"

"I drive sometimes," I reminded her.

"You not been dizzy lately?"

"I haven't, no." I thought about how long it had been. "It's been a while."

"Is you cured?"

I smiled at her. "Nah. Just something that comes and goes as it pleases."

"What makes it happen?"

"Sometimes if I turn around too quickly, sometimes if I'm stressed or upset, or sometimes when I do nothing at all."

"So, pretty much any time."

"Pretty much."

"But you been good lately?"

"I have. Everything's been pretty good lately," I said.

Claude gave me a small smile and nodded, and I realized how hard it must have been for her to hear that my life was perfect when hers was... really not.

"So," I said, changing the subject. "Shopping first, then we go and collect Oscar. How does that sound?"

"Good," she said, smiling a little more genuinely this time.

"Excellent. Because I want to buy a present for Arizona and Lashona's baby, and I don't know where to start. So you're in charge of that, okay?"

Now she grinned. "Cool."

So that's what we did. Claude picked out a teddy bear for the baby, and I threw in some tiny onesies that were marked for a newborn. The sales lady suggested a diaper bag to put them in, and so I bought that too. We checked out backpacks for Claude, but she screwed her nose up at all of them. I did manage to get her to pick out some new pajamas. I told her the old T-shirt I gave her probably wasn't too suitable, so begrudgingly, she chose some new ones. They were a pink and flowery shirt-and-shorts set and very girly.

The kind of PJs a little girl should have.

When we got back to my house, Claude went straight for Oscar. I don't know which of them was more excited. As Claude played with the dog out in the yard, I looked through the closet in the spare room when my cell phone rang. It was Yumi.

"Matty, I was thinking about your new dog."

"Um, why?"

"Well, he be at home all by himself."

"He's fine," I started to say.

"No, he not," she said, cutting me off. "He could be scared."

"Yumi, I'm at the house right now. He's just fine. We took him for a run this morning—"

"What you home for? You not at work?"

"I have to go back soon," I said. I found what I was after in the closet and threw it on the bed, then shoved everything back in and shut the door. "I have to finish at six and then pick up Kira."

"I'm on my way," she said, then I was listening to a dial tone.

I sighed and slid my phone into my pocket. I didn't have to wonder where Kira got his stubbornness from. Yumi was all of five foot nothing and an absolute force to be reckoned with. I adored her.

I picked up the bag off the bed and walked out into the backyard. I shook the old backpack out, giving it a good shake. "Here, Claude, what about this one?"

I held up Kira's old gym bag. It was an old Nike one, plain black with a small logo on the front and a tricky zipper. "The zipper doesn't work very well," I said. "But you can have it."

Her whole face lit up, and I knew we'd found the right backpack. "For real?"

"For real. It used to be Kira's, but he has a new one now. This was just a spare. It's all yours."

"Will he mind?"

"Not at all."

Claude raced over and took the bag. "It's cool, and kind

of like the other one I used to have. Like your old one, the one you gave me."

"Well, now you got a new one. And listen, Claude, sometimes things get taken. It sucks and yeah, it's not fair, but it happens. Don't worry about the bag or the kids that took it. Forget about 'em. They're not worth getting upset over."

Claude shrugged, still looking over the bag. "It don't matter none. I ain't goin' back to that place. It was real nice of you trying to help us out. Don't think we don't appreciate it, 'cause we do, it's just that place weren't for us."

Oscar lay down on his stomach in the shade and scratched his belly on the grass. He looked very pleased with himself. Claude laughed. "What's he doin'?"

"He's scratching his tummy on the grass. How about you go do it for him? And on his chest and neck. He likes it."

"Matty?" Yumi's voice called out from the side of the house. "You out there?"

"Yes, Yumi, come through. The gate's not locked."

"I knocked and you didn't answer," she said as she walked through, "then I heard laughing." She stopped when she saw Claude. "Oh. Hi, Claude. I think Oscar likes you."

Claude waved. "Hi."

"She had a bad morning," I signed to Yumi, so Claude wouldn't hear me talking about her. "So I brought her with me. She loves the dog."

Yumi smiled and patted my arm. "You such a good boy."

"Where's Sal?" I asked.

"Oh, he's gone to club with the boys." She shook her head and threw up her hands. "At least he leave me alone."

I laughed. "Oh, you love it when he annoys you."

She scowled at me, then she rolled her eyes and sighed. "All right. But don't tell him I said that."

"Wouldn't dare."

"I thought I would take Oscar. Just when you both at work, so he not lonely and make a mess in your house."

"Yumi, you don't have to do that."

"I want to. Plus, he be like my only grandchild. I take what I can get."

Oh.

I pulled her into my side. "Yumi..."

"That's not a bad thing, Matty," she said, looking up at me. "I resign for a long time to no grandkids. And that's okay. You know Gloria from bridge club? She has to buy her grandkids iPads for birthdays. Can you imagine?" She shook her head again. "Oscar not cost me that much."

That made me laugh. "No. I'm sure a chew toy and a box of treats will be just fine."

"I can take Claude too," Yumi said.

Claude, who had been playing with Oscar, heard and turned to face us. I looked at Yumi. "You don't have to do that."

"If I take Oscar to the park, Claude can come, yes?" She looked at me, then at Claude. "We can take care of him for an hour or two together, yes?"

Claude looked to me, not sure what to say. "You can go to the park with Yumi and Oscar if you want, squirt," I told her. "Yumi can drop you back to the FC later, or I can come get you. It's no big deal. I have to pick Kira up anyway, then go to Yumi's to pick up Oscar."

Yumi nodded, as though it was already a done deal. "We have lunch at the park."

"And ice cream," I said, making Claude almost smile.

"Ice cream?" Yumi asked.

"Yep," I said. "Claude loves it, and Kira tells her she shouldn't have it."

"Kira had some ice cream last time," Claude yelled across the yard.

"Don't listen to him. We can eat as much ice cream as we want," Yumi said. "Claude, go grab Oscar's leash and what he needs. Matty need to go back to work."

Claude raced inside with Oscar following right behind her, and I smiled at Yumi. "Thank you."

"You don't need to thank me, Matty," she said with a smile. A motherly smile. "It's what we do."

Claude raced back out to where we were, still in the backyard, holding the backpack. "I got his leash and the bone thing he was chewin' on his bed."

"Don't let him off his leash in the park. He can't hear you if you call him, so keep hold of the leash all the time," I said to Claude.

She nodded diligently. "I will. Promise."

I gave Yumi a shrug. "There's a few things to remember with a deaf dog."

Yumi raised one eyebrow at me. "I know, I know. You have a deaf dog. I have a Sal."

I burst out laughing and gave her a hug. "You're the best."

After grabbing a few other things, like an old plastic lunch container, a bottle of water, and his harness—and enduring a lecture from Yumi that Oscar '*Is just a dog and doesn't need the entire contents of Pets-R-Us despite what Kira thinks*'—they were on their way.

I had my appointment with Tamara, and again, I considered mentioning cutting back on my appointments, but didn't want to ruin the mood. It was a productive meeting—I told her all about Oscar and how the plans for the fundraising day were all going well, and how the mood in the club was one of excitement. We were counting down the days now, and there was a buzz amongst the boys.

When our time was up, Tamara bid me farewell, and I pretty much smiled all the way back to work.

I spent a few hours with Boss making sure everything was on track for the fundraising day. He'd had some phone calls from some people citing me as a point of contract, referred by the good Father Michael of St Andrews. We scored some free merchandise from one company, and apparently I was doing an interview in the *LA Times*.

"He said he had connections," I said with a laugh.

"Jesus," Boss mumbled.

"Yep. Him too."

Boss glared at me for the bad joke. "Maybe if he's that well connected, he can organize good weather for us in two weeks."

"Weather forecasts look good," I told him. "I've been watching them. All blue skies and sunshine."

Boss exhaled loudly and leaned back in his chair. He looked stressed.

"Boss, this will work. There's clothes stalls, arts and crafts, food stalls, cotton candy, fair rides for the little kids, we've got demos, and practice sessions. This is going to be massive. It'll be good for the club, good for the local businesses, and good for the community."

Boss ran his stubby fingers through his gray hair. "You right with the interview? Figure you're better with that shit than me."

"I've done dozens of interviews," I told him. And that gave me an idea. "When I was a cop, we did interviews all the time. It was always the same reporters and photographers. Maybe I can give some of them a call and see if we can do a promo interview on TV. Even as a follow-up to my work here, since I left the force. Any publicity is good publicity, right?"

"Not always, no," Boss grumbled back at me. "I seem to recall your face in the papers getting hauled out of a cop bar for fighting. That wasn't great publicity."

I smiled ruefully. "Actually, that was a show for Tressler. I needed him to see that I was serious about fighting, and being thrown out by old partners was the perfect way to do that."

His eyes hardened. "It was an act?"

"Well, it started out as one," I admitted. "It was supposed to be harmless, but I lost my shit and wanted to kill someone."

Boss sighed. "And that's the part they caught on tape."

"There's always someone with a phone these days. Everything and anything can end up online or on the news, and it usually does. It was a perfect way to be seen by Tressler, the man I came here undercover to take down." I sighed. "Sorry. I hate that I lied to you and everyone here. You know I'm sorry, right?"

Boss nodded. "Yeah, you only said it about a thousand times. I know you mean it."

I stood up. "I'll go make some phone calls and see if I can line up another interview before the kids come in for class."

I left a message on Berkman's phone for him to call me back and got organized for class. Then I called Yumi, who grumbled at me for checking up on her. "I need to let Ruby know when his sister will be back, that's all," I told her. "I know you're capable and wonderful and an exceptional cook."

Yumi giggled into the phone. "That's better." Then she said, "I can drop her off on my way. In an hour or two?"

I looked at my watch. "That'd be perfect."

I clicked off the call. I knew Ruby would freak out when I told him his sister was with someone he didn't know, so at least I had a time to tell him she'd be back.

Only he didn't come back in.

I checked with Arizona—Ruby had left at the end of his session, nothing out of the ordinary, Arizona said. "Just said he'd be back later."

I'd finished my class with the usual kids that turned up. Yumi dropped Claude off, and the little girl told me excitedly about everything she had done with Yumi and Oscar. She'd obviously had a great time. Yumi was grinning from ear to ear, gave Claude a hug, and told her she'd love to take her again.

Not long after that, Ruby walked in. I only saw him from across the gym, but I could tell by the way Claude was using her hands to describe whatever it was she telling him, she was recalling the details of her day.

It wasn't until I finished packing up the equipment and tidied the mats along the back wall, that I walked over to where they were. What I saw made my stomach drop.

Ruby's eyes were glassy, and his pupils were dilated.

My blood ran cold and my heart stuttered in my chest at the realization of what I was seeing. I felt almost physically ill.

Ruby was high.

CHAPTER FOURTEEN

"MATT?" Boss called out from the door to his office. "Phone."

Fuck.

I knew the call had to be important for Boss to come out and get me, and as much as I wanted to talk to Ruby, I had to choose.

"Elliot!" Boss yelled, this time.

Fuck.

"Ruby you don't go anywhere, you hear me?" I barked at him as I left to take the call.

It was another one of Father Michael's connections, who just happened to be a regional manager of a major sports drink company, and this time they wanted to meet with us to discuss a financial donation or sponsorship options. We arranged a time during the week, I thanked them again and again, and explained the details to Boss once I'd hung up the call.

He shook his head in disbelief. "Just what exactly does that mean?"

"We won't know what they're after until we meet with them."

"What do we tell them?" Boss cried. "Jesus. I dunno what to say to 'em."

"We see what cards they put on the table, Boss," I said. "If they want to give us a cash donation, we take it and say thank you. If they want to give us cash for sponsorship, maybe we could suggest a junior's tournament round with other clubs with them as the major sponsors."

Boss blinked. "How do you know all this shit?'

I walked over to him and put my hands on his shoulders. "Boss, do me a favor. You need to relax. Stop stressing, please. You're gonna have a heart attack or a stroke, and quite frankly, I don't have time right now to visit you in hospital."

He glared at me and I laughed. "Boss, we're gonna be fine. I promise. This meeting for sponsorship is huge. Like really huge. So do me a favor and smile. Please."

He grimaced what I think was supposed to be a smile.

"Okay, don't do that. You'll scare small children." Then I remembered Ruby. "That reminds me," I said, walking toward the door. "I need to go talk to Ruby. Remember what I said, Boss. You can't have a heart attack," I said as I walked out the door. "This place needs you."

I went back out onto the main floor area of the gym, and Ruby and Claude were gone.

Fuck.

I went out the front of the FC to look for them, but they were nowhere in sight. I walked the blocks on either side, looking for them in the shadows, and when I was in the car, I drove a few blocks looking for them. But they were gone.

I was a bit late picking Kira up, and when I got there, he

was waiting out front. He climbed in and threw his bag in the back. "Hey. You're a bit late. Everything okay?"

I pulled the car back into traffic. "Today has been... strange."

"Strange?"

"Good and bad."

Kira looked concerned. "What happened?"

"Well, we scored funding and sponsorship for the club. Well," I amended, "it's not signed off on yet, but they're interested and we have to meet with them. It's promising. I don't even know what they're offering yet, but any way we look at it, it's great."

"Oh, Matt, that's fantastic!" Kira said. "But the bad news?"

"Ruby came back into the club this afternoon, just after class."

"And?"

"And he was high."

Kira blinked. Then he blinked again. "What?"

I nodded. "His eyes gave him away."

"Oh, man."

"I had to take a call about that sponsorship, and when I came back out, they were gone. I looked for them, but they were nowhere to be found."

He slid his hand on my knee. "Babe, I'm sorry."

"I'm really mad at him," I told him honestly. "Like seriously pissed. But I know going off on him is the last thing he needs." I sighed. "I'll talk to him tomorrow and see what he has to say."

Kira leaned back into the passenger seat and exhaled loudly. "Man, after everything you've done for him."

I covered his hand with mine and gave it a squeeze. "I know. And Arizona. He'll be devastated."

Kira shook his head. "Are you sure he was high?"

As soon as he'd said it, he realized. Of course I knew. I was a narcotics detective. I knew the signs. He sighed again. "Goddammit."

"I know."

"What about Claude?" Kira asked. His concern was clear in his eyes. "Will she be all right with him tonight?"

"I don't know," I answered honestly. "Ruby's very protective of her and he usually looks after her better than anything, but he's not himself tonight."

"I don't like it, Matt."

"Neither do I, babe."

Kira looked at the passing streets. "Why are we going to Mom and Dad's?"

"They have Oscar."

Kira raised one eyebrow at me. "They what?"

I snorted. "Your mom wouldn't take no for an answer. She took him and Claude to the park for a few hours. Said she can look after him on days we're both at work. Also said she would consider it her grandmotherly duties because Oscar is like her grandson now. Which is fine, by the way. She'll take what she can get and because she won't have to buy him an iPad."

Kira stared at me and blinked slowly.

I laughed. "I told you today was strange."

Kira shook his head. "My mother is strange."

I snorted out a laugh. "Your mom is the best mom. Ever."

We pulled up out front of his parents' house then walked up to the front door. "Don't tell her that. You're already her favorite."

I was laughing as we walked inside, and as we took off

our shoes, Yumi came into the foyer. "You boys stay for dinner," she said, an order not an invitation.

I pulled Yumi against me into a big hug. "I was just saying to Kira that you were the best ever. And he said that's why I'm your favorite."

Yumi grinned up at me and swatted my chest. "I not have favorites."

Kira leaned down and kissed her cheek. "That's not what you tell me."

Yumi pushed her son's arm. "Oh stop it."

"Where's Oscar?" I asked, walking into the kitchen. "Has he been good?"

"He's such a good boy," she said, before walking to the stove, where she started stirring something in a pot. "We come home from the park, and he sleep all afternoon. Now he in the garden with Sal. Deaf man, deaf dog." She rolled her eyes. "I had to come inside."

Kira bit the inside of his lip, but I could tell he was trying hard not to smile. "I better go out and see which one's more confused."

Yumi looked at me and smiled warmly. Then a thought must have struck her. "Oh!" she cried, then scurried out of the room and into the dining room. "Come in here, Matty, I show you something."

I followed her dutifully. Across her dining table was an array of color selections, material swatches, wedding magazines, pictures of floral arrangements, and wedding cakes.

I didn't know whether to laugh or cry.

Yumi rifled through some papers, looking for something in particular. She held up a notepad victoriously. "Here!" she said. "I need to ask you."

Still bewildered at the sight before me, all I could do was nod. Or shake my head. I possibly did both. At the same time. I needed backup, possibly a SWAT. I needed Kira. "Um…"

"I need seating arrangements," Yumi said, flipping through pages of her notepad.

"Um, Yumi, I…"

She still flipped through pages, and I waited until she'd found the page she was searching for and looked at me.

I had to swallow so I could speak. "I don't have any."

She narrowed her eyes. "Any what?"

"Any family."

Yumi's face fell. "Matt…"

"I don't have any aunts or uncles or grandparents. There are no brothers or sisters, no cousins," I said quietly. "I don't have any family."

"You have the police boys and the gym boys," Yumi said with a nod. "They're your family."

"You're my family," I said, not meaning to say those words out loud.

Yumi gave a teary smile and hugged me. "You are family, Matty." She squeezed me. "You're one of my boys. We love you like a son. You no need to get married to be in this family."

I choked up at her words. "I want to," I squeaked. "I want to marry him. So much."

Yumi pulled back from me, smiling. "Oh!" she cried, remembering something else. "You need to sign this." And again, she started to rummage through papers on the table.

Kira spoke from the door, "Do I even want to know what's going on in here?"

I looked pointedly at the table. "Your mom's planning the wedding," I said slowly. I picked up the material swatches, an array of blues and silvers, and held them up for Kira to see. "We were just talking about seating arrangements, and I was just saying I don't have any family so I guess it didn't matter."

Kira walked over to me, smiling. He took my face in both hands and kissed me soundly. "Yes, you do. You have family."

"I already told him," Yumi said, not looking up from her papers, still rummaging for something in particular. "Here it is!" she declared and held up a single piece of paper. "You both need to sign this."

Kira slid his arm around my shoulder and kissed the side of my head. "What is it, Mom?" he asked, not sounding overly enthused. He seemed transfixed by the mountain of wedding paraphernalia on the table.

"It's your marriage license," she said. "You need to sign it."

"At a registrar office, Mom, not here."

"Is practice," she said, like it made sense. "I downloaded it."

"Oh, dear Lord," Kira mumbled, loud enough for even me to hear it.

"It's okay," I said, taking the piece of paper. "I'll sign it." I mean, it was a worthless document without being officiated anyway. I kissed Kira on the cheek and picked up a pen from Yumi's things on the table. Without hesitating, I signed the license.

When I was done, I glanced at Kira. He looked, well, he looked shocked. "It's just practice, right?" I asked. "Even if it wasn't, even if this was real, right here, right now, I'd still sign it."

Yumi gushed. "Oh, you boys will make me cry," she said, fanning her face.

Kira smiled, almost shyly, and I handed him the pen. "Your turn."

He took the pen, looked me squarely in the eye as he slowly leaned right across me and signed his name. Then he kissed me softly. "Piece of cake."

I laughed and pecked his lips, and Sal cleared his throat from the door. He pointed at the table and signed, "Are you cleaning up the mess?"

"Oh, shush," Yumi said, giving Sal the stink eye. "Oh, shoot," she cried, darting back to the kitchen. "Dinner."

Sal nodded toward Yumi's piles of papers and magazines and signed, "I haven't been able to eat at the dining table for weeks."

"We eat dinner tonight in the kitchen," Yumi called out.

"Okay," Kira called out. Then signed so his dad would know, "Mom said we're eating in the kitchen."

"See?" he said. "You two get married soon. Please. Tomorrow? Please? Put me out of my misery."

Kira laughed and clapped his dad on the shoulder. "Nice, Dad."

"Boys!" Yumi called out. "Dinner!"

I loved Yumi's cooking. It didn't matter what it was. Tonight's dinner was a Spanish chorizo stew-type dish, with rice and beans, and it was so good. Yumi told us about her day at the park with Claude and Oscar. I told them about the phone calls I took about sponsorship. I deliberately omitted the details about Ruby, not wanting them to worry, and after a night of great food, laughs, and good conversation, we took Oscar and made our way home.

Kira was driving, and after we'd driven a few blocks, I said, "Your parents are awesome."

"They are," he said quietly. And then he said... nothing.

"Kira? What's up?"

He looked a little stuck for words, then after a moment, he blurted, "I think tonight I might like to have sex."

I snorted out a laugh. "Oookay."

"I mean, I think I want to have... sex... without a condom... tonight. With you. Of course. I mean, you know what I mean."

I stared at the side of his face for a long while. When he looked at me, he was clearly nervous.

"Uh, Kira? I'm very okay with that."

He smiled. "I've been thinking about it. A lot. And our test results are all good, and I want to spend my life with you, and I don't know what I was scared of. But seeing you tonight, signing that marriage license without an ounce of doubt, it made me realize I don't want to wait."

"I don't want to wait either," I told him. The mere thought of it and I had to palm my cock, making Kira laugh.

Then, ruining the moment, my cell phone rang. The phone number of the FC scrolled across my screen. "Hello?"

"Matt? It's Jamaal."

"Hey, man. Wassup?"

"Uh, Claude's here. She said that you said if she ever needed you, she should come here and get one of us to call you. Is that okay?"

"Yes, of course. Is she still there? Is she okay?"

"Think she's all right. I asked her where Ruby was. She just said she wanted me to call you."

Goddammit. "We're on our way."

CLAUDE WAS UPSET. She was obviously relieved when we got there but a little embarrassed, I think, that she'd had to ask for us to come get her. She was quiet and didn't say much even when we asked her questions—just that Ruby had had to go somewhere and she'd got scared.

Even when we got home, she kind of clung to Oscar, always touching his neck, his ears, his collar. She ate less than half a sandwich for dinner and just wanted to go to bed. I tucked her in, and Oscar laid himself down on the floor at the side of her bed.

I stood, leaning against the doorway for ten minutes, and watched her toss and turn. Yes, I was mad at Ruby, but I was heartbroken for this little girl. Kira eventually took my hand and led me to the kitchen. He didn't say a word, just leaned me against the kitchen cupboards and wrapped his arms around me.

After the longest, most-needed hug, he pulled away, only to cup my face in his hands and kiss my forehead, the tip of my nose, and my lips. "She'll be okay," he said softly. "She's safe here."

I nodded and sighed deeply. "I think I'm going to have to report her to child services," I whispered, the words sounded strained and horrible. "I probably should have in the very beginning. I *know* I should have. But I wanted to trust them. But now this..." I shook my head. "Kira, she can't survive out there on her own. What if some sicko found her? I mean, Jesus. You don't want to know what I've seen happen to kids on the streets, Kira. There is shit that haunts me still."

Kira frowned. "No, I don't want to know."

"I know I have to call them, but she'll never forgive me for handing her in to the authorities."

Kira held my hands between us, twisting our fingers together. "Talk to Ruby tomorrow. Don't make any decisions tonight." He sighed. "I love you, Matt. I really do," Kira said seriously.

"I love you, too," I said. "And thank you." I played with his fingers. It had been a pretty shit day, but something else had been bothering me. "Kira, babe, can I ask you something?"

"Of course."

"Why do you tell me you love me like that? Like you think I wake up every day and have forgotten? Because I won't ever—forget that is. I mean, I love that you tell me, and I tell you every day too, but you say it so... I don't know... seriously? I don't think that's the right word..."

Kira sighed. He looked to the floor between us, and for a long moment, I thought he wasn't going to answer. "Because I can't remember if I told you enough, before... Before you went undercover. I mean, I know I did, but maybe it wasn't enough..."

I took his face in his hands. "Look at me," I said. "Everything you did was perfect. Everything. It was me that fucked it up, not you. You did everything right. It was me, *me*, who took it all for granted, who couldn't deal with the guilt and what you went through. So don't think you did anything wrong, okay?"

He nodded, and I pulled him against me. He tightened his arms around me. "Thank you."

"You don't have to thank me," I whispered.

Kira sighed and stood up straight. "Come on, bedtime. This day just needs to end," he said. He walked to the door and turned off the kitchen light, held out his hand and waited for me to take it.

When we climbed into bed, Kira wrapped his arm around me until his breathing evened out and he settled in to sleep. There was no attempt at sex, no mention of our earlier conversation about ditching condoms. My heart and head just weren't up for it.

Sleep didn't come easily. I stayed awake listening for sounds from Claude, and because my hearing was only half what it used to be, I got up a few times just to check on her.

———

I WAS UP FIRST. I let Oscar out to go pee and Claude came out not long after. "New PJs look good, Claude," I said, trying to be cheerful, when the truth was I was tired as hell and felt like crap.

I sat Claude at the table with a bowl of cereal then went in and climbed over Kira's still-sleeping body. I kissed his shoulder and rubbed his ass. "Time to get up, sleepyhead. And put some pants on. Claude's here, remember?"

He chuckled into the pillow, and I swatted his ass before I walked back out.

Kira went for a run while I watched Claude play with Oscar, then later, on his way to work,

Kira dropped me and Claude off at the FC. Ruby wasn't there waiting for her, and as the morning went on—as his class with Arizona came and went—he never showed.

She watched the door, and even though we tried to keep her busy, she was distracted and miserable.

Then half way through my lesson with the kids in the afternoon, he came in. He was wearing his UFC shorts we'd given him, his hideous fluorescent green high top sneakers, and a sleeveless T-shirt I hadn't seen him wear before. New or stolen, I didn't know. His clothes didn't matter, because something else stood out to me more than anything else.

His eyes were glazed over.

He had a stupid, shit-eating smirk on his face.

And my anger went from zero to really fucking high in one heartbeat. "Cody," I called out. "Take my class for me?" I didn't wait to see if he came over, I walked toward my office door. I pointed at Ruby. "My office. Now."

I waited for him to walk in, he took his sweet time, and I got fucking angrier with every chemically-slow step he took. I followed him in and shut the door behind us. My open door policy didn't apply here.

I bit back my anger as best I could. "Where the fuck have you been?"

Ruby took a step back and his heavy-lidded eyes widened. All his reactions were slow.

"Fuck, Ruby, what did you take?"

Ruby shrugged and frowned. "Dunno."

"What did it look like?"

He shrugged again, but didn't speak.

"Who gave it to you? You know what? Never mind, I already know. I told you to stay away from them, Rueben. They will do nothing but see you dead. So you do them some favors and they give you some cash, some pills, some powder. I know you think the easy cash is the way to go, but fuck, Ruby. You've got a real start here!"

Ruby shrugged again, like he couldn't care less. "Cash is

cash, man. Need it to buy food and stuff for Claude. Can't be stayin' at that shit hole you took us to. Claude hated it." His head lolled back a little and his dilated eyes took a second to focus on me. "Just tryin' to look after her."

"Look after her?" I pointed my finger at him. "You're not fit to look after her." I was so pissed off. "Do you know she came here last night and asked Jamaal to call me because she was alone and scared? She has spent last night and today miserable and worried sick about you!"

The kid paled and I took a moment to calm down. Don't get me wrong, I was still angry. Jesus, I wanted to grab this kid by the scruff of the neck and show him what he was throwing away. But that's all he was. A kid. A kid trying to do the best he could. I thought I'd taught him, shown him there was a better life for him. He just had to work for it. "I get that you need money. I understand that. I get that you want a better life, and you think the promise of quick cash is the answer, but I'm telling you, it's not."

"What the fuck would you know?" he bit back at me. "You ain't got a fucking clue what it's been like, how hard it's been. And you don't know Darius and Tyler. They a'right, look after me. So back the fuck off, man."

"You know what, Ruby?" I spoke through clenched teeth. "I can't even talk to you right now. But I'll tell you what. Claude's coming home with me tonight. She's not going anywhere with you, and you can be as mad as fuck as you want with me, but you know damn well where you're going is no place for her."

He looked as though he might argue, but he knew damn well I was right. And no matter how pissed off he was at me, he loved Claude more.

I pointed to the door back out into the gym. "So you go out there and tell her you're busy tonight and you want her to stay with us. Don't you dare upset her, because every time she cries, it breaks my fucking heart."

Ruby opened his mouth to say something, but in the end he looked to the ground and nodded.

I exhaled loudly, and as much as I wanted to hug this kid and tell him it would be okay, I just didn't know if it would be. He'd broken club policy for drug use, not once, but twice. It was a catch–22—he was about to lose his place in the scholarship program, which would push him further into drug-running, the very thing he needed to be in the program to avoid.

"I'll be here at ten tomorrow morning," I said, not even trying to hide the anger in my tone. "You better be here, and we're going to discuss your place in the program, because right now, I'm not sure you have one."

I turned and walked to the door, but before I opened it, I turned to face him. He looked downtrodden and miserable. "Can you please take a few minutes to see her? Talk to her, ask her about her day, ask her about the dog. Just listen to her. She needs you, Ruby. Just ten minutes. Please." My voice was quieter, sorrier.

I walked out and went back to my class, and as soon as Claude saw the door was left open, she raced inside. Cody looked at me and asked, "You okay, man?"

"I'm fine," I replied automatically. Then I took a deep breath and let it out slowly.

"I can finish up these guys if you want?"

I looked at the dozen or so faces who were staring at me. "I'm okay," I said to Cody, giving a smile. "Sorry. I'm better now anyway. I just hope that kid does the right thing."

Cody patted my shoulder as he left the class to me, and I finished them with some cool-down exercises, gave them all a high five each, and dismissed them. "See you guys tomorrow," I said. "We'll be sparring and putting all these moves into action."

There was some excited chatter between them while I packed up the mats and tidied the gear. After I'd given Ruby and Claude enough time alone, I stood in the doorway to my office.

They were both there, sitting on one of the tables at the back of the room. Claude was telling him all about Oscar and the hand signals she's been teaching him. I walked in, and her chatter died away.

I smiled at her and she frowned. "Matt, is you still mad at Ruby?" she asked innocently. "He said he was sorry for leaving me last night. He said he didn't realize it would take so long."

"Nah, I'm not mad anymore," I said softly.

Claude smiled genuinely and Ruby looked at me, I guessed to see if I was telling the truth. Claude looked at her brother. "See, Ruby? I told you he wouldn't still be mad." Then she turned to me. "But Ruby knows this time it might take too long and wants me to stay at your house. Is that okay? I won't be no trouble," she said. "I can look after Oscar for you."

"That's no problem, squirt." I gave Ruby a clap on the shoulder for at least telling Claude she should come home with me. "You ready, Claude? I'll call us a cab."

"I thought Kira was pickin' you up tonight?"

"I'll call him and let him know. I just wanna go home, squirt. I'm tired," I explained. "Plus, I'm sure Oscar won't mind."

She grinned and jumped off the table. I thought mentioning the dog would convince her. She grabbed her bag, which she'd obviously been showing Ruby, and said goodbye to her brother. I pulled out my cell, called a cab, and we walked out. I reminded Ruby about being back here at ten in the morning, and without another word, we left Ruby sitting in my office.

I thought maybe some reflection time might help him realize what he was risking. If I was honest with myself, I wanted him to realize on his own. I wanted his strength of character to shine through. I knew he had it in him. I just had to believe he'd make the right decision.

CLAUDE and I just started watching the second animated movie of the night and ate a very not-nutritious dinner of popcorn and ice cream.

Kira came home to find the three of us, me, Oscar, and Claude on the sofa. He was grinning at us, but had questioning eyes, so I followed him into the kitchen.

"What's going on?" he signed. He didn't want Claude to hear.

"Ruby was high again," I signed back.

Kira's shoulders slumped. "Oh, Matt. I'm sorry," he whispered.

I told him, in sign language—probably not very well— that I'd been angry, and I had yelled at Ruby but only said stuff that he needed to hear. I told him Claude had been upset all day, and while she was happy to see Ruby, I think she could tell something was amiss with him. "I don't know what he took."

Kira frowned. "So, a bad day, huh? I guess that explains the choice in dinner?"

I laughed. "Yep. Want me to make you some popcorn? The second movie hasn't been on long. It's about some monsters at a university."

Kira laughed and kissed me. "No, I'll pass on the popcorn, thanks, but the movie sounds pretty good."

I rolled my eyes but went back out and joined Claude and Oscar on the sofa. Kira came in after he'd fixed himself something to eat, and as soon as Claude had fallen asleep, he put her to bed and told Oscar not to leave her room.

Then he took me to our room and shut the door. "Matt, I really want you," he whispered.

"Then have me," I told him.

He pushed me onto the bed and kissed me so hard it made my bones turn to sponge. He quickly undressed us both and soon had our cocks in his hand as he lay over me, kissing me, rubbing against me.

And when I was getting close to the edge, he climbed off me, only to take my cock in his mouth while he offered me his.

I sucked him like my life depended on it, and he took me into his throat. We sixty-nined, fucking each other's faces while devouring each other. I loved the taste of him, the musky smell of his, and the feel of his hard cock in my mouth.

I loved that I turned him on so much, and I loved the way he gripped my hips and swallowed around me. His hips jerked as he tried not to thrust too hard, so I took him as deep as I could, and he gave a strangled cry as he came down my throat.

My cock surged with his, and his lips quickly closed around me while he drank every drop I gave him.

I licked him clean, nuzzling my nose into his pubic hair while he licked and sucked me. He hummed and moaned, then righted himself so his face was now near mine. I kissed him, hoping he could still taste himself on my tongue.

With languid kisses, soft touches and sleepy whispers, we fell asleep.

AFTER BREAKFAST, when Kira had gone to work, I asked Claude if she could take Oscar out the back. I needed a few minutes to get my head and heart in the right place before I made some phone calls. I had to call social services and arrange a meeting at the FC—I didn't want to do it here —to hand Claude over.

I watched her in the yard with Oscar, and I felt sick to my stomach. My eyes burned with tears, but I knew I had to do this. For the sake of the little girl, for the sake of Claude, who didn't stand a chance in this world on her own.

I had my cell phone in my hand, and blinking back tears, I was about to dial when the room went all quiet, the walls slanted left and the floor went right.

Everything went black.

I OPENED my eyes to see two white and purple sparkly shoes in front of my face, and two black and tan dog paws.

It took my brain a minute to catch up. Claude and Oscar.

I was lying on the kitchen floor.

Then the room spun again and it felt like my head was rotating in all different directions and a wave of nausea hit me.

Fuck.

"Matt. You okay?"

"Yeah," I said, and foolishly tried to get up. I swallowed

down the urge to vomit and couldn't even lift my head off the floor.

"Matt, you're bleeding."

Through the swirling and complete disorientation, there was a dull ache at my temple. I wanted to touch it to see if it was bleeding, but it was pressed against the tiled floor and I couldn't lift my head.

"Matt," Claude's voice squeaked. Her tiny hand shook my shoulder. "You're scaring me."

"It's okay, squirt," I croaked.

"Did you get dizzy?"

"Yeah." I exhaled slowly, trying to stem the urge to vomit. This was one of the worst vertigo spells I'd had in a long time.

Claude's feet disappeared from in front of me and came back a short time later. "I got a pillow. For your head," she said. She put her hand under my head and tried to cram a cushion from the sofa under my head. The action made my head spin in the opposite direction and my stomach lurched. I took some short, sharp breaths so I wouldn't be sick. It wasn't something a little kid should see.

I closed my eyes, but the spinning got worse and I knew I wasn't going anywhere for a while. "My phone, Claude. I had it." I had it in my hand before I fell so it couldn't be too far away. "It's here somewhere."

I felt her fumbling around me and behind me. The phone must have hit the floor when I'd fallen. I just hoped it still worked. She handed me my phone, but when I looked at it, I couldn't seem to get my eyes to focus. I couldn't even fucking call.

"Claude. Need you to call Kira, okay?" Even though I was whispering, I knew she'd hear me just fine.

She took the phone back. "Um. I don't know how."

"See the green square with a phone in it? Press it."

"Okay."

"Down the bottom there's some pictures. What are they?" I couldn't remember. I'd never had to actually take notice of what was on the screen.

"A star and a clock and a man's head and—"

"Press the man's head. It's got people's names and numbers. Find K for Kira and press the button that says call. Can you do that for me, squirt?"

"Um," she mumbled.

I guessed she pressed a number or something, but the voice I heard wasn't Kira's. It was Yumi's. "Hello?"

Claude didn't say anything for a moment. "Um, Matt's on the floor. He can't get up."

I couldn't focus on what she was saying anymore. The next thing I knew, Claude put the phone down near my head and sat down in front of me. Oscar licked my face. "You okay, squirt?" I asked. I didn't want her to be scared or get upset, any more than she probably already was.

"I'm fine, Matt," she said. "You don't look so great."

"I'm okay," I told her. "The dizziness sometimes makes me want to be sick. I'll be okay if I just lay here a while."

Claude touched my face, then my hair, almost the way I remember my mother doing when I'd been a kid. Maybe Claude remembered her mom doing the same, when her life had been a happier place. It was strangely comforting, and it made me feel like shit.

Not five minutes ago I was ready to hand her over to the State, and here she was sitting on my kitchen floor comforting me.

"Matthew!" Yumi yelled from the front door.

I had no doubt that Yumi had driven like a bat out of

hell, but what was probably ten minutes seemed to take a life time.

"It's Yumi," I said to Claude. "Can you unlock the front door for me?"

She disappeared from my line of sight, and a few seconds later, Yumi was kneeling in front of me. Her cool hands were on my face, and she was looking closely at what I presumed was a cut on my head. "Cut's okay," she said. "Bad one, huh?"

She was referring to the bout of vertigo. "Yeah."

"Can you get up?"

"Not yet. Feel sick."

Then Sal was there, and like a father would pick up a child, he slid his arms underneath me, and keeping me as horizontal as possible, he somehow lifted me up and carried me to the sofa.

I somehow put my hand to my mouth, because the nausea was overwhelming—and like Yumi somehow knew, she knelt before me with a bowl.

I couldn't stop myself from being sick, and while Sal took Claude out into the backyard, Yumi cleaned up my mess and wiped my face with a damp washcloth

Within about half an hour I could sit up, and half an hour after that, the nausea was all but gone. I felt foolish for being so helpless and needing Kira's parents to care for me. Yumi told me not to worry, she said it was a pleasure to look after her boys.

I had to make some phone calls. The first was to the FC. I'd been supposed to meet Ruby an hour ago, but after I'd spoken to Boss and told him what had happened, he said I needn't worry—Ruby never showed. Not for a meeting with me, not for his training session with Arizona. I told Boss I would be there for the sponsorship meeting later this afternoon, but I couldn't run my classes.

I called Tamara's office next and canceled my appointment with her at lunch time. I was supposed to be there in an hour and there was just no way I could get through that.

I called Mitch next. It went straight to voicemail. "Mitch, it's me. I need you to do me a favor. Keep an eye out for Ruby... Rueben Vaughn. The kid you met at the club? He's been gone for over a day. It's not like him to leave his sister this long. Let me know if you see him. Thanks."

My last call was to Kira. I left a message, explaining what had happened and that I was fine and not to worry.

Which didn't stop him, because he called straight back, worried. I told him again not to worry, but he sighed into the phone. Yumi took my phone and spoke to him. When she handed my phone back to me, she patted my knee. "He be here at three."

Now I sighed. I hated needing a baby sitter. "I'll be fine," I told her.

"You got that important meeting at four," she reminded me. "Kira just make sure you get there with no rushing."

I nodded. "I don't know what I'd do without you. Or Kira or Sal. I'd be lost without any of you."

Yumi sat down beside me and smiled. "You remember when you first met us? Me and Sal?"

"Of course. You hadn't heard from him in a few weeks because he was..." I cleared my throat. "*Preoccupied*... with me, so you came to Kira's old apartment and I was there." Then I admitted, "I didn't think I was ready to be meeting the parents, but you were great."

She got a faraway look in her eyes and smiled. "I spend years worrying Kira would never settle down. He date a lot of guys."

I frowned. "Um, I don't really need to know that."

She shook her head. "I tell him he'll find someone and he'll know. He'll just know. That's how it happens. You find the one that is your other half and you know. Kira laughed at me for years and told me I was dreaming. Said he'd never find someone like that." She smiled knowingly at me. "But he did."

"When we meet you that first time," she continued, "we stayed for dinner and you had to go to work, remember? Catch more bad guys, you said."

"I remember."

"When you walk out the door, I look at Kira, and I knew. *He* knew. He was smiling like I've never seen," Yumi said. "You know what he say to me?"

I shook my head.

"He said 'I've found him.' Just like that. *I've found him.*"

I smiled and my chest tightened.

Yumi patted my knee. "You're his other half. Like me and Sal. That big lump drives me crazy." Her eyes widened for effect. "Cray-zee, I tell you. But when I met him, I just knew. Our family not too happy with us, but we not care. We were together from that day on. We drive each other crazy. It's what we do."

I smiled warmly at her. "Sal adores you."

"I know," she said simply, with absolute confidence. "And Kira adores you."

"I almost lost him."

Yumi shook her head. "He never lose faith in you. You lose faith in you."

"I did," I said with a nod. "But I still don't know what I did to deserve him."

Yumi shook her head. "I just told you. Where you been for this conversation?"

I snorted out a laugh. "Huh?"

"You the one that make his heart whole. He saw you and he knew. You all there is for him. It's how it is for us Takeo-Francos. Even when you was stupid and undercover, he still love you. You made him crazy like Sal makes me crazy. It's what we do."

I couldn't help but laugh. "But Kira doesn't do anything to make me mad or crazy. He's kind of perfect."

"Give him time," Yumi said with a serious nod. "He's his father's son." She patted me on the knee again. "If he wants to come home at three and check you're okay, then you let him. He do it because he cares. So you let him, and you tell him you're thankful even though it make you crazy. Because it's what we do."

I grinned at her, at her philosophy on life, love, and being married for almost thirty years. "You're pretty amazing, you know that?"

"Yeah, I do. Been trying to tell him that for years," she said, nodding out to the backyard.

"I think he knows," I told her.

"He should," she replied. "I tell him all the time."

I laughed again, and Yumi told me to go get cleaned up while she made lunch. Still not too steady on my feet, I took my time. By the time Kira came home at three, I was feeling better.

Kira inspected the small cut at my temple. When he looked into my eyes, he was clearly concerned. "Are you okay?"

"I am now."

He ran his fingers down my hairline to my jaw. "If you're not feeling up to this meeting, I'm sure they'll understand."

"I can't miss it. It's too important for the FC," I told him.

And it was.

<hr>

IT WAS JUST a lot more low-key than I'd expected. I'd arrived a bit early, not wanting to rush my head. Kira was pretty much by my side the entire time, and Father Michael came in—even Boss wore a button-down shirt. I was expecting a business meeting.

What we got was a guy in his fifties, wearing jeans and a T-shirt, an obvious sports fan, who basically chatted about MMA and football, the local kids, demographics, and the importance of education. And of course how positive advertising with kids and sport was marketing gold.

He told us the programs we were trying to implement were great, including the fundraising family fun day, but we just needed some financial backing, which was very true. I suggested the junior MMA tournament and his eyes widened. He then, of course, stipulated major product endorsement and advertising in return for sponsorship or something similar, and I told him that it sounded great, though it may not be enough to keep the doors open long-term.

He wanted us to get back to him with a proposal of how we felt the donation or sponsorship allocation would be best spent. He went around the gym floor with Boss one more time, even watched some of the kids in my class go through their routines with Cody, then he shook hands with us all and left.

And just like that, things fell into place. It would seem we'd just found key financial backing for the FC. The doors would be open for another twelve months at least, and for these guys, for me, that was everything.

It was as though life was finally back on track.

Until we walked out onto the sidewalk and ran right into Darius and James McInnes. Darius laughed, surprised, like he couldn't believe his luck, then he reached his arm behind his back and pulled out a gun.

My world went completely silent, except the blood thumping in my head. Each heartbeat was slow and pounded in my chest. It was a Glock 17, standard issue, a dime a dozen handgun, and it was pointed straight at Kira.

I moved without thinking. And while the world around me erupted, my mind shut down.

Kira.

Not again. No, no, no.

CHAPTER FIFTEEN

IT HAD TAKEN all of three seconds from start to finish, and I still wasn't sure what the hell had just happened. I'd seen Darius and James walking toward us. In that split second, in my mind, I'd been torn between wanting to punch the shit out of both of them, and beg them to know where Ruby was.

But I hadn't got the chance to do either.

After all my years of police training, when all my instincts were rewired to run toward danger instead of from it, this time was different.

Without thinking, without a conscious thought, my body had moved away from danger, to protect Kira and Claude.

A team of cops, uniformed and not, had their guns drawn, and Darius and James were pinned face-first on the sidewalk.

There was loud yelling of "Police! Police! Stay down on the ground! Stay down!" Then the next thing I knew, I'd scooped Claude up like a ragdoll and pinned her to Kira's chest. I pushed them back through the gym—from the loud chaos, into the abrupt silence of the FC. Everyone inside was turned to face us, wondering what the fuck just happened.

My heart hammered and I was frozen. Like my mind had splintered, I still wasn't exactly sure what the hell had just gone down, but I knew they were safe.

"I'm sorry," I mumbled over and over. I was pressing them against the wall inside the door, still keeping myself in between us and the threat of whatever was happening outside. "I'm sorry."

Arizona was suddenly beside us, looking from me to the swarm of police we could see through the glass doors. "What the fuck? Man, are you okay?" he asked, pulling me back, giving Kira and Claude some room. "What the hell just happened?"

Kira gently put Claude down so she stood beside us, keeping his hand on her shoulder, but he didn't take his eyes off me. "Claude, you okay?" he asked.

The little girl nodded, wide eyed and confused. "I think so," she said.

"Jesus," Kira whispered, shaking his head. He was pale and clearly shocked, but just like always, his concern was for me. "Matt, you okay?"

I finally took a deep breath and my head spun. I rubbed my forehead to try to stem the spinning, and when my fingers touched the small cut from my fall earlier today, I blinked slowly as a familiar vertigo headache set in. "I'm fine," I whispered.

Boss was there now, looking out of the front doors at the swarm of police. "Jesus, Elliott. What the hell did you do now?"

"We just walked outside, right smack in the middle of a take-down," I said.

Whether Boss had meant for it to sound accusing or not, when he took one look at me, he could see it wasn't intentional. I could feel the blood had drained from my face, and I was taking long, deliberate breaths trying to keep my head on straight.

Kira put his hand on the side of my face. "Matt?"

"Just dizzy, that's all," I said. Then I looked right into his eyes. "He had a gun, Kira," I said—I wondered if I'd said that out loud.

"We're all okay," Kira said. "No one was hurt." He was trying to placate me.

I looked at Claude, then, and she looked more scared than hurt. "You okay, Claude?" I asked her again.

She nodded again but stayed close to us, almost still in between us.

Then Kira barked out a laugh, more through relief than humor, and ran his hand through his hair. "I'm still not sure what the hell just happened."

I leaned against the wall, resting my hands on my knees. My head was spinning and thumping, and nausea burned my throat. Kira held onto my shoulder ,and Boss and Arizona were on the other side of me when the front doors opened and a uniformed officer walked in. I didn't recognize him. "Everyone in here okay?" he asked. He looked directly at me and took a few steps closer. "Sir? Are you hurt?"

I stood up straight and put up my hand. "I'm fine."

And then Mitch came in, followed closely by Tony and Kurt. Mitch was smiling, until he saw me. He rushed over and lifted my chin, turning his head to inspect the small cut on the side of my head. "What happened? You okay? You hurt?"

I shook my head a little. "I'm okay."

"Man, you have the worst timing," Kurt said. "We were just about to bust them, and then you walked out."

I exhaled slowly, and I knew Kira could tell I was still struggling. "How about we go sit down? We can all talk in here," he suggested, taking my arm and leading me toward my office. He waited for me to sit down. "Do you feel sick?" he asked.

I nodded. "A little."

Kira pulled over the wastebasket and sat it at my feet, then looked at Mitch, who looked confused, and explained, "He had a bad bout of vertigo this morning."

"Oh," he said quietly. The three of my old cop partners stood there awkwardly, not knowing what to say.

"I'm okay," I said again. I didn't want them to look at me with pity. "Just wasn't expecting that. The asshole had a gun," I said, looking at Kira then. "You and Claude..." I exhaled loudly unable to finish that sentence. "Fuck. Never again."

"Hey," he said, still crouching in front of me. "Me and Claude are just fine."

Claude, who was now standing on the other side of me, said, "I didn't see anything. I was just walkin' along then you swooped me up. I was all smooshed in between ya's. I didn't see nothin'. Just yellin' then we was back inside."

I gave her a smile. "Didn't mean to scare ya, squirt. Just didn't want you near them bad guys, that's all." Then I patted her on the arm. "Can you do me a favor, Claude? Can you go check on Boss for me? I need to talk to these guys."

She nodded and gave the policemen a wide, wary berth as she walked out.

Mitch leaned against a table. "Matt, man, you haven't lost your edge. Your reflexes! You were quicker than us!"

I leaned back in the chair, and with a deep breath, shook my head slowly, still trying to get my head around what had just happened. "Was it coincidence that went down at the front door of this place? Because you know I don't believe in coincidences."

Mitch grinned. "We'd been tailing him for a while. He was a nasty piece of work but just a small fish in a big pond. There were six separate busts last night, took down a huge racket. Picked up the few loose ends today—Darius McInnes being one of them."

I nodded, as though it all made perfect sense. "Connections?"

Kurt answered, "Darius McInnes and Tyler James were just one team of many who recruited street kids to mule. Kids do the dirty work and they collect the cash. They got cocky, made some mistakes and we got 'em."

"Well, I'm glad they're gone," I said. Then I realized someone was missing. Mitch's new partner, the guy who had replaced me in the Fab Four. "Where's Ricky? Sick of your shit jokes already?"

Mitch's smile faded. "He was just getting some intel for us." Then his brow furrowed and he frowned. "I asked him to stay behind and get some information... for you, actually. I got your message earlier today, Matt. I wanted to be sure."

"About what?" Kira asked. I didn't need to. I could tell from the look on his face.

Mitch looked at Kira and spoke softly. "We found a body."

Kira looked at me. "Who?"

I took his hand. "I asked Mitch to keep an eye out for Ruby." I could feel my eyes burn and my head spin. I swallowed down the urge to vomit. I looked back at Mitch. "You sure?"

Mitch looked at me for a long moment, and finally he nodded. "The kid you introduced me to once here at the FC. But I wanted to be sure. Ricky was trying to find out what he could."

I swallowed thickly. I didn't dare look at Kira. I just squeezed his hand instead. "It was definitely the kid you met here?"

Mitch nodded. "I recognized him," he said, almost in a whisper. "But you know procedure. Did he have any distinct features that you were aware of? It might help in IDing him."

I shook my head. "No birthmarks, no scars. Not that I saw anyway." Then I thought of something. "Was he wearing shoes?"

Mitch tilted his head. "What?"

"His shoes?" I clarified. "Was he wearing any?"

Mitch nodded. He understood where I was going with this, which to me, confirmed what we both already knew. "Yeah, he was."

"Bright green high tops?" I asked.

Mitch nodded.

Kira sighed and his chin dropped to his chest. I squeezed his hand, and when he looked at me, his eyes were filled with tears. "Matt..."

I blinked back tears and turned to look at Mitch. "Don't tell me what they did to him," I whispered. "I don't want to know." The truth was, I couldn't handle hearing it. He was just a fucking kid.

Mitch nodded sadly, and his silence told me that no, no I really didn't want to know how he'd died.

"Was it McInnes? James?"

"We're pretty sure. You know how those things work."

I nodded. "Yeah."

"We'll know more when the ME's done," he continued. "There's DNA—"

"Mitch, don't," I said. My head felt light and spacey. *Jesus*. "Just tell me. Was he alone? Did he die alone?"

Mitch frowned. "Matt..."

"He was just thirteen years old."

Mitch stared at me for a long while, and he and I both knew... I wasn't dealing with this like a cop. Because I wasn't one. I was on the other side of the fence now. I didn't want them to think he was just another nameless, faceless, worthless street kid.

I squeezed Kira's hand again and told my old cop partners, "He was thirteen. He didn't have a home or parents. He was a good kid who was just dealt a really shitty hand, ya know? No one cared if he didn't come home, except for Claude." I turned to look at Kira. "Oh, Jesus... I gotta tell Claude."

"Tell Claude what?" she said from the door.

I spun to face her, and I saw her eyes go from my face to Mitch's, to Kira's and back to mine. "Claude..."

"They found him, didn't they?" she asked quietly. "Ruby? They know where he is?"

I nodded.

She stared at me for a heartbreaking moment. Her voice was tiny and broken. "He's not coming back, is he?"

I shook my head. "No, sweetie. He's not."

She turned and ran, and I leapt out of my seat to go after her "Claudia, wait!"

I didn't even get one step and my entire vision tilted, and my world went dark.

CHAPTER SIXTEEN

KIRA

WATCHING Matt struggle with vertigo was the hardest thing. He hated feeling vulnerable, he hated the loss of independence, and he hated how he thought that people looked at him with pity.

They never looked at him with pity. They looked at him with concern and love.

But he didn't see that.

Matt didn't see himself very clearly at all.

He leapt out of the chair, calling after Claude, took one step, and fell forward. I managed to half-catch him so he didn't hurt himself again, but two falls in one day had taken its toll.

This fucking day had taken its toll.

Vertigo, walking into a police takedown, and now the news about Ruby...

I lifted Matt by the shoulders and sat him in the chair he'd just got out of. I could almost see his head spinning, lolling back and forward. I grabbed the wastepaper bin and put it on his lap, knowing nausea usually followed bad vertigo. He lifted his head, slowly opened his eyes, and said one word, "Claude."

I nodded. "Okay. I'll go," I told him. I looked at Mitch. "Stay with him," I said, and ran out after Claude.

Arizona was near the door, standing with two uniformed police officers. "I tried to stop her," he said to me. "But she bolted."

Racing outside, there were still a few cops. "A little girl, black frizzy hair?"

One of the officers shrugged, and the other pointed right. "That way."

I couldn't see her anywhere up the street, which meant she hadn't gone far, and as I passed the alley adjacent to the club, I caught a glimpse of movement. It was the lid of a dumpster. Now shut, I wasn't even sure if I saw it move or if it was the sunlight playing tricks on me. But when I ran across the street I heard it—a sound that broke my heart.

The tiny sobs of a little girl.

I lifted the lid, and there she was, huddled in the back with her knees drawn up and her head down. She didn't look up.

"Claude," I said gently.

She shook her head.

"Can you come out?"

She shook her head again.

I sighed and lifted the lid right back. Putting both hands on the side of the bin, I climbed inside. It was a mix of flattened cardboard and garbage bags, and it stank. But it didn't matter.

"Claude, I want you to come with me," I said. "You can't stay here."

She finally looked up at me. Her big brown eyes were filled with tears and red-rimmed, her cheeks were wet. She didn't talk.

"Claude, I know you're scared and that's okay. But you're not alone."

"Ruby..."

"I know," I told her softly. "But you got us. And right now, Matt's back at the gym and he's not feeling very well, but he needs you, Claude. He told me you looked after him when he fell over this morning. He said you were the best."

Claude just stared at nothing.

I had no clue what I was doing. I had no idea what I should say, how I should act, but I needed her to get out of this goddamn dumpster. I added, "And Oscar, he needs you too."

She looked at me but remained silent.

"Yes, they do. We all do. And you know what?" I asked. "I can't be in two places at once. If I'm here with you, then I can't be there with Matt, but if I'm with Matt, then I can't be here with you. And I really want to be with both of you, so I need you to help me out, okay?"

She wiped her eyes with the back of her hand but made no attempt to move.

"I need to go back to see Matt, Claude. I can't leave him when he needs me, and I'm not leaving here without you, so can you help me out?"

Her lip trembled, and still she said nothing.

"Claude, I know you're scared. You know what? So am I," I admitted. "I don't know what I'm doing. I don't have a clue, and it scares me. But we will get through this together, okay?"

She looked at me with those big brown eyes and fresh

tears rolled down her cheeks. I held out my hand. "Come on, Claude."

She took my hand and started to cry, and by the time we got back to the FC, Matt was still sitting in the same chair, and she basically ran over to him, crawled into his lap, and sobbed.

She burrowed into his chest, and he wrapped his arms around her. He looked over the top of Claude's head at me.

For a while the room was quiet, except for Claude, who cried and cried. Matt held her tight and kissed the top of her head, and when he looked at me, silent tears fell down his cheeks.

"Matt," I said, walking over and kneeling in front of him. "I know you've got a lot going on right now, but I think we should go to the cabin. The three of us."

Matt's blue eyes were wide and teary. He nodded. "Okay."

FALLING in love with Matthew Elliott was easy.

From the first time I'd seen him, when he was running on a treadmill alongside Mitch and threw his head back and laughed, I just had to meet him. When my boss, Chris, had told me he was *the* Matthew Elliott always on TV or in the papers, I'd thought he might be some conceited asshole.

But he really wasn't like that at all.

I'll admit I was first attracted to his looks—blond, blue eyes, boyish good looks, and fit. But then I'd got to know him.

He was the very opposite of conceited. He was humble, but there was a quiet confidence, and above all else, the man had a heart of gold.

That's who I fell in love with. The man behind the badge, the man behind the media. The man that was brave and vulnerable, the man that blushed when I touched his face.

The Matt that no one else knew.

It hasn't been easy. Actually, there's been times when it's been downright fucking hard. Being kidnapped and having my arm broken by some crazy lunatic like Tomic didn't even come close to watching Matthew Elliott self-destruct. His physical and emotional injuries were soul destroying, but he'd come so far in these last seven months, and I did have to wonder what the effect the events of today would have on him.

First, having two serious bouts of vertigo in one day—a brutal reminder of his inner ear injury and how he got it—then the incident with that Darius guy and a gun, and of course, Ruby. I knew it could be, and probably would be, a huge setback in his progress. I didn't want him to go backwards—he'd worked so hard at moving forward, and he had come so far.

It was dark as I drove to the cabin. Matt was beside me in the passenger seat, and Claude and Oscar were in the back. I kept his hand in mine for most of the trip. Matt was tired and still a little dizzy, and even though he tried to tell me he was fine, I knew better. When I suggested the cabin as a getaway, even for a few days, he smiled and nodded.

We needed to decompress. We needed to regroup and take some time out, go somewhere we could be just us and talk. I didn't want to get caught up with our busy lives and not talk this through.

We learned that lesson the hard way before.

I squeezed Matt's hand. "You okay?" I asked, before getting out of the car.

Matt nodded. "Yeah." He gave a quick glance to the little girl in the back seat. "Let's go inside, huh?"

I grabbed the bags, and Matt walked slowly to the front door, letting Claude and Oscar in first. He flipped on the lights and showed them around the small house. "Mine and Kira's bedroom is upstairs in the loft," he explained. "You can sleep on the sofa bed with Oscar, okay? You can have a shower, some dinner, and watch TV till you fall asleep. How does that sound?"

Claude just nodded. She'd not said a word since I'd got her out of that dumpster.

She barely touched her dinner and spent the night just staring at the television screen, with one hand on Oscar. The dog had planted himself by her side since we'd gone home and collected him.

Matt was finishing washing up after dinner when I left Claude and walked into the small kitchen. I kissed the back of his neck, and he turned and wrapped his arms around me. "I love you," he mumbled into my neck.

I pulled back, so I could see his face, and touched his cheek. "I love you too," I told him. "You feeling better?" He looked better.

"Yeah. It just takes a lot out of me, that's all."

I kissed him softly. "You're okay coming here?" I asked.

He nodded and eyed me curiously. "I love it here. Why?"

I shrugged. "It's just been a place where we've come when things weren't great."

Matt nodded, then looked at Claude, who was still staring at the TV. "Do you think she'll be okay?" he whispered.

"I don't know," I answered quietly.

"I was about to call child services this morning," he

murmured so only I could hear. "That's what I was doing when I fell over. Then she sat with me until your mom got there."

"Oh, Matt."

He shrugged. "Made me feel even worse. I felt like such a prick. And now with Ruby..." He sighed. "I don't know what that means for her."

I ran my hands over his face and cupped both sides of his jaw. "We don't need to decide tonight. Actually, given everything that's happened today, we shouldn't make any decisions tonight."

Matt stared at me for a long moment, taking in the features of my face. "How did I ever get so lucky?"

I smiled and kissed him. I'd never get sick of the way he looked at me.

"We have had a lot of bad stuff happen here. But for what it's worth," he went on to say, "we've had a lot of good, too." Matt smiled. "I also told you I loved you here for the very first time. Actually, it was the first time I'd told anyone I loved them."

"Me too," I replied. "It was the first time I'd told anyone that either."

Matt smiled. There was a tinge of sadness to the curl of his lips. "I know a lot of bad stuff has happened, and we've always come here to the cabin to recoup. But I love coming to this place. It's like a second home."

I slid my arms back around him and kissed his neck. I chuckled when he shivered. I pecked his lips and went to pull away, but he stopped me. "Babe, can we talk later? When Claudia's asleep, I want to talk to you about every-thing that happened today."

"Is everything okay?" I asked cautiously.

"Yes," he answered assuredly. "I just want us to talk.

There's some stuff I've been thinking over, and I want to discuss it with you first. Then maybe even Tamara, but you first." He looked back at Claude, who I don't think had even blinked. "And we need to talk about Ruby."

I didn't really want to talk about Ruby. Not yet. It was still too awful to think about. "Okay," I said.

He smiled, then took my hand and led me out to the sofa. We sat in silence, staring at the TV until Claude fell asleep, then we finally went upstairs and got ready for bed. I was nervous about what Matt wanted to talk about.

When he came out of the bathroom, I had the covers pulled back for him and patted the bed. "Do you feel okay?" I asked. "Not dizzy at all?"

Matt smiled and climbed onto the mattress. "No, I'm okay." Then he took my hand. "Are you?"

"What do you mean?"

"Are you okay?" he repeated. "After today. I haven't really had a chance to ask you, what with the news of Ruby and then me taking another nose dive. I haven't really had the chance to talk to you about how you're feeling?"

"Matt, I'm fine," I told him, again. "I really am. Is that what you want to talk about?"

Matt frowned. "Well, yes. Of course it is."

"And?" I prompted. There was something else. I could tell.

"I'm going to leave the FC," he said simply. "I won't put you in that kind danger again. I just can't do it. He had a gun pointed at you! Every time I close my eyes, I see it!"

"It wasn't pointed at me," I countered quietly. "And both of those guys were taken down two seconds later."

"It's not the point," he replied. "My job is *still* a danger to you. First being a cop, and now at the FC. It just seems you're not safe around at me. No matter what I do."

"Matt," I started, but he stopped me.

"Kira, babe, it's okay. I'll find something else."

"But you love it."

"I love you more. A thousand times more," he said. "Maybe I could find a job in a library somewhere, where the most dramatic thing that happens is someone can't find a book."

I snorted, despite what he was saying. "Don't make any decisions just yet," I told him. "Thank you for telling me what's on your mind, but like I said before, let's not make any life changing decisions today."

Matt nodded, but I could tell he'd already made up his mind. One thing about Matthew Elliott was, once he'd made up his mind, there was no going back.

I lay down on the bed and left my arm out as an invitation. He put his head on my shoulder. I wrapped my arm around him and he snuggled himself into me.

I kissed the side of his head. "I love you, Matt," I told him again.

I could feel his lips smile against my chest, but his breathing soon evened out and he fell asleep.

I lay there thinking about what he'd said. I could understand the logic behind why he would want to leave—I just didn't think he should.

It had taken six months, but Matt was finally smiling again. Laughing and joking, even humming to himself. It was the old Matt, the Matt I fell in love with. The way his eyes shone and how they crinkled at the corners when he smiled.

It had been gone for a long time.

There were daily reminders, like the scar in my eyebrow, the slight discoloration across my left forearm—left behind by the metal bar Tomic had used to snap it—and the subsequent weakness of my left arm. It had been over twelve months. With specific exercises and weights, it was almost back to normal. Almost.

The scars on the inside took much longer to heal.

For Matt, the scars had festered until they'd nearly killed him. Literally. He had almost died from cage fighting —his time at the FC had almost killed *us*.

I'd never imagined it would be the FC that would save him.

The way he smiled, the kids he taught and helped. It had really made him live again.

He'd deny it and tell me it was me who saved him, and maybe that was partly true, but his work at the FC gave him purpose. He'd really found his place in the world.

I loved turning up and helping out, partly to help the kids and the guys like Arizona, but also so I could see Matt in his element. Seeing him run through classes with those kids and helping them find a better life—and seeing him thrive on it—reminded me of why I fell in love with him.

Matt rolled onto his side, so he faced me, and snuggled farther into me. If he was ever restless, I would simply kiss his forehead or touch him or speak softly to him, and even in his sleep, he would settle.

I wrapped my arm around him, pulled the sheet up over us, and closed my eyes.

I woke up to the sound of the TV on. It was still much too dark, and Matt was sound asleep beside me. I grabbed my phone from the bedside table to check the time. It was ten past three.

I walked downstairs to find Claude lying on her side, staring at the television. The only light was the flickering of the screen, and even then I could see the blankness in her eyes.

"Hey," I said softly. "Can't sleep?"

She shook her head a little.

"Want me to sit with you?"

She hesitated for a second but then shook her head again. "No," she said weakly.

"I can sleep down here if you want?" I tried.

"S'okay," she mumbled. "Can turn it off if it's bothering you." She reached out for the remote control.

"The TV's fine, Claude," I said. I rubbed her arm. "Just checking on you." I pulled the blanket up over her little body. Oscar stirred on his bed in the corner and sat up when he saw us. I patted my thigh, motioning for him to come over, and when he did, I picked him up and put him on the sofa bed with Claude.

She never took her eyes off the television, she never smiled. But her hand found the soft felt of Oscar's ear, and when he lay down beside her and closed his eyes, I watched them for a heartbreaking moment before I went back upstairs.

I climbed back into bed, and this time when a still-sleeping Matt pulled me into his arms and kissed the top of my head, I welcomed it.

THE NEXT DAY, we spent the morning taking Oscar for a walk. We thought the fresh air would do us good, and a slow walk along the trails we used to run might give Claude an appetite. She'd hardly eaten in days.

She certainly hadn't said a great deal.

She was quiet, withdrawn, and barely responded to anything. She was lost in her head, and Matt and I were at a loss for what to do.

Matt had spoken to Boss on the phone and told him he'd call him in a day or two. The fundraising day was fast approaching, but Matt had reassured Boss everything was organized. Then he spoke to Mitch for a long while, who just wanted to know his friend was okay. In the afternoon, when Claude was watching TV, Matt went out onto the deck and called Tamara's office.

He told her about Ruby, and how he'd yelled at him the day before he'd disappeared. I sat beside him and held his hand. He told her about his double episode of vertigo, and about Darius McInnes and Tyler James, and how there'd been a gun. He told her he was thinking of leaving the FC because he couldn't bear the thought of me being in danger.

"Tamara, I was considering cutting back my appointments," Matt said, giving my hand a squeeze. "I thought I was ready, but I'm not. Not even close."

I blinked at his words, not expecting them at all.

Matt swallowed hard. "The very last thing I said to Ruby wasn't very nice. It was warranted," he added. "Ruby was doing the wrong thing, and I chided him for it. I don't think it was unreasonable, but he must have."

I could hear the hum of Tamara's voice as she spoke to him through the phone.

Matt nodded to whatever she'd said, then he said, "No, Kira's right here." Tamara said something else and Matt looked at me. "Tamara wants to be on speaker. Is that okay?"

I nodded, and Matt pressed the speaker button. Tamara's voice came through loud and clear, "Kira, Matt said there was an incident outside the FC and there was a gun. I'm really glad Matt called, and I'm glad that you're taking time to reflect and talk. Are you okay?"

"I'm fine," I told her. "It all happened so fast I didn't

really see anything. Matt pushed me and Claude back into the gym. He kept us safe."

Matt rolled his eyes. "It wasn't exactly like that."

"It was exactly like that," I said.

Tamara chuckled.

"Tamara," I continued more seriously. "Claude's not doing so great. She's really retreating into herself, and I don't know how... I don't really even know what to say, but I was hoping maybe she could see you when we get back into town. We'll pay for it," I told her.

"We just don't know what else to do," Matt said.

"Certainly," Tamara said. "Though there might be a colleague better suited to dealing with children, but I'll be happy to do what I can."

"Thank you," Matt said. "It would mean a lot."

"Matt, are you feeling okay?" Tamara said. "Problems sleeping, nervous, anxiety? You know the symptoms, and I'll be honest with you, I'm worried that these events—"

"Tamara, I feel okay," he answered simply. "I was scared for Kira and Claude. I'm worried for her, and my stupid vertigo got in the way again, but you know what?" he asked rhetorically. "I feel okay."

"And what about Rueben?" Tamara asked.

I looked at Matt and swallowed down the lump in my throat. "I don't think that's registered yet," I said. He squeezed my hand. "It's hard because we need to be strong for Claude."

Matt nodded to me. "We'll need to organize the funeral too," he said softly. "He should have a proper funeral."

I nodded and my heart sank. "Yeah, he should."

"Matt, Kira," Tamara said. Her voice had taken on a serious tone. "I want you both to know something. What you're doing is commendable, and Matt, today you have shown just how far you've come." She went on to say how Matt should be proud of himself for his actions and his willingness to be open about everything, and how I'd done everything right.

It didn't feel like it, though. I kept thinking about Ruby, and when Matt ended the call to Tamara, I stood up and walked to the deck railing and looked over the trees. Matt followed me. "Hey. You okay?"

I nodded, but then because there was supposed to be only honesty between us, I shook my head. I looked at Matt. "Not really."

He put his hand on my arm, and his eyes were wide with worry. "Kira."

"I just keep thinking about Ruby," I said, my voice barely a whisper.

Matt's eyes softened and he gave me a sad smile. "I know. It's hard…"

"He was just a kid," I started to say, but then the glass sliding door opened and Claude stepped out.

She looked at each of us. "Oscar needs to go outside. Can you take him?" Her voice was quiet. Her face was emotionless, blank.

"You don't want to?" Matt asked.

She shook her head and went inside. When we followed her in, she was back to lying on the sofa, staring at the television screen.

"I'll take him," I said, grabbing the leash from the counter.

"You sure?" Matt asked. Then he signed, "Kira, are you okay?"

I nodded. "I am," I said, answering both questions.

I knew I shouldn't have been avoiding her, but watching her so sad and lost was hard to watch.

I didn't know what to say to her. Or how to fix her. Her brother was gone, and I couldn't even comprehend how alone she felt. I couldn't fathom being all of nine and not having a single person on the planet. I didn't even know where to start.

But Matt did. He'd been there—he'd experienced that exact, horrendous thing. Albeit he'd been older, but still a kid. If anyone could understand, if anyone knew what to say, it was him.

Even that night, I kept myself busy in the kitchen. I cleaned and prepped food for dinner, cooked and cleaned some more. We sat with her on the sofa until she finally fell asleep.

The next morning, she tore a piece of toast apart slowly, but I wasn't sure if she ate any of it. We went for a walk through the woods again, down to the main street of Wrightwood, and she still hadn't communicated with more than a nod of her head. We bought coffee to go and got Claude a hot chocolate, but she didn't finish it. Seemingly exhausted, she fell back onto the sofa and stared at the TV. It wasn't even on.

Standing in the kitchen, leaning against the sink, I signed to Matt, "I think we should call Tamara. For Claude. She's not good, Matt. I don't..." I took a deep breath. "I don't know what to do for her."

Matt nodded. Then he signed back, "We will call Tamara. But you just being here helps her. She might not know it now, but believe me, just being here is enough." He took my hands and kissed my knuckles.

I whispered, "I hate feeling helpless."

"I know you do," he said, staring into my eyes. "But you're not helpless. You're helping more than you realize. I've been in her place right now, so I know exactly."

I frowned. "I know you have," I murmured and squeezed his hands. "And I'm sorry you went through that. I can't even imagine..."

Matt gave me a small smile. "She knows you're here, she knows she's not alone right now, and that's all that matters. One day at a time."

I smiled and shook my head. "When did you get so smart?"

Matt leaned in and kissed me softly. "It's a work in progress." Then he said, "Just sit with her on the couch. Read a book, have a nap, whatever. It doesn't matter. As long as you're there."

So when Matt busied himself with laundry, I sat on the sofa next to Claude and picked a gossip rag off the top of the pile of magazines. They were all Mom's old ones, and it was absolute drivel—after the third or fourth magazine, I noticed Claude was rubbing her thumb on her shoes. I didn't say anything, just watched from the corner of my eye, but as she sat with her knees pulled up and her shoes on the sofa, she was brushing them off with her hands. First it was a gentle rub, but it soon became a frantic scrub.

"Claude," I said, gently putting my hand on her arm. "What's wrong?"

"They're dirty," she said. "They're new and I got them dirty." She was now pulling at her shirt to try and wipe them clean. "Ruby bought 'em for me brand new with his own money," she said, rubbing at her shoes frantically, becoming close to hysterical.

I tried to pull her hands away from her shoes, but she fought me. "I told him I'd keep them all shiny. I promised him!" she cried.

Then the tears started.

And they wouldn't stop.

"I told him," she sobbed. "I told him." She sucked back a breath then wailed, "I promised him."

Matt was now standing at the door, probably as wide-eyed as me. I didn't even think about what I should do or should say, I just did what felt right. I picked up Claude and tucked her onto my lap, wrapping her up in my arms the best I could.

And she sobbed, her tiny hands fisted into my shirt. She held onto me as though clinging to life.

I pressed my face into her mop of wiry hair, and when I looked up, Matt was in front of me. He put his hand to my face and wiped the tears from my cheeks. I blinked back more tears, and he kissed my forehead, then the top of Claude's head.

I could feel the fight leave her, and soon she was like a ragdoll in my arms. She'd cried herself out, and exhausted, she'd fallen asleep. It was a deep sleep, the only real sleep she'd had in three days. Matt propped up her pillow, pulled back her blanket, and I laid her down as gently as I could.

She stirred a little, and Matt shoved a cushion under her arm for her to cuddle, and soon her breathing evened out again.

Without a word, Matt took my hand and led me outside onto the deck. He turned quickly, pulling me into his arms, and held me as tight as he could. "Kira, babe, are you okay?"

I shook my head, buried my face against his neck. "I don't think so," I mumbled. I sucked back a deep, shaky breath. "Ruby was just a kid..."

He ran his hand through my hair and kissed the side of my head. "He was."

I nodded against him again. "It's not fair."

He pulled back and looked at me. He looked sad. Haunted. "I know."

"You can't leave the FC."

"What?"

"You can't leave the club," I repeated. "You're all some of those kids have got. No one else would care if they disappeared. No one but you. If you weren't there, what would happen to her? Who would care for Claude? What if those two guys took her? What would they have done to her tiny little body? How bad would they have hurt her?" I was almost sick at the thought. "You can't leave, Matt. You can't leave them."

"Kira..."

I wiped away my tears. "Don't leave them. They need you."

"I need you, too," he said.

"You will always have me."

"Even if some drug-running asshole pulls a gun on you?" His eyes were wide and scared. "I don't think I can deal with that. I can't handle the thought of something happening to you, because of me. Not ever again."

I smiled, despite my tears. "You know what? I think I'm getting used to it. It's just what happens when I'm around you."

Matt huffed out a laugh and shook his head. With his hands still to my face, he wiped my cheeks with his thumbs. "Kira..."

"You can't leave the FC. You love it, Matt. And they need you. Those kids need you. Boss and the boys, they need you."

"What about you?"

I smiled slowly. "I will always need you. That won't ever change. Matt, you're it for me, forever." I leaned in and kissed him softly. "For richer or poorer, to love and cherish, or something like that."

His eyes went wide, and he stared at me intently, searching for something. "We're not married yet."

"We will be."

He smiled warmly. "How did I ever get so lucky?"

"You punched me in the mouth, remember?" I said with a grin, despite the tears. "We were training and you jabbed me and split my lip."

"You were flirting and it distracted me."

I laughed quietly, though my eyes were still watery. "I seem to recall you flirting with me."

"I seem to recall not being able to form a proper sentence around you. You only had to smile and my brain went blank."

"Have I lost that effect on you? I used to make you blush..."

I kissed him and kept his forehead against mine. "You still take my breath away."

He kissed me then, softly, and pulled my bottom lip between his. He moved his hands to hold my face, and he deepened the kiss. But then I heard something. Ending the kiss, I pulled away and turned to the familiar sound. Matt obviously hadn't heard anything, but he quickly turned to follow my line of sight, and we saw a car had stopped in front of the cabin.

"Mom and Dad," I murmured. "Did you call them?"

"No, I didn't," he answered softly.

We went to the front door and opened it for them to come inside. When they got close enough to see, I put my finger to my lips. "Sshh."

As always, Mom came in first. She hugged me. "Where is Claude?" she asked quietly.

"Asleep," Matt answered.

Then Yumi walked over to Matt and hugged him,

fiercely. I don't think she'd ever hugged him that hard. Even when he tried to pull away, she kept him in her strong grip. Eventually she pulled away and put her hand to his face. "You okay, Matty?"

He kissed her cheek and nodded. "I'm fine."

I looked over at Dad, who had just walked in. He signed, "She's worried. About you. You, Matt, and Claude of course. Mostly Matt, though."

I signed, "Can we go out to the deck?" and quietly walked through, careful not to wake Claude.

When we were all there, I said, "Matt's okay. Actually, Matt's been the strong one this time."

Mom looked at me, and reaching up, she put her hand to my cheek. Someone else might not have seen that I'd been crying earlier, but I had no doubt she could tell. "Kira?"

"It's just been a hard day," I said, taking in a calming breath. "Claude kind of broke down earlier. She's asleep now, but she lost it today. She's been so quiet and withdrawn. She's hardly said a word these last three days."

"And she got upset today?"

I nodded and sighed. "Mom, it was awful. She was trying to clean the shoes Ruby gave her," I said quietly. "I didn't really know what to do."

Matt walked over and slid his arm around me, kind of squashing Mom in the middle of us. "You were great. You did everything right."

I looked at my parents. "I didn't know how to help her. I still don't know what to do."

"You do everything," Mom said, with sad eyes. "You both do so much already. You're good boys. You take care of those kids. No one make you. No one even ask. You just do it."

"We didn't take very good care of Ruby," I said. My eyes burned, and I bit my lip to stop any tears.

"No," Matt said seriously. He lifted my chin so he could look me in the eye. "Kira, we did everything we could. There's no blame here. There's no guilt. Ruby knew the dangers. He knew, but he did it anyway. It's a shitty life for a kid, but how he got to where he was isn't on us. We offered him all we could. Kira, babe, don't feel like we didn't try hard enough. There's nothing else we could have done."

I nodded but knew I must've hardly looked convinced. "We'll have to arrange something more permanent for Claude." I shrugged. "She can't just go back to the streets."

"She stay with us," Mom said, still standing beside us. We turned to look at her. "She need a home. And school. She can have your old room, Kira. She live with us and we look after her."

I looked from Mom to Dad. He just shrugged and nodded. "Yumi's made up her mind," he signed. He shrugged one shoulder as if to say there's no point in arguing. Then he smiled. "Your mom always wanted more kids."

I looked at my Mom and couldn't stop the tears this time. "You'd do that for us?"

"We do it for Claude," she replied. Then she put up her finger and pointed it at me. "But Oscar only when you need. Not full time. Not a kid and dog. I'm crazy, but I'm not that crazy."

Matt laughed and hugged her, kissing her cheek. "Sit down out here. I'll make some coffee."

We sat at the patio table, and I looked at them both. "Are you sure?" I signed. "It's a big decision, Mom. It's not a few weeks, it's years. She's just nine. She needs a lot of things. She needs therapy, Mom. She needs to talk to someone who can help her."

"You forget who raised you?" Mom said. "I know what kids need." Then her eyes softened. "But she will need you too. And Matt." She looked back to where Matt had walked inside. "Has he been okay? I been so worried. When you said you come up here, and the men with a gun and poor, poor Ruby..." Mom shook her head. "I worry that Matt not take it well."

"Mom, he's been great," I told her. "He's really taken care of me this time."

Mom smiled warmly. "He a good boy."

"He's the best."

Matt came out the sliding glass door carrying a tray of mugs and pot of coffee. When everyone had a cup, he sat down next to me, and we talked about the little girl who was asleep inside.

"She not going to some welfare place," Mom said, shaking her head. "If she wants to live with you, then that's fine. We'll help. But I just think she needs someone who done it before. We raised you," Mom said, looking at me. "And you turn out just fine. You both work funny hours and we retired, not work at all. We have the time she needs."

I nodded. As much as I wanted to argue, my mother was right. She usually was.

It was mid-afternoon when Claude woke up, and we were still sitting outside on the deck. When she came outside, she went straight to Matt and climbed up on his lap.

"You feel okay, squirt?" he asked.

She nodded but didn't say anything.

"Claude," Matt said gently. "We want to talk to you, is that okay?"

She looked at him for a long moment, probably deciding if she trusted him or not, and nodded.

"You know you're not alone, yes?" he asked, not waiting for her to answer. "Because you're not. You have people who care about you and who are worried for you."

Claude's bottom lip trembled and her eyes welled, but she didn't cry.

"We want you to know you have somewhere to stay, a real home. You're not going back to the streets. You don't have to live like that anymore."

Claude blinked back her tears and shook her head. "I don't got anyone." Her voice was soft and croaked.

Mom fought her own tears. "Yes you have. You have us. All of us."

Claude looked at me, then at Matt. She obviously still didn't know what was going on.

"If you want," Matt said, "and only if you want to, you can come live with Yumi and Sal. They want you to stay with them."

Claude turned to face my parents, and she kind of sank back into Matt. It was obviously a bit of a shock, and something she didn't seem too keen on.

"You can have my old room, Claude," I said, trying to sweeten the offer. "Your very own room! With your own bed, and we can go shopping for new quilt covers and make it all pretty."

Mom shrugged, sadly. "I know we are a bit different."

"No you're not," I said, almost offended that she would say that.

Mom smiled at Dad then patted my leg. "Kira, we are."

"You *are* different," Matt said with a warm smile. "And pretty damn amazing."

I looked at Claude. "Mom will make you eat your vegetables, she'll make you do your homework. You'll have chores, nothing too bad, like keeping your room clean and putting your laundry in the hamper. And Dad?" I went on to say, "Well, he'll wait until your first date and follow you to the movies, sit up the back and embarrass you so bad."

Dad laughed. "That was just for you," he signed.

I looked at Claude. "That was just for me, apparently."

She was quiet for a long moment, and we gave her time to think. Eventually she asked, "What about Oscar?"

"He'll stay at our house, with me and Kira," Matt told her. "But he'll come over a few days a week and you can see him when you come to our place."

Claude blinked a few times, then she looked at Yumi. "And I gotta go to school?"

My mom nodded once. "Yes."

"It's okay to be scared, Claude," Matt said. "I was scared when my Mom died. I didn't want to make decisions, and you know it was okay. I didn't have to decide straight away, and neither do you."

"We just want you to know you not alone," Mom said. "And you welcome to live with us."

Oscar put his nose on my leg. I scratched his head while we deliberately talked about other stuff. Claude didn't say much for a little while, just seemed quite content to sit on Matt, leaning against him. She seemed lost in her thoughts as we talked, and Dad asked us how long we were staying at the cabin for.

"Not sure," I answered. "I have to go back to work the day after next."

"Claude and I can stay here for another few days," Matt said. He gave her a squeeze. "Only if she wants to."

"We gotta go back, Matt," she said, her voice was quiet. "We got work to do before next weekend. The fun day's on, remember?"

Matt smiled at her. "You sure you want to?"

She nodded and shrugged. "Can't leave it all for Boss to do. You'll never hear the end of it."

We laughed around the table. Then out of nowhere, Claude said, "I really miss Ruby."

Our smiles died. Matt rubbed her back and said, "I know you do, squirt. And you always will. We'll help you remember him so he stays in here." He pointed to her heart. "We'll just take one day at a time."

The little girl nodded sadly, and a silence fell over us. After a short time, while Claude was still curled up on Matt's lap, she asked him, "If I do go with them, do I still get to see you and Kira sometimes?"

"Of course!" Matt answered. "All the time. You'll be sick of us. You can stay on weekends if you want, and if Yumi and Sal have to go out or something, you can stay with us. I'm sure Oscar will love that."

Claude smiled, albeit small and brief, for the first time in three days. She nodded. "I'd like that."

Mom grinned and leaned forward on her chair. "You will? You come stay with us?"

Claude gave a bit of a shrug and a nod. "Guess so."

Mom almost tackled her and Matt. "We have so much fun. And you have a nice house and good food, and I have another girl in the house. It's always been me and lots of boys. I been outnumbered for years."

"Mom," I said with a laugh. "You'll scare her."

After a bit of discussion, it was decided that Claude would go back to LA with Mom and Dad today. It was only mid-afternoon, and by the time Matt and I had cleaned up the cabin and stripped the beds, we'd only be an hour or two behind them. We'd stop by to see them on our way home.

When they were leaving, Mom was happy but

cautiously so. She was also concerned about me. I had been upset when she'd gotten there, and that worried her.

As Matt, Dad, and Claude were near the car, I had a moment alone with my mom. "You sure you're okay?" she asked me again.

"I am. Well, I will be. I just feel—" I searched for the right word "I don't know. Weird."

"Anything I can do?" she asked, looking up at me.

"You know what I need? I just need some time, Mom. I'm okay. I'm fine, I really am. I just need some time with Matt and no one else. And that's probably selfish, given everything Claude's been through, but I need to just be with him, in the quiet."

Mom looked at me, concerned. "That's okay," she said. "I understand. You feel off balance."

I nodded. I wasn't quite sure how I felt, but off balance was pretty close. "I do."

Mom kissed my cheek. "Let him look after you this time," she said.

"I will," I told her. "He really has been great this time, Mom. With everything that's happened these last few days, it's really shown how far he's come. He's been great."

Mom smiled at me. "I know."

We said our goodbyes, with promises to see them soon, and watched them drive away. When we walked back inside, Matt rubbed his hand on my arm. "You okay?" he asked. "I really think Claude's better off with your parents. Not that I would mind if she wanted to live with us full time, but it's not about what I want. It's about doing what's right for Claude. And I'm sure we'd do just fine, but I really think she needs people like your mom and dad. She's been without that kind of structured stability—not that someone needs a mom, I'm sure two dads could do just fine, but

Claude needs things I'm not sure I'm in the right place to give it to her. I mean, I'm still in therapy, and she needs more than I can give her..." He was rambling. He always did when he was nervous.

"You, we, would do just fine, Matt," I told him.

"You're not pissed off that she's gone with them?"

I shook my head. "Not at all. I'm pretty sure it will be all of us who take care of her."

Matt smiled. "I hope so."

"She adores you," I told him.

"And you."

"We did the right thing," I told him. "I think Claude and my mom will get on like a house on fire. And if she really doesn't like staying there, then we'll deal with that then."

"Kira, are you okay?" he asked, looking at me concerned. "You look a little...distracted."

"I can't explain it. I just feel... out of balance or something," I said, using my mom's words.

Matt's eyes were wide with concern. "Babe, what is it?"

I shrugged. "I don't know. I feel... I don't know."

Matt took my face in his hands and looked me right in the eye. "Tell me what to do, tell me what you need."

"I need... you."

"You have me."

"No, I need *you*. I need to be with you. I need to... have you."

"Okay," he agreed, took my hand, and climbed the stairs to stand beside the bed. He turned around and pulled off his shirt and bit his bottom lip. "You can have me anytime."

I shook my head. "I feel a bit stupid. I mean, I can't really explain it. It's not just sex. I need to feel you, and I need..."

"You need to feel alive. And validated. And whole," he said, like he could read me completely. "It's been an awful few days and you need some balance."

I nodded. "Yes."

He cupped my face and kissed me, slowly and perfectly, but then he pulled away. "Shit. I didn't bring anything with us..."

"I did," I told him. It was like packing underwear—I never *not* packed condoms and lubricant. "But I don't want to use it. I want it to be just you and me."

His eyes widened. "Are you sure?"

I nodded. "Yes. I've never been surer of anything. I want it to be skin on skin, no condom, no barrier. Just us."

Matt kissed me again, pulling my bottom lip in between his. "Just us."

With my forehead against his, I kissed him one last time before going to my bag to get the lube. I hadn't even unpacked it. It had been over a week since we'd used it last.

Matt stripped off his cargos and climbed onto the bed. I threw the small bottle beside him, and he quickly poured some onto his fingers while I got undressed. He smeared his hole first, then pressed a finger into his ass. I still hadn't even got my shorts off.

By the time I was naked and kneeling on the bed, he was adding a second finger. I licked his balls then the length of his cock. "You need to come first," I told him.

He shook his head quickly, urgently, and sank his fingers in up to the knuckle. "No. You first. In me, please."

Jesus. He was almost begging. He needed this as much as I did.

Leaning over him, I grabbed the lube and poured a small amount on my fingers, lathering my cock first. I was so hard. I was so turned on by the realization of what we were about to do.

Slowly, I pulled his fingers out of his hole, and taking both his hands in mine, I pinned them over his head. Our bodies pressed together as our mouths and tongues fused. Matt drew his legs up, bringing his knees to our chests, spreading himself open, giving himself completely.

My cock rubbed against his hole, and this was it.

"Are you sure?"

He nodded quickly. "Please."

I released one of his hands and guided my cock, slowly pressing into him. Matt's mouth opened with a gasp. and he threaded his fingers with mine on one hand, and when I reached up to grab his other hand, he joined our fingers again, holding both my hands so tight.

I covered his mouth with mine and gave him my tongue, while I slowly sank my cock inside him. Matt lifted his hips, rocking us, until every inch of me was buried in him.

When he let go of my hands, he wrapped his arms around me, pulling me closer, holding me tighter as we thrust and rocked. He was moaning with each push, sounds I had never heard from him.

He felt so hot and so, so good.

It had never felt so good.

"Matt, I'm close," I rasped.

He quickly locked his ankles behind me, holding me inside him, and he held my face in his hands. His eyes were dark and full of love, and he whispered against my lips, "Come inside me."

His words set fire to my blood, and I thrust harder, deeper, until my orgasm ripped through me. My cock swelled and surged inside him, filling his ass with my cum.

I'd never felt anything like it.

Still holding my face with his eyes wide, he watched me come. "Oh, fuck," he ground out, before pulling my mouth to his. And while I was still inside him, while my body jerked with pleasure, he slid one hand between us and gripped his cock, spilling hot cum between us.

I still didn't pull out of him.

I didn't have to.

I wanted to stay inside him forever.

When he lazily opened his eyes, I kissed his blissful smirk and reluctantly let my cock slip out of him. I rolled us onto our sides, then I pulled him against me and threw one leg over his thigh. I kissed the side of his head. "Do you feel okay?"

He chuckled and murmured, "Um, I feel so good right now."

I couldn't help but laugh. "That was... Matt, that was amazing."

He nestled himself further into my chest and kissed the skin there while we both caught our breath. He ran his hand down my side and over my ass, before pulling my hips into his. My still semi-hard cock pressed against him, and he shivered. "Mmm," he hummed. "Still hard. Do you want more?"

I chuckled again thinking it was a rhetorical question, but then he pulled my hips to his again, feeling my dick jerk between us. "Definitely more," he said, then he pulled out of my arms to lay face down on the bed.

"Matt..."

He replied by gripping the sheets above his head, spreading his legs and lifting his ass.

I considered telling him I'd be fine, but he knew me too well, and I had to give my dick a squeeze. Then he moaned. And lifted his ass higher. I almost growled as I kneeled between his thighs and leaned over him. I whispered in his left ear, "You're such a tease."

"Just fuck me again," he said.

I laughed low in his ear. "And you're bossy."

He waggled his ass, rubbing against my hard-on, so I gave him what he wanted. I pressed the head of my cock against his still-wet hole, and pushed right in.

Still slick from when I was inside him before, I slid into him so easily. Matt threw his head back and grunted, lifting his ass again and again to meet me. Every now and then he would react like this—wanting, *needing* a good, hard fuck.

I covered his hands with mine and drove into him, giving him exactly what he needed. What *I* needed. He needed to be owned, and I needed to claim him. We needed to reconnect.

I kissed and scraped my teeth on his shoulder as I fucked him, making him groan louder and buck his hips back to meet me. Pleasure built with each thrust, and it wasn't long until I came inside him again.

I collapsed on top of him, sweaty and well sated, kissing his skin where I'd marked him with my teeth. I was still inside him, and when I went to move, he stopped me. "Stay in me," he said.

I kissed the back of his neck. "We're a mess. We need to get cleaned up."

We stayed like that for a little while as we caught our breath, and Matt started to laugh underneath me. I slipped out of him and gave him room to roll over only to settle back on top of him. He spread his legs and arms wide, wrapping them around me only to chuckle again. "What's so funny?" I asked him, pleased to see him so happy.

He kissed me with smiling lips. "I'm such a mess. I'm covered in lube and cum and sweat."

His eyes were shining, and he looked so damn content, I couldn't help but laugh with him. I dragged him to the shower, and we both stood in the cramped space and scrubbed each other down. I washed the lube out of his hair, and he gave me a bubble beard. I took the hand held showerhead and sprayed the jet at his asshole, trying to make sure he was clean, which ended up as a water fight, which ended with us laughing hysterically, an absolutely drenched bathroom, and wet and smiling kisses.

He rubbed his towel over my hair. "I like your hair when it's a bit long," he said.

"I thought you liked it short and spiky."

He looked genuinely perplexed. "I can't decide."

I laughed at him and tied the towel around my waist. I grabbed his face and planted another kiss on his lips. "Thank you," I told him. "I really needed this."

He looked at me and tilted his head. He was still smiling, but his eyes were questioning.

I explained. "I needed this time with you, just an hour or so. I needed this laugh."

"Me too."

"We better get this cleaned up and head back to town," I told him. Then I remembered that we'd have to plan a funeral for Ruby, and my smile faded. "We have some not-so-nice stuff to deal with back home."

Matt stood up straighter and took my face in his hands. "Babe, we'll get through this. You and me, together? We can do anything."

I turned my face and kissed the palm of his hand. His words, his absolute conviction, warmed me through. "Yes, we can."

CHAPTER SEVENTEEN

TWO WEEKS LATER—THE **day of the fundraiser.**

WE GOT to the FC early, because even though Matt and the guys had done so much to be prepared, we still had so much to do. When they closed the street off, the stall vendors and carnival rides moved in and we pulled out heavy wooden picnic tables. We set up the temporary ring and floor mats, for the kids to do their exhibition shows, and were still taking the kids through their routines when people started to trickle in.

Then more people came. And more still.

Matt was in his element.

It was an effort to keep up with him. He did the PR rounds of the stall owners, he kept the FC boys organized and busy, and he kept Boss from stressing out completely. He even did some interviews for newspapers, a local community magazine and radio. He was really pushing how the gym was fitness-based, community-based, and how they focused on teaching kids drug awareness.

Claude was there, of course, with Mom and Dad in tow. It hadn't been an easy two weeks for Claude, or for any of us for that matter. We'd buried Ruby, and it had been a horrible, horrible day.

Watching Claude's little heart break all over again had been just awful.

But one good thing to come out of the grief and sorrow was Claude's relationship with my parents, in particular with my dad. They would spend hours together, in absolute silence —Dad being deaf of course—but it had almost a calming effect on Claude. She needed the quiet to collect her thoughts and found a peace in being around my dad—someone who offered a huge presence but also a gentle silence.

We'd all had a lot to sort out with taking Claude on, it wasn't as easy as just taking a kid off the streets and giving her a home. Tamara had explained there would be a lot of adjustment issues, a lot of emotional trauma for Claude to deal with, and it would need to be done one day at a time.

We'd all met with Tamara a few times in those two weeks, over and above our normal sessions. She'd laughed when she'd met my parents, telling me and Matt later that it explained a lot. But she took on Claude as a patient, calling it family therapy, and it was different to see how Tamara approached a kid, as opposed to me and Matt.

I think Matt developed a newfound respect for Tamara. He'd let go of the resistance, or the animosity he'd felt toward her, and had really shifted in his progress with not only Claude's development but also his own.

He'd even invited her to come down to the fundraising day, and it wasn't a polite invitation but more of an offer for her to see Matt's personal milestone in just how far he'd come.

At first I'd thought he might have wanted her to come along so she could see the kids, to show that they're not nameless or faceless and see the struggles they faced instead of spouting figures from some psychology textbook. But the more I thought about it, the more I thought it was out of pride—he wanted to show off his hard work, and he wanted her to meet the people he talked about because they mattered to him. And he should be proud of his work.

But whatever the reason, and for whoever's benefit, Tamara was there.

Matt introduced her to the FC boys, and she watched as Matt ran his kids through their routines in front of the gathered crowds. She saw how he'd taken a bunch of street kids, some of which had nothing, all of whom now had a sense of pride. And hope. She saw how he'd given them hope.

I thought Tamara would disappear not long afterwards, but she didn't. She stayed the whole day, talking to people we knew, people we didn't know, and I think she really saw why Matt fought so hard for this, why he defended it so much when they'd discussed his work.

Either way, there was a mutual admiration between them. Well, until they locked horns about something else in a few months, and I had no doubt they would. I was pretty sure Matt liked the challenge and Tamara knew it was an effective way to get Matt to communicate.

Whatever it was, and as much resistance as there was between them, they achieved a lot together.

She stood with me and my parents and we watched Matt take the makeshift stage. I guess all those press conferences as the spokesman for the Fab Four paid off, because he took the microphone like he was born to do it. He thanked the people for coming, for showing support in their community. He thanked the sponsors, then he thanked the kids.

He told the audience of the club's efforts to get street kids back into school, in conjunction with mixed martial arts programs. Then Matt put his hand to his heart and said, "I'm very proud to announce the FC, with the help of Hillvue Community College, and with a very generous sponsorship deal with Red Dog, we've now been fortunate enough to secure funding which will enable us to run a full MMA scholarship program to get homeless kids back in school."

A round of applause went through the gathered crowd, then Matt looked over to us. "It is with a very heavy heart that we announce the Rueben Vaughn Memorial Scholarship." Matt took a deep breath. "Because no thirteen-year-old kid should think they're forgotten, not loved, or not seen. And they most certainly shouldn't ever die alone on the streets."

Another round of applause went up, with the loudest cheering from the FC crew.

It was such a bittersweet moment, and I picked Claude up, giving her a big squeezy hug. Matt smiled at me, then turned back to the crowd. He thanked everyone again, and when he walked off stage, he came straight over to me and Claude and hugged us both.

With the formalities officially over, Claude wanted more turns on the carnival rides, so Mom and Dad took her. Tamara smiled warmly at Matt. "That's great news about the scholarship, Matt," she said.

"It is," he agreed. "We knew we were getting some sponsorship money and weren't real sure what to spend it on, and then at Ruby's funeral, we decided," he said, looking at me. "It just felt right."

"It did," I chimed in.

Tamara smiled like some inside joke was funny. "Oh, Matt."

He looked at her, unsure. "Oh, Matt, what?"

"You really should be very proud of what you've achieved. It's remarkable and certainly something you, your family, and kids can be very proud of."

Matt barked out a laugh. "Well, I don't think I have to worry about the kid part. I think it's pretty clear that being a parent is not something we'll be adding to the list too soon. One day, but I'm not in the right headspace yet..."

She smiled. "Matt, I'm going to tell you something, not as your doctor, but as a friend. You're already a parent, and you're doing a marvelous job."

Matt looked at her like she'd lost her freakin' mind. I'm sure it matched the look I was giving her.

"Matt, Kira," she said, looking at us one at a time. "You don't need titles for whatever it is you are to that little girl, be it a father, a big brother, or an uncle. Up until now, and even as a joint effort with Sal and Yumi, you've both taken very good care of her, and the thing is, boys, for all the horrible things she's been through, she's very lucky to have you."

Matt ran his hand through his hair, looking toward where Claude and my parents had disappeared to. "I don't know about that..."

Tamara shook her head. "Matt, you're better than you realize. You're doing a fabulous job, and like a true father, you'll doubt it every step of the way."

She put a reassuring hand on his arm before she walked

away, leaving Matt staring at me. "Well, that was weird," he mumbled.

I laughed, and just then Anna and Mitch joined us. As always, I gave her a kiss on the cheek, and we ended up sitting at one of the picnic tables talking about life and our men.

"You look the best I think I've seen you," she said. "Tell me, what's been going on?"

I couldn't help but grin. "Life's good," was all I said.

She smiled knowingly. "You mean, Matt's good."

"That too," I said with a laugh. "Things between us are almost back to the way they were before. Actually, despite everything, I'd say they're better. We're better now."

"Still talking it out like a *Dr. Phil* episode?"

I snorted a laugh. "Something like that."

"I'm really happy for you, Kira," she said. "You deserve it."

"And what about you?" I asked. She looked so good. "Looking a little bit amazing there. What's your secret?"

Anna looked over to where Mitch and Matt were still talking and smiled. "We might be talking about babies."

I nudged her with my shoulder. "Well, it's about time. And, by the way, you do know Kira can be a boy name or a girl name."

Anna laughed. "I'll keep that in mind."

Arizona and Lashona walked over to our table, and I introduced them to Anna. Anna was quick to take their little girl while a pregnant Lashona sat down.

Mom, Dad, and Claude came back not long after, and it seemed everyone we knew was there, and it was particularly great to see Matt's old police partners here. They'd come to support Matt, and it really meant a lot to him.

When the crowds had mostly dispersed, we were all at

the picnic tables out on the street, and as the vendors packed up their stalls, Matt finally got a chance to take a break. He was chatting with everyone, catching up with each group of people as he went.

He looked... happy.

I looked around at everyone still sitting in the setting LA sun to see Arizona was talking to Mitch, and Lashona was fussing over babies with Anna, Rachel, and Evie. Boss was there, talking to Tamara, of all people, and the way they laughed and chatted between themselves looked a little flirty, which was weird—and nice, I guess—but mostly weird. Ricky and Kurt were talking football with Cody and Amil.

It was a cool afternoon, the air was fresh, the light was soft, and it certainly didn't feel like we were sitting in the middle of a busy street. We only had a little while left before the street would be opened up again to traffic, so it was great to take the time to do it now.

A nice surprise to the end of the day was Berkman turning up. When I'd spoken to him earlier, he hadn't been sure if he could make it but said he'd do his best. Matt's old boss, Ross Berkman, walked over, interrupted Matt and Father Michael, and congratulated Matt on a successful day. He clapped him on the shoulder, then sat at the table with the rest of the boys and swiped Kurt's beer, taking a mouthful before he could protest.

The way everyone joked and laughed made me smile.

It actually felt kind of surreal, peaceful. Our friends and family were all there, and every single one of them was smiling.

I looked at Matt as he was talking to Michael, and when he laughed at something the priest had said, I had an overwhelming urge, an absolute certainty of what I wanted to do.

I stood up, kissed Anna on the cheek, then walked over to Matt and Father Michael.

"Hey," Matt said, smiling as soon as he saw me.

"Hey," I said, putting my hand on his lower back. "Father Michael, can I ask you to do one more thing for us today?"

The kind man smiled cautiously. "Sure."

"Marry us."

I looked at Matt, never more certain of anything in my entire life. He blinked then blinked again. "What?"

"Now," I said. "Let's get married. Right now."

Matt's mouth opened and shut, twice. "Um."

"Unless you don't want to," I added.

"I want to," he said quickly. "But we're not ready, we don't have anything..."

I pulled the leather necklace out from under my shirt so the ring sat on the outside. "You, me, two rings, and a priest," I said. "And everyone we know."

Matt was still staring at me with his mouth open, but Father Michael said, "It's not quite that easy. There's paperwork and registration forms and licenses. Those take time."

"It *is* that easy," I said. "It's really very easy. We have that signed marriage license that Mom made us practice on, we can bring that around tomorrow and finalize all the legal stuff then. Let's just do the ceremony part right now." I looked around at our friends and family. "Everyone's here."

Matt looked at me for a long, serious moment, then he looked at Michael. "Will you do it? Now?"

"I can go through a ceremony with you," Michael answered, unsure. But it won't be official or legal."

Matt waved his hand dismissively. "We can work out

details later," he said, undoing the leather strand that held the ring around his neck.

I did the same, and when Matt and I were both standing in front of him with rings in our hands, grinning like idiots, I don't think he had the heart to say no.

Michael mumbled something that sounded like, "I can't believe I'm doing this," then cleared his throat. "If I can have your attention, ladies and gentlemen."

It took a moment for everyone to stop talking, but eventually they were all quiet, looking at us.

"Matt and Kira have asked me to do something for them," Father Michael said. "Well, kind of. But while they are surrounded by family and friends here today, they've asked me to marry them."

There was two full heartbeats of silence. Then Yumi stood up. "They what?"

"Mom," I started.

She put her hand up as if stopping traffic. "I have all those plans. Color schemes and seating arrangements! Why you do this now?"

"Because I don't want to wait," I answered. "Not another day."

"Because I can't wait to be a part of your family," Matt said.

Mom softened with Matt's words, then my dad tapped her arm, asking what was said. He must have missed what Father Michael had said.

"They're getting married," Mom signed to him.

"Now?" he signed, clearly surprised.

"Yes, now," Mom signed and spoke at the same time.

Dad exhaled, relieved. "Oh, thank God," he signed, looking at me and Matt. "Does this mean I get my dining table back?"

Matt and I both snorted, and Father Michael said, "Do I want to know what he said?"

I shook my head, and Matt laughed and said, "He'd like it very much if we were married today."

Mom sat back down in a huff. Dad grinned and pulled Claude onto his lap so she could see better, and Father Michael told us to take each other's hands.

Then he started, "We are gathered here today to celebrate the love between Matthew and Kira as they become united in the house of God."

I couldn't stop smiling. I wasn't nervous at all—I was completely, with every fiber in my body, certain of this.

"Do you have any vows? Anything you'd like to say to one another? Matthew?" Michael asked.

"I do," Matt blurted out, making everyone laugh. He bit his lip and laughed, blushing a dozen shades of embarrassed. I cupped his face with one hand and pulled his face against my neck, laughing with him.

"I meant vows," Father Michael amended patiently, waiting for our audience to stop chuckling. "Do you have vows you'd like to tell Kira?"

He nodded. "Um..." He straightened up and ran his fingers through his hair. "Um, Kira, you..." He took my hand again and squeezed so hard he cracked my knuckles. He swallowed hard. Then he found his words. "Kira, for every wrong, for every mistake—and God knows I've made a few —you made me right. For every scar, for every wound, you have healed me. You are exactly the other half of me, the half that makes me whole. You make me strong. You have given me more than I could have ever asked for." Matt took a deep breath then exhaled shakily. "You are my everything, and I promise to you honesty, love, and faithfulness for the rest of my life."

I blinked back tears, the emotion of his words, the sincerity in his eyes overwhelmed me.

"Kira?" Father Michael prompted me.

I gave him a nod, trying to get the words right in my head. "Matt, I knew the second I saw you that you would change my life. And every time you say to me 'I don't know why you still love me' or 'I don't know what I ever did to deserve you' well, I wanna tell you something. You have so much heart, and so much love. You don't see yourself as anything special, you never have, but you're an amazing man, and I will spend my life trying to get you to see you the way I do."

His eyes welled with tears, and I moved my hands to hold his face, wiping my thumbs under his eyes.

Our foreheads were touching, and I spoke just to him, "This is why I love you. No one sees you like I do. It's a gift, and one I'll be forever grateful for."

Matt closed his eyes, as if basking in my words, and without any conscious effort, I kissed him. I just had to. I lifted his face and pressed my lips to his for a soft, slow kiss.

It wasn't until the priest beside us cleared his throat that I remembered where we were.

I pulled back, leaving Matt looking a little kiss-drunk. Then I heard the muted coughs and laughter from our friends and family.

Matt blushed again, laughing through his embarrassment while I looked at Michael. "Sorry."

"We're not up to that part yet," he said, trying not to smile. He held out the rings we'd given him. "Rings first."

"Oh," Matt said, taking the ring and handing it to me.

I took his left hand and slipped the metal band over his ring finger, then he did the same to me. Matt was teary again, but he was grinning now. He wiped his eyes with the back of his hand and asked Father Michael, "Can I kiss him now?"

Michael nodded, and Matt held my face and kissed me. Our friends and family were now standing and clapping and even other strangers, who had stopped to watch while Father Michael spoke about the power of California and announcing us as husband and husband.

And right there, in the middle of the street on a cool afternoon, surrounded by our loved ones and strangers and vendors and trucks moving equipment, we were married.

Matt buried his face in my neck, but we were soon pulled apart my mom, who was pulling us down so she could hug us. She was crying, but they were happy tears. Dad carried over Claude and handed her over to Matt, who hugged her as my Dad hugged me. Then Claude wanted to hug me, so Mom hugged Matt, fiercely.

When my parents were done, we were hugged and congratulated by everyone else. It was surreal. And wonderful. I didn't need some fancy wedding, with color schemes and flower arrangements. I just needed him.

It wasn't even technically official, and wouldn't be until tomorrow, but it didn't matter. It was real to me. And after everyone had wished us well, Matt found his way back to me. Without a word, he simply slid his arms around me, and again, buried his face into my neck.

He breathed me in, and while everyone was abuzz around us, he was absolutely still. I could feel the rise and fall of his chest, how his hands pressed on my back, and how his warm breath ghosted over my skin at my neck.

He was completely centered, completely at peace.

Running my hand up his side, over his neck and to his jaw, I pulled back slightly so I could kiss him again. Deeper this time, it was an emotional need. People around us heckled us, but I didn't care.

Mom tapped our shoulders. "Boys. Time for that later."

———

THE NEXT MORNING, we didn't take Oscar for a run. We slept in a little; after we'd made love almost all night, we were both tired.

And ridiculously happy.

After breakfast and showers, we were dressed and ready to go see Father Michael, but we needed to do something first. I'd arranged something for Matt and for me too, and I was nervous. I took a deep breath and let it out slowly. "Matt, I want to take you somewhere."

He turned to face me. "Take me somewhere? Like where?" he asked, looking at his watch. "We have to be at the church soon. We told Michael we'd be there first thing."

"I know. But it's still early and we have plenty of time," I said. "It won't take too long, and we really need to do this."

"Okay," he agreed cautiously. "Is it a surprise I'll like?"

I didn't answer him, and when we headed toward the airport, he was getting excited. "Did you plan a honeymoon or a holiday or something and not tell me?"

I shook my head. "No." And I think he could tell from my serious mood, that it wasn't anything of the sort. I drove into LAX, then turned into the service access area, and pulled up at a gate. I gave an access code I was given to a security guy and drove through the service gates.

Matt had gone from curious to concerned. "Kira? Where are you going?" he asked, though I'm pretty sure he knew. The row of old abandoned hangars came into view. "Why are you doing this?" His voice was calm and quiet.

"Because you need to see something."

"There's nothing here to see," he said, almost defiantly.

"Yes, there is."

I pulled up at the front and got out of the car. I waited for him to decide he would get out, and I walked to the side entrance door. The same door Matt had come through the night of my abduction.

"It'll be locked," he said, looking around. There wasn't a car in sight, and the only sound was the coo of pigeons roosting in the ceiling.

I turned the handle and let the door swing open. "I called Ross. He organized clearance for me to bring you here. He said it would be left unlocked for us."

I had spoken to Ross after our impromptu wedding and asked him for one last favor. I told him Matt needed to do this. That we needed to do this, and Ross had smiled, like he understood.

"Not a problem. Leave it up to me and call me if you need anything. Look after him," was all he'd said before clapping me on the arm then walking away.

And so we were about to come face to face with some demons.

Matt shook his head. "Why are you doing this?" he asked again. He almost looked scared. "Why today? We had such a great day yesterday, why do you want to come here now?"

And that was the reason I was doing this.

"I'm doing this to show you that there's nothing to be scared about. That what happened twelve months ago is over."

"I know it's over," he said quietly.

I smiled at him then pushed the door open, into the old

empty warehouse. "Then you won't have any worries about coming inside."

A thousand memories hit me as I walked in to the vast open space. The smell immediately taking me back to when Tomic had brought me here. The smell... a mix of dust, engine oil, and damp induced a flood of memories.

Matt was still at the door, waging an internal debate whether or not to come in.

A cold shiver ran through me, and it seemed to propel him into motion. "Are you okay?" he whispered beside me, his hand on my arm.

I looked around the old hangar, taking in the sights, the smell, the memories. Then I looked at him. "Yes." I nodded. "I am."

Matt tried to smile but then looked around behind us, like he was expecting someone to be there. "It looks different in the daylight. It was dark back then," he whispered. "And you were over there." He pointed his chin to the spot where Tomic had snapped my arm.

The table was gone, the boxes were gone, and in its place was... nothing.

There was some police tape with the faded words Do Not Cross in the far corner, but there was only filtered sunshine and a whole lot of dust.

"There's nothing here," I told him. "Just memories, Matt."

He nodded and frowned. He pulled me against him and buried his face into my neck, just like he had yesterday. But this was different. After a long, quiet moment, he said, "Why today? How come you wanted to do this today?"

"Because I wanted you to see that we are ready to move on. Our life together starts today, when we file those papers at the courts to officially be married, I wanted us to begin our lives together with no demons."

"Demons?"

I sighed and touched his face. "Your eyes would always give you away—the battles, the demons you fought always showed in your eyes." I found myself smiling, despite the conversation. "Your eyes are back to beautiful. Clear. Full of fire."

Matt shook his head, like he didn't understand.

"There are no demons," I told him. "Not here, in this old hangar. Not in our lives. The demons are gone."

Matt finally smiled. "They're gone because of you."

"No, Matt," I replied quietly. "Because of you."

He stayed quiet for a while and took a few steps back, looking around the abandoned hangar. "You know, I think I get it now," he said. "What this whole thing was for—losing my mom, becoming a cop. Meeting you, going through all that undercover stuff, and opening the FC for kids. It's like everything had to happen to get me to this point," I said. "To find Claude, to help her, to save her. We couldn't save Ruby, but we saved her. That's what this was all for."

I smiled at him. "You're a remarkable man, Matt."

"No I'm not. I'm just doing what's right."

"You're remarkable."

"It's remarkable how much my life has changed in the last two years."

"You thought you were going to be a cop forever."

"I did. And now, now I can see it's not what I wanted at all. What I'm doing now is what I'm supposed to be doing. And I owe it all to you."

"Me?"

"You were the turning point of my life, Kira. If the

course of my life were to be drawn on a map, there would be a very distinct point where I change direction."

A soft smile played at my lips. "And that's a good thing?"

He smiled back at me. "It's a very good thing." He looked around the empty hangar, and with a loud sigh, he turned back to me. "You're right, though. There are no demons here."

I grinned at him. "Life starts today, yes?"

He threw his head back and laughed. "Yeah, it sure does." He nodded toward the door. "Come on. Let's go see Father Michael and get this husband thing sorted out."

"Husband thing?"

He laughed again, walked over, and kissed me. "Yes, husband." He took my hand and we walked out of the old hangar, into the warm LA sun. The door closed behind us, and we never looked back.

MATT, Mom, Dad, and me stood at the side of the stage when Claude walked out up to the microphone with a piece of paper in her hands. Her once-wiry hair, now tamed and styled, she really looked more and more like the young lady she'd become. She was even wearing a dress.

For the first few years, she'd only do this if Matt went with her and did the talking, but now she'd do it on her own. She held her head high and smiled at the gym full of people, announcing the recipient of the Reuben Vaughn Memorial Scholarship.

It hadn't exactly been an easy road with Claude. There had been adjustment issues in the beginning, but as she'd settled into school, things had gotten easier.

I smiled as I remembered being called into the school to meet with her teacher. Claude had only been there for a month when the school—a private school—had requested her guardians be there, so the four of us had turned up—Mom, Dad, Matt, and me.

We'd sat across from the teacher, who had been surprised to say the least. I guess having one Spanish man, a

Japanese woman, a genetic mix of both, and an all American white man there as 'parents' of a little black girl might have been odd to some. But not to us.

When the teacher had made a comment on our family, my mother had taken offense to her tone. Me and Dad had leaned back in our chairs and sighed collectively. Matt leaned forward in his chair and grinned, and Mom proceeded to rip the poor teacher a new one, lecturing her on what a family really was.

Claude, dressed in her uniform, who had been sitting quietly up until this point, had got the giggles. Dad and Claude had exchanged a few words in sign language, then Matt had joined in. Claude had only known a few words at that stage, so it was a mixed-up conversation, all the while Mom was still ranting on at the poor woman across from us.

We must have looked like a circus act.

Anyway, as it turned out, Claude wasn't in trouble like we'd assumed. The teacher wanted to see us because apparently Claude was bright.

Like, really, really smart.

She couldn't read and write very well, but her aptitude tests were off the charts.

None of us were surprised. Proud but not surprised.

Six years later, the young lady on the stage in front of us could speak fluent ASL, Japanese, some Spanish, and was almost top of her class.

Between us and my parents, we just about shared custody of Claude. She'd spend equal amounts of time at either house, though Matt and I never really defined whether she was more of a little sister or a daughter—she was just family.

Matt and my fur-family, as we called it, had grown from just Oscar to include Elvis. Elvis was another rescue dog—

he had the body of a Labrador but the legs of a Corgi. He looked like he'd been put together wrong, but with our mix-matched family, he fit right in.

Matt and my human-family were a work in progress. We'd applied to adopt a child of our own two years ago, had many appointments, even came close once, but were still waiting to hear.

Our adoption support worker, a lovely lady by the name of Tann, was very sympathetic to us, and we kept in constant contact.

Matt tried not to act too bothered, but every time the answer was no, he deflated. He was incredibly busy with work, and at first he thought we might be too busy to afford the time a child needs, but after his workload simmered down, he confessed to me that he really wanted a child.

He wanted to give me a child.

Matt's work had taken on a whole life of its own. When he'd been at the FC for eighteen months, Berkman had approached him to take on another community gym, running classes for at-risk kids and getting the business up and running.

And then another gym.

He spent the majority of his time at the FC, but with three gyms to run, he had a team of people under him. By the fourth year, he was basically managing people. He had meetings in the city with head honchos and business executives, and theoretically worked as a liaison officer between the police, the city, and the community while still in daily contact with kids and keeping fit.

It was perfect for him.

I'd left my work and joined him as a head trainer, teaching the new teams how to run classes and get them qualified in health and fitness. I ran some classes at the FC and at the other gyms as well. It was still physical but a little more academic, and it suited us both perfectly.

It also gave us more time and more suitable hours so that bringing a child into our family seemed more doable.

Matt had really come into his own. He told me once that meeting me and eventually ending up at the FC was the starting point of his life, and I really think he was right.

He had a light that shined out of him now, a real sense of purpose, and a happiness that came from within. He would still smile when he saw me, he told me all the time I still take his breath away, that he's grateful for me, every single day.

I'd never loved him more.

Matt smiled at me as Claude gave a small speech on her brother, the scholarship, and the kid that earned it this year. Pauly had been one of Arizona's students for two years, and he really deserved this break. Claude called him up to the stage, shook his hand, congratulated him, and handed him the certificate.

Matt walked up onto the stage and shook Pauly's hand too, then despite the watching crowd, he hugged Claude. It was always an emotional day for her—the day her brother's memorial scholarship was awarded. She missed him terribly, and this day, in particular, was difficult.

For the last six years, every day afterwards, we'd go out to dinner as a family. And tonight was no different.

It was Claude's choice, so the five of us, Dad, Mom, Matt, me, and Claude, headed to a pizzeria. It was just like any other dinner—we squeezed into a booth, we ordered dinner, we argued, we laughed, and we laughed some more.

Then Matt's phone rang. It rang a hundred times a day, and even Claude said, "God, Matt, turn it off for one night."

He laughed her off, pulled out his cell, and when he read the name on the screen, his eyes shot to mine.

He put the phone to his left ear. "Tann," he said, letting us know it was our adoption worker. "No, we're out for dinner. We're all here, actually."

Matt was quiet while Tann spoke, and everyone was quiet, watching him, waiting for a sign. My heart was hammering, even though we'd been close before and were horribly disappointed, it was hard not to be excited.

Matt put the phone on the table. "She wants to be put on speaker phone," he whispered. He pressed the speaker button like it could bite him.

Tann's voice came through the phone, "Hello, Kira, are you there?"

"Yes," I answered. "My whole family's here. We can all hear you."

"Good," she replied. "I have news."

"Yes?" I was almost afraid to ask. Matt grabbed my hand, holding on so tight I could feel him shake. He was as nervous and excited as me.

"It's good news," Tann said. "Actually, it's wonderful news."

My mom put both her hands over her mouth and her eyes welled with tears.

"Your application has been assessed," Tann said. "And we have a perfect candidate."

A buzz went around the table, but Matt shook his head. "We've heard this before. Please Tann, are we..." He shook his head again and looked at me. His blue eyes looked hopeful, but he said. "Are we even close this time?"

I couldn't blame him for asking. When we'd been this close before only to be told no, Matt had cried for two days.

"I have the file in my hand," Tann said. "And I have your name on it, if you want."

Matt squeezed my hand to the point of pain, and he stared at me. I'm sure my expression matched his.

"You should know," Tann said, "this candidate is fifteen months old. Which is a little older than the norm. The reasons for this are medical reasons, but I didn't think you guys would mind."

I squeezed Matt's fingers now. My voice squeaked. "What medical reasons?"

"He's deaf."

My eyes sprung with tears, and when I looked at Matt, I covered my mouth and laughed.

"It's a he?" Matt asked. His grin was huge and he was buzzing with excitement.

"Yes," Tann answered. "Do you want me to send the file? I can email it to you now if you'd like?"

"Yes," Matt and I answered at the same time.

Tann laughed into the phone. "Sending it to Kira's phone now, so I can stay on the line to Matt's phone."

I pulled out my phone and clicked on the message icon. While we waited for the file to download, I looked at my family sitting with us. Mom was crying, even Dad was teary, and Claude was grinning and bouncing in her seat. I put my hand around Matt's shoulder, and with a shaking hand, I pressed the file.

The picture was of a little boy with longish brown hair, wide brown eyes, and chubby cheeks.

His name was Nicholas.

Matt choked out a ragged breath and tears fell down his cheeks. He looked at me and nodded. I leaned my head against his and looked back to the picture on the phone.

This little boy, this little perfect human, was going to be ours.

"He's perfect," I said, unable to hide the tears in my voice.

Tann laughed again. "So, are you ready for your lives to change forever?"

I looked at my family, and I looked at Matt, and together we spoke into the phone, "Yes."

~THE END

The Spencer Cohen Series, Book Two

The Spencer Cohen Series, Book Three

The Spencer Cohen Series, Yanni's Story

Blood & Milk

The Weight Of It All

A Very Henry Christmas (The Weight of It All 1.5)

Perfect Catch

Switched

Imago

Imagines

Red Dirt Heart Imago

On Davis Row

Finders Keepers

Evolved

Galaxies and Oceans

Private Charter

Nova Praetorian

Titles in Audio:

Cronin's Key

Cronin's Key II

Cronin's Key III

Red Dirt Heart

Red Dirt Heart 2

Red Dirt Heart 3

Red Dirt Heart 4

The Weight Of It All

Switched

Point of No Return

Breaking Point

Starting Point

Spencer Cohen Book One

Spencer Cohen Book Two

Spencer Cohen Book Three

Yanni's Story

On Davis Row

Evolved

Free Reads:

Sixty Five Hours

Learning to Feel

His Grandfather's Watch (And The Story of Billy and Hale)

The Twelfth of Never (Blind Faith 3.5)

Twelve Days of Christmas (Sixty Five Hours Christmas)

Best of Both Worlds

Translated Titles:

Fiducia Cieca (Italian translation of Blind Faith)

Attraverso Questi Occhi (Italian translation of Through

These Eyes)

Preso alla Sprovvista (Italian translation of Blindside)

Il giorno del Mai (Italian translation of Blind Faith 3.5)

Cuore di Terra Rossa (Italian translation of Red Dirt Heart)

Cuore di Terra Rossa 2 (Italian translation of Red Dirt Heart 2)

Cuore di Terra Rossa 3 (Italian translation of Red Dirt Heart 3)

Cuore di Terra Rossa 4 (Italian translation of Red Dirt Heart 4)

Intervento di Retrofit (Italian translation of Elements of Retrofit)

Confiance Aveugle (French translation of Blind Faith)

A travers ces yeux: Confiance Aveugle 2 (French translation of Through These Eyes)

Aveugle: Confiance Aveugle 3 (French translation of Blindside)

À Jamais (French translation of Blind Faith 3.5)

Cronin's Key (French translation)

Cronin's Key II (French translation)

Au Coeur de Sutton Station (French translation of Red Dirt Heart)

Partir ou rester (French translation of Red Dirt Heart 2)

Faire Face (French translation of Red Dirt Heart 3)

Trouver sa Place (French translation of Red Dirt Heart 4)

Rote Erde (German translation of Red Dirt Heart)

Rote Erde 2 (German translation of Red Dirt Heart 2)

www.ingramcontent.com/pod-product-compliance
Lightning Source LLC
Chambersburg PA
CBHW032210180726
48284CB00001B/267